MIRASOL

"This was our house," he said softly, "right here."

Leigh peered through the dusty window and saw a beamed ceiling, a huge fireplace framed with Spanish tile.

"I still think of Mirasol as home," he said, stepping closer to her. "That's why I came back."

His breath caressed the nape of her neck, and Leigh didn't dare turn around. She didn't trust her own shocking need for his touch.

"What do you think?" he asked. "Would this place fit in with the redevelopment plan?"

His hands were warm, and when he began to knead the tension from her shoulders, Leigh tipped her head back slightly. "I don't know," she whispered. "I can't think while you're doing that."

He leaned closer. "Shall I stop?"

"No. It feels wonderful." She closed her eyes and breathed in the crisp, clean air. "I love being out of the smog."

"Is that all you love?" he murmured.

Leigh had no time to answer before his mouth covered hers. A jay screeched nearby, but all Leigh heard was the pounding of her heart beating in time with his . . .

HISTORICAL ROMANCES BY PHOEBE CONN

FOR THE STEAMIEST READS, NOTHING BEATS THE PROSE OF CONN . . .

ARIZONA ANGEL	(3872, $4.50/$5.50)
CAPTIVE HEART	(3871, $4.50/$5.50)
DESIRE	(4086, $5.99/$6.99)
EMERALD FIRE	(4243, $4.99/$5.99)
LOVE ME 'TIL DAWN	(3593, $5.99/$6.99)
LOVING FURY	(3870, $4.50/$5.50)
NO SWEETER ECSTASY	(3064, $4.95/$5.95)
STARLIT ECSTASY	(2134, $3.95/$4.95)
SWEPT AWAY	(4487, $4.99/$5.99)
TEMPT ME WITH KISSES	(3296, $4.95/$5.95)
TENDER SAVAGE	(3559, $4.95/$5.95)

PARADISE

PHOEBE CONN

ZEBRA BOOKS
KENSINGTON PUBLISHING CORP.

ZEBRA BOOKS are published by

Kensington Publishing Corp.
850 Third Avenue
New York, NY 10022

Zebra and the Z logo Reg. U.S. Pat. & TM Off.

First Printing: September, 1995

Printed in the United States of America

There is only one happiness in life, to love and be loved.
—George Sand

One

Leigh wondered what other women did with their wedding rings after a divorce. Diamonds could always be reset in attractive mountings which gave no hint of their history, but she had had only a wide gold band whose purpose could not be disguised as a sparkling gemstone's could. The circle symbolized eternity, and a wedding band was a visible token of everlasting love, but her marriage to Doug Bowman had lasted only nine years.

They had met at eighteen, and at twenty-one had wed with ecstatic hopes for the future, but now all that was left of those precious dreams was a wedding band she no longer had the right, nor desire, to wear. She was leaving Los Angeles for a new life, and the ring was a poignant reminder of the old. She could have sold it for what the gold would bring, but considered money a poor compensation for parting with what would have become a treasured heirloom had the marriage endured.

With a restless sigh, she focused her thoughts on the future, slipped the bittersweet souvenir into the satin bag with her other jewelry, and eased it into the bottom of her purse. Ready to leave her apartment for the last time, she toured the rooms to make certain nothing had been left behind. She wanted no lingering attachments to the past and had given Doug first pick of the furniture, and then sold the rest. Her footsteps echoed through the empty rooms, but her memory, playing cruel tricks, still rang with the laughter of far happier times.

"Good-bye," she whispered at the door, and dropped her keys

through the mail slot for the manager to find. Her Camaro was parked at the curb, and as she hurried down the walk, she didn't look back. It was time to move on, and she was doing so, but she had never dreamed how painful it would be.

The Sunday morning traffic was light. Leigh made good time leaving town, and then chose the winding Pacific Coast Highway rather than the wide 405 freeway that stretches inland through rolling hills. The more leisurely scenic route suited her mood, and she welcomed the exotic beauty of the majestic eucalyptus lining the road. Native to the forests of Australia, the graceful trees' ragged bark was peeled away to reveal trunks as pale and smooth as naked flesh. Blue-gray, the drooping leaves scented the air with the pungent aroma of camphor.

Farther on, scrub oak dotted the landscape with clumps of bright green, and cypress, the branches grotesquely sculpted by the sea breeze, added a deep layer of emerald. Peeking above them, palm trees shook their shaggy heads. Oleander, blooming in pink and white profusion, crowded the median of the road the Spanish *padres* had christened *El Camino Real*. Ice plant with crisp yellow flowers spread across the sandy soil interlaced with a sprinkling of delicate orange nasturtiums; but an occasional proud yucca or thorny cactus invaded the verdant beauty in a defiant reminder that this was still desert land.

When Leigh began her trip north on the undulating highway, the skyline of Los Angeles was veiled in coastal fog, but as she neared the exit sign for Mirasol, the sun finally burst through the haze. Within minutes, the sky brightened to a vivid azure, and the ocean took on a quicksilver gleam. Relieved that it would be a glorious day after all, Leigh grabbed for a last bit of freedom before beginning her new job. She waited for a break in the oncoming traffic, and turned her car across the highway onto the narrow shoulder of the rocky cliff.

Anticipating warm weather inland, she was dressed in navy blue shorts, a white T-shirt sprinkled with gold stars, and white eyelet tennis shoes with lace ties. She grabbed a red baseball cap from off the backseat to shade her face, locked her car, and pocketed the keys. After a brief search along the bluff, she found a worn path and followed it down the steep incline to the beach.

More than a dozen surfers were already in the water, their wet suits forming glistening black commas on the bottle-green waves. Farther out, a young man tugged on a flashy rainbow sail and skimmed by on his sailboard. It was still too early for families with small children to crowd the beach with their striped umbrellas and plastic sand toys, or for bikini-clad sunbathers to be basking on colorful towels. Bound for the tide pools, Leigh walked along the scallopped edge of the lapping waves to reach the treacherous jumble of rocks.

She chose her footing carefully and braced herself with her hands each time she stepped on a boulder that teetered with the surprising suddenness of a carnival fun house floor. She scrambled over a hunk of brick wall that might have washed up from Atlantis, and at last reached the shallow pools fed by the constant ebb and flow of the tides. Teeming with marine life, they offered endless amusement to those with patience and a keen eye.

The rocks lining the pools were fringed with furry lichens and spotted with oval limpets. Tiny fish darted through the water in a furious game of tag, while flowerlike sea anemone languidly waved their smokey-aqua petals. The sea anemone above the waterline had folded inward and resembled dozens of small bran muffins frosted with colorful bits of shell.

Sea snails, their spiral shells miniature replicas of the Taj Mahal domes, slid over the sandy bottoms of the pools, while hermit crabs dragged their borrowed shells from one dark crevice to another. An occasional crab crawled out upon the rocks to sun himself, his pale green back decorated with a fanciful design as beautifully executed as Japanese calligraphy.

The waves had worn some rocks smooth, and filled others with shallow pockets that provided the perfect resting place for a shy snail. Climbing over the spray-kissed stones, Leigh paused to follow a fleeting trail of shadows across the sandy bottom of a pool and found a starfish she would have otherwise missed.

Pleased by the discovery, she knelt down to observe the pool more intently, drank in the salt-scented air, and hummed along with the rushing gurgle of the sea.

The last time she had been at the beach, the scene had not been nearly so tranquil. It had been one of the last times she and her ex-husband were together. She had hoped for a relaxed afternoon when they could finally make some serious plans for their future. Doug had brought along a script to study for a part he had hoped to play in a new Robert Altman film, but he had swiftly grown bored with memorizing lines and joined in an impromptu volleyball game with a crowd of boisterous teenagers.

Leigh had sat alone and watched him play in a seething, frustrated silence. When they met in college, she had admired his ability to make friends so easily; he had teased her about being far too serious. Tall and athletic, he had a magnetic appeal that drew people to him, but it had taken her years to realize just how desperately he needed their attention.

He had the classic features of a film star, but lacked the determination to become a serious actor. He had worked in several films made for television, and had appeared briefly on a couple of soaps. He had flashed his engaging grin through a great many commercials, but spent far more time working out at the gym than he did in a studio.

Leigh had never doubted his love, but it had become increasingly difficult to support his dreams when he refused to allocate even one afternoon to acknowledging hers. It had been the volleyball game that had finally made her accept the fact that Doug would never be more than a handsome child. They were opposites who complemented each other beautifully in many respects, but in others, they were so hopelessly out of sync that she could no longer pretend a happiness she did not truly feel.

She needed strength from Doug, and an ambition to match her own, and she could no longer carry the weight of all the responsibility a marriage entailed. She had loved him with all her heart, but had received far too little in return. He had cried when she told him she was leaving him, and tears filled her eyes as she thought of him now.

She removed her sunglasses to wipe her eyes on her arm, and made a conscious effort to leave the past where it belonged. Her future lay in Mirasol, and she had every intention of creating a good one. A sea gull's piercing cry drew her attention back to the tide pool where two hermit crabs were now actively battling. The larger yanked the smaller this way and that in what was surely a life and death struggle. Intending to give the little fellow some help, Leigh looked around for a stick that might have washed up with the tide.

"Have you found something exciting?" a man called out.

Leigh glanced up to find him making his way toward her. Dressed in khaki shorts and running shoes, he carried a T-shirt wadded up in his hand. "I'm not sure yet, perhaps," she replied. When he reached her, he pulled his shirt on over his head, raked his hair with his fingers, and then knelt on the opposite side of the pool. He looked close to forty, but possessed a sleek runner's build. His dark hair was laced with gray, but his brown eyes held a youthful sparkle.

"What's your view on interfering with nature?" Leigh inquired. "I can't stand to watch a bully, even if he's only a hermit crab, get the best of a little guy."

The man leaned closer to the water to get a better view of the miniature war. "If we were filming a nature feature for 'National Geographic,' I suppose we'd have to let the crabs battle it out, but I'm with you. Let's give the underdog a hand, or in this case, a claw."

Leigh remembered her car keys and pulled them from her pocket. The pool was only a few inches deep, and she could reach the crabs easily. She gave the larger one a poke with her ignition key to scoot him backwards, but he failed to release his smaller prey. "Well, so much for that approach. What do you suggest?"

The man appeared to give her question serious consideration, and then chuckled. "Getting them to declare a truce and sidle up to a bargaining table is obviously out."

"Obviously." Leigh laughed at his proposal, but could not think of a better one until the crabs inched closer to her side of the pool. "Oh, wait a minute. Maybe they're not fighting after all. It looks as though the larger one's claw is caught inside the smaller one's shell."

Intrigued, the man shifted position to improve his view. "You're right. Are you carrying a Swiss Army knife that includes a pair of tweezers?"

"Unfortunately, no." The crabs where tugging each other around in a furious circle now, and realizing the larger one's predicament, Leigh's sympathies began to shift. "I'm afraid we're going to have to pick them up."

The man looked up. Deeply tanned, his even white teeth lit his grin with a teasing warmth. "They couldn't pinch us too badly with such tiny claws."

"Let's hope not." Leigh slid her keys back into her pocket, but before she could reach for the crabs, the man scooped them up in his hand. Neither was more than half an inch long, but with their claws and feet a wiggling fury they were difficult to hold. He gave a slight tug in a vain effort to separate them. "I don't want to break off a claw. Come on you two, cooperate."

"I don't believe teamwork is in a crab's nature," Leigh said.

"Then they're lucky it's in ours, aren't they?" he replied. Forced to adopt a more inventive approach, he closed his fingers over the crabs and shook his fist as though he were rolling dice. When he relaxed his grip, the little creatures tumbled into the pool, shaken apart, and scurried away in opposite directions.

"All right!" he cried in an ecstatic whoop.

Her spirits buoyed by his success, Leigh returned his smile. "Good for you. I never would have thought of that. Do you suppose it left them with dreadful headaches?"

He laughed at that prospect and straightened up. "I doubt it. They're used to being whisked back and forth by the waves. Did you sight anything else worth watching?"

Only you, Leigh thought to herself. She knew women who would tell him so too, but turning shy, left the compliment unspoken. "Not really." She slid her fingertip along the edge of a sea anemone's petal-like tentacles and felt a slight tug. "Do you have any idea how these lovely creatures reproduce?"

The man circled the pool and hunkered down beside her. "As a matter of fact, I do. One method is from eggs, but they also form buds around the base that grow and break free. Let's see if we can find some."

Intent on locating a bud or two, for several minutes Leigh didn't notice the man was actually studying her rather than the sea anemone. She hadn't met anyone interesting since her divorce, and hadn't dated at all. She had begun to wonder if her emotions weren't permanently numbed, so the pleasure this man's inquisitive glance brought was a delicious surprise. She still had her standards, though. She wouldn't pick up a stranger on the beach.

She rose in a graceful stretch. "I've got to be going."

"Yeah, me, too."

Leigh heard a shading of regret in his voice, then scolded herself silently for being flattered. She picked her way back over the rocks, and he followed by his own route, coming out closer to the water. He bent down to grab one of the small stones scattered along the shore, then hurled it out over the top of the incoming wave where it skipped across the surface in three bounding hops.

"I wish I could do that," Leigh called.

The man turned and beckoned for her to join him. "How much have you practiced?"

Leigh crossed the damp sand. "Not at all, I'm afraid. Is that the secret?" At five feet two, she had to look up at him, but then she had to crane her neck to speak to most men.

"Actually, there are several secrets," he revealed in a conspiratorial whisper. He looked around for another stone, and handed it to her. "That's a good one. You need a flat stone or else when you throw it, it will just drop like a . . ." he paused, waiting for her to fill in the word.

"Stone?" she offered in a lilting giggle.

"Exactly. Now when you throw it, let it roll off your index finger. Here, watch me another time."

Leigh stepped back as he scouted for another smooth stone. He picked up a couple, and then bent low. "You have to get close to the water, and use your whole arm." He whipped another stone out over the waves lapping the shore and it skipped first one way and then another before dropping out of sight.

"Very impressive," Leigh told him.

"Now you try it." He rested his hands on his hips and waited.

"I've never been any good at sports," she hedged, and sure enough, when she tossed the stone it disappeared without a single bounce. "I'm sorry."

"Don't apologize. It took me years to perfect my technique. Come on, let's find some more stones and keep trying."

Leigh reminded herself it was Sunday, successfully fought the impulse to check her watch, and began looking around. Fortunately, a wealth of small stones littered the beach and she did not have to look long to find several that fit his specifications. He also gathered a handful, and plunked them down by her feet.

"Let me watch you a few more times," Leigh asked.

He shook his head. "You'll never learn watching me. Try it again."

STANFORD was stenciled across his T-shirt in faded letters and it suddenly struck her that he was unusually adept at providing relaxed instruction. "Are you a college professor?" she asked.

He winced. "Retired. Does it still show?"

"You're awfully young to have retired."

"And you're stalling." Although he had refused, he picked up another stone and gave it a graceful heave over the waves. It took one long hop, and then two smaller ones.

"You're really good." Leigh tried to remember his tips, and to her utter amazement, she skipped a stone over the water in two neat little hops. "I did it!" she exclaimed. The incoming wave washed up over the toes of her shoes, and she danced back out of the way. "Maybe it was just beginner's luck."

"No. Inspired coaching," he replied. He skimmed another stone on the water, and then handed her a smooth one stained bright yellow from rusty iron debris.

Leigh attempted another smooth, low, angled throw, but the stone simply fell with a plop and she moaned in disgust. "I'm just no good at this."

"Are you always so hard on yourself?"

Taken aback by that question, Leigh debated replying with the truth, then decided nothing else would do. "I suppose, but if I don't expect the best from myself, who will?"

"We're just skimming stones here," he chided. "Now keep going. Mozart didn't learn to play the piano in a day."

Leigh sighed wearily, but gave it another try and again succeeded in getting several bounces out of the throw. It hurt her whole arm, though, and she grabbed her elbow. "I must be doing something wrong. It's not supposed to hurt, is it?"

He laughed, and nodded. "I forgot to warn you, didn't I? Putting a spin on the stone does tend to hurt, but it's a small price to pay." He sent another couple of stones flying out over the water with spectacular results, and then pulled a watch from his pocket. "I'd like to stay and tutor you all day, but I own an antique shop in Mirasol, and have to get back to open the place. If you ever come through there, drop by and say hello. It's the Victorian house on the southwest corner of Mirasol Avenue and Ventura Street."

Leigh slipped the last of the stones he had given her into her pocket as a memento of the unexpected fun. "I'm on my way to Mirasol right now."

"Great. Why don't you follow me, and we'll have brunch together. I make the best avocado sandwich in town."

Leigh hadn't expected him to ask her for a date, if it could be called that, but he was a charming man who owned his own business and could cook. What more could a woman want? Her whole face lit with a delighted smile. "Thank you. I'd like that."

"Where are you parked?"

"Right above us on the bluff."

He moved close to gesture. "The white van is mine. I'll wait for you just past the turnoff for Mirasol."

For an instant, Leigh couldn't decide if such a protective attitude was condescending or merely considerate. Mirasol was sixteen miles inland, but she had made the drive several times and knew there was absolutely no danger of becoming lost. There was a vast difference between being independent and being rude, however, and she smiled rather than stubbornly insist she could get there on her own.

"Thank you. I'll see you there." She followed him up the bluff, but after getting into her car, hesitated before turning the key in the ignition. She tossed her cap aside, and fluffed her dark hair with her fingers. Several inches long on top, her hair dipped to her earlobes at the sides, and only tickled her nape. It was a sophisticated style that not only accented her blue eyes, but projected the polished image her profession required.

She wanted desperately to be taken seriously in Mirasol, and while accepting a luncheon invitation offered on the beach might seem a peculiar way to go about it, she did not want to waste the opportunity to get to know one of the local businessmen. She laughed at herself then, because he had definitely inspired more than a purely professional interest. She started her car and slipped a Stevie Ray Vaughn cassette into the tape deck.

Completing the turn to get back out onto the highway took a while, but before long, she reached the turnoff for Mirasol, and as promised, the man was waiting in his van. She waved, and he pulled out to lead the way. Shaded by ancient oaks and towering sycamores, the road followed the graceful curves of the Ventura Riverbed, now thickly overgrown with chaparral, and brightened with shimmering clumps of goldenrod. Farther on, they passed oil fields where the wells, like gigantic grass-

hoppers, bobbed in a chugging rhythm in perfect time with
Stevie Ray's bluesy guitar.

Past the pale green refineries' tangled pipes and squatting
vats, the road split yellow-ochre fields littered with freshly
baled hay. There were lacy pepper trees, and saffron tipped aca-
cia. Horses with glossy coats grazed in pastures bordered by
miles of white fences. Nestled between the rocky slopes of the
Topatopa Mountains on the north, and the Sulphur Mountains
on the south, the fertile valley was scented with orange blossoms each spring. Now, early in summer, the fruit was ripening
in the orchards.

Along the road, power lines drooped with the lazy ease of a
trombone solo, and the tranquil rural vistas soothed Leigh's
soul. Just as on her previous visits to Mirasol, the unhurried
drive into town drained away the tension that often brought an
annoying ache to her neck and shoulders. Three months ago,
she had had only a vague inkling of the city's existence. Now
she felt as though she were coming home.

The orange and avocado groves surrounding the town were
lush, but most of the houses were modest wooden bungalows,
along with an occasional adobe with a red tile roof. The Victorian dwellings provided infrequent reminders of Mirasol's historic past. Leigh had heard their whimsical architecture
described by some as picturesque, and by others as ridiculously
ornate. She had always tended toward the latter opinion, but as
she parked in front of her new friend's residence, she considered
it the perfect place to showcase antiques.

Queen Anne in style, the three story house was embellished
with turrets, bay windows, and verandas. Two fancifully crafted
brick chimneys soared above the roofline. The exterior was
covered in shingles and half-timbering painted in gradually softening shades of sea-green, while the window trim and doors
provided bright terracotta accents. Set back from the street by
a wide green lawn, the house was framed with beautiful rose
bushes heavy with yellow blooms. Pansies and Queen Anne's

lace bordered the walk. A discreet sign read: Jonathan Reid Antiques, open afternoons and by appointment.

"Jonathan Reid," Leigh let the name roll off her tongue. She had seen the sign and should have recalled his name. Without asking, she knew he went by Jonathan, never Jon, nor Nate. He had parked his van in the rear, and come through the house to meet her on the front porch. True to the Victorian era, casually arranged white wicker furniture made it an appealing spot to rest and enjoy a lazy afternoon.

Jonathan welcomed her inside. "I hope you like antiques," he said.

Leigh had expected the dusty heaps of quirky junk usually sold as such, but a single glance at the ornate furnishings in the front hallway disabused her of the idea. "My goodness, this is more like a museum than a store. You have a beautiful collection."

Jonathan beamed with pride. "Thank you. I spend a great deal of my time searching out pieces at estate sales. I restore them myself, display them here to every advantage, and have built up a regular clientele who come from as far away as San Diego and Seattle. Why don't you look around a bit, and I'll take a shower and change my clothes."

Leigh glanced down at the wet toes of her tennis shoes. "You needn't dress up on my account."

Jonathan unhooked the velvet rope that barred the second floor as private and started up the oak-paneled staircase. "Thanks, but I'd like to look my best if a customer wanders in."

"Oh, of course, I'd forgotten about them." Embarrassed, Leigh turned toward the parlor where a floral carpet in tones of russet and peach covered the oak flooring. Elaborately carved Carrera marble framed the fireplace, and what could be seen of the walls between the multitude of paintings and portraits was covered in rust and forest green striped silk. The bay window was draped with velvet curtains in a rich russet shade, and potted ferns and philodendron enhanced the view.

There were marble topped mahogany tables, rosewood side chairs covered in peach velvet, and a Chippendale sofa, its rococco curves resplendent in russet satin. There was a pump organ which looked as though it had come from a country church, and everywhere she looked knickknacks and glassware vied for her attention. Dizzy from the sheer volume of items on display, Leigh sat down on the window seat, and looked out toward the mountains. She did not understand how anyone could live amidst such a riotous confusion, and wondered how the Victorians had managed to keep their sanity. She was relieved when Jonathan called to her from the doorway.

He had dressed in Levi's, rolled up the sleeves of a white shirt, and donned a pair of loafers. Lean and fit, he was every bit as handsome as he had been on the beach. "Come on in the kitchen and keep me company."

Leigh was only too glad to leave the crowded parlor and hurried down the hall after him. When she discovered the kitchen was completely modernized, she felt much more at home. "How may I help?" she asked.

"Set the table if you like." Jonathan nodded toward the cupboard drawer. "I usually eat in here. The dining room is too elegant for anything less than Christmas dinner for twelve."

Leigh had gotten only a quick peek as she had walked by, and while the room was as artfully decorated as the parlor, she had to agree that it was too formal a setting for lunch. The kitchen, however, was papered in a blue and white floral print with bright yellow accents. The counters were covered in butcherblock formica, and the cupboards, table, and chairs were oak. An impressive cast-iron gas stove, the type used in restaurants, dominated the back wall.

"This is a charming room," Leigh replied. She glanced out at the veranda facing Ventura Street where a wicker chaise lounge and table heaped with Sunday papers created an inviting scene. Potted geraniums and hanging baskets dripping with fuchsia added color.

"I've never had much luck with plants, but yours are spectacular. Do you do all the gardening yourself?" she asked.

Jonathan plucked an avocado from a wooden bowl on the counter, and removed a tomato, a plastic container of alfalfa sprouts, and a bottle of ranch style dressing from the refrigerator. He opened a loaf of whole wheat bread and popped two slices in the toaster oven. He answered as he began to peel the avocado.

"I can't grow anything except cactus, which I've discovered thrive on neglect. Ron Tate's my gardener. He deserves all the credit for the landscaping. He's what people used to call a handyman and he's good with everything. I've discovered I have a gift for working with wood, but not much else, I'm afraid, with the exception of avocado sandwiches." He looked over his shoulder and winked at her.

Leigh set the table with blue placemats and napkins and sat down to stay out of his way. "From what I saw on the beach, I'd say you were a gifted professor as well."

Jonathan removed the toasted bread from the small oven, and added the other two slices. He hesitated a long moment before responding. "Yeah, I was, but working with students was only a fraction of the job."

Curious as to why he had changed professions, Leigh waited for him to add more and when he didn't volunteer the information, she gave him a little nudge. "But the best part?"

Jonathan slathered the ranch dressing on the toast, and added layers of avocado, tomato, and sprouts. "Definitely. My field was American history, which I'll always love, but it doesn't necessarily follow that all history professors get along. Money's tight everywhere, which compounds the internal politics and constant jockeying for position among the faculty. Department meetings were more like the hellacious dinners dysfunctional families suffer through than professional conferences."

Jonathan turned toward her. "In my opinion, there were too damn many professors who looked upon tenure as a form of early retirement. I said so quite often too, and I'm sure you can imagine how popular that made me."

"Only too well. The security of tenure didn't appeal to you?"

Jonathan looked as though he had just caught a whiff of something absolutely vile, then shook his head. "Security can be a form of golden handcuffs, and bondage doesn't tempt me." He topped the sandwiches with the second piece of toast, put them on bright blue plates, and carried them over to the table. "Ice tea all right with you?"

"Yes, thank you." His relaxed manner had made Leigh feel at home. "I've always loved history, too," she said. I've watched Ken Burns' series on the Civil War a couple of times, and even saw Ted Turner's *Gettysburg* in a theater full of cheering southerners. My ears hurt for hours from all the cannon fire, but I felt as though I'd actually been there. I was so touched by Jeff Daniels' masterful portrayal of Joshua Lawrence Chamberlain, that I wish I could have known him."

Delighted by her enthusiasm, Jonathan replied. "It was the people involved, not the battles, that got me excited about history. Chamberlain has always fascinated me too, and not simply because he was a college professor before he enlisted in the Union Army. It isn't surprising, that *Gettysburg* attracted an audience partial to the Confederacy. If you ever spend any time in the south, you'll soon discover the Civil War commands enormous interest there. Some Georgians are still cursing Sherman's march to the sea."

"As well they should," Leigh agreed. She took a bite of her sandwich, and moaned appreciatively. "This is every bit as delicious as you promised."

Jonathan's reply was slyly suggestive. "I'd not realized you were a history buff, or I might have done even better."

Leigh doubted she would ever tire of his teasing smile and couldn't help but wonder if his kiss wouldn't be memorable as well. An athlete's build along with a scholar's sensitivity was a marvelous combination. The few times his slim fingers had grazed her palm on the beach, the sensation had been very pleasant indeed. Ashamed of how hungry she was for a man's touch, she quickly rechanneled the erotic direction of her thoughts.

"I don't know how," she insisted. "I'm really impressed with your talent as a chef, and it certainly looks as though you've put your knowledge of history to excellent use here in your house." She took another bite of sandwich, and hoped he wouldn't notice her hands were shaking.

Jonathan took a sip of the tea he brewed daily in a glass jar left out in the sun. "Thank you. I do everything I can to authenticate a piece, and return it to its original condition. I enjoy working with my hands. Actually, I enjoy everything about owning this place. I run on the beach most mornings, then work in my shop on the back porch. Sometimes I just sit out on the veranda and read while I wait for customers. I don't miss the pressures of academic life one bit."

Leigh nodded politely, but Jonathan's description of his life as a celebration of leisure rang in her mind with an alarming echo. She tried not to sound judgmental, but failed to hide her concern. "You must have some goals."

"Not a one," Jonathan said. He finished his sandwich, wiped his hands on his napkin, and sat back in his chair. His guest had eaten only half of her sandwich, and he waited before offering dessert. "That's enough about me. Tell me something about yourself. My God, we didn't even introduce ourselves, did we? I'm Jonathan Reid, as you must have read on the sign out front."

He was a bright and attractive man, and a moment ago, Leigh had been thoroughly enjoying herself. Now she was filled with the uncomfortable suspicion that Jonathan's charm masked a personality as exasperatingly irresponsible as her ex-husband's. That he had been a rebel in a university setting wasn't at all surprising when viewed in that dreary light. Just as quickly, she scolded herself silently for dismissing him as tragically flawed before having had the opportunity to get to know him.

"How do you do, Mr. Reid. I'm Leigh Bowman."

Jonathan's easy smile slipped into a perplexed frown. Lacking the silver highlights of his hair, his dark brows drew a sharp emphasis to his scowl. "Your name's familiar, but I know we've not met before today."

Leigh blotted her lips with her napkin and took a deep breath. She was proud of her new job, but tried not to sound as though she were bragging. "I've just been hired as Mirasol's city planner to oversee the redevelopment project. If you ever attend the city council meetings, you might have heard my name mentioned there."

She had expected a polite show of interest, but the expression of utter dismay that crossed Jonathan's face took her by surprise. "Is something wrong?"

"I'll say." Jonathan left the table and nearly threw his plate in the sink. He leaned back against the counter, and crossed his arms over his chest. "It's my opinion, and it's not unsupported, that the council's plan to revitalize Mirasol is ill-conceived at best and disastrous at worst. I was away on a buying trip when the council voted to hire you, and I'd assumed Leigh Bowman was male. If I'd had any idea that's who you were, I'd not have invited you here."

He was delivering a lecture now, and Leigh did not need to be asked to leave in any stronger terms. She promptly rose from her seat, but kept a firm grip on her temper. "Mirasol has a charming past, Mr. Reid, but if it's to have a future, it has to look forward to the twenty-first century rather than back to the nineteenth. Restoring antiques is one thing, but preserving an antiquated town is quite another."

Jonathan shook his head regretfully before offering a bitter retort. "Well, they say looks are deceiving, and I mistook you for a pretty tourist when the truth is you're out to bulldoze the town."

Leigh felt as though she had been blindsided. They had been having an enjoyable lunch one minute, and the next, Jonathan Reid had leaped to his feet and declared her an archenemy. She refused to accept such a ludicrous label. "That's a gross exaggeration."

"No. You're very pretty, and if you push the city council's plan, there won't be anything left of Mirasol." He walked over to the door leading out to the veranda and opened it. "I won't keep you, Ms. Bowman."

Leigh cast a knowing glance around the kitchen before moving toward the door. "You're scarcely the purist you believe yourself to be, Mr. Reid, or you'd not have modernized your kitchen. That's what I intend to do with Mirasol—not destroy it."

As she slipped by him, she felt him recoil slightly as though he feared she had poison spines. That hurt, but she wasn't disappointed to learn he had the character to fight for what he believed in. It was a damn shame, however, that they had ended up on opposing sides so quickly. She moved down the driveway with an angry stride.

"Welcome to Mirasol," she muttered under her breath, but she had no intention of leaving before she had completed what she had been hired to do. Jonathan Reid certainly didn't lack for brains, and she hoped he was bright enough to stay out of her way.

Two

Leigh sent a cautious glance over her left shoulder before easing her Camaro out onto Mirasol Avenue. There was never much traffic on the two lane road, but she did not want to risk plowing into anyone in front of Jonathan Reid's, and in her present mood, such a stupid accident was a very real possibility. The library, which sat on the corner opposite his shop, was closed on Sundays, but the aroma of popcorn was thick around the movie theater down the block.

The light was red at Signal Street, appropriately named as the site of the town's lone traffic light. The post office, with an impressive bell tower, was located at the intersection's southeast corner. A brass plaque on the front dedicated the town's tallest structure to the memory of Elijah Keene, an ambitious local rancher, who in the 1920's had succeeded in transforming Mirasol from a sleepy agricultural village into a popular tourist retreat. Inspired by California's gracious Spanish heritage, Elijah had convinced the shopkeepers to remodel the town with extensive use of adobe and red tile.

He had advertised Mirasol's splendid climate in publications back East and built the Mirasol Inn, an elegantly appointed resort hotel, to house the tourists who responded. With an eye to the future, he had founded an exclusive preparatory school to attract the sons of his wealthy guests. In response to his efforts, tourists crowded into Mirasol each winter and spring, swelling the population from 3,500 to nearly 10,000. Operas, symphonies, and theatrical entertainments were common. After vacationing there, several wealthy families returned to take up ranching and added to the town's new cosmopolitan flavor.

For one glorious decade Mirasol had sparkled with a glittering brillance. Then the stock market crash of 1929 brought an end to Elijah Keene's dreams of civic pride. The tourists he had courted vanished, and so did the town's newfound prosperity. The beautiful Mirasol Inn sat vacant, and heartbroken, Elijah joined the majority of the locals in a return to ranching. Gradually the years when Mirasol had been a popular winter resort were all but forgotten.

As Leigh drove through the heart of the city, all that remained of Elijah Keene's creation was the Spanish architecture, and after nearly seventy years, it was in desperate need of restoration. The uniqueness of the city's history, as well as the city council's enthusiasm, had influenced her to apply for the position of city planner, but there had been a great deal of competition for the job. She had won the appointment not only because she had the most impressive educational background and experience, but because she shared the council's desire to recapture Elijah Keene's vision.

She had been led to believe the redevelopment project had wide support, but if Jonathan Reid's claim were true, then she was in for some strenuous opposition. She had the city council's confidence, however, and was convinced she would eventually win over whatever foes the plan might have. Except for Jonathan Reid. She might have to resort to using a bulldozer on him.

She turned left at Montgomery Street, and left again at Aliso to reach the duplex she had rented. Recently whitewashed, the one-story adobe house had turquoise shutters and doors. Four rough-hewn posts supported the overhanging red tile roof to form a wide veranda. Native plants filled the yard: purple sage, orange tipped Indian paintbrush, stiff stalks of lavender statice, delicate golden California poppies, and cacti in a multitude of hairy, lumpy, and sharply spined varieties. Olive trees added the final touch of southwestern charm.

Leigh had thought the place ideal when the rental agent

showed it to her, but despite having made several trips to Mirasol to transport her household goods, she had yet to meet her neighbor. Her clothes had been the last of her belongings to be removed from her apartment in Los Angeles, and the Camaro's backseat and trunk were full. She parked in the driveway, and unlocked the side door to her new home.

She was on her third trip, carrying an armful of garments in slippery cleaners' bags, when she heard a knock at the open door. After quickly hanging everything in the closet, she went to answer and found an attractive brunette waiting in the driveway. Her short hair was more tangled than stylish, and her huge hoop earrings might have gotten better reception than a satellite dish, but her expression was one of impish delight.

"Hi, I'm Bonnie MacNair, your next door neighbor. Well, not next door really, since I rent the other half of the duplex, but you know what I mean. I thought we ought to get acquainted." She peered past Leigh to get a peek at her kitchen. "Could you use some help?"

Leigh introduced herself as the new city planner and was relieved when Bonnie responded with an enthusiastic welcome. "There's not much left to bring inside, but if you'll carry that bag of shoes, I'll grab the last of the clothes."

Bonnie grabbed the handles on a shopping bag brimming with stylish leather pumps and sandals, and followed Leigh through the kitchen, and down the hall to the bedroom. The unit came furnished with sturdy oak pieces and neutral carpets and drapes, but Leigh's quilted bedspread brightened the whole room. With an heirloom technique, but a thoroughly modern design, it featured a heavenly array of gold stars on a field of midnight blue, and shams with a glowing sun and crescent moon.

As Leigh hung up the last of her garments, Bonnie set the bag down beside the closet and ran an appreciative touch over the spectacular quilt. "This is gorgeous."

"Thanks. It will probably last a hundred years. I put some

Cokes in the refrigerator on my last trip. Would you like one?" Leigh asked.

"Thank you. Are you sure there isn't something more I can do?" Bonnie glanced into the bathroom as they moved down the hall. Midnight blue towels hung on the racks, and she caught a glimpse of a poster with blues and greens.

"Not a thing, thank you. I've cut what I own to the mininum to travel light." Leigh handed Bonnie a soda, and got one for herself. "It's rather stuffy in here. Shall we go out on the front porch?"

"The backyard is nicer," Bonnie replied, and led the way around the duplex where a grassy lawn encircled an orange tree heavily laden with fruit. Two director's chairs with faded green canvas seats and backs provided the only seating and she slid into one and stretched out her legs. She was wearing worn Levi's, a red tank top, and sandals.

"I hope you don't mind sitting back here. I'm the librarian and I spend so much time smiling during the week, that on Sundays I just like to sit back here and hide. How do you like Mirasol so far?"

With her ears still ringing from Jonathan Reid's rebuke, Leigh chose to rely on the tact her job required. "I'm sure I'll enjoy my stay." She took a long sip of Coke. The day was growing warm and she rolled the cool can against her cheek. Because the library was right across from Jonathan's house, she could not resist asking about him.

"Jonathan Reid gave me his opinion of the redevelopment project this morning. I was rather surprised by the vehemence of his opposition. Do you know him well?"

"Ah yes, the professor," Bonnie pronounced the title with Daffy Duck's stuttering lisp. "I was born here, so I know everyone well. My mother owns the Beauty Spot, and she put my playpen right next to the manicurist so you might say I cut my teeth on gossip." She took a long drink, and wiped a slight dribble from her chin.

"Jonathan isn't a native, but he might as well be. He moved

here when his father became headmaster of the prep school. His mother taught there, too. He has a Ph.D. in history from Stanford, but taught in Colorado and Arizona before coming back here. He's divorced. Most definitely eligible, but I've never gotten anywhere with him."

Leigh's feelings about him were ambivalent at best, but that didn't stop the painful tightening in her chest. She leaned down to pluck a bright yellow dandelion from the grass, and asked nonchalantly, "Do you want to?"

"No. Not really. I want to leave Mirasol, and he's as rooted in place as that old mansion of his. I apply for every position that becomes available, but with most cities cutting their budgets, more librarians are losing their jobs than are being hired."

She frowned petulantly. "Nothing ever goes right for me. My mother sent me to college so I could make something of myself, but I ended up right back here in Mirasol. How could you bear to leave Los Angeles? Oh, I know there have been riots and earthquakes, but still, it's got to be a lot more fun than here."

A tall oleander hedge bordered the chain link fence enclosing the yard but the happy laughter of children playing with a barking dog drifted over from next door. "I was intrigued by the redevelopment project," Leigh answered truthfully. "I've only been divorced a year, and right now, work is much more appealing to me than social life."

"Oh, I'm sorry." Bonnie leaned forward slightly. "What happened?"

No wonder Bonnie knew everyone's story if she were always so curious. Certain whatever she said would be repeated all over town, Leigh again chose her words with care. "Doug and I met in college, and just grew apart over the years. The divorce was painful for us both, but we've survived. What about you? Are you dating anyone special?"

Bonnie leaned back and scuffed her feet in the grass. Her long acrylic nails were painted a bright red, and she tapped them against her Coke can in an impatient staccato. "No, not really. I'm sure it must be much easier to meet nice men in Los Angeles. Did you ever go to any of the clubs where the movie stars hang out?"

Leigh tried not to laugh, but her life was so far from what Bonnie imagined she could not help but be tickled. "No. Dancing all night has never appealed to me. Now let me ask you another question. Are there many people opposing the redevelopment plan? I'd hate to walk into the council meeting tomorrow night, and find the only support is from the elected officials."

"Oh, no, that's impossible. Lots of people want changes made. The library is one of the newest buildings in town, and I'm really proud of it, but anyone can see the rest of Mirasol is crumbling faster than we can patch it. There are always people who will stubbornly oppose progress, and we've got our share of those fossils, but you needn't worry you'll not feel welcome here. I just hope you don't find Mirasol so unbearably dull that you'll quickly move away."

"There are nice people everywhere and I'm looking forward to making some good friends," Leigh assured her. "I love to read, and I'll come by the library soon to get a card."

"Please do. Well, I promised to stop by my mother's this afternoon, and I better get going. I like your hairstyle. My mother has a lot of talent and she can keep it looking good for you."

Judging from Bonnie's windblown curls, Leigh seriously doubted it. "I hope to meet all the merchants in the next few days. I'll be sure to tell your mother we're neighbors." They parted in the backyard and Leigh went back inside and opened all the windows to let in some fresh air. She needed to go to the market, and sat down to make a list.

Her duplex was small. There was just the front room, a kitchen, bedroom and bath, but she intended to make it home. She still had pictures to hang, but with her television set and microwave already in place, little else to do. As she had told Bonnie, she liked to travel light and that meant she wouldn't clutter her home or her life with a lot of possessions.

She recalled Jonathan Reid's congested parlor with a shudder, then wondered if the private rooms upstairs were filled to overflowing with antiques. The Victorians had liked massive beds, but certain she was unlikely ever to see Jonathan's, she swept that thought from her mind. She concentrated on her shopping but when she arrived at the market, avocados topped her list.

Monday morning, Leigh dressed in a navy blue silk suit and matching silk T-shirt for work. City hall was located on Ventura Street, two blocks south of Jonathan Reid's, but rather than drive by his place, she cut down Signal Street, and then across on Santa Ana. Only two blocks off the main avenue, the city hall was shaded by a giant oak tree, and surrounded by rolling lawns. Beyond the south lawn, an herb garden framed a fish pond, and organically grown produce was featured in a large demonstration garden.

The one-story stucco structure had the requisite graceful arches and red tile roof, but an arbor shading the northern entrance was covered with thickly entwined wisteria vines rather than bougainvillaea. Only a few of the fragrant lavender flowers remained, but the plant's velvet soft pods dangled over the sidewalk as thick as rain. A terracotta fountain fed by four lions, home to several goldfish, gurgled softly amidst a bed of feathery Alaska fern.

The atmosphere at city hall was one of refreshing calm when compared to the frenetic activity Leigh had observed in so many other cities. Business was conducted at the slower pace of rural California, but city hall was nevertheless home to the far-reaching redevelopment plan she had been hired to supervise. Preliminary sketches and diagrams of the project were prominently displayed at the entrance.

Leigh stopped at the receptionist's desk. Opal Lingard had been with the city for more than thirty years. Council members came and went, but she was entrenched. Nearly six feet tall, she wore her sandy-gray hair atop her head in a twisting knot that added another couple of inches to her height. She favored tailored dresses with lace collars and narrow belts which did little to soften her angular figure. Fifty-eight, she had been married for forty years to the rancher who had been her high school sweetheart.

Opal peered over the top of her glasses, and smiled. "Frank's waiting for you, Ms. Bowman. I'm afraid there's bad news about your office, but I'll let him tell it."

Leigh nodded appreciatively and went on down the hall to the mayor's office. Franklin Pierce, who claimed to be distantly related to the fourteenth president, owned the shoe store in Mirasol, and divided his time between there and city hall. His door was always open, but Leigh knocked lightly on the jamb.

"Ms. Bowman!" Frank was on his feet in an instant, and quickly circled his desk to greet her. A balding man in his fifties, he wore lifts to boost his height two inches but had to stand very straight to make the five feet eight he had given on his driver's license. Nearly two hundred pounds, he worked in his shirtsleeves, left his collar unbuttoned, and wore his tie loosely knotted. He greeted Leigh with an enthusiastic vigor, and her delicate hand disappeared in his meaty clasp.

"We had every intention of having your office ready by today, but the painters aren't quite finished. Would you feel comfortable working in the council chambers for a day or two?"

He seemed almost pathetically eager to please her, and Leigh hastened to reassure him. "I'd planned on taking several days, perhaps the whole week, to introduce myself to all the merchants. People are often too intimidated to speak up at large meetings, but when they're given the opportunity to express themselves in private, they are generally eager to share their views. I probably won't have any need for an office until next week so the painters needn't rush."

"You are indeed a treasure, my dear, but I do want to offer a word of advice. Because you're new to town, gathering opinions will be a worthwhile exercise, but should you come across anyone who isn't behind the redevelopment project, please remember that it's already been approved."

Leigh feigned complete ignorance as to his meaning. "Perhaps I misunderstood, but when I interviewed for this job, didn't you tell me all of Mirasol was behind the plan?"

An anxious frown crossed Frank's face before he nodded. "Yes, I did say that, and I meant it, but there's always a certain element that delights in causing the rest of us problems."

"Really? Are they well organized?"

"No, of course not." Frank began to back away. "I don't want to keep you. We have only a few pieces of business for the meeting tonight. I'll introduce you, but no one will expect a full report after one day on the job."

Leigh knew better than to believe that and would be well-prepared for whatever came her way. "I'm familiar with the plan, Mr. Pierce. I'll have no trouble answering whatever questions there might be."

"Frank," he offered as he returned to his chair. "There's no need for formality between us. We're like a family here."

As Leigh turned away, she wished she really could be regarded as part of the delightful community rather than an outsider. She had nearly ten years experience working with city governments, and had learned long ago that whenever people were involved, Murphy's law was sure to apply. Because Mirasol was small, she had hoped the problems would be few, but she had never been so naïve as to imagine there wouldn't be any.

Armed with a clear acrylic clipboard etched with her name, and plenty of paper and pens, she left the city hall for the walk to the business district. At the corner, she decided it would be ridiculous to continue using circuitous routes to avoid passing by Jonathan's house, and headed on up Ventura Street with her head held high. When she reached the library, she entered through the patio. She wanted to say hello to Bonnie and get a card, but as she came through the door, she saw her neighbor was busy with a young man dressed in a denim jacket, Levi's, and work boots.

His shiny black hair brushed his broad shoulders, and he was leaning across the front desk for what was clearly not a discussion of the latest bestseller list. Not wanting to intrude, Leigh moved to a display case filled with a collection of dolls dressed in period costumes, and continued to observe Bonnie and her companion in the reflection on the glass. The man's voice was hushed, but Leigh caught the urgency of his tone. He slammed his fist on the counter for emphasis, then nearly collided with a frail, white-haired woman as he headed toward the door.

Leigh turned to get a better look at him. A Chicano with eyes nearly as dark as his hair, he sent a piercing gaze right through her, but despite his furious expression, he was remarkably handsome. He pushed the door open with both hands and strode out, but an almost palpable hostility lingered in his wake. Leigh waited until Bonnie had checked out a book for the elderly patron, and then approached the desk.

"Are you all right?" Leigh asked. "That guy didn't look as though he was here to inquire about the summer reading program."

Bonnie was dressed in a demure crinkle-pleated dress in a pale peach print. She had done her nails in a bright apricot shade and the tips clicked on the counter as she moved aside a stack of books returned that morning. When she finally found the courage to look up, her cheeks were still tinted with an incriminating blush.

"That was Miguel Fuentes. He works out at the Keene Ranch, and only comes into town to torture me." She reached into the drawer beneath the counter and withdrew a small card tucked inside a plastic sleeve. "Here's your library card. I knew you'd come by soon, and wanted to have it ready."

"Thank you." Leigh slipped the card into her shoulder bag. "Do you have any security here?"

"Security? Well, sure. There's an alarm system I set every night before I leave, but no one has ever tried to rob the place. After all, we never collect more than a few cents a day in fines, and the copying machine doesn't take in all that much."

"I was thinking about you," Leigh stressed. "If Miguel's a problem, perhaps you ought to report him to the police."

"Oh, my God," Bonnie gasped. She covered her open mouth with both hands, then moved to the end of the counter and motioned for Leigh to come close. She lowered her voice to a pleading whisper. "Miguel's a nuisance, but he's no threat and I'd never file a complaint about him. I've known him my whole life, and—"

Now believing she must have observed a lovers' quarrel, Leigh's expression softened, and she nodded sympathetically. "I understand."

Bonnie merely looked frightened rather than relieved. "No. You don't. There's nothing between us. Nothing at all."

Leigh moved aside as a heavy-set man came through the door and approached the desk. He smelled faintly of garlic, and was wearing a pair of suspenders that yanked his sagging trousers up around the middle of his wrinkled shirt. He sent an appraising glance down the sleek lines of her suit, and licked his lips. Leigh had hoped to make friends in Mirasol, but not this badly. She started for the door.

"Thanks for the card. I'll stop by again as soon as I can." In a hurry to get on with her canvas of the merchants, Leigh left the library and moved down the sidewalk with a brisk step. The theater wasn't open in the mornings, but the salty scent of popcorn still lingered in the air.

Leigh made a mental note to buy some microwave popcorn on her next trip to the market, crossed Signal Street, and passed the post office. The major portion of the long block was taken up by Keene Park. Snowy Madame Hardy roses, a favorite of Victorian gardens, framed the plaza entrance. Spanish tile decorated the fountain at the center, and Leigh paused to watch a sparrow dip into the bubbling water for a cooling drink.

Inside the park, small children were climbing over the colorfully painted play equipment, while their mothers sat talking on benches shaded by trees as old as the town. Another of Elijah Keene's projects, the beautifully landscaped park had a bandshell in the far corner for outdoor entertainments. As the city grew, the park land would become increasingly valuable, but Leigh had been pleased to learn Elijah had donated the land with the stipulation it was never to be used for any purpose other than the public's enjoyment as a park.

In Los Angeles, too many parks were scarred by gang battles, or filled with homeless clad in ragged clothes sleeping on the grass. With the redevelopment plan, the city of Mirasol intended to manage its growth, provide incentives for its youth, and employment for its citizens. Leigh believed in those goals, and the sunlit beauty of the park was clear evidence of the value of long-range planning. She sat down by the fountain to make a few notes to herself for that night's meeting, then continued her walk.

At the end of the block, a newly constructed building with a stair-stepped Pueblo facade was the site of Marmalade, an elegant cafe decorated with French country charm, and Silken Shadows, an expensive boutique. The cafe would not open for another hour, and Leigh moved on to the boutique. The window display featured charming lace fashions that were as artfully arranged as flowers in a bridal bouquet. Because of her diminutive size, she avoided such extravagantly feminine styles for fear she would look more like a doll than a grown woman wearing them, but she could not help but admire such pretty clothes.

The summer sun was warm, and she welcomed the rush of an air-conditioned breeze as she pushed open the plate glass door. Silken Shadows was as handsomely appointed a shop as any on Rodeo Drive. Carpeted with plush white wool, and scented with expensive perfume, it featured fashions attractively displayed by designer rather than color or size. Soft chamber music added to the shop's luxurious atmosphere.

As Leigh entered, a statuesque brunette left a tall stool behind a counter filled with exquisitely crafted Tabra jewelry, and came forward to greet her. She was wearing a knit tunic in a taupe and white abstract print, a taupe skirt slit high to show off a tantalizing glimpse of slender thigh, and taupe flats. Her thick sable hair was pulled back in a sophisticated chignon, and her make-up had been applied with a delicate hand. Perhaps in her mid-thirties, she was easily the most beautiful woman Leigh had ever seen.

"Good morning," the woman greeted her in a soft, sultry tone. "I carry only a few petite sizes, but I'll be happy to special order anything you find appealing."

Leigh turned over the price tag on a silk jacket trimmed with a jumble of print patches and tried not to gasp. "Everything looks appealing, but today I just want to introduce myself." As she explained her mission, Leigh had to assume that this elegant creature was on her side.

"Welcome to Mirasol," she responded. "I'm Denise Keene. That's a beautiful suit, by the way. Navy is a good color for you. I was just about to have some mineral water. Would you like some?"

"Yes. That would be very nice, thank you."

Denise stepped through a louvered door at the rear of the shop, and returned with two beautiful blue bottles of Tŷ Nant, and crystal water goblets. "Sit down with me." She gestured toward the chairs clustered near a full-length mirror and placed the glasses on the small gilt table between them. Covered in nubby white silk, the chairs were deep and comfortable.

"What a marvelous bottle," Leigh said, for not only the vivid blue glass, but the graceful shape made it distinctive.

"Yes, isn't it pretty? The spring water's imported from Wales, but I buy it simply for the bottle rather than the taste." She split one between them, and left the second unopened. Her nails were beautifully manicured with clear polish tipped with white. A three carat diamond solitaire adorned her right hand and she wore diamond studs in her ears. She raised her glass in a silent toast before taking a sip.

Leigh eased back in her chair. "I'm not used to being pampered like this and I could sit here all day, but I do want to become acquainted. If your name is Keene, are you a descendant of Elijah's?"

Denise crossed her legs and adjusted the drape of her skirt. "I was married to his grandson, and because the name is an asset in Mirasol, I decided to keep it. Eli is also my ex-hushand's name, and his late father's as well. I swore if we had a son I was going to name him Conrad, or Virgil, or anything other than Elijah, but we failed to produce an heir so the opportunity never arose. My ex and I are still on friendly terms. I imagine you'll be seeing a great deal of him during the redevelopment project."

Denise's voice flowed with the effortless grace of the classical accompaniment piped through her shop, but Leigh was not certain if that were merely a casual comment or a threat to stay clear of a man she still considered hers. Not knowing how to respond, she chose to disregard the subject entirely. "I hope to see the whole town renovated as beautifully as this building. You've set a high standard."

"Well, I could afford to after the divorce. I don't want to see Mirasol lose any of its uniqueness, however. I'd welcome the business more tourists would bring, but I really believe the musty quaintness is part of the city's charm."

Leigh took a long drink of water, and tried to decide if Denise Keene were purposely giving her mixed messages, or merely confused in her outlook. "Musty charm isn't what most tourists want, Ms. Keene, or they'd tour archaeological sites. What Mirasol hopes to attract is suffcient wealth to enliven the local ecomony. The whole town will need not only a facelift, but shops as sophisticated as yours to accomplish that."

Denise smiled slightly. "Please call me Denise." When Leigh nodded, she continued. "I hope that you don't believe taste and wealth are synonymous."

"No. I realized that a long time ago." Again Leigh had the unsettling sensation that Denise was talking around the issue rather than about it. She preferred a straightforward approach herself, and doubted they would become friends. She placed her goblet on the table, and sat forward.

"I don't want to take up any more of your time. I'll come back another day to shop."

"Please do." Denise rose with the graceful ease common to tall women and walked Leigh to the door.

There was a ceramics studio located around the corner, and as Leigh made the turn she looked back to find Denise standing out on the sidewalk. The woman waved, and stepped back to study the merchandise in her window before returning to her shop. Denise looked as though she had just stepped out of Vogue, but despite her hospitality, Leigh could not recall ever meeting a more coldly forbidding woman.

She shivered slightly, and again resolved not to make snap judgments, but without even knowing Elijah Keene III, she was grateful he was the one who would be involved in the redevelopment rather than Denise, who obviously had exquisite taste, but very little heart.

Three

Ornately scrolled wrought-iron chandeliers lit the city hall auditorium with warm pools of light. The dark beams of the twenty foot ceiling were decorated with flowing arabesques accented with gold leaf and the intricate pattern was repeated in bright frescos around the four open windows and both doorways. The heavy oak doors were trimmed with wrought-iron and carved with rows of deeply incised rectangles and squares.

By 7:20, the auditorium was nearly full and the janitor began setting up additional chairs in the rear. Friends greeted each other across the room with friendly jests that echoed off the high ceiling and added treble notes to the low rumbling conversation. The five council members were seated in front at a mahogany conference table, each with a notepad, pencil, decanter of water, and glass. Opal Lingard had a small desk near the windows, and sat poised to keep the minutes while she enjoyed the fragrant evening breeze.

An extra chair had been placed at the end of the conference table for Leigh. She had spent so much time in town, she had had to rush to bathe and dress for the meeting, but her choice of a slate gray suit had already been made that morning. She had her notes in front of her, but sat in a relaxed pose with her hands folded in her lap. She had met with the council members on her initial visit to Mirasol, liked their willingness to hire a professional to oversee their project, and looked forward to working with them.

Zoe Kunkel was at the opposite end of the table. Her ample

figure draped in a pink and green print, she exuded the same lively charm dispensed at her store, Fish, Feathers, and Fur, one of the most complete pet shops Leigh had ever visited. In the window, Dalmatian puppies had been scrapping playfully on a field of shredded newspaper. Just inside, a miniature potbellied piglet rooted around the small sawdust-filled plastic shell originally intended as a child's wading pool. The dear little piglet's silver hide was covered with coarse black hair and although he had grunted in pleasure as Leigh had petted him, she just could not see herself owning a pig as a pet.

Zoe also carried lop-earred rabbits, calico guinea pigs, golden hamsters, white rats, and tiny mice. Tiered cages held a colorful assortment of kittens sleeping in blissful heaps. In a dimly lit side room, gurgling fish tanks displayed an exotic array of tropical fish. Leigh had lingered by the Red Cap Orandas, white fish with bulbous bodies, beautiful lacy fan tails, and bright red beanies. Above them, Bubble Eyes, black fish with inflated pouches beneath their shiny eyes, seemed to be watching her.

Near the cash register, electric-green tree frogs used suction-cupped toes to climb the sides of their glass tank. Beside them, there were Australian Walking Sticks, brown-speckled insects that resembled the cork at the bottom of their cage. An informative note said the curious creatures ate rose stems, leaves, and fresh catnip.

Birds filled the back of the shop with an incessant cacophony, while on the side, snakes lay coiled in silent splendor. Leigh had bent down to examine an iguana, and found his striking fluorescent color came from skin as perfectly patterned as fine bead work. She had given the piglet a last tickle before leaving the shop, and smiled as she thought of him now.

George Culbert was seated next to Zoe. A gaunt man in his sixties with a sparse gray beard, he had said hello to Leigh when she called at his garage, then promptly stuck his head under the hood of a pickup truck. She wasn't certain if he was a taciturn individual, or merely shy, but she had taken the hint, wished him a good day, and gone on.

Frank Pierce had the center seat at the table, with Bruce Stiz, a CPA, at his left. Bruce was in his early fifties. Tall and broad, with graying blond hair and glasses, his thin lips formed an unfortunate downward curve that reminded Leigh of a bullfrog's pompous pout, but he was among the most vocal supporters of the redevelopment plan.

The last of the council members was Dr. Randall Hubbs, a tall, rawboned dentist whose features seemed to droop from his bushy black brows. Leigh had yet to see him smile, but he had greeted her warmly that night. It wasn't the council which caused her nervousness, however, but the townspeople she had yet to meet. Frank Pierce had already picked up his gavel to call the meeting to order when Jonathan Reid took the last seat in the front row. He leaned over to thank an older man dressed in khakis, who had apparently saved the seat for him.

Leigh rose for the salute to the flag, and repeated the words clearly. She wasn't actually addressing the group, but she had learned that speaking in a determined manner before she was called upon to do so lent her voice a confident timbre later. It was part of the calm, professional manner she strove to project. As soon as everyone had been seated, she did her best to direct her attention to the council, but the few times her glance strayed in Jonathan's direction, he was staring at her with a virulent contempt.

They might have opposing views on the redevelopment issue, but Leigh thought it very unfair of him to target her for his anger. After all, the plan had been discussed for more than a year before she had been hired, and she thought he should have come to terms with the fact it had been approved long before this. Maybe he was the type who delighted in holding a grudge, but she thought it a shame such an intelligent man could not see the benefits to Mirasol when they were so plain to her, and to nearly everyone else.

After the minutes of the last meeting were approved as read, the agenda contained the usual city business: a proposal to solicit bids for tree trimming in Keene Park, a discussion of the necessity to purchase new radio equipment for the fire department, and the question of how to deal with a resident who had built a wall without first obtaining a building permit. Not surprisingly, the last item inspired a heated debate as many of those present believed merely levying a fine would invite other residents to build whatever suited them without bothering to first get a permit.

Leigh had lost count of how many council meetings she had attended over the years, but she had long ago mastered an expression of polite interest while allowing her mind to wander over more diverting topics than those under discussion. Because she was so new to Mirasol, she studied the people in the audience, and recognized several she had met that day. Rhonda Boyle's hair was dyed the incendiary red of a road flare, making her easy to spot.

Rhonda was thin as a zipper, and when Leigh had arrived at her shop, she had been standing out on the sidewalk smoking. She had taken one last drag on her cigarette, drawing her heavily made-up features into a contorted prune, and then had flicked the butt into the gutter from curved burgundy nails. Easily sixty-five, she had been wearing one of the leopard print jumpsuits featured in her shop window, and Leigh had been distressed to discover it was easily the most tasteful item she carried. The woman had a passion for gold lamé that would have put a Las Vegas showgirl to shame, and Leigh had found it difficult to believe she sold many of her things to local ranchers' wives.

Beverly MacNair, Bonnie's mother, was also easy to identify. Clearly not a natural blonde, she bore only a slight resemblance to Loni Anderson, but emphasized it by copying the beautiful star's wildly dramatic hairstyle. Leigh had found her as refreshingly natural as Bonnie, but still doubted she would patronize her shop.

Dr. Hubbs leaned over to whisper, "I hope you're not bored. This is one of our better meetings."

Leigh smiled to assure him she was still awake, but the wall issue was taking far longer than she had anticipated. Her glance drawn to Jonathan, she found him again speaking with the man by his side. His expression was relaxed now, tempting a lingering look, but she forced herself to turn away before he caught her. She was greatly relieved when in the next minute a decision was made to fine the owner of the wall built without a permit, but to force the removal of any other residents who attempted to slip past the city inspectors.

Frank Pierce then rose to welcome Leigh to Mirasol. He briefly reviewed her qualifications, and complimented her on her charm to inspire a warm round of applause from the audience. Leigh rose, thanked everyone for their enthusiastic greeting and spoke without having to refer to her notes.

"As the mayor described, I've been involved with redevelopment programs in several southern California cities, but none has offered the opportunity to work with as comprehensive and exciting a project as the one here in Mirasol. Too often towns are allowed to spread out from the center in a series of tacky strip malls and congested shopping plazas that not only destroy business in the central city, but fail to create any sense of community in the outlying areas.

"Mirasol has chosen instead to build on the best of its historic past to assure a bright future, and I want to congratulate all of you for your obvious love of your city and your inspired vision for its renovation. I'm so proud to be here, and I look forward to working with you to make Mirasol all it can be. Please drop by my office here in city hall to share your ideas, and feel free to speak with me any time you see me on the street."

Leigh nodded to Frank Pierce, but before he could continue the meeting, Jonathan Reid raised his hand. Leigh wasn't in the least bit surprised, and called on him immediately. "Yes, Mr. Reid. Do you have a question?"

Jonathan rose, took a step forward, and jammed his hands into his pockets. He was dressed as he had been when she had last seen him; not even his sour expression had changed. A sarcastic edge slanted his every word.

"Mirasol is undoubtedly fortunate to have a woman with your

extraordinary abilities working for us, but I can't help but wonder what you'll do after you've completed your contract with the city."

That was scarcely the hostile challenge Leigh had expected, but she could see where he was leading. Like playing chess, her only hope was to block his move before he could call her an outsider who would soon pack up and move on. She came around to the front of the conference table and leaned back against it in a deliberately provocative pose.

"Why, Mr. Reid, we barely know each other—are you hinting at giving me a reason to stay?" Just as she had known the audience would, they erupted in loud guffaws and hilarious giggles while Jonathan's expression filled with a frustrated rage. Rather than dent the table, Frank whacked his gavel against a small wood block with a syncopated rhythm a jazz percussionist would have envied. A lesser man would have walked out, but Jonathan stood his ground.

"What an enchanting thought," he replied as soon as the last titterings of amusement died down. "We've heard a great deal about how much revenue this project will generate when it's completed, but I'd like to hear the specifics as to how shopkeepers are going to cover their expenses during the construction of the new commercial corridor."

Giving his question the consideration it deserved, Leigh stepped away from the table and straightened her posture. "The project will be built in several phases, Mr. Reid. The merchants now in business in Mirasol will be given the first opportunity to rent space in the new buildings. When they have all been relocated, the present stores will be razed and replaced with exact replicas of the original structures."

"So the shops with the choicest location, those across from the park, will go to newcomers?"

This time the audience responded with loud and unmistakable grumblings. Leigh raised her hands in a request for silence before Frank could again pound his gavel. "At present, the success of the shops beside the park—Marmalade and Silken Shadows—prove the value of expansion. With the next block constructed of equally beautiful buildings, all the downtown shops will have a prime location. In fact, I fully expect the block past the park, with shops on both sides of the street, to be the most popular."

"That's merely conjecture," Jonathan pointed out.

"No," Leigh argued. "It's an opinion based on the considerable experience for which I was hired."

"Tourism is at all time low in California," Jonathan said, swiftly taking a new tack. "People are terrified of earthquakes, and if they can stand the thought of the ground moving under their feet, then the threat of urban violence alienates them. Just where are you going to find the numbers of tourists the expanded business district will require to succeed?"

This time the crowd leaned together in twos and threes for whispered exchanges that gave clear evidence of their fears. Again Leigh was ready to defuse them. "You're absolutely right, Mr. Reid. But the very problems that will keep out-of-state tourists away will make Mirasol a paradise for the harried Los Angeles resident, and with seven million from which to draw, we may find ourselves having to turn people away. The public's memory is mercifully brief, and by the time the redevelopment is complete, we should be experiencing an upswing in tourism from throughout the United States." She smiled as heads bobbed in the rapt audience. Her comments were not only logical, but had been readily believed.

Frank punctuated Leigh's final remark with a forceful swing of his gavel. "That's all the time I can allow you, Jonathan. Is there anyone else with something to contribute?" He surveyed the crowd, and called upon a man seated in the rear. "Come on up here, Eli, so we can all hear you."

Leigh returned to her seat, but she had a clear view of Elijah Keene III as he walked up the side aisle. He was perhaps five foot ten, blond, slender, and dressed in a blue silk shirt with the sleeves rolled up and a pair of well-tailored gray slacks. She would have bet on the fact his black loafers came from Gucci,

and his Rolex was gold, but there was no arrogance about the
man, only a boyish charm. When he reached the front of the
room, he winked at her before turning to address the crowd.

"It's getting late, but before Frank adjourns the meeting, I
want to remind everyone that the expansion downtown, and the
proposed resort hotel and golf course, will be built on land I
currently own. I wouldn't have encouraged the project had I not
believed it would benefit the whole town by bringing in jobs
and increased revenue. The Keene family has always stood for
what's best for Mirasol, and this is no exception. Let's all give
Ms. Bowman our support in bringing our city into its second
great era of prosperity."

When he began to applaud, the whole auditorium joined in.
Leigh couldn't help but be pleased, but she read the oath on
Jonathan's lips before he left his seat. As he started for the door,
he was joined by Denise Keene, who slipped her arm through
his on the way out. Even knowing she and Jonathan had little
chance of becoming friends, to see him with Denise caused
Leigh a sharp stab of disappointment. She simply couldn't picture the man who had taught her how to skim stones on the
ocean being happy with a woman who was so stylized and cold.

She didn't let her feelings show in her expression, for indeed
she was pleased with her portion of the meeting, and bid the
council members good night with a relaxed smile. But her insides felt hollow, as though she had lost something precious. It
was a feeling she knew only too well. She gathered up her notes,
but as she turned away from the table, she found Eli Keene
waiting for her.

He offered his hand. "I'm sorry we haven't met before tonight. Don't let Jonathan get you down. He has the temperament
of a pit bull and isn't happy unless he has a neck to chew on.
I'm sorry it had to be yours tonight. The least I can do is provide
a more appropriate welcome to Mirasol. Let me take you out
to the Inn for a drink."

Now that he had moved close, Leigh noted the laugh lines
at the corners of his blue eyes, and decided despite his youthful

manner, he was probably Jonathan's age. She had not had a date in a year, and now she had been asked on two in as many days. Haunted by the scene of Jonathan leaving with Denise, she made up her mind in an instant.

"That's very nice of you. I've driven by the Inn, but haven't had a chance to stop and I'd really like to see it."

Eli feigned deep disappointment. "I'd hoped your interest would be in me rather than the Inn."

He was teasing her, but Leigh feared she had been tactless. "I'm sorry. That didn't sound right, did it? I really would like to talk with you. I'll bet you know all kinds of interesting stories about Mirasol."

Eli shook his head slightly. "That's not really my favorite subject, but because you're new to town, I'll indulge you just this once."

"I better take notes, then."

"No," Eli leaned down to whisper. "You won't even want to."

As his breath caressed Leigh's cheek, she caught the scent of Obession cologne and shivered with a longing that brought a bright blush to her cheeks. She had been so busy wrapping up her last project before taking the job with Mirasol that she had not realized just how lonely she was. Jonathan Reid had taken advantage of that sorry fact, invited her home, and then thrown her out. Well, she knew more about him, and about herself, than she had yesterday, and she wouldn't make the same mistake twice. Being lonely was sad, but accepting a date with the first attractive man to come along had simply been stupid.

"I'll meet you there," she answered, but she intended to keep their conversation focused on business, where she could safely rely on her expertise rather than worry about being sabotaged by her aching heart.

Elijah Keene had built the Mirasol Inn in the ornate mission revival style to capitalize on the tourists' natural fascination with California's colorful history. His architect had borrowed so liberally from the graceful arched façades and domed bell towers of the missions at Carmel and San Gabriel that many tourists assumed the new hotel was in actuality a refurbished eighteenth-century mission. Elijah was amused by their mistake, and made no effort to dispel it. He decorated the spacious rooms with heavily carved furniture from Spain, used bold Mexican fabrics for drapes, and left the austere white walls as devoid of ornamentation as a monk's cell.

In sharp contrast to the starkly decorated rooms, the lounge, restaurant, bar, and ballroom provided a feast for the eye with open beams painted in bright floral designs enhanced with gold leaf. The lighting fixtures were Mexican silver, and the furniture upholstered in deep red velvet. On every wall, large paintings of California landscapes were displayed in ornate gilt frames. Off the main lobby, an exquisitely beautiful chapel contained a massive gold-leafed altar carved in Mexico, and striking windows of Tiffany glass.

At present, only a few of the Inn's rooms were available, but the restaurant was popular with locals for its delicious cuisine, and the chapel and ballroom were frequently rented for weddings and receptions. On a Monday night, however, the restaurant was closed, and the bar would draw only a few regular patrons. As Leigh turned into the parking lot, Eli left his black Porsche and waited for her to pull into the space beside his.

The Inn was located on Mirasol Avenue, a mile from the business district, and while the drive had been short, Leigh was confident she had had sufficient time to clear the council meeting from her mind, and focus on the questions she wished to ask Eli. When he took her hand as they started for the entrance, she quickly pulled away, but smiled as she explained why.

"I do want to get to know you, Eli, but let's keep it on a purely professional basis."

Looking sincerely pained, Eli pulled open the heavy oak door and waited for Leigh to precede him. The lobby of the Inn was lit with a soft golden glow designed to flatter the aging furnishings, but Leigh felt as though she were stepping into a classic film noir; it would not have surprised her to have seen Humphrey Bogart and Lauren Bacall standing at the desk waiting to check in. The bar was located on the right, through an arched doorway, and even more dimly lit than the lobby.

Eli waved to the bartender behind the long mahogany bar, and directed Leigh toward a secluded red leather booth. He waited for her to be seated, then slid close and rested his arm along the back of the booth. "I'm the most professional man you could ever hope to meet," he announced with mock seriousness. "In fact, I'm so adept at separating business from pleasure, that I rival my Porsche at ease in shifting gears."

Leigh shook her head. "You're simply incorrigible, aren't you?"

"That's precisely the word my teachers used to describe me, but it's been a long while since I've been in school." Eli ran his fingertips up the side of Leigh's neck in a lazy caress and laughed when she shivered.

The bartender approached to take their orders before Leigh could tell Eli to keep his hands to himself. "Perrier with lime, please," she said.

"Wouldn't you rather have something stronger?" Eli asked. "If you're worried about driving home, I'll gladly make my personal suite available for the night."

A sly smile tugged at the corner of his mouth, and Leigh readily understood that rather than simple hospitality, his company would be included. He used his every opportunity to come close, touch her, and make suggestive remarks, and she knew instinctively that he was not merely teasing. Were she to accept his offer, he would definitely make the night memorable. She thought his slim build due to the same nervous energy that kept her slender, but whatever the reason, he was extremely attractive. She addressed her reply to the bartender.

"Perrier is *all* I want, thank you." She waited until the bartender had turned away to answer Eli. "Please don't think I'm not tempted. I definitely am, but for all the wrong reasons."

Eli arched a brow. "It's only my wealth that appeals to you?"

Athough her laugh failed to reassure him, it served to melt Leigh's tension. "You do have a wealthy man's polished manners, but no, it's not the smoothness of your approach that provides the only appeal. You're very handsome, and because I was raised in an affectionate family, a man with an easy touch always appeals to me. But—"

"Damn. For a minute, you had me believing I was really doing well."

The bartender returned with their drinks, and Leigh took a quick sip of hers while Eli poured the jigger of Scotch over his glass of ice. "My first priority in Mirasol has to be my job, Eli. If we were to become involved, it could present terrible problems for us both. The people opposed to the plan would call me your whore, and—"

"My God. I'd put a quick stop to that," Eli assured her.

"Yes. I'm sure that you possess the influence to silence them, but their feelings wouldn't change and it would make my stay here doubly difficult. There's also the very real possibility that having a personal relationship might create conflicts which would spill over into implementing the plan, and then the whole town would suffer."

"No. You were hired to direct the plan, and as far as I'm concerned, whatever you say goes." He reached for her hand, and planted a whisper-soft kiss in her palm. "Now, do you have any other objections? I'm certain I can discount them as easily as your first two. If you like me, and I most definitely like you, then let's just enjoy it."

His expression was as blatantly seductive as his words, and suddenly it wasn't merely the evocative decor that reminded Leigh of the movies. She felt as though she had stepped into a scene Eli must have rehearsed innumerable times with other women. One actor had been more than enough for her, and she withdrew her hand from his and moved over slightly to put more distance between them.

Technically, she worked for the City of Mirasol rather than

for Elijah Keene III, but that didn't mean she couldn't file a sexual harassment lawsuit against him if he continued propositioning her. She preferred to defuse the situation with humor rather than threats, however, and turned flippant. "Do women usually leap into your bed within minutes of meeting you?" she asked.

Eli's mood changed as abruptly as hers, and he downed half the Chivas Regal before he answered in a harsh, clipped tone. "You're the first woman I've invited into my bed in a damn long time, Leigh, and if you want character references, I'll have everyone on the city council mail you one first thing in the morning."

That a provocative question from her could have prompted such an angry response, after the way he had come on to her, shocked Leigh, but she had no choice but to stifle the impulse to walk out. "There, do you see?" she asked pointedly. "Once you mix a professional relationship with a romantic one, conflict is inevitable. Now I want to be able to work with you without having to constantly worry about being pressured for more, or hurting your feelings. I need you, Eli, but it would be dangerous for us both to move past friendship."

Eli opened his mouth to respond with a crude expletive, but caught himself before it escaped his lips. "You're right, of course, but that doesn't mean what might be the wisest course tonight will be the best decision forever."

Leigh liked him ever so much better now that he had dropped the sophisticated moves which must surely devastate the local ranchers' daughters. She offered her hand, and after a slight hesitation, Eli took it. "I can't make any promises," she confided truthfully. "I'm recently divorced, and quite frankly, the prospect of becoming involved with anyone scares me."

Eli nodded. "Now I understand. Maybe you're suffering from post-traumatic stress disorder."

"No, not at all. My husband and I didn't have awful fights. We merely had different goals in life. I've met your ex-wife, by the way, and I'm not sure what to make of her."

Eli finished his drink and signaled the bartender for another. The man already had it ready and brought it to their table. Eli dribbled the Scotch over the ice, but didn't take a sip. "Denise is like a chocolate Easter bunny. She has a delicious shell, but there's nothing inside and she'll leave you with an awful stomachache. I was lucky that all she cost me was money. We all have 20/20 hindsight, but I sure as hell wish I'd let Jonathan have her back in high school."

Leigh would not have mentioned Jonathan, but because Eli had, she felt free to pursue the topic. "You and Jonathan knew each other in school?"

"Sure. It never had more than two hundred students and everyone knew everybody else. Denise went to Mirasol High, but she made certain all the guys at the prep school knew her. She's always attracted attention the way blue serge gathers lint. Even at sixteen she was adept at playing Jonathan and me off one another. One week she'd be with him, the next me. We were both eighteen, and when we graduated, she still had a couple of years of high school to finish. Jonathan went to Stanford, but I was never much of a student and stayed here.

"I think it broke Jonathan's heart when Denise married me, but he was the lucky one." Eli closed his eyes, obviously shutting out memories too painful to relive. When he opened them, he regarded Leigh with a weary smile.

"Jonathan's objection to the redevelopment plan is sincere, but because he lost his first love to me, he'd fight me no matter what I proposed. You handled him well tonight. In fact, you made him look ridiculous, and that's precisely the tactic to take with him. Wounding his pride will hurt him far worse than anything else you could ever do. Don't get me wrong. There's a lot I admire about him, but Denise came between whatever chance we had to be friends."

Finally inspired to discuss the plan, Eli straightened up. He withdrew a gold pen from his pocket, and made a quick sketch of an avocado on his cocktail napkin. He then added a cute face, and a crown. "I'm more than just the avocado king, Leigh. You must have read *The Good Earth* in high school, and that book makes it plain that wealth always lies in the land. I'll never part with all my groves, but I can sacrifice enough acreage to build a luxury hotel and resort complex with facilities for golf, tennis, and swimming. That's what's sparking the redevelopment plan, so it really doesn't matter how loudly or eloquently Jonathan protests. We're moving ahead on it."

Leigh reached for the napkin. "I didn't realize an avocado could have a personality. May I keep this? It might make a good logo."

Eli quickly signed his name on the corner of the napkin, pocketed his pen, and handed it to her. "Frame it if you like." The bartender caught his eye; he checked his Rolex, and sighed unhappily. "It's getting late and I still haven't told you much about Mirasol. Of course, we could always go upstairs and continue our discussion without having to worry about being interrupted."

"That's enough, Mr. Keene," Leigh cautioned, but she was confident they had reached an accord and her smile was genuine. "You've told me more than you may have realized. I saw Jonathan leave tonight's meeting with Denise. Now that I know they have a history, there's always the hope she'll keep him too distracted to complicate my life."

"She'd certainly like to," he agreed.

As they left the booth, Eli swung by the bar to leave the bartender a generous tip. "I own the place, so the drinks are on the house," he told Leigh as they walked beneath the arched doorway, "but it's important to keep my employees happy. Now what about keeping me happy? When can we get together again to talk about Mirasol?"

Even in the lobby's dim light Leigh caught the teasing sparkle in his eyes. "It will be a business discussion, of course," she warned.

Eli raised his hands to protest his innocence. "Of course, Ms. Bowman. I wouldn't dream of asking you to compromise your professional ethics."

When they reached the parking lot, Leigh leaned back against her car. The night had turned cool, and she hugged her arms. "First, I'd like to really get acquainted with the town. Then perhaps you'll share more of your valuable insights."

Eli cocked his head. "Knowing just how uncomplicated the townsfolk are, you'll only need until the end of the week. I'll give you a call then." He pulled his keys from his pocket, and tossed them between his hands. "How do you like your apartment?"

Surprised that he would ask, Leigh frowned slightly. "It's very nice, thank you." Her eyes widened as he stepped close, but for once, he refrained from touching her.

"I own that duplex," he confided with a sly wink, "so you see, you're sleeping in my bed whether you realized it or not."

Leigh just shook her head and got into her car. She turned her key in the ignition, but heard the low, rumbling purr of Eli's Porsche rather than her own engine. As she turned out onto the road back toward town, she watched his headlights glow in her rearview mirror. She felt certain he would respect the line she had drawn between them, but knowing how vulnerable she truly was, she feared maintaining her own distance might not be all that easy.

Four

Leigh shut off her alarm clock's jarring buzzer and rolled out of bed. After waking comfortably snuggled in Doug's arms for nine years, she couldn't curl up and catch a few extra minutes sleep without feeling so utterly alone that she could not bear to face the new day. To get up before becoming overwhelmed with loneliness was a race she ran every morning. The weekends were the worst, but she had learned to get up at her usual time even if she lacked a compelling reason to do so.

She chose another of her many tailored suits, this one in a sandy beige, and low heeled shoes to make touring the town as painless as possible. She ate a quick breakfast and then drove to city hall to check in. As she came through the front doors, she was amazed to find Opal Lingard peering around a philodendron of truly magnificent proportions. It was decorated with a big red bow, and when she read her name on the attached envelope, she assumed it was from the city council.

"What a wonderful surprise," she exclaimed.

Opal clucked her tongue. "Can't be that much of a surprise after last night."

Leigh had no idea what had prompted such a cynical remark until she opened the envelope and read the card. The plant was indeed a welcoming gift, but from Eli Keene, rather than the council. She noted Opal's smirk, and knew without having to ask that the receptionist had also read the card. Leigh fixed her with a steady stare.

"Because you obviously know who sent this, I won't pretend

that you don't, but from now on, anything which arrives here with my name on it is to be considered private. I don't care whether it's an official surveyor's report for the redevelopment project, or a bouquet of flowers. It's to go straight to my office with the envelope unopened."

Suddenly preoccupied with typing the minutes of last night's meeting, Opal's hands fluttered over her notepad. "Yes, Ms. Bowman. I'm only here to make your job easier, but if you want my advice, you'll avoid Eli Keene and find yourself a nice young man who doesn't get bored with a woman faster than a ripe avocado rots."

Though Leigh considered Opal's comment a novel, if perhaps appropriate, way to describe Eli's relationships as fleeting, she didn't appreciate it. "I didn't ask for your advice, Mrs. Lingard, nor do I ever intend to on personal matters. Is my office ready?"

Opal removed her glasses and polished the lenses on her skirt. "Well, the paint's dry, but the furniture hasn't been moved back in as yet. Lester Cornell—he's our janitor—should get to it today, but sometimes he's a bit forgetful." She paused to don her glasses. "I suppose I'll have to remind him."

"Yes. Please do." Leigh picked up the beautiful plant, and marched it right down the hall to her empty office. The telephone hadn't been removed, and she sat the plant beside it on the telephone book where the pot wouldn't soil the pale beige carpet. She brushed off her hands and opened the miniblinds to give the philodendron plenty of light. With an exuberant abundance of heart-shaped leaves, it was the most beautiful one she had ever seen, but she knew better than to ask Opal for the number of the Keene Ranch to thank Eli. Deciding to look it up later, she left to spend a second day strolling through the downtown.

As she passed by Jonathan's, she recognized the man who had saved a seat for him at last night's meeting. Again dressed in khakis, he was running an edger along the grass bordering the sidewalk. Gathering her courage, she crossed the street to speak with him.

"Mr. Tate?" she called.

Ron quickly tipped his frayed straw hat. Years of working outdoors had given his deeply tanned skin a leathery toughness, but his dark eyes held a bright twinkle, and his smile was warm. "Good morning to you, Ms. Bowman."

"Good morning. You keep Mr. Reid's yard as beautiful as the gardens featured in Martha Stewart's magazine. I've just been given a philodendron, and I'm not sure how to care for it. Do you have any advice?"

Ron leaned against the edger's long handle. In his late sixties, his posture was still proudly erect, and hard work kept him slim. "Yes, ma'am, I sure do. Buy yourself a little box of Miracle-Gro at the market, and follow the instructions. Philodendrons are thirsty plants, so keep it well-watered, and it will make you a small jungle in no time. If the stems get too long, just snip them off, root them in a jar of water, and start yourself a new plant."

Leigh made a note of his suggestions on her clipboard. "Thank you. I'll do that. I've not had much luck with house-plants, but maybe I've just lacked an incentive."

Ron regarded her with a skeptical glance. "After what I saw last night, it's difficult to imagine you ever lack purpose. I'm as opposed to the scourge as Jonathan, by the way, but that don't mean I'm not glad you're here in Mirasol."

"Thank you, but what's the 'scourge'?"

Ron removed his hat to wipe his forehead on his sleeve, then plunked it back in place. His dark brown hair was still thick, and he wore it combed straight back. "In my opinion, that's all this redevelopment plan is: a scourge that will ooze over the city.

Leigh considered his words before she responded. "Mr. Tate, the plan won't cause widespread destruction. I'll not debate the issue with you but I'm confident that when you walk through a revitalized downtown, you'll be pleased rather than sorry."

Ron shook his head. "Ain't nothing but greed behind this,

Ms. Bowman. Tourists won't just bring money. They'll bring all their petty gripes in their luggage, and nobody, not them or us, will be any happier for it."

Small towns were known to be clannish, but his view of tourists struck Leigh as unnecessarily harsh. "Did you share your opinion with the city council when the plan was first proposed?"

"Every chance I got," Ron assured her, "but once the merchants caught the scent of money, I could have more easily gone swimming with sharks in a feeding frenzy."

"We all have to earn a living, Mr. Tate." Believing they would never see eye to eye, Leigh was about to thank him for his gardening tip and be on her way when she heard the screen door slam. She had not intended to speak with Jonathan that morning, but when she turned and saw him striding toward her, it was too late to walk away.

"Good morning, Mr. Reid," she said brightly, but his expression held not a hint of welcome.

Jonathan failed to return Leigh's greeting, and dismissed Ron Tate with a quick nod. The gardener again tipped his hat, and went back to work. "You're wasting your time with Ron," Jonathan told her. "He's every bit as opposed to your plan as I am."

Jonathan was standing two feet away, and despite the hostility of his mood, Leigh felt his heat coil around her with a stirring intensity that made Eli's gentle caress seem absolutely chilly by comparison. It was easy to dismiss the attraction that sizzled between them as a mere trick of chemistry, but that rationalization failed to ease her disappointment. She had found life to be filled with malicious pranks, and surely this was another of them.

Eli had complimented her on wounding Jonathan's pride, but as she viewed the stubborn set of his jaw, she felt ashamed rather than proud. "I shouldn't have said what I did last night," she offered in hopes of at least a partial reconciliation, "but I want this project to succeed. Humor is one of men's favorite tactics to dismiss women's concerns, and—"

Although startled by her apology, Jonathan quickly interrupted. "I regard this as a war, Ms. Bowman, and if I'd been able to make you look ridiculous in front of half the town, believe me, I'd have done it."

He had stated his position so forcefully, Leigh didn't doubt his resolve, and remained on guard. "I won't keep you," she said. "I merely asked Ron for a gardening tip. I wasn't attempting to subvert your employees."

"He's his own man," Jonathan argued, "and I won't dock him for the time."

Jonathan was still glaring at her, his dark eyes smoldering with what Leigh recognized as hatred rather than Sunday's desire, and she began backing away. Thinking it a damn shame he wasn't Eli Keene, she grasped her clipboard more tightly, and with a last faint smile, turned and went on into town.

Ron waited until Leigh had crossed the street, and then came up behind Jonathan, who was still watching her. She had a girlish bounce rather than a seductive sway, but it was vastly entertaining. "She's cute as a bug," Ron whispered. "Sure makes me wish I was twenty years younger."

"She's a spider, not a bug," Jonathan argued, "and she's going to strangle Mirasol in her web."

Both men continued observing Leigh closely. Jonathan made no effort to hide his frustrated rage, but Ron had an openly appreciative gaze. "Every garden needs a few spiders," Ron offered. "They catch flies, for one thing, and—"

"Christ!" Jonathan cursed under his breath. "She's not going to rid the town of flies! She's going to suck the life right out of it."

Ron leaned close to whisper. "Well, I'd put politics aside real quick if she ever offered to suck the life out of me, if you know what I mean." He could tell from Jonathan's startled expression that he most certainly did. Chuckling to himself, he went back

to edging the lawn, which was a lot more enjoyable now that
he had the delectable Ms. Bowman on his mind.

The Mirasol Fitness Center was located a block north of the
business district, in what had once been the sanctuary of a Naza-
rene Church. A sign out front boasted the latest in fitness equipment, and conveniently scheduled aerobics classes. Carpeted in
pale gray, and brightly lit by fluorescent fixtures in addition to
the sunlight filtered through the panels of stained glass at the
arched windows, that morning it was being used by only a handful of women.

Leigh introduced herself to Pam Akers, the African-American
beauty who managed the center. Pam was tall and lithe, with
long, springy curls she kept off her face with a zebra print head-
band that matched her leotard.

"Welcome to Mirasol," Pam greeted her. "There's obviously
not an ounce of fat on you, but I'd recommend a membership
just the same. It's important to keep limber, and a supple figure
makes any woman look younger."

"Looking young has never been a problem," Leigh confided.
"In fact, it's just the opposite in my case. You're fortunate to
be tall. I really envy you."

Pam called out a word of encouragement to a pudgy patron
using a stationary bicycle, and then took Leigh into her corner
office. Walled in glass, it provided the privacy to talk while still
allowing her a clear view of the floor. "I've been in the fitness
business ten years, and I've yet to meet a woman who's pleased
with herself. Isn't that a shame? Now I might be able to see
over the crowd whenever there's a parade, but let me tell you
something, girl—I'd much rather be your size. Men love petite
women." She gestured with her whole body. "It makes them
feel big and strong even if they can't hold their own with other
men."

"There's more to life than pleasing men," Leigh replied, an
opinion that prompted an amused howl from Pam.

"The day the women in Mirasol believe that, I'll be out of business, and I'm not a bit worried it's going to happen any time soon. I was able to rent this place at a reasonable price because most people don't want to do business in an old church, but I'm hoping to move into one of the new buildings once they're completed."

She reached into her desk, pulled out a pink card, and wrote Leigh's name on it. "I want you to have a complimentary trial membership," she explained. "Our schedule's printed on the back."

Leigh couldn't accept the card, but tried not to offend the friendly woman. "I work for the city," she reminded her, "so I can't take gifts from the merchants."

Pam shook her head, sending her curls bouncing over her shoulders in a wild punctuation of her words. "Do you honestly believe I'm trying to bribe you?" she asked.

The calendar on the wall featured a female bodybuilder with bulging muscles and skimpy red satin bikini that hid very little of her well-oiled body. Distracted a moment, Leigh looked out on the floor where a plump woman in gray sweats was doing situps on a slanted board. "Bribe is much too strong a word," she responded, "but if you're eager to change locations, there are undoubtedly some who'll accuse you of trying to influence me to help you. I don't need that kind of criticism, and I'm sure you don't either."

Pam shrugged, tore up the card, and sifted it through her fingers into the wastebasket. "You don't mince words, do you, Ms. Bowman?"

"I'm sorry if I was too blunt, but my job is to bring the redevelopment project into reality, and I can't have people accusing me of playing favorites."

Pam grabbed a sport bottle from her desk, and took a sip of water. "Even if I can't convince you to exercise, be sure to drink plenty of water," she advised. "At least eight glasses a day."

"Yes. I know that's important."

Pam reached for the doorknob, then hesitated. "I'm trying

to admire you for avoiding any charges of conflict of interest, but I'm sure I'm not the only one who's heard you were out at the Inn last night with Eli Keene. Even if you two are on the same side, it wouldn't be a good idea to get too friendly with him, either."

Leigh heard the underlining message in that remark loud and clear. "I told him the same thing myself," she replied, "so if you're dating him, you needn't worry I'll be any competition."

Pam had to cover her mouth with her hands to stifle her laughter this time. "Girl, every woman in this town, with the possible exception of Rhonda Boyle and Opal Lingard, has dated Eli. He's like a rich dessert, delicious on special occasions, but a steady diet of Eli Keene will ruin more than your figure."

Leigh barely knew the man, but she found Pam's description disturbing. Despite the glass walls, the office suddenly seemed far too confining, and she edged toward the door. "As I said before, there's more to life than pleasing men, Ms. Akers, and now I'll have to ask you to excuse me so I can continue learning my way around town."

Pam pulled open the door. "I'd say you already know your way around, Ms. Bowman."

Leigh smiled, but she was accutely aware of the women who stopped exercising to follow her with their eyes as she strode the length of the room. There were mirrored panels between the colorful windows, and as she moved along, she caught a glimpse of herself out of the corner of her eye. She wore a size two, and knew the gym's patrons must surely envy her petite size, but all they saw was the illusion of success, and it was no more real than her reflection in the mirrors.

Her next stop was Brown's Hardware where the merchandise ranged from pink plastic flamingos to chain saws. She had always gotten by with a hammer and a couple of screwdrivers, but she could not help but admire the wide array of tools on display. When a tall, red-haired clerk approached her, she recognized him from Monday night's meeting.

"I need one of those little gadgets you put on the kitchen faucet to make a spray."

"You're in luck. We've got the Faucet Queen in several colors." He led her down an aisle crowded with light bulbs, and electrical cords and switches to the plumbing department. "Which did you need, the threaded model that screws on, or the kind that just slips on?"

"The slip-on one, I suppose." Leigh chose a white one and followed him up another aisle through a forest of rakes and hoes, and past a revolving rack containing assorted rolls of Con-Tact paper to reach the cash register. "Are you Mr. Brown?" she asked as she paid for her purchase.

"I'm one of them. Not *the* Mr. Brown, of course that's my father."

When he didn't give his first name, Leigh knew where he stood on the redevelopment project, and decided to make a chart to keep track of her potential friends and foes. "The pink flamingos are tempting," she confided. "I know just where I'd like to put them, but I really ought to get the owner's permission before I buy a pair."

Bob Brown leaned across the counter. "You wouldn't believe how many of those things we sell. It's damn near impossible to keep them in stock."

"Is that a fact?" Leigh had thought the tacky plastic birds had gone out with fins on Cadillacs. Apparently gossip was the only news that traveled quickly in Mirasol. "Is your father in today? I'd like to speak with him, if I may."

"Sorry. Dad's been in his grave more than ten years. Bob's my name. My brother, Carl, and I run the store. Or at least we're running it until the building's torn down. We're calling it quits then."

"But why? Mirasol will still need a hardware store."

Bob rocked back on his heels. "Take a good look at this place on your way out. We don't carry a thing a tourist will need, and once the town's crawling with them, the locals won't drive into town to shop. Besides, it would be just too damn much trouble to move all this junk. We'd rather just slash the prices, sell it all cheap, and move to Idaho."

"Idaho?" Leigh thought the choice odd.

"Yeah, Idaho. We figure there must be lots of little towns there that aren't in any danger of being overrun by snotty tourists toting fancy camcorders."

Leigh made a mental note to improve the image the townspeople had of tourists. "I'm sure you're right, but I still say Mirasol will need a hardware store."

"Fine. You open one."

"Thank you. I'll definitely consider it." Leigh slipped the Faucet Queen into her purse and bid him a good day. Her next stop was the yardage shop. It was filled with colorful fabrics, and pattern books were displayed on a long table surrounded by comfortable chairs, but the lineoleum was badly worn, and a large sheet of plastic had been strung over a corner where the stained acoustical tile made it plain the roof leaked. The owner, Patsy O'Dell, was so pleasant, however, that Leigh accepted her offer of a cup of herb tea and sat down with her in her cluttered office.

Patsy was dressed in pink slacks and a matching top that flattered her silver hair. She took only a tiny sip of her tea before yanking open the bottom drawer on her desk and pulling out a rag doll. It had the Cabbage Patch Doll's cherubic expression, combined with an endearing old-fashioned charm. "My family has been selling yardage in this town for three generations," she revealed, "and I intend to keep right on doing it, but I'm smart enough to know tourists won't drive a hundred miles from Los Angeles to buy Laura Ashley prints to make their bedroom curtains. What I plan to do is sell history."

Leigh was lost. "History?"

Patsy shook the doll to fluff out its pinafore. "Everybody loves these dolls. Here, hold her a minute."

Leigh reached for the doll, and was surprised by how soft and cuddly it was. From its yarn pigtails to little leather shoes, it was immensely lovable. "This is awfully sweet," she agreed.

"Sure is, and a much better companion for a little girl than a plastic Barbie. Now, I figure mothers and grandmothers will buy them as much for themselves as for their children. They're cute as a decorator item just sitting in a chair, too. I'm thinking of making a whole line of rag dolls and stuffed animals. There are lots of women in this town who can sew, and they could sure use the extra money I'd pay them."

Patsy sat back in her chair and folded her hands in her lap. "Well, you're the expert, Ms. Bowman. What do you think? Can I make a success with my dolls, or not?"

From the width of Patsy's confident smile, Leigh was convinced she could make a success of anything she tried. "Yes," she assured her. "I'm sure that you can. I like your idea of continuing to serve the needs of the locals while expanding your merchandise to appeal to tourists. That should give you a steady business year round. I wish everyone had your enthusiasm."

"So do I!" Patsy agreed. "We don't have much mud around here, but there are too many people stuck in what little there is. So, what do you think of Eli? I heard you went out with him last night."

Leigh handed Patsy the doll. "I'm beginning to feel sorry for the man," she confided. "It's a shame he can't meet a business associate for a drink without the whole town knowing about it."

Patsy slid the doll back into the bottom drawer and closed it. "Following Eli Keene's love life is one of our favorite pastimes, honey. He's the star of our own little soap opera, you might say. A girl can't do any better than Eli in this town. I had my chance with his father." Her eyes sparkled with the memory. "He wasn't quite as handsome as his son, but he excited me clear to my toes. You know what I mean?"

Leigh nodded. "Yes. I most certainly do."

Patsy shrugged. "Well, it just wasn't meant to be."

Leigh rose to her feet. "I know that one too," she replied. "Thank you so much, Mrs. O'Dell. You've made my morning."

It was nearly noon when Leigh left the yardage shop, and

she went on down to Mama Bee's Kitchen on the corner. Lace curtains with blue ribbon trim screened the cafe's windows, and the tables were covered in red and white checked tablecloths. The pine plank floor, blue plastic chairs, and dozens of potted plants added to the restaurant's informal charm.

Not wanting to sit at a table by herself, Leigh walked on back to the counter at the rear and took the blue leather stool at the end. Ron Tate and George Culbert, in stained coveralls from his garage, were seated a couple of stools away. The men were engaged in a heated argument over how to buy cheese. Ron quickly looked to Leigh for an opinion.

He handed her a catalog featuring specialty cheeses. "George orders from this place all the time, but because they sell the cheese by weight, I told him he was a fool to order the Swiss when it's so full of holes all he's paying for is air."

Leigh shot Ron a disbelieving glance, and he winked at her. Obviously he was having a little fun at George's expense, but he had just put her in an extremely awkward position. George was on the city council, and while she knew he backed the plan, he had been the least cordial of the group. If she laughed at him now for not seeing the absurdity of Ron's argument, she knew he would never forgive her.

"Just a minute," she begged, and appearing to give the matter serious consideration, she read the descriptions of the cheeses George had circled in the catalog. "My, but don't these sound good." She looked past Ron and smiled at George. "I'd go right ahead and order the Swiss, George. After all, holes don't weigh anything, so you'll get all the cheese you pay for."

When she handed the catalog back to George, he rolled it up and swatted Ron's shoulder with it. "See. I told you there was nothing wrong with buying the Swiss."

"Yeah," Ron agreed, "but you couldn't tell me why!"

Ron again turned to wink at Leigh, and than offered his opinion of the cafe's food. "Avoid the special," he whispered. "Don't matter what it is, special it ain't."

"Thank you." Leigh was used to eating a carton of yogurt at

her desk, but until she had a desk, her usual wasn't an option. She perused the menu, and tried to remember if she had ever eaten in a restaurant that offered biscuits and gravy a la carte. Before she had, the waitress appeared. A young woman with permed hair drawn up in a frizzy ponytail, she was squeezed into a tight blue T-shirt and short white skirt. She pulled her order pad, and a plastic pen topped with a bunny on a spring from the pocket in her tiny black apron.

"What can I get for you, hon? The day's special is pot roast."

Ron shot Leigh a warning glance, but she wasn't even tempted to order it. "I'll have a BLT on whole wheat toast, and ice tea." She laid the menu aside.

"You want avocado on that?"

Leigh's mind instantly flooded with the memory of Jonathan looking over his shoulder to wink at her as he sliced an avocado and she had to swallow hard to find her voice to answer. "No, thank you. Let's just keep it simple."

The window opening into the kitchen was at the opposite end of the counter preventing Leigh from seeing the chef as the waitress handed him her order, but when she heard a pan clatter to the floor followed by a loud curse in a deep male voice, she grew curious. "Is there really a Mama Bee?" she asked Ron Tate.

"Sure, but she's gotten too heavy to come into town everyday, and her son, Albert, does most of the cooking. When the pots don't just fly off the stove, that is."

"He still uses her recipes though," George leaned around Ron to add.

"I'll bet they're delicious," Leigh hoped aloud.

"Hell, no," George assured her, "but everyone's used to them by now."

That wasn't at all encouraging, but Leigh's sandwich proved to be surprisingly good. She ordered BLT's often, and frequently had to scrape off excess mayonnaise, but this one was perfect. By the time she had finished, the cafe had filled with the luncheon crowd and she scanned the faces for any she might recognize. Some people smiled and waved, but several, like Bob Brown, pointedly ignored her.

When she left Mama Bee's, she sat down on the bench outside to review her notes and plan the afternoon. The Marmalade Cafe was across the street, and she would try it soon. In the distance, the rolling slopes of the Sulphur Mountains beckoned. She sat back and sighed. Mirasol wasn't nearly as peaceful a place as she had imagined, but she was a long way from disillusioned.

In fact, the derogatory remarks she had heard about tourists had inspired her to plan ads with the most wholesome family she could create. The man would be carrying a baby boy, while the mother held their daughter's hand. The little girl would be skipping along clutching one of Patsy O'Dell's rag dolls. If such an appealing family didn't implant a more desirable image of tourists in the citizens' minds, then she would find something that would.

She had just stood when Ron Tate left the cafe. He fell in step along beside her. "George thinks you're awfully cute," he confided. "He won't ever admit it, so don't let him know that I told you."

Leigh was tempted to tell Ron to speak for himself, but felt certain he already had. "When I stopped by his garage yesterday, I got the impression he prefers carburetors to women."

"Well, yeah, but he's just shy. I'll bet he gives you one of them damn cheeses for Christmas."

"I'll look forward to it." They soon parted, but Leigh couldn't help but laugh as she thought of two life-long friends arguing over something as silly as the weight of holes in Swiss cheese. Ron Tate was clearly a man who could remain friends with people who disagreed with him, and she admired him for that.

It wasn't until she walked by Jonathan Reid's later that afternoon that she began to wonder if the depth of anger she had seen from the former historian weren't prompted by something more personal than the redevelopment plan. She slowed her step, thinking she might catch sight of him working on his back porch, but he wasn't there. Maybe he had a customer, or was adding up his sales figures, but as she continued on down the street, she felt the eerie sensation of being watched.

She smiled to herself and hoped Jonathan was peering out of an upstairs window. It was an awful shame the whole town was obsessed with Eli Keene, when Jonathan Reid was ever so much more intriguing. She turned suddenly and waved, then walked on back to city hall eager to improve the image of tourists, and perhaps in the process, enhance her own in a certain handsome, dark-eyed resident's heart.

Five

  While Leigh had not really expected Opal Lingard to prod Lester Cornell, when she returned to city hall, she found her office furnished. The spectacular philodendron was now displayed on the corner of a mahogany desk with a wood grain as luscious as a dark chocolate caramel. There was a matching cabinet which contained a lateral file against the wall, and two chairs covered in a nubby oatmeal fabric to accommodate visitors.

  Leigh would have been delighted had Eli Keene not been seated at her desk writing a memo. That he had taken her chair behind the desk, rather than one of those placed in front of it, said a great deal. He had an unassuming charm, but she thought when pressed he would turn as demanding as a feudal lord. It was difficult to suppress the impulse to do just that.

  Leigh laid her clipboard on her desk. "I would have called to thank you for the beautiful plant, but Opal is such an industrious receptionist, I didn't feel the telephone lines here were secure. I'm glad I can thank you in person. It was very thoughtful of you to welcome me to the city, and at the same time help me decorate my office."

  Eli's expression had lit with a bright smile when Leigh entered. He crumpled the note he had been writing and shoved it into his pocket as he stood. "You're welcome." He then lowered his voice. "You're right about Opal. Because she works for Mirasol, she believes anything that happens within the city limits is her business." He pulled out an eelskin wallet and handed

Leigh a business card engraved with his first name and a telephone number.

"I should have given you one of these last night. It's my private line, and no one else listens to the voice mail. If I can help you in any way, don't hesitate to call."

Leigh watched a slow grin spread across Eli's lips, and knew exactly what type of calls he hoped to receive. Thinking he would be sadly disappointed in what she had to say, she laid the card on her clipboard. "I've made it clear to the merchants I've met that I'll not accept gifts from them. Your position in the redevelopment plan may be unique, but this lovely plant is the last thing I'll accept from you while we're working together. As for your private line, I'll keep the number in the event of some rare emergency, but your regular office number is all I'll need for business."

Leigh's request erased Eli's lazy smile in an instant. He tossed one of his regular business cards on top of the first one he had given her, then jammed his wallet back into his hip pocket. "You don't simply draw the line, do you, Ms. Bowman? If I filled the trench you just gouged between us with sea water, I'd be able to float the Queen Mary."

He started around her desk, but Leigh stepped into his path to prevent him from leaving. She pitched her voice at the same discreet level as his. "The whole town's talking about the fact we were together last night at the Inn. Now I realize you're used to being something of a celebrity here, but I don't want whatever I do, and whomever I wish to see after hours, to become common knowledge."

Eli regarded her with a wary glance. "Now I understand. People didn't just remark on the fact we were together last night, did they? I'll bet they all had an opinion about me, with a special reference to my fondness for women."

He was wearing the same gray slacks, but his shirt was a pale green rather than blue today; although it was again silk and worn with the casual elegance that marked all his gestures. Leigh's glance reached the fringed ties on his black loafers before she again looked at him directly. "I'll not fault you for liking women, Eli, but let's not add my name to your list."

"I haven't kept one," he assured her, "and there aren't any notches on my bedpost, either. Just because I'm one of the few men in Mirasol who doesn't go to work wearing a Stetson or a baseball cap doesn't mean I actually live up to some of our citizens' more imaginative fantasies." He chuckled softly to himself. "Not that it wouldn't be fun to try, but I intend to live my own life rather than animate a fanciful illusion."

Leigh understood that desire so well her attitude softened. "We're all caught in illusions, aren't we?" she replied. Jonathan had been such fun until he had discovered she wasn't just a pretty tourist. At least he liked tourists, which was definitely a plus. In the next instant, she realized she might have discovered a compelling way to reach him.

Eli could actually see the conflicting thoughts colliding in Leigh's mind. Mentally, she had put him on hold to consider something else entirely and he was surprised to be more intrigued than insulted by her thought processes. "I came by to make certain you'd received the plant, and also to suggest that you come with me up to Santa Barbara on Saturday. It's a much larger city, of course, but they've done aggressive redevelopment and I'd like your opinion on how it's working. On my last trip through there, I noticed a lot of vacant stores, and we can't afford to have it happen here."

"No, that's certainly true." Leigh was reassured by the seriousness of Eli's manner. She debated going by herself before the weekend, but she had really planned to concentrate on Mirasol that week. "I've not been to Santa Barbara in years. They have a magnificent mission, as I recall."

"Yes. They do. We'll stop there if you like. They're doing the exact same thing we're doing here: capitalizing on a Spanish heritage."

"Which in their case is authentic," Leigh reminded him.

Eli raised his hands. "Please. You mustn't ever let on that Father Serra himself didn't tread our main street in his sandals."

Leigh was certain if the Spanish cleric actually had, the first Elijah Keene would have placed a bronze statue of him at the entrance to the park. "You realize, of course, that you're asking me to maintain another illusion?"

When Eli appeared to be appalled by that grim prospect, Leigh took it as a good sign, and decided to trust him. "I'll go with you on the condition that business is the only subject we discuss."

"Absolutely," Eli assured her. "I'll even be happy to charge the city for mileage and meals if you like."

"Please do." Leigh checked her watch and was relieved she would still have time to organize her day's impressions before five o'clock. "I'll look forward to Saturday, but right now, I need to get back to work."

"That's *all* we've been doing," Eli stressed, and he left without trying to make it more.

Leigh sat down behind her desk, and leaned back. She had been on her feet all day and it felt so good to kick off her shoes and wiggle her toes. She inhaled deeply, and caught a faint trace of Eli's cologne. He definitely had a model's cool good looks, and she could easily imagine him playing the father in her ideal tourist family, but he was totally wrong for the part. What she needed were models the townspeople didn't know, and would easily accept as personable tourists.

She closed her eyes for just a moment, and when Frank Pierce called her name, she jumped in surprise. "Yes, Frank? Come on in, or we can go to your office if you'd like. I have an idea I want to discuss with you."

Frank came on in and eased his bulky frame into the closest chair. "Let's talk here. I hope you like your office. If there's anything else you need, just let me know."

The room wasn't really large enough to hold another item of furniture, and Leigh assured him it was fine. She reviewed the stereotypical descriptions she had heard of tourists, and described how she intended to counteract them. She had traced the cartoon avocado Eli had drawn for her onto a piece of plain paper, so she did not have to show him the original on the cocktail napkin.

"I thought the avocado might make a clever logo, and it still might for some phase of the plan, but giving the tourists an appealing image is what's needed now."

Frank nearly burst with enthusiasm. "Splendid idea!" he exclaimed. "You're as perfect for this job as we all knew you'd be. I'm sure we can fit this into the promotion budget, so go right ahead with it." He hauled himself out of his chair with a weary sigh. "If you wear out your shoes going back and forth into town, put in a voucher for a new pair."

"I've plenty of shoes, Frank."

He hesitated at the door. "Don't work too late. Lester likes to lock up as soon as he can after five."

In the last year, Leigh had fallen into the habit of taking her work home to fill her otherwise empty evenings, and she assured him she would leave on time. She had made a good start, but there were many more people to meet. She hoped tomorrow would bring a lot more merchants with Patsy O'Dell's zest for life, and a lot fewer with Bob Brown's gloomy resignation.

"And what about your own mood?" she asked herself softly. She loved working with cities because she could actually see the results when the well-designed projects she managed were completed, but she lacked any kind of optimism in the other facets of her life. When Bonnie MacNair brought her a present that evening, she felt as though the librarian had read her mind.

Bonnie thrust the bottle filled with a bright blue liquid into Leigh's hands. "I wanted to get you a housewarming present to make you feel welcome here, but I thought you'd enjoy this a lot more than another salad bowl, or throw pillow."

"Sensual Harmony?" Leigh read on the label. "Oh, it's bath oil! I was afraid I was going to have to drink this. Come on in."

"Well, it's made of natural oils and scents so I bet you could drink it if you were desperate."

"For what? A potent laxative?" The rounded bottle had a cork stopper like an old-fashioned patent medicine, and she leaned forward to place it on the coffee table as she and Bonnie sat down on the sofa. Bonnie was a neighbor, obviously eager to be a friend, and Leigh had no reason to refuse her gift, but accepting it made her uncomfortable all the same.

"It was very sweet of you to want to give me a welcoming gift. Thank you."

"It's not just any bath oil," Bonnie explained. "It's designed for aroma therapy. Have you ever burned incense, or scented candles and found they lift your spirits?"

"My ex-husband was fond of incense, but I've not bought any since we separated. Thanks for reminding me. I'll have to get some just for myself."

"It's important not to starve the senses," Bonnie cautioned. "Wait until you have the time for a leisurely bath before you try the Sensual Harmony oil. It's wonderfully relaxing, and creates a real sense of inner peace just like it promises on the label."

"When you give such enthusiastic endorsements, I'll bet the company that makes Sensual Harmony could use you in sales."

Bonnie had changed out of the dress she had worn to work, and was now wearing Levi's and a knit top. She kicked off her sandals, and curled her legs up underneath her. After resting her arm along the back of the sofa, she propped her head on her elbow. "You're right. I probably could. My mother agreed to sell the fragrant oils in her shop on a trial basis at first, but they've been so popular that she's reordered several times. There's another formula for stress, and one for sweet dreams, but I like this one the best."

"I'll look forward to using it."

"Be sure and give me a report." Bonnie leaned forward slightly. "Well, what did you think of Eli? I heard you went out with him Monday night."

Leigh knew she should have seen that question coming. "Would you like something to drink? A Coke, or iced tea?"

"No, thanks. Just tell me what you thought of him."

Leigh picked up the bath oil, and turned the rounded bottle in her hand. It had such a pleasing shape, she would keep it for a vase once she had used all the oil. She seldom indulged in leisurely baths, though, and doubted it would be empty before Christmas. She had nothing to hide, and no reason to stall any further, but she didn't want to encourage Bonnie's curiosity, and replied with a nonchalant shrug.

"I've been absolutely amazed by the number of people who've asked me about Eli. We were just talking about Mirasol, which I guess disappoints everyone."

Bonnie ran a long nail down the side seam of her Levi's. "Does it disappoint you?"

"No. Not at all. I think Eli's going to be easy to work with."

"Oh, yeah. He's easy all right." Bonnie rolled her eyes and then burst out laughing. "I shouldn't laugh at him, but since he and Denise were divorced, I don't think I've seen him with the same woman twice. I want to believe he was so deeply hurt that he won't risk becoming involved with another woman, but that's probably just wishful thinking. After all, if a man can get any woman he wants, he's bound to continually exchange the one he has for someone better."

Leigh considered Bonnie awfully young to be so cynical, then remembered where she had grown up. "Did you hear that opinion voiced often at the Beauty Spot?"

Bonnie frowned slightly and brought her hands to her lap. "Not just there. You've seen how pretty my mom is, but my dad still left her. She had lots of boyfriends while I was growing up, but none of them ever stuck around long enough to keep their promises and she's been stuck a lot of years giving perms and covering gray. That's what I hate about Mirasol. This town's so damn small women don't have much of a choice, and if they make the wrong one, they're doomed."

Leigh had not meant to depress Bonnie with her question. "Would you like to borrow this bottle of perfumed oil for the night? It sounds as though you're in more need of inner peace than I am at the moment."

"Thanks, but no. I have my own. Well, I guess I better get going. I didn't mean to take up your whole evening. Maybe we could have dinner together some night and go to the movies. We don't get the new films right away, but eventually everything plays here."

Leigh stood to walk Bonnie to the door. "Yes. Let's do that as soon as there's something we want to see. Every time I walk by the theater my mouth starts watering for popcorn."

Bonnie stepped out, but kept her hand on the screen door. "One night a couple of years ago, the projectionist just put on the film, and went home to eat dinner."

"You don't mean it."

"Wait. This gets better. The film broke, everyone started stamping their feet and calling for someone to fix it. When nothing happened, they realized there wasn't anyone there. Rather than wait around in a dark theater, people started to leave. Some figured they sure hadn't gotten their money's worth, and helped themselves to a couple of candy bars on their way out, while others threatened to report them to the police as vandals or thieves. Before you know it, there was this big fight going on in the lobby and pretty soon it spilled right out into the street.

"I mean there was popcorn flying everywhere, and people were hurling handfuls of Milk Duds at their neighbors. About that time, the projectionist comes ambling up the street sucking on a toothpick and when he sees the crowd, he's terrified the Blob must be loose in the theater. Luckily the police arrived before the crowd got hold of him, but every time I go to the movies, I remember the 'Great Popcorn Riot' and laugh."

Although Leigh had spent less than a week in Mirasol, she could so easily picture the ridiculous scene, she laughed, too. "I'll bet there were people who demanded refunds on their tickets, weren't there?"

"Of course! No one was ever certain just who had grabbed the first Snickers, so the owner had to refund everyone's money.

The theater was closed for a nearly a week while they sham-
pooed all the chocolate and caramel out of the carpet."

"Does Eli own the theater too?"

"No. That's one of the few buildings he doesn't own, but I'll
bet we'd get good films a lot faster if he did. Oh, that's my
phone ringing. 'Night." Bonnie dashed across the porch to her
door, and hurried inside.

Leigh remained at her open door. The porch lights only par-
tially illuminated the yard, and the desert plants, which were so
handsome during the day, created a host of menacing shadows.
Bonnie's story about the theater had been so amusing, however,
that Leigh was still smiling as she went back inside alone.

Eli called to confirm their Saturday date, and to say he would
pick Leigh up at ten o'clock. Expecting him to be as nicely
dressed as she had always seen him, she gave a great deal of
thought to her clothes. The suits she wore to work were much
too formal, but she didn't want to dress too casually when she
had insisted upon making it a business trip rather than merely
a pleasant outing. She finally chose a pale blue crinkled gauze
skirt with a matching T-shirt, and tan sandals that tied at the
ankle.

When Eli appeared at her door in Levi's, a blue chambray
shirt, and boots, she worried aloud that they appeared to be
color-coordinated. "Not that anyone will notice what we're
wearing, or care, but—"

Eli took her elbow. "No. I hope everyone we pass in the street
thinks we're trying to look like Barbie and Ken."

"I'm too short to be mistaken for Barbie." Eli's Porsche was
so low to the ground, she had a difficult time gathering up her
flowing skirt to enter it gracefully, and hoped that he hadn't
noticed how perilously close she had come to just falling in.

Eli pulled a pair of Carrera sunglasses from his pocket, circled the car and slid in behind the wheel. "All right, so you're
a diminutive version of Barbie, and I'm probably too old to be

mistaken for Ken, but I really don't give a damn what anyone thinks anyway. Do you?"

Leigh fastened her seat belt, and then grabbed hold of the dash as Eli started his car and made a tight U-turn in front of her duplex. Now that they were seated together in the close confines of his car, she had to admit clothes had merely been a convenient worry. Simply spending the day with Eli, when it would present so many opportunities for serious problems to develop, had been her true concern.

"I spend most of my time at work," was all she would confess, "where appearance is always important."

"All the city of Mirasol requires is that your clothes be clean and safe," he answered.

Grateful Eli was driving below the speed limit, Leigh leaned back in her seat. The black leather was as soft as a glove, and she thought how easy it would be to become spoiled by the luxuries he took for granted. "Yes, but that's the minimum, and my job requires that I be stylish rather than merely presentable."

Eli shot her a sidelong glance. "Have you always been obsessed with your work, or is this something new since your divorce?"

"I'm not obsessed, Eli. What a ridiculous thing to say."

"Preoccupied, then?"

"Focused," Leigh insisted.

As they left town, Mirasol Avenue was shaded by giant oaks and bordered on the right with a bicycle trail and bridle path separated by the same type of wooden fence that enclosed the outlying paddocks. They passed a couple on sleek racing bicycles dressed in matching black shorts and crazily striped yellow shirts. The lean pair were hunched over their handlebars, their legs pumping fiercely as they rounded a curve. Such a strenuous sport looked exhausting to Leigh, but she supposed racing was their idea of run.

"Do you ride?" Eli asked.

"No. I haven't owned a bicycle in years."

Eli chuckled to himself. "I was talking about horses. I own

several, and if you like to ride, it would give us an additional way to tour the resort site."

Embarrassed to have misunderstood, Leigh quickly apologized, then added, "I went horseback riding at Girl Scout camp, but that was nearly twenty years ago."

"Well, do you recall it as being fun?"

"All I remember is how far off the ground I was. All the horses were gentle, and there wasn't any danger that we'd be thrown or injured along the trails, but no. I think I was too frightened to have any fun."

"I have a nice little pinto mare. She's as petite and delicate as you. I'll lead you around the front lawn until you've gained the confidence to ride on your own. Would you like that?"

"No, thank you. I may not be very tall, but I'm not a child, Eli, and I certainly don't need to be treated like one."

When the road split into highway 33 for Ventura, and 150 to Santa Barbara, Eli swung right to follow 150. They passed old frame houses shaded with shaggy pepper trees, and newer stucco residences with solar panels on the roof. There were lots of RV's parked beside the garages, while glistening black crows dotted the lawns. A trailer park, with an imposing rock wall feathered with pampas grass, proclaimed itself the home of Mobile Estates.

"Can an estate be mobile?" Leigh asked.

Eli was still smarting from her caustic remark about the pony, and just shrugged. Eucalyptus shadowed the curving road here, and dusty-blue California jays squawked insults to each other through the curtain of leaves. They crossed the bridge over the Ventura River and leaving the chaparral behind, entered rolling hills dotted with well tended citrus and avocado groves. When they reached the stone arch at the entrance of the Keene Ranch, Eli guided his Porsche to a stop. He turned toward Leigh and draped his arm over the steering wheel.

"You're hanging onto your seat as though you're afraid we're going to fly off the road at every turn. Is it me you can't stand, or is it this car? If it's just the car, I'll pull in and we can take one of the ranch's trucks. They aren't nearly as comfortable, but you're sure to feel a whole lot safer."

Leigh hadn't realized how tightly she was gripping her seat until Eli mentioned it, and then she had to apologize again. "I'm not worried about your driving," she assured him. "I'm just used to driving myself everywhere I go, so I'm out of practice at being a passenger." She folded her hands in her lap. "There. Is that better?"

"Better than what?" Eli shot right back at her.

The mammoth avocado trees bordering the massive stone gate were heavily laden with tiny avocados that would grow to the size of a man's fist by the autumn harvest. Leigh concentrated on the big, old trees, and swallowed hard. "You were right earlier," she confessed in a hushed whisper. "I do concentrate on work because it's easiest for me, and bears the best results. My husband and I were together from the time we were eighteen until last year, and the other men I've known have all been acquaintances or colleagues from work."

She paused to scrape away the memory of the brief time she and Jonathan had conversed easily, and then continued in her normal tone. "If we stick to discussing the plan, I'll be fine," she insisted more to herself than him. "If you're going to push every occasion we're together into an opportunity for something more, I'll have to ask you to take me home, and I'll drive myself to Santa Barbara."

Eli waited a moment to make certain he had a good hold on his temper, and then let her have it. "I asked if you liked to ride so we could tour the resort site, and for no other reason. Do you honestly believe I might enjoy playing the Cisco Kid and seducing women on horseback?"

Leigh would have been as insulted as he if she had not had such a vivid imagination. "Is it even possible to seduce a woman on horseback?" she asked.

Eli cursed under his breath. "Yes, but it's a lot easier riding bareback than with a saddle. You'll have to be the one to suggest it, though, because I sure as hell won't mention it. Now do you want to trade the Porsche for a truck, or not?"

When Leigh frowned slightly, Eli was positive she was trying to figure out exactly how to go about making love on horseback. "You'd have to face me, Leigh, and put your legs over mine."

Instantly the erotic image became clear, but for some reason what Leigh pictured was a woman with Lady Godiva's long, trailing curls, and the man, well, he bore an unfortunate resemblance to Jonathan Reid. "Oh, now I understand."

"I'm so relieved." Not waiting for Leigh to finally make up her mind, Eli started the Porsche and after turning to make certain the road was clear, he pulled out on the two-lane highway. "These groves all belong to me," he announced proudly. "Only a small portion of them border the highway, but you can at least appreciate how large an operation the ranch is. The resort is going in on land we've held for expansion. It's just up ahead. I think you'll see how perfect it is at first glance."

Leigh nodded, and when the road curved through open land surrounded by low, rolling hills dotted with scattered oaks, she could easily envision a modern resort hotel with beautifully landscaped grounds, swimming pools, tennis courts, and golf courses. "I've seen the drawings, of course, but not the actual site. This is almost too perfect as it is."

"Now you sound like Miguel Fuentes. He's the best man I've got, or I'd fire him for constantly railing against me for planning to pave over prime agricultural land." Eli pulled over to let another car pass. "You'd think I was burning the Amazon rain forest to hear him talk."

Leigh recalled Miguel's furious scowl as he had stormed out of the library, and thought he must be a very good worker indeed for Eli to keep him on if he expressed his opinions with the same fiery anger she had glimpsed. "But you'll still have most of your land under cultivation, won't you?"

"Yes, but the loss of even an acre is agony to Miguel."

Leigh could understand the young man's view. She drank in the peaceful pastoral scene, thought of the miles of open prairie the pioneers had crossed to reach California, and wished she were an expert rider and could explore the land on horseback. "Do you come riding out here often?" she asked.

"Not nearly often enough, but I want to include stables and riding trails in the resort." He was sorely tempted to offer to satisfy whatever lingering curiosity she might have about sex on horseback while they were still in his barn, but he much preferred this quiet awe to the resentful belligerence he had inadvertently sparked in her earlier. She had impressed the city council with her knowledge, but he knew for a fact one councilman had voted to hire her simply because she was the most attractive applicant for the job.

"It's far easier being a man," he confided softly. "We're judged on how well we can get a job done, but women are always expected to look good while they're doing it. It's money rather than looks that causes my problems, though. I've had more people pretend to be friends of mine for what it can get them than I care to count and I wouldn't wish that on anybody, Leigh, least of all you. I'm going to be the best friend you've ever had, with no strings attached, and we're going to turn this valley into the most successful resort of its kind in the state. Now let's see what we can learn from Santa Barbara."

After Eli had pulled out onto the highway, Leigh waited until a man with a bushy gray beard like Jerry Garcia's rode by on a Harley-Davidson; then she rested her hand lightly on Eli's sleeve. "Maybe I will call your private line. Whenever I get discouraged with the project, will you please give me that same speech?"

Eli couldn't help himself and responded with a low growl. "I'll give you whatever you want," he promised.

Leigh took a deep breath and held it. All she wanted was for the pain to go away, but using Eli as salve would be a far worse betrayal than cultivating his friendship for profit. "Say, did you ever hear about Mirasol's Great Popcorn War?"

"You mean the night the projectionist went home, and there was a riot in the theater when the film broke? Sure. That incident is one of the most colorful in the city's history. Do you suppose we could capitalize on it somehow?"

"I think it's a hilarious story, but I wouldn't want anyone to think we were holding the city up to ridicule."

"Of course not," Eli agreed. "The theater isn't part of the redevelopment plan, so it will remain a historic site. Maybe we could have an impressive brass plaque made for the building to commemorate the incident as though it were a momentous Civil War battle."

"Tongue in cheek?"

"Of course."

Leaving the valley, the road began to climb through sandstone canyons where sharply angled layers in shades of buff and rust left clear evidence of ancient seismic activity and upheaval. They were entering the Los Padres National Forest and pines, interspersed with sycamores, and yucca grew right up to the road. Leigh caught a flash of sun on water to the left and called excitedly, "Is that Lake Casitas?"

"Sure is. I should have thought to take the turn-off and stop there for a minute." Eli pulled into the next turn-out, and shut off the engine. "There's not much traffic. We can cross the road and take a look at the lake if you like."

Leigh hadn't thought to bring a camera, and now was sorry. "I've seen the lake on the map, but didn't realize it was this close." Eli took her hand as they crossed the road, but then quickly released it and stepped away. "Is the fishing good here?"

"I haven't been out here since I was a kid, so I can't say. I don't have the requisite patience to be a fisherman, but there seem to be plenty of people scattered along the shore in boats, so it must be fairly good."

The lake was nestled in the valley, and from the highway they could see only a fraction of its irregular shape. They had a clear view of the parking lot and launch area for boats, but most appeared to be of the inflatable variety with outboard motors. Leigh watched a man below them casting his line from the boat he had eased into the reeds. She would have liked to have talked with him, but there was no trail through the underbrush down to the lake, and even if there had been, she couldn't have made the trek in a gauze skirt and sandals.

A lone hawk was circling overhead, and she shaded her eyes with her hand to watch him until the annoying whine of a motor drew her gaze back to the lake where someone was now riding a jet ski right down the middle. He was sending up a wild spray, and the ski's wake made waves that rippled clear across the water. The fishing boats rocked and wobbled, and while Leigh was too far away to hear anyone cursing, she knew they surely must be.

"What's the matter with him?" she cried. "Can't he see people are trying to fish? And what about the poor fish? Doesn't all that noise make them frantic?"

Eli laughed and looped his arm around Leigh's shoulders to guide her back across the highway. "The fish have probably gotten used to the sound of the outboard motors and jet skis and are no longer addled by it. Think of them as urban fish, who are used to the raucous sound of progress."

Leigh waited until they were both seated in the Porsche to reply. "That's not my idea of progress, Eli. That's just noise pollution."

"Careful, Leigh. You don't dare let anyone hear you bad-mouth progress or they'll think you've defected to Jonathan's side."

"Not bloody likely!" she replied. She crossed her arms over her chest and frowned sullenly. "We've got to have superbly managed progress, Eli, or else we'll just have the same chaos in Mirasol that blasted jet ski is making on the lake."

"Yes, ma'am. I'm right behind you on that."

Leigh glanced over in time to catch his smile, and knew precisely what he would sneak up behind her to do. Although they had exchanged cross words earlier, he was in exceptionally high spirits now, and as she leaned back to enjoy the mountain scenery, she was amazed to find she was, too. Obviously she needed to get out more, but she was still convinced it wasn't a good idea to spend her free time with Eli.

Today would be the first and last time, she promised herself silently, but after all, the trip to Santa Barbara was strictly business and easily justified. That was also danger, however. What she would call business the seasoned gossips of Mirasol would surely describe in much more scandalous terms. For an instant she hoped Jonathan would believe she and Eli were lovers and fume with a jealous rage, but with her next breath, she feared he wouldn't care at all.

Six

Leigh propped her feet on the lower rung of the extra chair at their table and covered a wide yawn with both hands. "I'm sorry, Eli, but I doubt there's an inch of Santa Barbara we've not covered." They had visited the historic eighteenth-century mission first, then come into town and had lunch at a cafe on the courtyard of the *Paseo Nuevo,* the new downtown mall.

After lunch they had walked the length of State Street to study the city's revitalized business district. Eli had challenged her to a game of pool in one of the sports bars, and while Leigh had not played in years, she had accepted and had even sunk a few balls with her fumbling shots. Now they were relaxing at a copper-topped table on the patio of a charming Mediterranean cafe.

Leigh had made extensive notes on the most popular shops, and while she had seen a great deal of appealing merchandise, she had purchased only a small box of jasmine incense and a festive windsock to hang by her front door. Shaped like a giant swallowtail butterfly with long flowing streamers, it was crafted of a tough nylon fabric in bright purple, red, and orange. It would add a whimsical touch of color to her attractive duplex, and make her feel more at home.

She had had to argue with Eli about who would pay for it, but had eventually won. She snuggled deeper into her chair, and watched him divide the thick chocolate brownie he had cajoled her into sharing. She seldom ate sweets but it looked sublime. It was after four o'clock, but the six hours they had spent together had disappeared so quickly that had she not had her notes, she would never had been able to account for the time.

Eli laid his half of the scrumptious dessert on his napkin, and pushed the plate toward Leigh. "Eat," he encouraged. "There ought to be enough sugar in that to keep you going until midnight."

Leigh took a tiny bite, and held it on her tongue until the fudge frosting melted before she began to chew the walnut-laced confection. "This is positively decadent," she murmured.

Eli took a sip of espresso and nodded. "Definitely. Shall I order a couple more?"

"Don't you dare." Leigh savored another delicious bite of brownie and then took a long drink of her cinnamon-flavored iced tea. "We've seen so many unusual shops today, like the one devoted entirely to windsocks and kites, or the one filled to the rafters with fanciful rubber stamps, but I keep thinking of the tattoo parlor. It was as bright and clean as the Beauty Spot."

"The tattoos weren't bad, either. I didn't see a single heart with the word MOM across it up on the wall. I'm not all that partial to skulls, but the Celtic designs were really striking. In fact, I can see myself with one of those elegant patterns swirled around my arm."

Leigh wasn't certain if Eli were teasing her or not, and thought it best not to encourage him. She let a mouthful of tea trickle down her throat and felt only increasingly lazy rather than energized as he had predicted. It was a beautiful day, sparkling clear and warm. The downtown was crowded and she scanned the faces of the passersby searching for further inspiration for her tourist family. When she spotted Bonnie MacNair walking along the opposite side of State Street, hugging Miguel Fuentes' arm, she sat up with a start. Bonnie recognized her in the same instant, but quickly looked away without waving, and she and Miguel ducked into the next shop.

"How odd," Leigh murmured.

Eli was fast growing accustomed to the way Leigh's attention wandered. It certainly wasn't flattering, but it was a damn sight better than having a woman fawn all over him just because he was Eli Keene. When she straightened up, he followed her glance and also recognized Bonnie and Miguel in the crowd.

"What strikes you as odd," he asked. "That she'd be with him, or that he's with her?"

Leigh provided a brief description of the whispered scene she had witnessed in the library. "Bonnie made the attraction sound one-sided, but from the way she was hanging onto Miguel's arm just now, it certainly doesn't look that way."

Eli was also puzzled, but for an entirely different reason. "You're divorced, so you have to know how volatile relationships can become."

Leigh took immediate exception to his assumption, as well as his patronizing tone. "Leave my divorce out of this," she insisted. "Women are often too ashamed to admit they're being abused, and if Bonnie won't even acknowledge the fact she and Miguel are a couple, then that may very well be what's happening to her."

Alarmed, Eli sat up and rested his arms on the edge of the shiny table. "You ought not to jump to such dire conclusions about men you don't know," he cautioned, "and in Mirasol, where gossip is more pervasive than the scent of orange blossoms, it's doubly dangerous. Miguel's been a surrogate father to his younger brothers and sisters since his father died. If you'd ever seen the way they rush into his arms, you'd know how gentle a man he is."

"I'm happy to hear it, but you said yourself that he's fighting you on the redevelopment plan."

"That he is, but just because he has a passionate nature doesn't mean he's abusive. Miguel's a good man. Don't cause him trouble by voicing unfounded suspicions."

Eli had given her a clear order, and Leigh leaned close to respond in a pointed whisper. "Gossip may be a world class sport in Mirasol, but I'll not stoop to spreading it about Miguel or anyone else. Now it's been a long day, and I've seen enough. Let's go home."

Leigh was concentrating solely on him now, but Eli wasn't at all pleased by her motivation. He watched her gather up her purse and the long, blue bag holding the windsock, but he sat back in his chair. "I'd like to finish my espresso, if you don't mind."

Leigh did mind, but because they would be traveling back to Mirasol together, she chose to be gracious. "Go right ahead." She continued to sit forward, and watched the crowd moving by on the sidewalk. There were retired couples holding hands, families with strollers bouncing over the terra cotta paving stones, and an occasional swarm of teenaged boys in long, baggy shorts and oversized T-shirts emblazoned with the logos of heavy-metal bands. Most wore their hair so long in front it dangled in their eyes while the rest of their heads were shaved up the back and sides.

"How does a man know when he gets a bad haircut anymore?" Leigh asked. "We've seen a lot of young men today who would look better if their mothers were to cut their hair with a bowl."

"Leigh?"

Leigh turned toward him. "Yes?" Eli's silvery blond hair was slightly longer than hers, and expertly cut; it brushed his collar.

"There are couples who have fierce fights only to make up with renewed passion. It's not a pattern I enjoy, and it's clear you wouldn't either, but if it's the way Miguel and Bonnie want to behave, then that's their business and no one else's."

Regarding that as one condescending piece of advice too many, Leigh left her chair with an agile leap. "I'll wait for you at the car."

"No," Eli scolded, but he was on his feet just as quickly, and threw down ten dollars to cover their bill and tip. "I'm ready to go home, too."

They walked back to where he had parked without speaking, and rather than returning on the winding road they had taken from Mirasol, Eli remained on highway 101 until they reached the turn-off Leigh had always taken for the city. She knew this terrain well, but with Eli driving in sullen silence, the pastoral view wasn't particularly soothing. Now she was sorry she hadn't urged him to get a tattoo. It would surely have been painful and she would have preferred to listen to him wimper about it all the way home rather than suffer through this sad effort to ignore each other.

"You're an only child, aren't you?" Leigh asked him suddenly.

Eli shot her a quick, challenging glance. "Yes, but what's that got to do with anything?"

"Birth order is extremely important," she explained. "I'm also an only child, and only children and first-borns simply don't get along well. It's a control issue. We're both used to getting our own way, you see, which makes conflict inevitable."

Eli shook his head sadly, but he was intrigued. "You mean we're doomed?"

"I'm afraid so."

"Was that the problem with your ex?"

Leigh hesitated a long moment before deciding she would answer his question, but not reveal another thing about Doug. "No, he was the middle child. They're the sociable ones."

"Denise has an older sister," Eli confided, "but clearly that was no help."

"I never said birth order was the only problem in relationships," Leigh stressed.

Eli glanced out at the horses grazing in the pasture bordering the road. In the late afternoon sun, their legs cast the same long angular shadows as the fence posts. "It's been my experience that some people search for creative solutions to problems, while others simply use their talents to stir up trouble."

The warning edge had crept back into his voice, and Leigh was certain he was referring to her fears, as yet unsubstantiated, that Miguel was abusing Bonnie. He hadn't seen the fear in Bonnie's eyes though, and she had. Not wanting to run through the same argument when it was clear neither of them would give an inch, she kept still, but she liked her comically nosey neighbor too much not to speak with her again about Miguel. If Bonnie were being abused, then Leigh would not simply encourage her to report Miguel to the police, she would drive her right down to the station.

Miguel tossed the motel key on the formica topped desk, and began to unbutton his denim shirt. "Quit worrying about them, Bonnie. So what if they saw us? We're both single, but you're acting as though you'd just been caught cheating on your husband. We've got no reason to be ashamed."

Bonnie walked past him into the bathroom and splashed cool water on her face, but when she looked up, her eyes were still bright with fear. She gripped the sides of the sink, but couldn't stop shaking. "What will Eli do?"

Miguel peeled off his shirt, tossed it over the chair at the desk, and came to the door she had left open. He raked her slender figure with an insolent stare. "Do about what?"

"You know damn well what I mean! Will he talk about us to everyone he meets?"

Miguel leaned back against the doorjamb, and unbuckled his belt. He often worked without a shirt, and his broad chest, flat belly, and muscular arms were a smooth bronze. "He's got a lot more on his mind than the women at the Beauty Spot. Besides, if I know him, and I do, he'll spend tonight fucking your new neighbor and forget all about us."

Bonnie brushed by Miguel, kicked off her sandals, and stretched out on the bed without bothering to remove her dress. She flung her arm over her eyes and tried to fight down the panic that was churning in her stomach like the wash in her mother's old Bendix. "Leigh isn't like that," she said.

Miguel sat down on the side of the bed and pulled off his boots and socks. "Like what? Doesn't she like men?"

Bonnie searched for the right words. She admired Leigh enormously, and didn't want to say anything that would make Miguel dislike her any more than he already did for her part in the redevelopment project. "She'll have been in Mirasol a week tomorrow. I doubt that she sleeps with men she's only known a week."

Miguel stood to yank off his levis and then, naked, lay down beside Bonnie and pulled her into his arms. "A week is a life-time to Eli, so she better not waste her chance. You ought to be grateful I had the patience to wait more than twenty years for you." He slid his hand up under her dress, and began tracing lazy circles just above her bikini panties. Her bare skin was invitingly warm, and he soon slipped his fingers beneath the elastic to comb the dark curls she kept waxed to a narrow strip.

Bonnie raised her elbow slightly to peer up at him. "You can't count the years you were growing up, and you didn't wait for me either." Miguel had the most incredibly light touch, and yet he knew exactly where to press. Her breath caught in her throat as he found her most sensitive spot, and she arched up against his hand. "Damn you, Miguel," she murmured in a sul-try sigh. "You know you didn't wait."

Miguel lapped at her ear, then nibbled around her hoop ear-ring, and drew her earlobe through his teeth. "I didn't want to practice on you, *querida,* and that's all the other girls were: just practice for this." He thrust a finger up inside her then, and with fluttering strokes quickly coaxed a shuddering response.

Bonnie waited to let the last tremors of joy wash through her before she rolled toward him. She ran her hand over his bare hip, then down between his thighs. She wrapped her fingers around his cock and felt him swell to rock hard. She stroked him with the demanding rhythm he liked, and smiled when he moaned way back in his throat.

She released him when his passion began to tear in small drops, and scooted off the bed to pull her dress off over her head. It was one of the tight prints she saved to wear with him, and she slung it over his shirt, stepped out of her panties, and unsnapped her bra. With his dark eyes nearly closed, Miguel's lashes shadowed his cheeks, but he was watching her as he kept pleasuring himself with the brisk motion she had begun.

He was the best lover she had ever had, and she knew from the whispered complaints she had strained to overhear from the day her mother had told her about sex, that most of the women in Mirasol would kill to have a man like him. He was only twenty-six, so his stamina came naturally, but he always took care to bring her to climax first, and often. She climbed back up on the bed and straddled his hips.

He reached up to roll her rosy nipples between his finger and thumb, and she guided his cock along the length of her cleft before allowing only a bit of the velvet tip to penetrate. He thrust up with his hips, striving to enter deeply, but she straightened up to elude him. She loved teasing him like this, and again lowered herself down on him, only to rise before he could begin pumping.

"Where's all that patience you were bragging about?" Bonnie whispered. She twisted above him, but allowed him no more than a shallow sample of her charms. "I love taking you inside me." His hair fanned over the pillow like black silk, and she used her free hand to drag her long fingernails up the taut muscles of his belly. "I wish I could keep you inside me all the time, the whole hot, hard, length of you."

She shut her eyes to imagine how glorious that would be, but slid down only a fraction of an inch more. "I wish I could wear your cock deep inside me to work, and come whenever I got bored."

"Would you let me carry your tits in my pockets to squeeze when I missed you?"

Bonnie tightened her vaginal muscles and gripped him with a rolling rhythm. "Like this?" He arched up beneath her, and this time she slammed her buttocks against his thighs and let him drive home. "Oh, yes," she sighed. "God, if you were any bigger, we wouldn't fit."

But they did fit, perfectly, and she pressed down each time he lifted his hips. He gave her breasts a last adoring squeeze, then slipped his hand between them to rub her clit. He slowed his motions, then stilled them to hover right below release until he felt her tremors surround him and her juices flowed out over his hand. He grabbed for her waist then, and pushed her down on the bed so he was in control of their coupling. He tickling her with shallow thrusts, then driving deep, brought her to another climax before losing himself in a blinding release.

He fell asleep locked in her arms, confident they would have each other again later.

First thing Sunday morning, Leigh went out on the porch, and hung up the butterfly windsock from a hook she nailed into an overhead beam. She walked out to the street to admire it, then inspired by its bright exuberance, felt compelled to get away. She took a quart of bottled water, the weekend edition of the *Los Angeles Times,* a beach towel, and drove out to the coast. She didn't care if Jonathan Reid came jogging by. She intended to enjoy the sun in solitary splendor.

She parked along the bluff where she had the previous week, and after making her way down to the sand, spread out her towel and sat down. She took a few sips of water, opened the newspaper, and scanned the headlines before reading the comics. She seldom had the time, or inclination, to read the entire paper, but she never missed the comics. It was one of her few diversions. Even before Eli's impertinent question about her being obsessed with her work, she had been well-aware her life consisted of little else. Believing the move to Mirasol provided the perfect opportunity to break old patterns and achieve a new sense of balance, she vowed to take off every Sunday.

She watched a couple nearby put up a green beach umbrella with scalloped edges. Designed to resemble a palm tree, it created an instant tropical shelter. Tickled, she wondered where they had bought it, and thought she just might spend enough Sundays at the beach to justify owning one of her own. While she had not admitted it to Eli, buying the windsock had been a start on recovering the simple joy of life. She wouldn't change the seriousness with which she approached her work, but she wanted so much more out of life. It was what had prompted her to strike out on her own.

The cool green sea was again dotted with surfers out to challenge the waves, and Leigh kicked off her tennis shoes, and wandered down to the shore to watch them. She had grown up in Southern California, but she had never ridden a surfboard. Perhaps it was high time she did. Most of the surfers were young men, but even with their figures disguised by wetsuits, Leigh recognized a young woman or two.

"Good for you!" she cheered. She watched the surfers lie down to paddle their fiberglass boards out to catch the cresting waves, but when they went flying off them more often than they were able to stand and ride within the cascading curl, she gained a whole new respect for the sport. The surfers didn't appear to discourage easily though, and continued to battle the sea for an infrequent but spectacular ride. She was positive the fact it didn't come easily made the thrill all the more exciting when it was finally achieved.

After a while, she picked her way across the rocks to reach the tide pools, but rather than study the marine life she found a rock that made a fine bench, and sat down to observe the sailboats skimming the horizon. She had never lived this close to the shore, and the serenity of the Pacific invited a lengthy stay. She looped her arms around a bent knee, shut out the insistent urgings of her conscience to get back to work, and refused to leave.

Rather than risk another confrontation with Leigh Bowman, Jonathan Reid had briefly considered staying home that morning, but, determined not to alter his routine just to avoid her, he had come down to the beach anyway. He had been so relieved not to find her at the tide pools when he had begun his run that he had added a couple of extra miles. Now, walking back up the beach to cool down, he recognized her by her red cap, and braced himself. When he realized she was lost in the beauty of the view, rather than waiting for him, he didn't know what to think.

He pulled on his T-shirt, skipped a few stones, and while he resented it deeply, had to finally admit he wasn't truly upset to find Leigh there. She hadn't shifted position in the time he had been watching her, so he doubted that she had seen him, but leaving without speaking to her struck him as cowardly. Ron Tate had dropped hints about the new city planner all week. Clearly taken with her, Ron had not let a single day go by without mentioning her name.

And every time Jonathan had complained that he didn't want to hear about Leigh Bowman, let alone devote any of his precious time to talking about her, Ron had said that was just fine because she was dating Eli, but that revelation had only made Jonathan feel worse. Last Sunday he had gone after her as fast as a hungry trout leaps for an expertly tied fly, and to his everlasting shame he still felt as though he had bitten down on a painfully sharp hook. Except it wasn't the roof of his mouth that ached. He knew Leigh Bowman's kind all too well, but while he cursed with every step, he made the trek out over the rocks to reach her.

"Nothing in the pools today?" he asked with forced calm.

Jonathan hadn't called to Leigh until he was close enough to touch her, and with the roaring noise of the sea, she had not heard him approach. She felt him now though, and turned toward him slowly. Her hat had slipped down, and she gave the bill a quick push so she could see him without having to cock her head at an odd angle.

Along with everything else, she had dismissed him from her mind shortly after arriving at the beach, but as their eyes met a heart-stopping thrill jolted her clear through. He had intrigued her from the beginning, but like someone plagued by a dangerous allergy, every time they met the power of his appeal rocked her more strongly. He exuded a pure masculine magnetism and his shorts and faded T-shirt hid so little of his muscular body she could easily imagine him nude.

Overcome with an intoxicating need, she hoped the gods were amused by the joke they had played on her, because she certainly wasn't laughing. When Jonathan quirked a brow, she grew uncomfortably aware of how long it had taken her to respond. "I haven't looked," she admitted with a careless shrug.

Leigh's manner was as guarded as when Jonathan had struck up their first conversation, and he knew it was his fault. "It was thoughtful of you to apologize for the joke you made at my expense at the meeting, especially after the way I'd thrown you out of my house. That was unforgivable of me." He waited a beat, hoping she might contradict him, but she nodded instead.

"Just because I'm not pleased with the project you've been hired to oversee, doesn't give me the right to be ill-mannered."

The breeze off the water fluttered his hair and he reached up to swipe it out of his eyes. The silver at his temples blended so perfectly with his deeply tanned skin Leigh believed he would grow more handsome with each passing year. Few women were as lucky. Self-conscious, she pulled off her cap and ruffled her short curls.

"Definitely not," she said, "but if in the future you'll confine your attacks to the project, rather than to me, I'll refrain from making personal comments, too."

"That seems fair." He extended his hand. "Come on. Let's look at the tide pools. There might be another pair of hermit crabs in desperate need of rescue."

Taking his hand would be lunacy when just looking at him made her heart pound. She fully intended to rise without touching him, but slipped on a loose stone, and he reached out to catch her. His grasp was firm, and he held on even after she had regained her balance. His hands were warm as his fingers closed around her upper arms and his flesh was so compatible with hers that she slid her arm around his waist without thinking.

They stood together, neither wanting to step away until finally

Leigh found the courage to look up at him. What she saw shocked her, for beneath the desire that lent his dark eyes a smokey glaze, she glimpsed a bright hint of loathing. He might have blamed their initial argument on his disgust with her job, but her vague suspicion that there was far more to his objection to her was now confirmed. In another instant he would bend to kiss her, but she feared it would be a bruising, punishing kiss meant for someone else entirely.

"Thanks. I shouldn't have taken off my shoes." Using far more care, she crept across the rocks without slipping a second time but she was so distracted she couldn't find the pool where they had met, and thinking it really didn't matter, she stopped at another.

Jonathan wasn't certain what had prompted him to apologize, other than a basic sense of fairness, but Leigh had eluded him so quickly he felt cheated. He knelt down beside her and tried to concentrate on the pool, but it took him a long moment to realize there wasn't a damn thing in it. "What are you watching?" he whispered.

Embarrassed to admit she hadn't even noticed the tide pool was empty until he had spoken, Leigh gave him a hushed reply. "I'm waiting for something to appear."

"Waiting," Jonathan repeated numbly, but he couldn't think of anything better. "Okay."

Exquisitely aware of the man by her side, Leigh prayed for any sort of a sea creature to wander into view so there would be something to comment on before they went their separate ways. After enduring several unbearably long minutes without so much as a tiny fish swimming by them, she started to excuse herself at precisely the same moment Jonathan chose to speak her name.

"Sorry," he murmured. "Go ahead."

He was so close, Leigh could have touched his cheek just by raising her hand. He had shaved before coming to the beach, and she knew his skin would be warm, and smooth. She wrapped her hand around her ankle to fight the temptation to caress him.

"I was just going to say this doesn't seem to be a good morning for observing aquatic life."

Jonathan nodded, but remained crouched beside her. "You were sitting so still when I first saw you. Did I interrupt you while you were sorting out something important?"

Leigh sighed softly. "I can't say now, but it's unlikely. Do you sort out your problems while you jog?"

Jonathan responded with an amused smile. "No, but I learned a long time ago that I can't outrun them." His voice deepened slightly. "Be careful with Eli."

Startled by his sudden shift in subject and tone, Leigh waited for him to elaborate on his warning, but his glance was now focused on the still empty pool. "What are you talking about?" she prompted. "Are you afraid we'll not practice safe sex?"

Jonathan's head snapped around, and knowing she now had his full attention, she capitalized on it. "Everyone describes him as promiscuous, but that doesn't mean that I am." Leigh used his shoulder for leverage as she rose. She crossed the rocky shoreline with a series of flying leaps, then strode across the sand with her arms pumping wildly.

Jonathan overtook Leigh easily, but she didn't slow down. "Christ! I wasn't talking about sex. I was referring to his motives for backing the redevelopment plan. It's been his baby from the beginning and he's the one who's going to reap the most benefit, regardless of how often he proclaims it's all for the good of his beloved Mirasol."

Leigh grabbed up her towel and shook off the sand. She folded it quickly, then gathered up her shoes, bottled water, and newspaper. Only then did she look up at Jonathan.

"You rotten son-of-bitch. You want to discuss business, you call city hall and make an appointment, but don't you dare sidle up to me on a Sunday to warn me about another man's motives when it's clear yours aren't ever so pure!"

Leigh was absolutely livid with him, and herself as well for ever dreaming he might be interested in her when obviously all he had wanted was to score a few points for his team. "Watch

Eli, my ass," she swore under her breath. Eli was a veritable prince compared to Jonathan Reid, who would pretend to want her company and then take advantage of her.

Jonathan watched Leigh start up the bluff. "You and Eli are a real pair!" he shouted up at her.

Leigh paused on the narrow trail. "Yeah, but we're nothing compared to you and Denise!" She was being most unprofessional, but damn it, it was Sunday, and today was her day off!

Seven

Bonnie MacNair had been listening for Leigh's car, and the instant she heard her neighbor arrive home she bolted out her front door and chased her up the driveway. As soon as Leigh opened the Camaro's door, Bonnie lunged for her.

"God! I thought you'd never get home. We have to talk."

Leigh was no calmer than when she had left Jonathan gaping at her on the beach, but Bonnie's tear-streaked face immediately captured her sympathetic attention. "Let's go inside. I haven't had breakfast yet. Have you?" She picked up the things she had taken to the beach, and led the way to her back door. "Why didn't you wave to me yesterday in Santa Barbara?"

Bonnie followed Leigh inside, and flopped down at the kitchen table. She held her head in her hands, and sniffed loudly. "I know that was stupid. I didn't mean to snub you."

Leigh took a jug of orange juice from the refrigerator and poured them each a glass. She carried them to the table, and sat down opposite Bonnie. The day had begun so poorly she was afraid Bonnie's story was going to be all too predictable and tragic. There weren't any bruises on her face and arms, but something had to have happened to prompt such anguished behavior. Not wanting to upset Bonnie further, Leigh waited for her to pull herself together and confide in her on her own.

Bonnie took a sip of juice, choked, and then recovered after a sputtering hiccough. "It's not what you think," she blurted out. "I'm not ashamed to be seen with Miguel. He's so handsome there are times it hurts to look at him and he's the best lover I've ever had, but he works in Eli's groves, and that's all he'll ever do. If my mother found out I'd been with him, she'd be so disappointed in me she'd just die, Leigh. She really would."

Although reluctant to be drawn into whatever conflict Bonnie might have with her mother, Leigh still tried to be helpful. "From what I saw at the library, and yesterday, I'd assumed whatever trouble you had was with Miguel. If it's with your mother instead, you're a grown woman, Bonnie. It's time you made your own choices."

Bonnie slumped back in her chair. She was dressed in Levi's and a wrinkled blue shirt. Not helped by her perpetually tousled curls, she looked thoroughly bedraggled. "Yes. I know. But Miguel offers everything I want, and everything I don't want all at the same time. He's smarter than any of the men I dated in college, or since, but everything he wants is right here in Mirasol. Nothing I want is."

"Except Miguel?" Leigh asked softly.

Bonnie wiped her eyes. She hadn't bothered with make-up that morning and looked pale without her usual touches of bright color. "Yes, that's certainly true, but I'll only see him in Santa Barbara. I won't go out with him here."

"Miguel accepts your conditions?" Leigh couldn't understand why he would.

Bonnie rolled her lower lip through her teeth. "He wants us to get married, but he's supporting his whole family and he can't afford a wife even if I'd agree, which I won't."

"You have a good job."

"I know, and please don't think I don't know how lucky I am to have it, but I don't want to be a librarian forever, and even if I did, I'd not want to be one here in Mirasol. You've got to promise me you won't tell anyone you saw me with Miguel because it'll get right back to my mother, and she'll never forgive me. I've told her I'm dating a Santa Barbara man who's in real estate. That's why he's always too busy on the weekends to come here and meet her."

Leigh had such little appetite now, she didn't offer Bonnie more than the single glass of juice. Bonnie's comments about her childhood had made it plain she didn't think much of men, but Leigh certainly didn't share her negative views. "There must be a thousand books available on how to have successful relationships. Doesn't the library have some good ones?"

Bonnie nodded, then shrugged. "So?"

"So read some! No one knows better than I do how difficult it is for couples to blend their lives and careers, but when two people love each other, and sincerely work toward the same goals, it can be done. Miguel wouldn't have offered marriage if he didn't love you, but other than complimenting his looks and prowess in bed, you've not said how you feel about him. Do you love him?"

Leigh watched Bonnie squirm uncomfortably as she tried to come up with an answer, and was thoroughly disgusted with her. "If you're not proud too be seen with Miguel, then you ought to break it off rather than simply use him for sex until someone better comes along. Now I've got to do my laundry, so you'll have to excuse me."

Bonnie stared wide-eyed as Leigh left the table. "I'm not just using him," she said.

"The hell you aren't." Leigh leaned back against the counter. "I'm all for equality between the sexes, but you're treating Miguel the way some men treat a pretty waitress or sweet clerk they'll sleep with on the sly but never introduce to their friends, or marry. Eli described Miguel as his best man, so clearly he deserves better. Any man does."

Seized with a sudden inspiration, Leigh walked back to the table. "I'd like nothing better than a hard-working man who wants a wife and family."

Huge tears welled up in Bonnie's eyes. "You can't really be interested in him. He did graduate from high school, but he never even considered going away to college."

"So what? You said he's bright, and if he let his hair grow a tad longer, he'd be even more handsome than the Indians in

Dances With Wolves. It's been a while since I slept with a man, and if he's as good in bed as you claim, then I'd be sure to enjoy sleeping with him."

"But he's only twenty-six!"

Leigh shrugged. "Women usually outlive men, so it's a good idea to marry one several years younger to avoid having to grow old alone. Twenty-six is the perfect age for me."

Feeling at a great disadvantage, Bonnie rose to face Leigh. "I'll bet Eli doesn't pay Miguel half what you earn."

"That's no problem, either. It's all a matter of priorities, Bonnie. You just want out of Mirasol. I want a loving husband and father for my children. If Miguel is devoted to his family, then he'll surely be equally devoted to the family he creates with me."

Leigh turned away to hide her smile and walked over to open her backdoor. "You'll need a few days to break up with him, then I'll give him a call out at the ranch. He'll undoubtedly need a little consoling, and I'm very good at that."

Bonnie gestured helplessly. "He'll not have anything to do with you as long as you're part of the redevelopment plan."

"I'm sure he'll change his mind when I describe the new opportunities it will bring. If he enjoys working in the groves, then he could just as easily manage the grounds of the new resort complex. That would provide a much higher salary and increased financial support for his family."

Dumbfounded by the response she had received from Leigh, Bonnie started out the door with trembling steps. "I thought you'd understand, and want to help me," she murmured.

Leigh gave her a comforting pat on the shoulder. "After you've had some time to think about it, I'm sure you'll realize just how helpful I've been. Why don't you fill your bathtub, pour in some Sensual Harmony oil, and compose a touching farewell to Miguel. Leading him on as you have been is cruel, Bonnie. Make a clean break with him now."

Leigh closed the door after her. Bonnie had looked even more distraught than when she had arrived, and Leigh hoped she had given her plenty to think about. She had certainly learned something herself and would not jump to conclusions the next time she overheard a few angry words. She owed Eli an apology, but if she called his private line now, he would probably suggest a way for them to spend the day together and she did not want to mislead him the way Bonnie had Miguel.

For the moment, she would allow him to remain angry with her, along with Jonathan and Bonnie. At this rate, she would alienate the whole town before the first shovelful of earth was turned for the new commercial buildings. She needed to make friends rather than enemies, but for now, it couldn't be helped.

"Laundry," she reminded herself. She had a list of chores, and planned to spend the rest of the day on them. She stopped worrying about being popular and got busy.

Eli called Miguel into his office first thing Monday morning. "I'm your boss rather than your best friend," he began, "so I didn't expect you and Bonnie to join Ms. Bowman and me for an espresso Saturday afternoon, but the way you two ducked out of sight has me worried. It's your business who you date, but I've always thought you were man enough to be up front about it."

"I am!" Eli was seated behind an oak desk, but Miguel didn't regard the massive piece of furniture as the most significant barrier between them. "I may work for you, but I don't see how anything I do on my own time is any business of yours."

"I'm making it my business," Eli informed him calmly. "I'm on the library board, so naturally I also have an interest in Ms. MacNair's welfare. She didn't look happy on Saturday. Times have changed, Miguel. If a man gives a woman a reason to complain, she's likely to do it down at the police station."

Miguel took another step closer to the desk. He'd kicked the mud off his boots outside, but he still feared he was tracking up Eli's rug and didn't dare look down. Sunlight streaming in the windows left Eli's face in shadow, but ringed his fair hair with a bright halo. No one had ever described Eli as angelic, and Miguel was badly offended by his condescending attitude.

"Just what is it you're talking about? Bonnie's got no reason to file any complaints against me. Absolutely none."

Eli picked up a yellow pencil and drew it through his fingers. "Some women like rough sex, or claim to, and then change their minds. You're strong. Haven't you ever put a few bruises on Bonnie without realizing it until you saw them later?"

Eli was only eleven years older than Miguel, and despite the fact he owned the ranch, Miguel had never regarded him as a father figure. "If you're accusing me of beating Bonnie, then we'd better step outside."

Miguel was glowering at him, but Eli shrugged off his threat with the same cool disdain that enabled him to get the best of most men in his business dealings. "Look, if you don't want anyone to know you're seeing Bonnie, fine, but it looks suspicious when the two of you hide from friends. If she's ashamed to be seen with you, then dump her."

Miguel folded his hands behind his back rather than wrap them around Eli's neck. "You have some work for me, I'll get right on it. Otherwise, I'm walking out because you're the last man who ought to be giving advice about women."

Eli got a good laugh out of that comment. "I do just fine, Miguel—better than fine, actually."

"Save it for the new city planner, or have you already gotten bored with her and moved on?"

Eli tossed the pencil aside, stood, and jammed his hands into his pockets. "Ms. Bowman and I were in Santa Barbara on business."

"Yeah, right. Bonnie and I were just picking up a few books for the library at the Earthling Bookshop."

"Damn it, Miguel. I'm not just jacking you around by prying into your personal life. I'm trying to keep you out of trouble. I'll have my hands full once the redevelopment gets underway and I need to know I can depend on you to keep the ranch running smoothly."

"Or what's left of it," Miguel shot right back at him. "There aren't enough people in Mirasol to staff that monster hotel you have planned. That means people will have to come from outside. They'll need apartments, homes, grocery stores, Blockbuster video, you name it and you're going to sell off the ranch bit by bit. In five years, you won't have enough left of your avocado groves to make a quart of *guacamole!*"

"If you don't want to work here, then pack up and leave," Eli threatened darkly. "Just load your mother and the kids in your truck and take off. Oh, wait a minute. You don't even own a truck, do you? Well, because you've been with me so long, I'll rent you one for the day. Just have it back by nightfall and I'll have one of the other men drive you back into town."

Eli sat down and began to sort through his mail. "Or," he added drily, "maybe Bonnie will lend you her car."

Had Miguel not been responsible for his family, he would have walked out and never looked back, but he had grown up in one of the houses Eli's father had built for his workers and it was no tar-paper shack either. It was a nice house, and his family's home. They lived in it rent free, and he couldn't move everyone into some tiny apartment he could afford while he looked for other work. There were other ranches, but none as large and properous as Eli Keene's.

He nearly choked as he swallowed his pride. "You know I can't leave."

Eli glanced up, and appeared to be surprised to find Miguel still standing in front of his desk. "And neither can I. Now get back to work."

Miguel left, but he was seething. Eli wouldn't last one day in the groves, but the ranch was his. It was land Miguel's father and grandfather had worked and if sweat were gold then they would have paid for it a thousand times over. Their labor was worth so damn little, however, that Miguel didn't even own enough dirt to dig himself a grave.

"Cabrón," he snarled under his breath. Eli managed the ranch from behind his desk while Miguel and the other men did all

the real work. He might not own a truck, but he knew the hillside groves so well he could drive a tractor through them blindfolded. While Eli ate fine meals in his big air-conditioned house, Miguel's lunch always tasted of dirt. By all rights, the ranch should have been his, and he would rather die than see a single acre sold.

With a proposal to resurface the roads the main item on the agenda, Monday night's council meeting drew a smaller crowd than the previous week's. Leigh noted one stirring similarity, however: Jonathan Reid and Ron Tate were again seated in the front row. Ron smiled warmly at her, but Jonathan's expression hovered between a sneer and a smirk. Leigh couldn't understand why he would have such a supercilious attitude until Frank Pierce announced the portion of the meeting devoted to new business and Jonathan immediately asked to speak.

When he was recognized, Jonathan stood and turned to address the crowd. The evening was warm, and the windows were open, but there was little breeze in the auditorium. "I want to state clearly, so no one will mistake my intentions, that I'm willing to do all I can to enhance Mirasol's economy. I want more tourists, better job opportunities, and greater prosperity. I just don't want to see the city torn up to do it."

Jonathan scanned the crowd for Eli, and found him seated in the rear. "Eli intends to build a mammoth resort complex on his land, and that's certainly his right, but it doesn't necessarily follow that we have to rebuild the town. Last week Ms. Bowman described both phases of the redevelopment plan, but I believe the most obvious means to improve the town has been overlooked.

"Structurally, the original buildings are sound. A fresh coat of paint, along with greater attention to attractive landscaping, and we can welcome an increase in tourism without having to suffer though a couple of years of construction that will create so much noise and dirt we'll have doomed the city to extinction before the first new store opens."

Leigh had worked at city hall all day, making her own chart of the business district with discreet plus and minus signs to indicate which merchants backed the plan, and which were outright hostile. She had drawn a cross for the few who projected an air of complete indifference. She had already noted which group was in the majority tonight, and expected trouble from the moment Jonathan raised his hand.

Frank rapped his gavel. "Jonathan, please. The redevelopment plan will provide far more than a facelift. If you've forgotten the details, come by my office tomorrow and I'll give you a copy. Now is there anyone with any real new business to discuss?"

"Yeah, I have some." Bob Brown rose to his feet, but doggedly pursued the same subject. "I think Jonathan has a damn good point. Some of us, and that includes my brother and me, have gotten a bit sloppy over the years. We might have kept up with the basic maintenance on the hardware store, but we've not made any effort to improve the place. Now all we've got are a lot of old buildings some folks think are begging to be torn down. Well, like Jonathan suggests, maybe if those of us who aren't looking forward to being uprooted were to show the same initiative as the crowd who wants to level the city and start over, we'd have a town that anyone would be proud to visit."

Frank whammed his gavel to silence the mutterings rolling through the crowd, but Leigh was on her feet, ready to respond before he could speak. "You've both raised good points," she began, "but failed to consider Mirasol's most pressing need is for a future that includes positive growth rather than simply maintaining the status quo."

"We might be able to hold the commerical buildings together a few more years with some creative use of plaster, paint, and flowering plants, but it would be purely a stopgap measure, and Mirasol deserves better. What we really need to do is to open the resort and revitalize downtown simultaneously; otherwise, we'll miss our best chance to grow ahead of the increased demand for services. The comprehensive plan was approved by the voters because it's not only sound, but vital for the life of the city."

Jonathan was about to get back on his feet, but Leigh raised her hands to keep him in his seat. "I spent Saturday in Santa Barbara." She paused while a wave of strained looks passed through the crowd. "It's a beautiful city, isn't it? And very close. Do you honestly believe tourists will prefer to spend their vacation dollars on Mirasol Avenue if we don't give them something better than the charming *Paseo Nuevo* on State Street?"

Jonathan left his chair. "Now wait just a minute," he cried. "No. I'll not wait, Mr. Reid," Leigh replied firmly, "and neither will the tourists. Either we get behind the redevelopment plan, or lower the flag on city hall and move out, because that's the only choice we'll have if we miss what is surely Mirasol's last chance for survival."

Patsy O'Dell leapt to her feet cheering, and Frank Pierce adjourned the meeting as soon as he could be heard above the noise. Leigh held Jonathan's gaze in a silent duel until Denise slithered up beside him. She was dressed in a handpainted silk sheath whose undulating scalloped pattern bore an appropriate likeness to a serpent's scales. The woman certainly knew how to dress, but Leigh wondered if she ever voiced any of her perplexing opinions in the council meetings. As Patsy approached, Leigh lost sight of Jonathan and his statuesque lady friend.

"You just go right ahead and remind them of Santa Barbara every chance you get," Patsy urged. "We've got a lot to offer, but as it stands now, we just can't compete. The whole character of Mirasol has to change if we're ever to generate the excitement the town used to have. Lordy. Why can't everyone see that?"

"Change is always frightening," Leigh responded, "so it's not surprising some would prefer to paint over the decay and keep on going as best they can. Fortunately, it's been my experience that the same people will become the most enthusiastic supporters once the plan is complete."

"I'll look forward to that," Patsy assured her, and then moved on down the table to talk with Zoe Kunkel.

Leigh had hoped to speak with Eli, but by the time she could get away, he was nowhere to be seen. Thinking she would have to call his private line after all to deliver the apology she had intended to make, she was relieved to find him leaning against her car. "I was afraid I'd missed you," she called to him.

"I wasn't certain you'd want to see me after the way we parted on Saturday, but I wouldn't have left without telling you that mentioning Santa Barbara was inspired. Did you see how many people slumped down in their seats? Santa Barbara is a great place. I really like it, but it doesn't have a bit of quaint charm and we're dripping with it here."

Leigh leaned back against her car. "Yes. That's just the problem. The city would make a perfect location for a film set in some sleepy village in the fifties, but this is the nineties and everything needs to be rebuilt. Damn it, Eli. I wish everyone believed in the redevelopment as strongly as you and I do. When we can make such a beautiful place of Mirasol, why would anyone oppose us?"

Eli was amused by her fiery eloquence. "Frankly, I think a lot of them fear if everything changes they'll no longer fit in. They'll get over it, eventually."

"That's what I told Patsy O'Dell, but I don't want to have to argue the issue every Monday night for the next two years."

"Hardly anyone shows up during football season," he quipped.

"I'll look forward to autumn, then. Do you want to go out to the Inn? I'll buy the drinks tonight."

Eli was so startled by that unexpected invitation, it took him a moment to realize what Leigh had asked. "Sure, but I'd swear you complained to me last week that you didn't want people talking about us being together."

Leigh knew she had, but now she just didn't care. "Is that why you waited for me out here?" The parking lot was behind city hall, and most people had parked on the street. Shaded by huge oaks, it was lit by bulbs strung along wires between the trees. The atmosphere was spooky rather than romantic, but Leigh parked there during the day, and hadn't worried about parking there at night when the police station was just across the street.

"Actually, no," Eli admitted. "I was afraid you'd refuse to speak with me if I tried to talk with you inside and that would have started a whole new round of imaginative speculation about us."

"God forbid."

Eli started toward his Porsche, and Leigh climbed into her Camaro to follow him out to the Inn. There were a few people seated in the bar, but it was a long way from full. Leigh slipped into the booth Eli apparently regarded as his, and again ordered Perrier.

"I owe you an apology," she began, and without revealing more than a brief hint of her conversation with Bonnie, she assured Eli that Miguel wasn't guilty of abuse. Then relaxing into the booth's comfortable folds, she described how she had convinced Bonnie she was interested in Miguel herself.

"My God," Eli moaned. "Were you serious? Miguel's undeniably handsome, but I'd no idea he was my competition."

Leigh was so amused by his pained expression that she rested her hand on his arm without realizing how seductive the gesture would be. "Miguel is no competition for you." Eli covered her hand with his own then, and she realized her mistake. She quickly pulled away, and took a sip of her drink.

"I deplore gossip, but that's really all we're doing, isn't it? One week in Mirasol, and I've been sucked into the worst of pastimes. I've been putting off going back to the Beauty Spot for fear I'll hear a secret that's too tantalizing to keep."

"I hope that you do, and call me to share it," Eli encouraged. "While we're playing true confessions, tell me what's going on between you and Jonathan Reid."

Leigh had been so careful to display her most polished professional manner at the council meeting, she hadn't realized anyone would question her relationship with the opinionated historian. She found it far easier to glance around the room than face Eli as she replied. "I've only spoken with him a couple of times outside of the council meetings, and unfortunately, those conversations went no better than the ones you've observed."

"That's not what I meant," Eli chided. "I swear it's damn near impossible to get the truth out of a woman. Denise didn't even understand what it was, but I expect better from you. Let's try again. I'll bet everyone in the auditorium felt the tension crackling between you two, and it sure didn't feel like hostility. Now what's going on?"

Leigh hadn't realized anyone else would have identified the force she recognized as purely sexual. That Eli had picked up on it so easily was appalling. "I admire people who are direct," she said.

"Good. Why don't you give it a try?" Eli finished his first Scotch, and signaled for another.

The bar was dim, and faint music blurred the conversation from other tables. She was confident she wouldn't be overheard, but doubted confiding in Eli would be wise. Not confiding in him when he was so open in his admiration for her was probably equally unwise, however.

"He's a very attractive man," she finally admitted, "but even if we weren't on opposite sides in the redevelopment issue, I doubt I'd date him. I barely know him, but I've gotten the impression he doesn't approve of me. Maybe he mistrusts all women, the way Bonnie mistrusts men."

"Then he's smarter than I thought."

Eli was still regarding her with a suspicious stare, and Leigh knew she had failed to make her point. "I want to concentrate on the project rather than romance, but even if I were hoping to meet someone here, it wouldn't be Jonathan. I'll bet he's an only child too, and it just wouldn't work."

"Christ," Eli muttered under his breath. "You're right; he is, but every couple is bound to have some element out of balance. If you're clever enough to recognize it, then you ought to be clever enough to know how to work around it. If you want to, that is."

"Jonathan's a born leader, and I'd love to have him on our side. You know him better than I ever will. How can we overcome his objections, and make him an ally?"

"I told you, he's harboring a grudge against me over Denise, and he'll never willingly support any cause I endorse."

Leigh considered that bleak prediction a moment. "Then I'll have to approach him on my own and work on the 'good of the town' angle. Otherwise I'm afraid we're going to find the opposition spreading as the date approaches for the project to get underway. Dissension has a way of gnawing away at a town and we won't have gained anything if we have new buildings no one is willing to occupy."

Eli downed his last swallow of Scotch and slammed down the glass. "This may sound like treason, but I really don't give a flying fuck about the people who are so far behind the times they can't see that Mirasol's disintegrating all around them. Jonathan's right. I am going to build the hotel, and I can run shuttles into Santa Barbara just as easily as I can ferry tourists into Mirasol. I'm providing the perfect opportunity to save the town, but if people continue to fight us on the redevelopment project, then I'll withdraw my support, and let them sink Mirasol and themselves with it."

Astonished by his mean-spirited threat, Leigh lowered her voice to deliver one of her own. "As I recall, you told me I'd be running the plan, and I don't appreciate your behaving like a spoiled brat who'll take the game elsewhere if the townspeople won't play by your rules." Incensed with him, Leigh shoved her finger into his chest.

"Do you understand me? The redevelopment is going through as planned, and I won't have you drop so much as a faint hint that you might withdraw your support. That's precisely what I meant about dissension tearing up a town, and I won't let it happen to Mirasol."

"Damn, but you're cute when you're angry."

Leigh opened her mouth to tell him how little she appreciated that remark but before she could, Eli raised his hands to frame her face and leaned over to kiss her soundly. He tasted of Scotch, but she broke free before he could slide his tongue over hers a second time. She swung out of the booth, and yanked open her purse to remove her wallet.

"Your money's no good here," Eli told her as he stood. He tossed a bill on the table for the bartender's tip, then took her arm. "Now let's try and walk out of here without yelling at each other, and the gossip will be no worse than last week's."

Leigh kept her voice down, but didn't soften her words. "You're being insufferably rude, Eli."

Eli waited until they had reached the parking lot to reply. "Do you think I enjoy having the money to buy and sell the whole valley? Do you honestly believe it's fun knowing how easily I can scramble several thousand lives?" He grabbed Leigh by the shoulders, and came within a breath of shaking her. "No," he whispered softly. "Once I have the hotel open, and the town rebuilt, I'll have completed whatever obligation I may have inherited to help Mirasol regain its prosperity. Then I'm getting out."

Leigh stared up at him shocked as much by the intentions he had just revealed as by how fiercely he had stated them. "That's what this whole project means to you? A ticket out of the valley?" she asked numbly.

Eli released a strained sigh, and nodded. "Do you blame me? I've been a prisoner here my whole life."

When he inclined his head, Leigh reached up to meet his kiss, but it was only to acknowledge his pain rather than to invite his passion. He was very gentle this time, slow and sweet, but his affection didn't even begin to touch the loneliness she strove so hard to hide. The longing for another man swelled within her, and when Eli at last drew away, there were tears in her eyes.

"Hey. What's wrong?" he asked.

"Damn near everything," Leigh replied with complete candor.

Eli pulled her into his arms and hugged her close. "If you won't stay with me here, what about the ranch? My staff is discreet."

Leigh rested in his arms, and wondered aloud. "Don't people go out on dates anymore?" she asked. "Do they just meet and sleep together instead?"

They were standing by her car, and Eli pulled her back with him so he could lean against it. "Are you talking about people in general, or me?"

His embrace was warm, but light, and yet Leigh felt more frightened than comforted and pushed away from him. "I think I'm going to be sick."

"Good lord, I've never had that effect on a woman. Maybe we better go back inside."

Leigh waved him away. "No. It's just been a long day is all. I want to go home." She fished her keys out of her purse, and unlocked her car door. "I was speaking of people in general," she finally answered as she slipped behind the wheel.

Eli grabbed hold of her open door. "From what I've heard, most people are scared to death and avoid anything that even remotely resembles commitment. I'm an optimist, though, and keep hoping I'll find a woman who can promise love without lying in the same breath."

"Was Denise really that bad?"

Eli closed the car door, and waited for Leigh to roll down the window. He leaned in to give her a quick good-night kiss. "Denise was the absolute worst. Now I'll follow you home to make certain you get there safely."

He turned away before Leigh could object, but because they were going the same direction, she really didn't mind. She took a deep breath, and wondered how any woman could lie about love when just kissing the wrong man made her feel awful. Then with a burst of delighted glee, she hoped Jonathan's stomach lurched every time he kissed Denise.

Eight

Tuesday morning at eleven, Leigh pressed Jonathan Reid's doorbell. As the musical chime echoed down the long hallway, she hoped that if nothing else he would be sufficiently impressed by the boldness of her gesture to allow her an opportunity to explain why she had tracked him to his lair. She had given him time to return home after his run, but when he did not swiftly appear, her courage began draining away. It was a large house, and she forced herself to wait longer than she would have at a smaller one, but she had already turned toward the steps when he finally came to the door.

The screen door's hazy mesh blurred Jonathan's expression, but it was clear he wasn't pleased to find Leigh on his doorstep. "I don't open for another hour," he said, "and I don't recall your calling to make an appointment."

There wasn't a trace of humor in his voice or manner, but Leigh had not expected a cordial greeting and produced a smile. "I was hoping you'd have time to take a walk with me through town. You see things so differently, that I believe I'd benefit from your insights."

"You've got to be joking."

"No. I'm completely serious, Mr. Reid. You obviously see things in Mirasol that are invisible to me, and I'd be grateful if you'd point them out. If this isn't a convenient time, then I'd like to schedule another that will be."

In a blatant attempt to disarm him with a softer image, Leigh had dressed in a pale blue suit. As Jonathan's glance drifted over her with a languid rather than hostile sweep, she was relieved by how well the ploy had succeeded. She was still standing on his porch, however, with the screen door between them. He appeared to be weighing her invitation, but against what?

"I want to be candid with you," she confided. "If this is a misconception, then please correct me, but do you have some objection to me as a person that has nothing whatsoever to do with my job with the city?"

Startled by her frankness, a long moment passed before Jonathan stepped out on the porch, and he kept his hand on the screen door handle. "What makes you think that?"

"I've learned to rely on my intuition. People are often reticent to express their feelings, but their emotions color their every gesture, and fill the spaces between their words."

"And you pick up on those subtle nuances?"

"Yes, and yours aren't in the least bit subtle. I'd call your hostility palpable, and if there's any way to dissolve it, I'd like to try."

Jonathan let go of the door and it swung closed. He gazed off toward the Topatopa Mountains rather than look at Leigh. "You're a very bright woman, Ms. Bowman, and no one could mistake your ambition."

He pronounced the last word as though it were an obscenity. Refusing to take it as an insult, Leigh leaned back against the porch railing. "Do you regard ambition as a general character flaw, or only as a failing in women?"

Jonathan turned toward her. "I'd not fault a woman for possessing a trait I admire in a man," he explained, "but an ambitious woman makes a terrible wife."

"You're speaking from experience?"

"Oh, yes," he breathed out in a poignant sigh.

Leigh had coaxed him into revealing his true complaint, and while he had confirmed her suspicion, he had failed to take the next step, and admit that his anger toward her was misplaced. She waited, hoping that he would, but he remained silent. They had strayed from the initial reason for her visit, but she thought this conversation had proven to be far more valuable. Unconsciously, her grasp tightened on her clipboard.

"Expectations can change over the life of a marriage," she offered softly, "and it's tragic when love isn't enough."

Jonathan's gaze darkened. "For some women, *nothing* is ever enough."

"But not all women," Leigh amended.

Jonathan took a step toward her. "What would it take to satisfy you?"

He was dressed in Levi's and a beige shirt. His hair was still damp from the shower, and he smelled faintly of soap rather than expensive cologne, but Leigh liked the scent ever so much better. He had asked a challenging question, but she wasn't even tempted to offer a provocative reply. Because she had given it so much thought, she had a ready answer. "I'd like to have balance in my life, a harmony between love, work, and family."

Jonathan dismissed her goal with a harsh laugh. "In other words, you want it *all.*"

Again his words were laced with sarcasm, but Leigh didn't respond in kind. "It's not an impossible dream, Mr. Reid. What's your heart's desire?" She didn't realize she was holding her breath as she awaited his answer until her chest began to ache.

A slow smile tugged at the corner of Jonathan's mouth and his glance wandered slowly down her figure. "I already have it right here, Ms. Bowman."

When his taunting gaze at last met hers, Leigh's mind filled with an erotic scene tinted in a faded photograph's sepia tones. Jonathan and Denise were angled across an ornately carved Victorian bed. Tangled in the lace-trimmed sheets, Denise was as exotic a creature nude as she was in her elegant clothes, and Jonathan, well-muscled and lean, was magnificent, too. He was lunging into Denise with deep, savage strokes but the expression gracing her perfect features was one of predatory triumph rather than wild passion. Her long nails raked his shoulders, drawing blood that dripped down on the ivory sheets.

Sickened by the lurid sketch, Leigh hurriedly blinked to dispel it. She turned, leaned over the rail to caress a fully opened rose, then confessed almost shyly, "I envy you. Now what about the walk? Do you have time this morning?"

Jonathan had been flippant, if not downright rude, and envy was the last thing he had expected to prompt in Leigh. The wistfulness of her tone revealed a touching vulnerabililty and he made the only choice he could. "I'll make the time." He closed and locked his front door, shoved his keys into his pocket, and gestured for her to precede him down the steps.

Once they reached the sidewalk, Jonathan fell in beside Leigh, and gauged his step to her shorter stride. Had their walk not had such a serious purpose, she would have looped her arm through his. She quickly discounted the impulse as absurd, but it lingered, unaccountably recalling the time she had invited a boy to her high school's Valentine dance. He had gone with her, but she had felt awkward the whole evening and when he had never called to ask her out in return, she had finally realized he had merely wanted to attend the dance. He hadn't liked her at all. After all these years, she was still embarrassed to have had such a terrible crush on him.

She felt the same sense of shame and loss now, as though she were asking for something Jonathan would never willingly give. Only now she was smart enough not to ask. She refocused her thoughts on the present and came to a halt in front of the theater. "We've a good view of the commercial block from here. The colonnade itself is attractive, which is why it will be rebuilt, but what do you think of the signs?"

Jonathan had never given them any thought, but now that he took the time to really look, he was appalled to discover they ranged from garish to faded, with the most attractive being Zoe Kunkel's for Fins, Feathers, and Fur. "With few exceptions, they're a mess," he admitted, "but putting up uniform signs won't be a major project and it will give the colonnade a whole new look."

Leigh raised her clipboard and printed the word, signs, in

block letters. She added a check. "So we agree on the signs then. They ought to be more attractive, and uniform."

"Well, you could say that," Jonathan conceded grudgingly, "but it's a small point."

"I disagree, Mr. Reid. The Spanish architecture of the business district provides a unified theme, but the present signs merely detract from, rather than enhance it. You've agreed that needs to be corrected."

"Yes, but—"

Leigh regarded him with an attentive gaze until he finally came to the realization they were indeed in agreement and shrugged. They crossed Signal Street, then Mirasol Avenue. Leigh drew Jonathan close to the window of the liquor store on the corner. "Jake has the most extensive display of limited edition decanters I've ever seen. I realize they're popular as Christmas gifts, and I'm sure that Elvis bottle must be worth quite a bit to collectors, but it doesn't appear to have been dusted in years."

Jonathan couldn't recall the last time he had been in Jake's, but he quickly defended the man. "All right, so Jake could use some help to clean up his window displays, but lots of tourists like to keep a bottle of booze in their hotel room, and his store is well-stocked."

"Oh, yes, it certainly is." Leigh led Jonathan through the door. Neon signs advertising popular brands of beer lined the walls above the shelves of liquors and racks of wine. In addition to refrigerator cases loaded with cold beer, the store also had a freezer filled with popsicles and ice cream bars. There were more racks of candy, gum, and snacks than a convenience store carried. There were comic books, but also magazines of a decidedly adult variety, and the cash register stand was surrounded by glass cases filled with airline-size, single-portion liquor bottles.

Jake Reynolds, a tall, balding man in his fifties, merely nodded to them, and continued waving the sports page to emphasize a point while he and a customer argued about the Dodgers' chances to make the World Series that year. Leigh looked up at the bare pipes overhead, and made certain Jonathan had noted them. "I don't want to say too much while we're here," she whispered, "but it bothers me that kids come in here after school to buy popsicles and snacks, or comic books, and have to walk by racks of Penthouse magazine to pay for them."

Jonathan would have made a spirited defense of freedom of expression, but he couldn't defend the practice as it appeared in Jake's and strode out the door ahead of her. "Okay. I'll admit Jake is probably the only one in Mirasol who's proud of that store, but it can be upgraded without tearing it down."

"Yes, it can, but when you consider the expense of gutting the place, redecorating, replacing the fixtures, and revising the stock to cater solely to an adult clientele, he would be much better off to begin with a brand new place. The redevelopment plan isn't just about the outside of the shops, Jonathan. It's about having the appropriate merchandise and presentation to bring in tourists' dollars. Jake is selling booze and sleaze and there's no other way to describe it."

Jonathan promptly changed the subject. "Come on, let's keep going or this will take the whole day." They walked in and out of the stationery store without finding anything badly in need of repair, but the sleepy atmosphere and uninteresting merchandise did worry him.

"They're way behind the times in there, aren't they?" he asked.

"I'm afraid so, and it's a shame when there's so much colorful stationery, clever greeting cards, and delightful gifts on the market. The owners are near retirement age, and stock the same items they have had on the shelves for forty years. They may have done a slow, steady business, but they won't be able to compete much longer without modernizing."

"I doubt they have the necessary energy. They may just choose to close."

Leigh looked up at him. She had not expected him to be so reasonable, but he was observing everything as closely as she had hoped he would and coming to the inevitable conclusions.

"I want it to be their choice, though," she explained. "I don't want anyone to feel as though they're being forced out."

"You can't possibly be that naïve. How do you expect them to feel?" Before Leigh could reply, Jonathan took her arm to escort her through the door of Fins, Feathers, and Fur. He didn't own a pet and had never been inside, but the sight of the piglet stopped him cold. He watched Leigh scratch its back, and then gave it a try himself.

"I don't think I've ever touched a pig," he said. "I didn't realize they had such wiry hair."

"He's cute though, isn't he? Pot-bellied pigs don't get very big, but still, I can't see myself owning one."

Zoe Kunkel came up behind Jonathan. "That's the perfect pet for you," she exclaimed. "You've got a nice big yard, and your customers will get a real kick out of him."

"He's a pig, Zoe," Jonathan argued. "He belongs on a farm."

"Not this pretty baby," Zoe cooed, and the piglet rubbed his pink snout against her palm. "I swear I haven't eaten a slice of bacon since we got him, and a pork chop would be impossible to swallow. If you don't want a piglet, how about a kitten? I've got some beautiful kittens now."

Jonathan started backing toward the door. "No thanks. I have too much trouble taking care of myself to want to take on any added responsibility. Ms. Bowman is sure to want a couple of kittens, though."

Zoe's expression brightened. "Come look at the kittens, Leigh."

"He's teasing, Zoe." Leigh loved cats and missed owning one, but she would be moving often, and too many apartments wouldn't accept tenants with pets. "We're looking at the building, rather than shopping today."

Zoe glanced from Leigh to Jonathan. "I'd not noticed what a handsome couple you two make. We could sure use your expertise, Jonathan. I hope Leigh convinces you the redevelopment's worthwhile."

"Not a chance," Jonathan swore, and pushed out the door.

"Still," Leigh added, "he likes the piglet, and that's a point in his favor." She left Zoe laughing, and rejoined Jonathan out on the sidewalk. It hadn't occurred to her that anyone would imagine they were a couple, and Zoe's remark had embarrassed her as badly as she feared it must have embarrassed Jonathan. She would have apologized, but because that would only have made matters worse, she pretended not to care.

"Zoe's shop is the best of the lot. Did you have a chance to see anything?"

"More than enough," Jonathan assured her. He moved ahead as they walked past Frank Pierce's shoe store. "We know Frank will be delighted to sell more shoes, but what about Rhonda?" Her shop was only open in the afternoon, and he peered in the window where mannequins clad in sequins and leopard skin prints were on display.

"You've been here awhile," Leigh commented. "Have you ever seen anyone wearing anything Rhonda sells?"

Jonathan regarded her with a knowing smile. "No, but Ron Tate once hinted that there are several men in town who like to dress up in women's clothes when no one's home. Apparently Rhonda's happy to help them out with special orders."

At first Leigh thought he was teasing her again, but she soon realized he wasn't. "My God. I didn't even consider it, but Rhonda's shop would be a paradise for transvestites, wouldn't it?"

"Are you asking me?"

Jonathan had a marvelous laugh, and Leigh couldn't help but laugh with him. "No. I just can't see you in a bustier and garterbelt—thank God."

"I'll take that as a compliment."

"Yes. Please do."

The Beauty Spot was next door, and as they passed by, Leigh waved to Beverly MacNair. The beautician had been very friendly during their initial conversation, but she turned away now, and much too quickly. Leigh could think of only one reason why the woman's opinion of her would have changed, but she could not imagine how Bonnie could have revealed she had offered to take Miguel off her hands without admitting she had been dating the ranch hand.

"Do you want to come in?" Leigh asked Jonathan.

"No thanks, but I'll wait for you here if you want to."

Leigh promised to take only a minute, but as she came through the door, all conversation ceased in the shop. The manicurist was applying a set of acrylic nails; Beverly was touching up the roots on a dye job. Another stylist was coiling a redhead's hair on tiny perm rollers. All six women turned toward her, but their eyes were narrowed, and none smiled.

"Sorry. I'm booked solid for the day if you wanted an appointment," Beverly called to Leigh.

"No. I just wanted to say hello. Bonnie gave me some of the Sensual Harmony oil, and I've really enjoyed it."

"That's good."

The shop was small, but attractively furnished, and decorated with colorful prints and lush tropical plants in bright ceramic pots. The atmosphere was extremely chilly, however, and Leigh quickly excused herself and left. "The Beauty Spot is one of the best maintained shops, but it's also one of the smallest. Beverly's eager to expand and there's no way for her to do it here."

Jonathan waited while Leigh wrote herself a note on the corner of her notepad, but he was puzzled by her frown. "What's wrong?"

"I'm not sure." His expression was merely curious, and Leigh found it easy to confide in him. "Bonnie MacNair and I share a duplex. I gave her some advice on her love life, and from the reception I just received, it looks as though it might have backfired."

"Never," Jonathan advised, "and I mean never, give anyone advice on matters of the heart. No matter how it turns out, it's the surest way to lose a friend."

"I know you're right." Feeling far from an expert on romance, Leigh pushed on to the hardware store, and let Jonathan wander around on his own while she searched the carefully categorized clutter for lightbulbs. As she paid for them, Carl sent Jonathan a skeptical glance.

"Never thought I'd see you two together," Carl greeted him.

"We're on a fact finding mission," Jonathan informed him coolly, "not a date."

Carl's grin widened to a smirk. "Is there a difference?"

"Yes," both Leigh and Jonathan answered too quickly. She grabbed the bag containing her purchase and hurriedly led the way out. "The hardware store is too crowded by half, and I'm surprised the fire chief hasn't shut them down. I'm not certain how wide the aisles of a retail establishment are supposed to be, but I don't believe they have the minimum."

"Is it the mess that bothers you, or the fact Carl thought you were with me?"

Leigh brushed a stray wisp of hair off her forehead. "Why would that bother me?"

Jonathan shook his head. "Just answer my question."

It was difficult when everything about Jonathan Reid bothered Leigh. She glanced across the street, and saw Denise watching them through one of her windows. She was holding a handknit sweater from the display, and appeared frozen in place. Leigh took a particular delight in waving to her, and Denise turned away.

"I didn't throw you out of my house," Leigh reminded him. "When I went to see you this morning, it didn't even occur to me that people might think we were doing anything other than discussing the redevelopment project. We can't control other people's thoughts, though, and I've learned not to try. Now the yardage shop is next and in the most pressing need of major repairs."

As Leigh started toward the door, Jonathan was amazed by how deftly she had avoided answering his question. He had apologized for the way he had shown her the door after they had had brunch together, but he knew whenever women went on the defensive, they would use whatever ammunition they had.

Patsy O'Dell came out from behind the counter to greet Leigh, then stared in shocked surprise as Jonathan followed her into the shop. "Don't tell me that you two have joined forces," she exclaimed. "Not that I wouldn't welcome it, you understand."

Because Jonathan dealt with designers and upholsterers who supplied their own fabrics, he had never been inside the yardage shop. When he needed a spool of thread or a few extra buttons, he bought them at the market. He noted the bolts of cloth were arranged in rainbows of color, and the long wall where notions were displayed, but what caught his attention was the large sheet of plastic suspended from the ceiling.

Patsy followed his gaze. "I know that looks awful, but it keeps us dry, and with the whole building coming down soon, it would be a waste of money to patch the roof."

"You're eager to move?" Jonathan asked.

"I sure am. Do you have a minute? I want to show you my doll."

"Sure. We have plenty of time, don't *we,* Ms. Bowman?"

Leigh thought his question odd, but also assured Patsy they would stay a while. As soon as Patsy headed toward her office, Leigh turned to Jonathan. "Was it my imagination, or did you just stress the word, *we?* "

Jonathan rocked back on his heels. "Well, *we* are together, aren't we?"

"Only if you're considering the fact that we're occupying adjacent space," Leigh corrected. "Other than that, the word 'together' is a real stretch."

Patsy waved her rag doll as she approached them. "I don't expect you to appreciate this doll as a woman would, but take my word for it, she's awfully cute. I intend to sell a million of them and share the profits with the women who sew them."

Jonathan responded with an amused smile as Patsy described

her plans to make certain no tourist left Mirasol without owning one of her cuddly creations. "I wish you good luck," he said.

As he backed toward the door, Patsy followed him, gesturing with the doll. "With more tourists, you're going to sell a heap of old tables and chairs, Jonathan, but I sure wish you'd side with us now."

Leigh hugged Patsy to turn her around and point her back toward her counter. "Thanks for showing him your doll." She followed Jonathan out to the sidewalk. "I think she's right. You stand to gain as much or more from the redevelopment as anyone."

Jonathan looked down the long colonnade. The arches gave the view an ancient feel, but he had noted how far decay had eroded the charm. "Patsy's forgetting that you're bringing in new shops. Her doll is cute, but what if someone opens a toy store with dolls that are doubly appealing? She's going to feel betrayed, and I for one won't blame her."

Mama Bee's Kitchen was on the corner, but Leigh wasn't in the mood to stop for coffee, and when she started walking on by, Jonathan followed her. "I won't debate the fairness of the free enterprise system, but the city intends to offer a variety of shops rather than several in any one category. Patsy's clever. If her dolls don't sell, I'm sure she'll design something else that will."

As they crossed Montgomery Street, Jonathan caught a whiff of greasy steam coming from the popular cafe. "Has someone already warned you never to order Mama Bee's specials?"

"Yes. Thank you, they have. Now George Culbert's garage is moving out of the business district, but what do you think of the pool hall next door?"

Jonathan waved to a mechanic as they walked by George's where the crowded service bays provided ample evidence business was good. "I haven't been in here in years," he admitted as they neared the entrance of the pool hall. A dusky cloud of stale smoke hung around the open door, and a Jimmy Buffet tune on the jukebox carried out into the street.

Unsavory was the only word Leigh could think of to describe the place and she was relieved to see Jonathan hang back rather than walk right in. The owner, Max Beadle, was the rotund fellow with the suspenders who had given her the eye in the library when she had first come to Mirasol. She was no more eager to cultivate his acquaintance now than she had been then.

"Many cities have family billiard parlors that are well-lit and provide relaxing entertainment, or sports bars with satellite dishes and big screen TVs so fans can watch their favorite teams play, and shoot a few games of pool. This place, however, caters to ranch hands, and they can get rowdy. They need a place to hang out, but it doesn't belong in the heart of town."

"What does Max have to say about that?"

"Frankly, he's probably my least favorite person in Mirasol, and my conversations with him have been brief. He wants to move, however, because he knows his regulars won't mix with tourists, and he doesn't want to find himself sitting alone in an empty bar."

Jonathan leaned back against the side of the building and shoved his hands into his pockets. "That makes sense, but I hate to give up the honor when I would have sworn that I'm your least favorite person in Mirasol."

Leigh wondered if he felt even a tinge of the thrill his presence brought her, then decided he must have experienced a tingle or two that first Sunday or he would not have invited her home. The urge to reach out and run her fingertips along his arm was difficult to resist, but she fought it by looking down at her clipboard where the few notes she had made added up to very little. "Believe me," she finally admitted, "there's no comparison between my reaction to you and Max Beadle."

Jonathan studied the blush filling her cheeks and whispered an enticing offer. "Let's get out of here."

Leigh's head came up with a start. "What did you say?"

"You heard me. I'll concede the fact the shops we've visited leave something to be desired, but I won't give in on how to go about achieving the improvement. I'll bet you haven't been out to the prep school yet, and it's worth seeing. No one has mentioned re-opening it, but with so many parents decrying the violence in the public schools, this might be precisely the time to do it."

His tone was persuasive, but the seductive light in his eyes made it plain he was far more interested in luring her away from Mirasol than touring the school he had attended. She could scarcely catch her breath, and if her clipboard hadn't been so heavy, she would have used it as a fan. She had seen the weathered sign for the prep school on the way into town, but it was located down a long private road and wasn't visible from the highway.

"Well, I suppose I should see it," she replied, "but isn't it too late today? It must be nearly noon, and I wouldn't want you to miss a customer."

"I'll risk it." Jonathan straightened up. "Come on back to my place and we'll drive out there in my van."

Leigh tried to think of a compelling excuse not to go, but her usually inventive mind failed to provide one. She licked her lips nervously. "You were so good about coming with me this morning, that I don't see how I can refuse."

"Just say no," Jonathan teased.

The word filled her mouth, but Leigh couldn't force the air from her lungs to speak. When he offered his hand, she took it.

Nine

The Mirasol Preparatory School had been built to conform with Elijah Keene's desire to maintain a uniform Spanish architecture throughout the city. The classroom buildings were one-story whitewashed adobe structures with the same gracefully arched colonnades and red tile roofs that were built downtown. The offices, cafeteria, auditorium, and dormitories were two-story mission style buildings with wooden balconies and shutters that had once been painted bright green. Extensive grounds had allowed ample room for athletic fields, but now served only to isolate the school from town.

As they drove up the road Leigh had noticed from the highway, Jonathan explained that a failure to attract sufficient numbers of students had forced the school to close in the late seventies, but the police still patrolled the grounds, and the landscaping was trimmed back twice a year to prevent the whole complex from becoming overgrown. An iron gate barred the entrance, but Jonathan produced a key to unlock it, and swung it open easily. When he climbed back in the van, he smiled at Leigh.

"My father was headmaster here when I was a student, and when he locked up the place for the last time, he gave me one of the keys as a souvenir."

"And you've kept it all these years?"

"Well, it hasn't been that long," Jonathan exclaimed, "but yeah. I've kept the key. I've always had an affinity for old junk, and the key to an abandoned school certainly qualifies."

The sun lent the faded buildings a rustic charm, and Leigh had no difficulty imagining the campus filled with noise and laughter as it must have been when Jonathan and Eli were students. As soon as Jonathan parked in the circular drive in front of the administration building she climbed out of the van without waiting for him to help her, and moved off the gravel drive onto the path. "Where are your parents now?" she asked.

"My father's headmaster of a prep school in Sedona, Arizona, and my mother teaches English there. It looks remarkably like this place, but it's coed, which has to be a lot more fun."

"At least for the students," Leigh added.

"Right. Mirasol Prep wasn't the only private school to fold in the seventies, but my folks hated to leave. Come on—I'll show you where we used to live. There were houses for all the faculty, but ours was the largest, as my parents were expected to entertain fairly often."

Jonathan had relaxed as soon as they had left Mirasol, but Leigh was all too aware of him to feel completely at ease. She took note of the buildings he pointed out, and remarked upon how well the facility had been maintained, but the silence was eerie and reminiscent of the movie sets on Universal's back lot.

"Does all this belong to Eli?" she asked.

"Yes, but his grandfather stipulated the site was to be reserved for a school, so he can't raze the buildings and put in an apartment complex. If Mirasol grows large enough to need a second public high school, this campus can be reopened."

"But you'd like to see another private school here?" Like her front yard, the grounds had been landscaped with native desert plants which required little care. Gnarled old olive trees interspersed with graceful pepper trees provided attractive accents while purple sage and bright orange California poppies grew wild along the walks.

"I think there's a real need for it. Too many kids come home to empty houses every afternoon, and when they reach their teens, it's too damn easy to get into serious trouble with drugs

and gangs. A boarding school offers a structured, safe environ-
ment. This was our house, right here."

The adobe house was built around an attractive courtyard,
but the fountain which had once bubbled into a small tile-lined
pool was empty. Leigh moved up to an arched window that
would have provided his family with a splendid view of the
school. She peered through the dusty glass, and saw a high,
beamed ceiling, and a huge fireplace framed with Spanish tile.
"What a pretty place this must have been."

Jonathan stepped up behind her. "Yes. It was. We moved
several times while I was growing up, but I still regard Mirasol
as home. That's why I came back."

His breath caressed her nape, and Leigh didn't dare turn
around with him standing so close. It wasn't him she didn't
trust either, but her own shocking need for his touch. "Eli said
you were an only child," she murmured in a vain attempt to
distract herself.

"Yes, but because I was brought up in a succession of private
schools, it was never lonely." Jonathan rested his hands lightly
on Leigh's shoulders. "What do you think? Would reopening
Mirasol Prep fit in with the redevelopment plan?"

His hands were warm, and when he began to knead the tension from her shoulders, Leigh tipped her head back slightly.
"I don't know," she confessed. "I can't think while you're doing
that."

He leaned down to whisper in her ear. "Shall I stop?"

His voice was low, smoothly enticing a predictable response,
and Leigh didn't want him to ever move away. "No. It feels
wonderful." She closed her eyes, and breathed in the crisp, clean
air. "I love being out of the smog."

Jonathan hadn't been trying to elicit a comment on the air
quality, and laughed as he took a firm grip on Leigh's upper
arms to turn her around. "Is that all you love here?"

Leigh had no time to answer before his mouth covered hers.
He exerted only light pressure at first, but she was so eager for
more she flicked her tongue across his lips to invite the passion

she craved and he didn't disappoint her. He slid his arms around her waist, and lifted her clear off her feet so he could kiss her more easily.

Leigh wrapped her arms around his neck, then grabbed a handful of his silver-tipped hair. She had known exactly how delicious his taste would be and how much she would want even more. He curled his tongue over hers, sweeping her mouth with a tenderness that felt so right she could scarcely remember to breathe each time he gave her a few seconds to gasp for air. Surrounded by his strength, she felt safe, and the energy that flowed between them had an indescribable sweetness.

With no barrier to separate their hearts, his response became hers, and when he moaned way back in his throat, Leigh held onto him even more tightly. His arms dug into her back as his hold became more possessive, nearly crushing her ribs, but the pain mattered little compared to the joy of his kiss. A jay screeched nearby, but all Leigh heard was the pounding of her own heart beating in time with Jonathan's. She refused to think of anything but him, but all too soon he broke away with a shuddering sigh. He cradled her head on his shoulder momentarily, then eased her back down on her feet.

Leigh understood how inappropriate the time and place were, but she was too happy to care and smoothed the wrinkles from her suit with trembling hands. When she looked up at Jonathan, however, his angry scowl instantly dissolved her smile. "What's wrong?" she asked breathlessly.

Jonathan closed his eyes as though the sight of her actually caused him pain, then looked away. "God help me, I knew just how good it would be with you, but I shouldn't have done that."

Leigh couldn't believe he was sorry when every glorious second had been precious to her. "Why not?" She quickly caught herself before she launched into Eli's speech about two consenting adults enjoying each other. Then she remembered Denise, and her heart fell. Jonathan looked consumed with guilt, and she couldn't abide that.

"It was just a couple of kisses, Jonathan. You needn't worry

I'll tell Denise you've been unfaithful to her." She turned away, but he reached out to catch her arm.

"Leave Denise out of this. It's just between you and me. That was a hell of a lot more than a couple of kisses, and you know it."

Leigh straightened up to her full five feet two inches. "All right, I'll admit it, but that doesn't mean we have to jump back and analyze the passion right out of it."

Jonathan swore under his breath. "I was a hell of a lot closer than you think to hiking up your skirt and slamming into you right where we stood."

Leigh sincerely doubted he ever let himself get that far out of control. She crossed her arms over her chest. "Aren't you forgetting that I would have had a say in it?"

Jonathan gestured expansively. "Look at you. Do you even weigh a hundred pounds?"

"Not quite, but that doesn't mean you would have gotten any farther than I wanted you to go." *And just how far was that?* Leigh chided herself silently. She had definitely wanted him, but a fevered coupling in a dusty courtyard was not what she had had in mind.

Jonathan shook his head. "You were as lost as I was, Leigh. Would you have even wanted to stop me?"

It was now Leigh's turn to glance away. A jay had landed on the edge of the fountain, and cocked his head as though listening to their exchange with rapt attention. "No, but I would have. Is the strength of the physical attraction between us what's bothering you?"

"Hell, yes. I'm too old to think with my cock rather than my head."

Leigh inhaled a deep breath and released it slowly. "What about listening to your heart?" she inquired softly.

"There's not enough left of my heart to speak above a whisper, and I was breathing too hard to hear it." Jonathan took a step toward her, then jammed his hands in his pockets. "I've been down this route before, Leigh, and I'll not travel it again."

"Excuse me? I seem to have missed an important clue here. What route do you think we're on?"

Remembered sorrow furrowed Jonathan's brow. "Let's just say passion can be a dead end. Leave it at that."

"Save the travel metaphors and speak to me in plain English, because I still don't know what you're talking about. I'll agree being on opposite sides in the redevelopment issue won't make things easy, but it would be a whole lot more difficult to pretend we're not attracted to each other."

Jonathan shrugged. "Nevertheless, that's exactly what I intend to do."

Leigh couldn't allow him to make such an important decision so hastily. That he would kiss her as if she were the great love of his life one minute, and then shut her out in the next infuriated her, but she knew losing her temper with him wouldn't improve things and fought to remain calm. "I'll admit that you caught me by surprise just now, but that doesn't mean I didn't enjoy it too much to see it end before it even begins. I don't rush into bed with men. I'd rather get to know you, and I mean really know how you feel about a variety of issues, in addition to Mirasol's future.

"I know you have to get back into town now, and so do I, but couldn't we get together tonight and talk? We could sit on your front porch if you like where we wouldn't even have to hold hands if you don't want to."

"You'll have to comb your hair," Jonathan replied as he raked his hands through his own. "Come on. Let's go back to the van and you can use a mirror there. As for tonight, no thanks. It just wouldn't work."

As he started past her, Leigh caught his arm this time. "Because you see me as being too ambitious?"

Jonathan winced. "Something like that."

"You don't even know me," Leigh reminded him, growing angrier by the second. "Don't try and shove me into your ex-wife's mold, because I just won't fit."

Jonathan pulled away and continued down the path. "Sure

you would. You should see the way your eyes sparkle when you talk about the redevelopment plan. When you can rebuild a whole city, how can a mere man compete?"

Leigh had to run to catch up with him. "Is that what happened? Your wife was so involved in her career that she had no time for you?"

Jonathan's eyes took on the glint of obsidian. "Cheryl was a high-powered attorney when I met her, so I've only myself to blame for not realizing I'd never be number one on her list of priorities. Rehashing it won't do either of us a bit of good. Let's just forget what happened here and leave."

Leigh opened her mouth to tell him what she thought of him, but it was a long walk back to town and rather than risk having to make it, she kept still. As soon as they were back out on the highway, however, she went to work on him again. "Everyone makes tragic mistakes in life, and I'd no more get involved with another man like my ex-husband than I'd attempt to fly, but—"

The van nearly veered off the road before Jonathan got over his surprise. "You've been married and divorced?"

"Yes. While the circumstances were nothing like your experience, I'd rather not share them with you until we know each other better. Oh, I almost forgot. You consider me too dangerous to know. That's the real tragedy, Jonathan. You look at me and see a reflection of your fears, and it's only an illusion. Frankly, Miguel Fuentes is beginning to look better to me every day."

"Who's Miguel Fuentes?"

"Merely one of Mirasol's most eligible bachelors."

"I've never even heard of him."

Leigh waited until he had pulled up in front of city hall to reply. Then she smiled seductively. "You needn't worry. I'll not even hint to him, or anyone else, that we were doing anything more than touring the prep school today." She left the van before she remembered she had meant to comb her hair, but ducked into the women's restroom as soon as she entered city hall.

When she looked in the mirror, she was shocked to find the bright blush in her cheeks was far more incriminating than her tousled hair. "I look as though I've adopted Bonnie's hairstyle," she murmured, but she had to splash her face with cold water and re-touch her make-up before she dared go on to her office.

"There you are!" Eli cried. This time he had waited for her in one of the chairs meant for visitors, but he had leaped out of it the instant Leigh came through the door. "I was hoping to take you to lunch. Have you already eaten?"

Leigh licked her lips, tasted Jonathan's lavish kisses through a fresh coat of lipstick and a new wave of frustration rolled through her. It was unfair of him to blame her for his wife's failings, and it was also terribly unfair of her to take advantage of Eli's interest in her. She adopted her most professional tone. "Why no, I haven't. Is there something we need to discuss?"

"Of course. Would I be here if there weren't?" His grin made it plain he would. "Several developers have expressed an interest in the redevelopment plan, but I've advised the city council to hold out for Lloyd Channing's firm, and it looks as though he's as intrigued by what Mirasol has to offer as I'd hoped he'd be. I assume you've heard of him."

"Of course. I've not worked with him, but know his reputation. His projects are exquisite right down to the smallest detail."

"Exactly. Come on. Let's go on over to the Marmalade Cafe and eat while we talk."

Leigh would have preferred to go home and take a quick shower, or better yet, a long soak in a bath scented with Sensual Harmony oil. She couldn't very well explain why she had such a need, so she had to accept Eli's invitation. The morning had provided far more turmoil than she could sanely handle but it was difficult to concentrate on Eli's conversation with Jonathan's stinging rejection still ringing in her ears.

Jonathan did not spend an easy afternoon either. With no appetite for lunch, he went out to his back porch to strip the paint from a ladderbacked chair he planned to refinish. When Ron Tate stopped by, he barely looked up to say hello.

"I was just over at Mama Bee's," Ron remarked casually. "Saw Eli taking Leigh Bowman to lunch at the Marmalade. He looked real pleased with himself, but I can't say that I blame him."

Astonished by Leigh's powers of recovery, Jonathan straightened up slowly. "I don't know why you think I'm interested in Eli's lunch dates, but now that you've mentioned it, how did Leigh look?"

"As cute as always. She's smart, too. I'll bet if she wants Eli, she'll be the second Mrs. Keene before Christmas."

"Not if Miguel Fuentes has anything to say about it."

"Whoa. When did she start seeing him?"

Jonathan pretended great interest in the ladderback chair. "How should I know? Maybe she doesn't bother with sleep. Do you know him?"

Ron leaned back against the work bench, and crossed his arms over his chest. "Sure. He works for Eli. His mother's a real pretty little widow. If she didn't have a passel of kids, I'd be calling on her myself."

"And if you were twenty years younger you'd be after Leigh."

"That's right."

Jonathan gestured with his paintbrush. "You offer a lot of excuses but I'll bet you're seeing every woman in town who'll invite you in."

Ron laughed, but he didn't deny it. "How did you find out Miguel's got the hots for Leigh?"

"Don't quote me on that."

"I got better things to do than spread gossip about field hands. Of course, if Leigh's involved with one of them, that would really be news and I just might make an exception."

Jonathan hadn't meant to start what could quickly become a disastrous rumor, and moved toward him. "Don't even think about it."

Alarmed by the seriousness of Jonathan's expression, Ron

edged toward the door. "Hey. You're the one who mentioned Miguel."

Jonathan was well aware jealousy had provoked it, but once he had wrapped his arms around Leigh her response had been so wildly pleasurable he had felt more alive than he had in years. He was going to have to refinish an entire houseful of furniture to fill the hole walking out on her had torn in his gut, but it had been the only choice he had had when she reminded him so strongly of everything he had despised about Cheryl. "Yeah, I did, and I'm sorry. Now did you come by to work, or use my side porch for a *siesta?*"

"A little of both," Ron admitted, and he moseyed on out. He was certain Jonathan was the one with the hots for Leigh Bowman, and if he thought he hid it well, he was sadly mistaken.

Leigh was exhausted when she got home, but rather than finally sink down into a steaming bath, she knocked on Bonnie's door. The librarian looked startled to find her on the doorstep, and unlike her earlier displays of friendliness, she didn't invite her in. Leigh pretended not to notice she had been slighted.

"I went into the Beauty Spot today, and got the most peculiar reception from your mother. Did you tell her I was interested in Miguel?"

Bonnie really looked horrified now. "No, of course not. I'd never mention Miguel's name around her."

"Good. Now suppose you tell me just what you did say about me?"

Bonnie gave a nervous shrug and chewed on a hangnail. Her nails were polished a garish red which made her gestures seem all the more frantic. "I don't remember saying anything."

Leigh had found silence was often more intimidating than probing questions and just looked at Bonnie until she began to shift her position uncomfortably. "You recall every word, Bonnie, and I need to know what it was. If you've decided you want Miguel, then fine. After all, you had him first, but I wish you'd spoken with me rather than spice the conversation at the Beauty Spot with insulting innuendos about me."

"It wasn't like that at all!"

"Then you do remember," Leigh complimented warmly. "I'd hoped we could be friends, and I certainly don't want Miguel to stand in the way."

Bonnie had changed her clothes as soon as she had come home, and now began fiddling with the buttons on her blouse. "I need more time," she mumbled. "There's such a huge gap between what I want and what I have that sometimes I think I'm just stupid for needing so much."

Leigh knew that disheartening feeling all too well. "It's not wrong to have dreams."

"I know, but if they'll never come true, what's the point?" Her mood softening, Bonnie moved aside. "You want to come in awhile?"

"Not tonight, thank you. It's been a real difficult day."

"My mother didn't say anything rude to you, did she?"

"No, but she didn't look happy to see me either, and that was a disappointment. What did you say about me that upset her so?"

Bonnie swallowed hard. "I just said you weren't nearly as nice as I'd thought you were, but I'll call her right now and tell her I was wrong."

"Would you please?"

When Bonnie promised she would, Leigh bid her good night, but Beverly MacNair's opinion of her was such a slight problem she quickly forgot it. It was a lovely night, and she would have much preferred to spend the evening sitting in one of the white wicker chairs out on Jonathan's front porch. There were no messages on her answering machine, and she did not even harbor a faint hope that he would call, but the silent apartment was a constant reminder of just how alone she truly was.

Eli wanted more than she was willing to give, and Jonathan didn't want anything at all. She remained in a scented bath until her fingertips began to wrinkle, but when she got out and wrapped herself in a towel, she was no more happy than when she stepped in. There was Lloyd Channing to think about,

though, and rebuilding the town. For tonight that wasn't nearly
enough, but tomorrow, she would again be her most professional self, and pretend nothing would give her greater happiness than to bring progress to Mirasol.

Jonathan usually read in the evenings, but that night he
couldn't concentrate on any of the books he opened. Restless,
he stepped out on his front porch, but the sight of the empty
chairs drove him right back inside. Leigh's suggestion that they
get to know each other had been reasonable, and for any other
couple, wise, but he already knew too much about her.

From her carefully coiffed hair to her beautifully tailored
suits, Leigh was a picture of professional perfection. Not merely
bright and inquisitive, she took command of the crowd at council meetings with an attorney's skill at manipulation. He was
surprised she hadn't pursued a career in law. While she had lost
her temper with him a time or two, she was more often in complete control of herself and the situation.

She would surely expect to exert that same steely control in
a relationship, which meant she could have been Cheryl's twin.
So why did the way she felt in his arms touch him so deeply?
Why did her kiss taste so sweet? Why did he long to possess
the very woman who could destroy him?

The telephone rang, and certain it was Denise calling to ask
about his day, he let it ring. He had gotten over her a long time
ago, and she posed no threat to his emotions, but she also offered no solace to his aching soul. He wanted to believe a
woman existed somewhere who would make love possible
again, but Leigh Bowman was only a taunting reminder of what
he had lost.

"Miguel Fuentes can have her," he murmured to himself, but
as the words left his mouth, he heard the lie. Now he wished
he had not stopped that morning because once he had had Leigh,
maybe the hunger she aroused would be eased and he could
again live in peace. The danger was that such an unruly passion

could never be sated, but only fed with more and more of her until there was nothing left of either of them worth saving.

He went upstairs to his room, carefully avoided looking at the bed he never shared, and put on his jogging clothes. It was too late to drive down to the beach, but not too late to run until he was too tired to think of anything but sleep, and too exhausted to dream of a love that could never be.

Ten

Leigh arrived at city hall an hour early to make certain everything was ready for the council's first meeting with Lloyd Channing, but Opal Lingard already had the coffee brewing and fresh donuts arranged in a pyramid on one of her best china plates. The developer had asked for a television set equipped with a VCR, and Frank Pierce had provided his own. Pleased with what she found, Leigh greeted the council members warmly as they entered, but she was as nervous as the rest of them by the time Eli arrived with Lloyd Channing.

Eli was dressed in a dark gray suit, and Channing in navy blue with a red and blue regimental stripe tie. Tall and slim with close cropped silver hair and a deep tan, he not only resembled a political candidate, he shook hands with the enthusiasm of a man running for office. Leigh had admired his work, and expected to like him, but after observing how effusively he dispensed compliments—many were about the council's wisdom in consulting him—she began to suspect his engaging manner was as carefully rehearsed as his formal presentation.

She blamed the harshness of her impression on a lingering resentment over the way Jonathan Reid had treated her, and attempted to focus her attention on Channing's remarks. The problem was he skirted the very details she wanted to hear. This was a preliminary meeting, of course, but still, she believed the council expected a more substantive discussion.

"I've seldom seen a project with so many advantages," Lloyd exclaimed. "The location is superb, and with ready access from both highway 33 and 150, we'll do a tremendous business. Eli and I drove through your fine town this morning. While it's been years since I've been through Mirasol, I was elated to see it's kept its original charm."

Which was precisely the problem, Leigh thought to herself. She smoothed the skirt of her black suit over her knee, and surveyed the engrossed expressions worn by the others at the table. George Culbert was actually smiling, and Randall Hubb's thin lips were crimped by a smile. Zoe Kunkel looked ready to burst with pride, and Bruce Sitz, a CPA ever mindful of figures, had his calculator in his hand. Frank was nodding apprecia- tively, and Opal's pencil was flying across her pad as she strug- gled to catch Lloyd's every word.

"I've brought a video tape featuring several of my most re- cent ventures, which I trust you'll find interesting." He handed the tape to Eli, who walked to the end of the table to insert it in the VCR. He turned on the television, and adjusted the sound as the music swelled. Titled, "Channing Enterprises Builds the Future," the video was an expensively produced commercial narrated by the developer himself. It began with aerial views of a spectacular ski resort in Telluride, Colorado, then pro- gressed to an equally luxurious hotel and resort complex in Sante Fe, New Mexico.

Channing Enterprises was known for its innovative architec- tural designs and quality construction, but as the next segment of the video began detailing the features of an ocean front inn near San Diego, Leigh became increasingly uneasy. Channing's firm had handled urban renewal projects with the same sense of style shown in the resorts presented in the video, but none were included. Revitalizing the city of Mirasol would be an extremely modest endeavor for Channing Enterprises, but Leigh still wanted the assurance it would be done well.

Fortunately, Randall Hubbs also noted the lack of urban projects and asked about it at the conclusion of the video. Lloyd Channing flashed a wide smile before responding. "I'm glad you mentioned that, Dr. Hubbs. Frankly, we haven't done many municipal projects in the last few years. The recession has forced many cities to slash their budgets and postpone much-needed redevelopment plans. Rather than showcase ventures that are several years old, I chose to present new ones, but should you wish to see urban sites, I'll send that information immediately."

"Please do," Hubbs replied. "Has your firm handled any urban renewal in a city our size?"

Again, Channing responded with a ready grin. "Dr. Hubbs, please. You must be aware that there aren't many cities the size of Mirasol with a city council as progressive as yours. It's a tragedy too, because too much of rural America is being lost."

Leigh watched the council members nod as Lloyd praised the virtues of hard work and thrift which had made the country great. It was another campaign speech rather than the specifics Randall Hubbs had sought, but the dentist appeared to be satisfied for the moment. Leigh wasn't.

She caught Eli's eye, and he glanced toward the ceiling, clearly as unimpressed as she by the slickness of the developer's spiel. She had expected Channing to be as solid as his work, but talented architects designed the innovative structures, and men employed by his construction firm brought them into reality. Lloyd Channing simply headed the operation, and his expertise obviously lay in public relations where he was a master at winning the confidence of the people involved.

Clearly he had won the city council's approval, but as the meeting adjourned, Eli whispered to Leigh. "I've invited Channing to dinner at my place tonight and I want you to join us. I hope he'll cut the bogus charm and get down to business. Shall I send a car for you about seven?"

Leigh had no idea whether or not Miguel Fuentes ever served as a chauffeur for Eli, but she knew without having to ask that Miguel would be precisely the one he would send. "No. That's not necessary, but shouldn't the dinner include everyone?"

"No. I'll wait until the contracts are signed to hold the banquet."

Leigh supposed that was wise, but felt uneasy about attending a meeting without the council's knowledge. "Do you mind if I tell Frank?"

"Why would I? He knows the hotel complex is a separate project and I have every right to discuss it in private with whomever I choose."

That was certainly true and relieved Leigh of her primary concern. "Fine. I'll see you tonight, then."

After Lloyd Channing left with Eli, the council remained to hold an informal session. Zoe wanted to show the videotape at the next council meeting, and the others agreed it would inform as well as entertain.

"Make the video the first item on the agenda, Opal," Frank directed. "It's about time we had something more tangible than the preliminary drawings we have on display."

"I'd still like some city scenes," Randall repeated. "Most of us are never going to stay at any of the luxury hotels Channing's built, including the one here."

"We don't have to stay in the hotel to draw the tourists' business," Zoe pointed out, "and that's what's going to save the town. People are always freer with their money when they're on vacation, which means they're far more likely to go home with one of my purebred pups, or a fancy pair of shoes from your store, Frank. Our neighbors will finally have the money to have their teeth fixed, Randall, and Lord knows we'll all need Bruce's help figuring our taxes so our profits don't all go to the IRS. As for you, George, there are a lot of us who've been putting off making car repairs, and once we've some extra cash, I'll bet your garage is swamped with business."

"Amen to that," George replied. "I'm sold." He rose and shoved his chair back into the table. "Now this job doesn't pay enough for me to stay here all day. I'm going back to work. Anyone else going back into town?"

The last of the donuts disappeared off the plate, and Opal unplugged the coffee maker on her way out. Leigh, however, sat back and watched the video again. The Telluride resort was magnificent, constructed of jutting angles in wood and glass it captured a snowflake's geometric perfection. The Santa Fe complex was built of adobe in the massive Pueblo style. Shown in silhouette against a spectacular sunrise, it sprawled across its desert site with the commanding presence of an ancient kingdon.

Gleaming white against the azure Pacific, the inn in San Diego recalled the classical simplicity of the Greek isles. The artfully produced video presented each resort at the precise moment of the day when the sunlight and shadows were most complimentary. Lloyd Channing had described them succinctly, and yet with unmistakable pride. Each venture reflected a harmonious relationship between design, building material, and site, and yet when viewed together, they lost their uniqueness and projected the artifical perfection of a fantasy world.

Certain she was allowing her misgivings of Lloyd Channing's sincerity to color her perceptions, Leigh turned down the volume to silence his resonant baritone, but that only served to sharpen her complaints. She wanted something better for Mirasol than Channing's anonymous ideals crafted of wood, stone, and glass. Because his was the most prestigious firm to show an interest in the redevelopment, she doubted a smaller firm, one with a more personal approach, would be chosen.

It was to Leigh's advantage to oversee the city's portion of a project built by Channing Enterprises. It would be a stunning accomplishment for her résumé, but as she carried the videotape down to her office for safekeeping, she felt torn by the sure knowledge the dynamic developer's vision of the future might not be the best one for Mirasol. She sat down at her desk, and went through the brief notes she had made during her walk through town with Jonathan. She had wanted him to see just how badly Mirasol needed more than spackle and paint, but she had not been immune to his fierce desire to preserve the town where he had grown up. Convinced there was a way to do both, she searched the files she kept on urban renewal for an inspiration.

* * *

Hidden from the highway by a high stone wall and long curving drive, Eli's house was not the Spanish style home Leigh had anticipated finding, nor a quaint Victorian mansion, but instead a beautifully detailed California bungalow. Although solidly constructed of wood and stone, it had the superb proportions of elegant Japanese architecture. The circular drive and grounds were brightly lit, providing Leigh with a clear view of the impressive two-story residence.

She parked behind a black Jaguar she felt certain must belong to Lloyd Channing, and started toward the house, so intrigued by its design she failed to notice Miguel Fuentes moving toward her with a long, determined stride until they nearly collided. Startled, she gasped slightly, then recognized him and relaxed. He was every bit as handsome as she had remembered him, but unfortunately, he looked as furiously angry as when she had first seen him in the library.

Miguel moved to block Leigh's way on the path. "You know who I am," he began, "so don't pretend that you don't. What have you been telling Bonnie? She's not been herself since you came to Mirasol, and I want to know why."

Leigh glanced toward the house, hoping Eli might have heard her car and stepped out on the wide porch to greet her, but there was no one in sight. "I haven't said a thing that wouldn't work to your advantage. Now I must ask you to excuse me. I don't want to be late for dinner."

Confused by her comment, Miguel stepped closer rather than move aside. "Destroying Mirasol isn't enough for you?" he asked in a hoarse rasp. "You want to tear out my heart as well?"

"No, of course not. I've nothing against you, and I'm not out to destroy Mirasol either. On the contrary, I hope to—"

Miguel swore at her in Spanish. "If you get your way, you'll pave the whole valley for parking for the new hotel and no one will remember what fine ranches we had here."

Miguel's fists were clenched at his sides, but Bonnie had assured Leigh he wasn't violent, and even if he were she doubted he would strike her in front of Eli's house. Still, it was an effort to remain calm. "I understand your concern for the local ranches, and I know this is prime agricultural land, but Eli has every right to do what he wishes with the acreage he owns. If he wants to build one hotel, or a dozen, he can. My primary responsibility is for the city itself—not the resort complex."

Miguel's eyes were as dark as wrought iron. "Get out now," he ordered, "or you're going to regret the day you ever heard of Mirasol."

He sprinted away, and his boots sent up a shower of gravel in his wake. Leigh stared after him, shaken by his threat, but she suspected he was far more worried about losing Bonnie than he was about the hotel. She was afraid she had handled the encounter poorly, but that did not give Miguel the right to threaten her. She remained on the walk, uncertain what to do. She ought to tell Eli what had happened, but certainly not while he was entertaining Lloyd Channing.

She took a moment to compose herself, and then climbed the steps. The front door was oak, with a leaded glass panel depicting a spray of orange blossoms with a graceful, Oriental simplicity. Her hand shook slightly as she pressed the bell, but Eli was there in an instant and his wide smile put her at ease. He was in his shirtsleeves and had loosened his tie, but otherwise was dressed as she had seen him that morning.

"Lloyd has part of his crew here," Eli warned. "I hope you weren't expecting an intimate dinner for three."

Leigh had gone through her entire wardrobe searching for something neither too severe nor too casual for what she had thought would be essentially a business discussion over dinner. She had finally chosen a pearl gray knit with a high neck and long sleeves. Now she felt overdressed and hurriedly pushed up her sleeves.

"No. That's fine. I'm eager to meet them."

"Not too eager, I hope," Eli teased.

"Certainly not." As she came through the door, Leigh turned to admire the entryway where an overhead fixture of exquisite

Tiffany glass provided a warm amber light. The mahogany paneling was as beautifully finished as fine furniture and prompted an immediate question. "Your home is marvelous. Is it a Greene and Greene?" she asked.

"Sure is. My grandfather's originial home was adobe brick, but when the earthquake destroyed so much of San Francisco in 1906, he decided he wanted something more substantial than mud and straw and hired the Greene brothers to design this house. Do you like it?"

Leigh noted the hint of doubt in Eli's expression and quickly assured him that she most certainly did. "Of course. I don't think anyone has ever equaled the Greene brothers in richness of detail, but I promise to pay more attention to your guests than the architecture tonight if you'll invite me back another time for a tour."

Eli looked very pleased by her request. "You'll be welcome here any time. Why don't you just stay the night, and explore after breakfast?"

Leigh could hear male voices coming from the front room, and knew they ought not to neglect his guests, and yet she was tempted to accept Eli's bold invitation just to see his jaw drop in surprise. "Not tonight, Eli," she said instead. "Now who's here?"

Eli clasped his hands over his heart as though she had just broken it, and then led her into the living room. Navajo rugs, their geometric designs woven in colors of rust, cream, and black, spilled across the oak floor. The walls here were also paneled in mahogany polished to a lush patina. The space above was painted a rich cream, and additional Tiffany lamps in amber glass provided the lighting. The massive fireplace was bordered with copper and amber tile which repeated the orange blossom motif. The furniture was the simple oak of the craftsman era, padded with deep cushions covered in rust-colored fabric.

In color and design, it was a thoroughly masculine room, and yet Leigh felt instantly at home there. Lloyd Channing was standing at the long table which served as a bar fixing himself a drink, while three other men were poring over sketches spread out on the coffee table. They all rose as Leigh stepped down into the room.

"Jack Slate," the first greeted her. "I'm the architect for most Channing ventures." He was forty-six, with a trim build and a full head of dark, wavy hair. His sharp features were striking, if not handsome, but his smile was genuinely warm. He was dressed in his shirtsleeves, as were the others.

Eli stepped up to introduce the other two men as Pete Ballard and David Ortega. They managed projects from design to completion and were as enthusiastic as Lloyd. Thirty-eight, Pete was sandy haired and slim. He apologized for the laryngitis which had reduced his voice to a whispered squeak, while the slightly older, and more robust David Ortega had a booming baritone that echoed off the beamed ceiling.

"We've been talking about the hotel all afternoon," Eli explained. He went to the bar, poured Leigh a Perrier, and dropped in a twist of lime before handing it to her. "We toured the site, and have been trying to reach a concensus on exactly what to build."

Lloyd Channing waited for Leigh to take a place on the oversized sofa, then sat down beside her. "What did you think of our video? The resorts were all built with Jack's plans, so whatever impression you received, most of the credit goes to him."

"It was an impressive presentation," Leigh responded truthfully. "You have Frank Lloyd Wright's remarkable talent for marrying a building to its site." Jack shrugged off her compliment as though he heard it often. "I'm curious as to what you've planned for Eli's land," she continued. "The rolling hills would be the perfect backdrop for natural stone, but perhaps you've thought of something more creative."

Leigh reached for one of the sketches scattered in front of her, and found a twelve-story building that looked more like a cubist fortress than a hotel. Faced with red marble, it was both beautiful and forbidding. It was difficult to hide her disappointment, but she tried. "Is this what you've planned?" she asked.

Jack handed her several other views of the same structure but from every angle it was equally stark rather than inviting. "For any hotel to succeed nowdays, it has to function as a conference center. This design allows for groups of well over a thousand while still reserving most of the land for swimming pools, tennis courts, and golf courses. It's the ideal site, actually, because the rolling hills are so completely monotonous that anything will look good there."

Leigh glanced toward Eli, who was leaning against the back of Pete's chair. If he had formed an opinion, it didn't show in his expression, but she thought it likely he had just been as insulted as she. "I'd describe the setting as one of tranquil beauty rather than monotony. Wouldn't you, Eli?"

David Ortega quickly made a note of her comment. "I like that," he said. "We're not pushing a Las Vegas image here, but a healthful, back-to-nature theme."

"There's a rhythm to the hills that rivals the shifting folds of the sea," Eli added. "I don't see anything monotonous about it, either."

Jack quickly acknowledged their complaints. "So it was a poor choice of words. At any rate, the land where we intend to build is flat, which is a hell of a lot easier to design for than a mountain top. We've enough experience to know just what succeeds and what doesn't and a conference center with such splendid on-site recreation is unbeatable."

"Indeed it is," Lloyd echoed, "which is why it interests me."

Leigh saw the perfect opening and seized it. "What about Mirasol itself?"

For once, Lloyd suppressed the width of his smile. "Let's wait until we've broken ground for the resort complex before we worry about it. After all, the hotel is the heart of the deal."

Leigh noted a dismissive glance pass between Lloyd and Jack Slate and readily understood how little either man cared about the town. "I understand," she offered with a mirror image of the developer's deceptive smile. "It's only natural that your main interest would be in the resort."

"Precisely."

Leigh settled into the sofa cushions, and Jack continued offering his opinions on how to create the optimum design for the hotel. Because Eli owned the land, he would be a full partner with Lloyd Channing or any other developer chosen for the project, but like Leigh, he listened with a reserved skepticism rather than the ready approval the less sophisticated city council had shown.

When dinner was announced, they moved into the dining room, which was another masterpiece of beautifully crafted wood, furnished with the original long mahogany dining table and chairs the first Elijah Keene had used to entertain. The fine porcelain was decorated with an orange blossom pattern, as was the sterling silver and the Baccarat crystal. As Leigh spread her napkin in her lap, she saw the same design woven into the linen. A unified theme was a hallmark of Greene and Greene, and that Eli had preserved it impressed her deeply.

"What do you think of this house, Mr. Slate?" Leigh inquired. Eli had seated her at the end of the table as though she were the hostess rather than another guest. Lloyd Channing was at her right, while the nearly always silent Pete Ballard sat at her left.

"It's magnificent," the architect replied, "but construction of this quality is prohibitively expensive now."

"It was expensive when it was built," Eli reminded them, "and I'm sure it still pays to use the very best materials and most experienced men in any project."

"Don't worry," David Ortega cajoled. "The hotel won't go over budget. None of our projects ever do. Channing Enterprises is not only good, but fast."

"You misunderstood me," Eli replied smoothly. "Quality costs money and always has. Your firm is noted for the excellence of its work, and I expect to see it here."

"That goes without saying in a Channing venture," Lloyd assured him, and he bathed them all in a radiant smile before engaging Eli in a discussion of the fine California wines he intended to feature at the hotel.

Eli's cook had prepared a crisp green salad laced with thinly sliced apples and walnuts in a light Italian dressing. Leigh really enjoyed it, but when it was followed by roast pork, she remembered Zoe Kunkel's newly acquired aversion to pork, and also thinking of the adorable potbellied piglet, could not even taste it. The sweet potatoes and green beans were good, and with a little sly rearranging, no one noticed she hadn't touched her meat. Dessert was a cheesecake flavored with rum, providing a perfect end to the delicious meal.

As they returned to the living room for coffee, Lloyd again dominated the conversation with an involved tale concerning a recalcitrant zoning commission which had required months of intensive lobbying to convince them to grant him the variance he required. "By the time they finally agreed," he revealed, "I'd lost all interest in the project and chose another which posed no such petty problems. It's a joy to come here, Ms. Bowman, and find everyone so wonderfully cooperative. It is the absolute best of opportunities."

Leigh had grown accustomed to the way Lloyd Channing peppered his conversation with superlatives. He was a veritable whirlwind of excitement, but also possessed the wisdom to hire able men like the three present that night to complete the work he secured for his firm. She couldn't fault his ambition, nor his many accomplishments, but recalling the icy perfection of his resorts, she wasn't sorry she had never spent the night in one.

"Thank you. The city council has sold the community on the redevelopment with vague sketches. I'm sure they would prefer to display scale models. Can you prepare them for us?

"That's no problem," Jack assured her. "As soon as the final plans are chosen, and contracts signed, I'll have my staff begin working on them."

"Good. Please construct the models for the commerical corridor first. It's imperative the town doesn't feel slighted. I realize it's a small endeavor compared to the hotel, but it's vital as well."

Lloyd flashed his familiar grin. "You needn't worry. We'll see Mirasol doesn't languish another day."

Leigh had had ample opportunity to observe how Channing's smile never brightened the cool depths of his hazel eyes. He might rely on abundant charm to manipulate people, but she saw his need to control for what it truly was. Confident Eli did also, she was relieved when his three guests left, and she could ask the questions which had bothered her all evening.

She kicked off her shoes, and curled up comfortably on the sofa. "Have you ever stayed at one of Channing's resorts?"

"Yes. I drove down to San Diego last fall to look at the inn he showcased in the video. It's every bit as fine as he claims, and rooms are available at a wide range of prices so it's not as exclusive as it might seem."

"But there are very few rooms at the low end of the scale?"

Eli joined her on the sofa, but took care not to crowd her. "That's true. What do you think of Channing?"

"I think there's probably a lizard beneath his heavily layered charm, but he has the successful projects to prove he delivers on his promises. What worries me is that he and Jack actually believe that red marble monstrosity is perfect for the valley. It isn't."

Impressed by her observations, Eli leaned back and propped his feet on the coffee table. "I think what we're going to have here is a royal battle of wills. I won't sign a contract that doesn't guarantee me approval of the plans, and I didn't like the marble palace either."

"I think that's very wise. You have a tradition to uphold, and I'll back you on it. As for the town, I'm not concerned Channing will do too much, but too little. It's plain he hasn't much interest in Mirasol but the redevelopment and the hotel have been presented to the city as a package, and I'd hate to have to separate them now."

"Jonathan would love it though, wouldn't he? He'd see it as

a crack in the plan and do his damnedest to blast it into an unbridgeable chasm. We can't allow that to happen."

"I know," Leigh agreed, but she refused to dwell on Jonathan. "I have another concern, or perhaps it's along the same lines." She described her conversation with Miguel. "Both you and Bonnie have assured me he isn't violent, but he's a deeply angry young man, and I don't want to dismiss his hostility as unimportant, when it might be a very costly mistake."

"I thought I'd straightened him out. Obviously I didn't. We've always treated our workers as extended family here, and sometimes that's a problem. I liked what you told Bonnie about getting Miguel the job supervising the resort grounds. Maybe I can bring him into the project using that angle." Eli's glance softened. "Now tell me what angle to use on you."

"You're doing fine," Leigh assured him. "It's just me. For the present, Mirasol is going to require my full attention, but once we get the redevelopment underway, perhaps things will be different."

"There's a sadness in your pretty blue eyes that's absolutely heartbreaking. Don't neglect yourself, Leigh. You're far more important than any work you could ever do."

Leigh had taken only a sip of the Ruby Cabernet served with dinner, but she was sleepy, and quickly covered a wide yawn. "Well, sometimes it's difficult to believe I even exist outside my work, but I'll heed your advice and do what I can. It would be so nice to have a life that was a harmonious whole rather than sharply splintered fragments."

"Like this house," Eli pointed out softly. "Are you sure you wouldn't like to stay for tomorrow's tour?"

"Didn't I just explain why I couldn't?"

"Women are known for changing their minds." Eli stood and pulled Leigh to her feet. He waited until she had slipped on her black pumps, then took her hand to walk her out to her car. "I doubt I'll get much sleep tonight. Will you?"

"Probably not." When Eli drew her into a fond embrace, Leigh didn't resist, but unlike the last time they had been together she didn't lift her lips to his. He offered a comforting warmth, but she knew that wasn't enough for either of them and stepped out of his arms. "Thanks for including me tonight."

"Is it too soon to ask you out for New Year's Eve?"

"Yes, a bit," Leigh laughed. "Good night, Eli." She got into her car, and quickly locked the doors before starting the engine. She turned on her lights, and waved to Eli before following the gentle curve of the drive. He waited in front of his house, and she saw him silhouetted against the open door. He looked very lonely. For a painful instant she wished they had been a better match. They weren't, and each would have to find their way alone.

Eleven

Denise rapped lightly at the open door of Eli's den, then entered without waiting to be welcomed. She had dressed in a sky blue silk shirt and gray pants, not because the outfit flattered her, although it did, but because it was how he dressed. It was an effective tip she had gleaned from an article by a woman who had made a study of how easily men could be influenced by a woman's choice of attire.

According to the article, men were drawn to women who mirrored their taste in clothes without ever realizing their appeal lay in what was essentially a clever disguise. Denise had thought the theory absurd until she had tried it and found how beautifully it worked in the initial stages of an affair. Not that she ever had to resort to tricks to attract men, but with Eli, she needed every bit of ammunition she could gather.

Eli was adding a long column of figures, and would not have quit in the middle, but Denise's sweet perfume was unmistakable and wreaked havoc with his concentration. He threw down his pencil and looked up just as she perched a well-toned hip on the edge of his desk.

"I can't even imagine what brings you here," he greeted her coldly. She looked as exquisitely lovely as always, but he had become inured to her perfect beauty long ago. He would have offered any other visitor coffee, but he just wanted Denise gone and didn't even provide a stick of gum.

Denise licked her lips slowly and affected what she believed to be an appealing vulnerability. "I suppose you could call it a business matter," she disclosed in a hushed voice designed to draw rapt attention. "You were generous when we parted, which I appreciated greatly, but now your situation has improved, and I believe you ought to adjust mine accordingly."

Wanting to get her out of his house as swiftly as possible, Eli left his chair and came around to the front of the desk. He took care to stand far enough away so that Denise couldn't flutter her hands over him in a possessive caress. "I've still no idea why you're here. Why don't you go home and send me a registered letter."

Denise laughed, as though she truly believed he had made an attempt at humor. "There are some issues which are better approached in person," she argued, "especially between us, Eli."

Eli glanced at his watch. He had absolutely nowhere he had to be that morning, but because it might be the only way to get rid of Denise, he would definitely announce he had a pressing appointment. Just being this close to her was giving him a headache and he knew it wasn't entirely due to her insipid perfume.

"I'm still lost, and if you don't hurry up, I'm going to be late." To emphasize his point, he took a determined step toward the door.

Denise moved off the desk. They were near equals in height, and she had worn low-heeled shoes to again maximize her allure. "I know you're a straightforward person, and I've always admired it in you. I'll do the same. You stand to make a fortune from the hotel complex, and as your former wife, I was in on the initial planning when you first began to consider it. I believe that entitles me to a share of the profits, and my attorney agrees."

Eli stared at Denise, astonished that he had ever had any feelings for a woman who had no more depth than an egg cup. "This is a new low even for you," he replied. "During our marriage, we discussed all manner of things as I recall, including the love you're totally incapable of giving. As far as I'm concerned, you're not even entitled to so much as the hotel's discount rate for conventions.

"If you actually have an attorney who'll believe your lies, then sue me. Just remember that even if we broke ground to-morrow, the complex wouldn't open for more than a year, and there's no guarantee that it will ever show a profit. Who knows? We might have to sell at a loss to some Japanese consortium, so forget whatever twisted idea you have for extorting money from me and get out."

Denise's already proud posture stiffened. She dug her white-tipped nails into her leather shoulder bag, but spoke sweetly. "There's no reason for you to be rude, Eli."

"The hell there isn't." Eli was sorely tempted to list the reasons she had been a sorry excuse for a wife, but chose to concentrate on the present. "I thought you and Jonathan would have at least announced your engagement by now. What's the matter? Won't your tarnished charms work their old magic on him?"

Eli saw her fierce slap coming and raised his hand to catch her wrist before she could hurt him. "Careful, baby. You let Jonathan catch a glimpse of that foul temper and you'll never be Mrs. Reid; although why you'd want to be is beyond me. Perhaps it's the challenge. I tell you what. If by some miracle you do wring a proposal from his lips, and actually get him to the altar, I'll provide the bridal suite in the new hotel free of charge for your honeymoon."

He chuckled at such an unlikely possibility ever coming to pass, and saw a flicker of fear cross Denise's dark eyes. He couldn't resist adding another taunt. "You already know I'll never have to make good on that offer. Jonathan came home to lick his wounds after a nasty divorce and he's no more interested in you than he would be in Rhonda Boyle wrapped in her slinki-est gold lamé."

Denise yanked her hand free of Eli's grasp. She wanted Jonathan so badly she refused to believe Eli's malicious prediction. He was just jealous because he knew she had always loved Jonathan more than him.

"I hate you," she cursed angrily.

"The feeling is entirely mutual." Eli walked to the door, and waved her on out. "Give Jonathan my love, because it's obvious he doesn't want yours."

Denise replied with a coarse expletive, and raked Eli with a glance crusted with loathing as she strode from the room. The scent of her perfume lingered, and Eli immediately opened the windows behind his desk to clear the air. He stood gazing out at his groves, and knew he had wasted far too many years with Denise to ever give the bitch a dime of the hotel's profits. He quickly made a call to his attorney to make certain there was a record of her ludicrous demand, and then went to find the large bottle of aspirin he needed whenever he was forced to speak to his shew of an ex-wife.

Leigh finished out the week working on her project to improve the image of tourists but she was so frequently interrupted by phone calls she made slow progress. After Lloyd Channing's presentation, the council spread their enthusiasm throughout the town, at the same time unwittingly galvanizing the resistance, and the citizens who called city hall were more often angry than not. Leigh simply listened to their fears rather than argue, and extended invitations to attend the next council meeting, but it made for long and harried days.

Thursday evening she found an egg splattered on her windshield. The sun had baked it on the glass, and it took a long time to scrub off, but she considered herself lucky the damage wasn't permanent. Saturday she drove down to Los Angeles to attend a baby shower for a friend and deliberately returned home too late to accept the dinner invitation Eli had left on her answering machine. She called to apologize, only to get his machine in return.

Sunday morning she was too restless to stay home, and believing Jonathan would surely avoid her, she again took the *Los Angeles Times,* and drove out to the coast. A flock of pelicans were floating on the waves near the tidepools, and having never seen a gathering of the large birds, Leigh left her things on the sand, and again discarding her tennis shoes, waded out into the sea. The water was icy cold, and she couldn't really get near the pelicans, but as they took flight and began to dive for fish in a frantic swarm, she was fascinated.

They were strange birds, in flight as ungainly as pterodactyls, and yet they dove for fish with unerring precision. Despite their comical appearance, they were superbly designed. When they swam, their necks took on the same graceful curve as a swan's, but with their long bill and handy pouch, they would never be mistaken for the far more attractive bird.

The water's chill finally drove Leigh back to the shore. There were plenty of smooth stones scattered about and taking careful aim, she skipped one over the incoming wave. Delighted to think she had finally gotten the knack of it, she scooped up another, but when thrown, it just dropped from sight. Discouraged, she would have gone back to read her paper, but Jonathan came up behind her, and handed her another rock worn smooth by the waves.

"Your first shot was good. Don't give up."

Leigh wasn't certain whether she was relieved he was speaking to her or not. "I could give you the same advice." When she looked up at him, she was surprised by the dark shadows beneath his eyes. He looked thinner too, although only four days had passed since she had last seen him. Her first thought was that he had been ill, quickly followed by the far more discouraging suspicion that their last conversation had *made* him ill.

Her fingers closed over the stone. "Are you all right?"

Jonathan wasn't even tempted to lie. "No. The whole town's buzzing about Lloyd Channing, but I've no faith in rumors. Does it really look as though he and Eli will be able to work together?"

Leigh ground the stone into her palm. Jonathan had done it again, and she had walked right into it. "I don't discuss business on weekends," she reminded him. "Why don't you just come to the council meeting tomorrow night and ask your questions then?"

Leigh wasn't wearing any make-up other than lipstick, and Jonathan was surprised to find her flawless skin was lightly dusted with freckles. Her lashes were long and dark without mascara, and her brows gently arched. The sea breeze had tangled her hair, completing a look of such youthful charm she could have easily passed for a teenager. He felt ancient.

"Sorry." He glanced down the beach. The sun was already warm, and the sand would soon be crowded with people like him who grabbed every chance to come to the shore. "I've been thinking about what you said on Tuesday."

Leigh assumed he was about to make a comment on Mirasol. "I mean it. No business on Sunday."

Jonathan plucked a rock from the sand, and hurled it way out across the cresting waves where it took three high hops. "I'm not talking about business," he corrected. "I was referring to what you said about my trying to shove you into my ex-wife's mold."

From the awful way he looked, Leigh thought he must have really taken her advice to heart. Apparently she had shocked him into seeing the truth, and he hadn't liked it. "It happens all the time, Jonathan. People get hurt, and throw up barriers to protect themselves from ever having to go through the same pain. It's all too easy to divide people into categories, and dismiss them without ever giving them a chance to prove they're not a threat."

Jonathan had refused to repeat his mistake so assiduously he couldn't very well argue with her. In fact, he was now a master at the sorry skill she had just described. "It's going to get too warm here," he predicted. "Will you come back to the prep school with me? It's quiet, and we can talk without fear of being interrupted. If you're still willing to talk with me, that is."

The teasing light was gone from his eyes, and Leigh doubted he felt up to holding her hand, let alone kissing her again. She hadn't expected her remarks to affect him so profoundly and because they obviously had, she couldn't very well refuse to take the next step.

"Yes. I'll follow you." She went to pick up her newspaper and towel, then climbed the narrow trail to the bluff. A little gray lizard crossed her path about half the way up, and she hoped there was a culture somewhere who regarded the tiny reptiles as good luck. Badly distracted, she didn't listen to Stevie Ray Vaughn or any of her other tapes as she drove back toward Mirasol.

She had no idea what to do now that she had Jonathan willing to talk with her. Tuesday it had seemed like such a logical suggestion, but now that she had met Lloyd Channing, their personal lives were going to be even more difficult to keep separate from the redevelopment project. She had real misgivings about Channing, and she would have liked to discuss them with Jonathan, but he was the very last person she ought to confide in on that subject.

She had forgotten to wear her hat to the beach, and hurriedly drew a comb through her hair as Jonathan unlocked the gate. She wiped her sweating palms on her shorts, and then gripped the steering wheel tightly as they drove onto the campus. She really liked Jonathan, and thought he must like her, too, or he would have forgotten her advice rather than dwell upon it.

She had a talent for providing sound advice to others, but as she left her Camaro, she wished she had some for herself. She was surprised when Jonathan pulled a blue blanket and wicker hamper from the back of his van. That he would have been sure enough of her answer to bring a picnic was unsettling, but that he had gone to the trouble to make a lunch for them impressed her far more.

"I hope this doesn't look too contrived, but I'm sorry about the way our first lunch ended, and I'd like to make it up to you."

Leigh grabbed the handle to help him carry the basket. "This is awfully heavy. What did you bring, several jugs of wine?"

"No. That's just the plates and thermos of iced tea."

Leigh managed a smile, but she was so nervous she doubted she could eat. Jonathan merely looked sad rather than anxious, but she couldn't think of anything to say to cheer him up when it would only sound as though she wasn't taking his sorrow seriously. She didn't even want to comment on the weather and remained as silent as he as they walked across the central courtyard and out onto the grassy edge of the soccer field. When he stopped under a pepper tree, she stood back, and waited for him to spread out the light blanket before she sat down.

It was still early, and rather than offer something to eat now, Jonathan poured them each a glass of iced tea, and then closed the hamper. He leaned back against the tree and got comfortable. "Perhaps it's the fact I was a college professor with an easy command of the facts, but it's difficult for me to admit when I'm wrong. Clearly I was wrong about you when I mistook you for a tourist. I had certain expectations then, but when you introduced yourself as the new city planner, they shifted abruptly.

"You were absolutely right, too. I saw you as a clone of my ex-wife and couldn't have reacted more negatively. Frankly, I'm surprised that you don't despise me. Which is another expectation that isn't based on my experience with you." He smiled slightly, as though amused by his own mistakes.

Fearful everything would go wrong again, Leigh relied upon an encouraging smile to prompt him to continue. She didn't want to ask specific questions, anyway. She wanted him to reveal what he would of his past in his own way. As for herself, she didn't think she could relate more than a few brief details without dissolving into tears.

"I had the benefit of growing up with parents who not only loved me, but adored each other," Jonathan continued. Naively, I expected the same kind of long and happy marriage. When I met Cheryl, I admired everything about her: her blond good looks, her intelligence, her dedication to the law. She was also intensely competitive, active in politics, and thought she might like to run for public office some day.

"We could talk for hours about world affairs and because so much of what's happening today relates directly to history, I loved it. It never even occurred to me than neither of us ever revealed much about ourselves. As for the sex, it was great. That's why it took me so long to realize there wasn't much love behind it. We complemented each other well for the first few years, but then I began to feel as though I were suffocating at the university.

"I was careful not to take my frustrations out on Cheryl, but all the same, our marriage unraveled faster than a cheap sweater. I thought people were supposed to change, to keep on growing over the life of a marriage, but the more I questioned my choices, the more threatened and hostile Cheryl became. She'd allocated me to a convenient corner of her life, and when I stepped out, she left me. There are certain advantages to being married to a college professor, especially for a woman with political ambitions. It's a solid, respectable career, but when I began talking about refinishing antiques, and opening a shop, I became an eccentric liability.

"I'd thought of us as a team. As it turned out, Cheryl wasn't a team player."

Leigh took a sip of tea in a vain attempt to dispel the tightness in her throat. She had left Doug not because he had outgrown his profession, but because he couldn't grow as a man. Jonathan might say that she had also put her needs above her husband's, and had not been a team player either. Believing it was far too dangerous to confide her own experience in light of his, she relied on generalities.

"Nowadays it's difficult to find anyone who isn't nursing a broken heart. Marriages begin with such high hopes, and it's tragic when they don't succeed. Often the conflict that will eventually destroy a couple is there from the beginning, but not recognized for the terrible threat it is. Then later people don't understand how they could have been so blind, but rather than gaining valuable insight, they become overly cautious. There are times I'm afraid that no matter how hard I try, everything will always go wrong." Leigh choked on her tears then, and fell silent.

The sunlight was filtered through the pepper tree's branches, and shaded Leigh's face with the delicacy of a black lace *mantilla,* but for the first time, Jonathan truly saw her. She was a woman who possessed not merely beauty and strength, but true depth of character as well. His chest still ached for all he had lost, but as he reached out to her, the last of his doubts were dissolved by her tears.

Jonathan pulled Leigh into his arms, and held her in a fierce grasp until she at last overcame her sorrow and relaxed against him. "You feel so good." He rubbed his cheek along hers. His instincts had trusted her from the beginning, and when his rational mind hadn't, the torment had had to sink clear to his soul before he had realized his mistake. He had brought her there to talk, but he had no further need for words. He tilted her head with his fingertips, and kissed her with the same passion he had shown her the last time she had been in his embrace.

Leigh raised her arms to encircle his neck and they were soon sprawled across the blanket. Her past remained a sad secret as she slid her hands under his T-shirt to feel the warmth of his bare skin. She could no longer dismiss the strength of their attraction as mere chemistry, and when Jonathan released her to pull his shirt off over his head, she missed him terribly in the few seconds they were apart. His chest was covered with dark curls, and she splayed her fingers through them before tracing the curve of a nipple with the tip of her tongue. She felt him shudder, and teased the tender bud between her teeth.

Jonathan rolled over to capture Leigh beneath him, and ravaged her mouth with fevered kisses. A deep boom in the distance rattled the windows on campus, but barely registered in his consciousness. He wanted Leigh out of her clothes, but afraid he would rip them in his haste, he ran his hand up her thigh, and tried to content himself with the touch of her silken flesh. When it wasn't nearly enough, he reached down for the laces on her tennis shoes, and started to undress her there.

By the time he had tossed her first shoe away, Leigh knew where Jonathan was going. She wanted him too, but not so desperately she couldn't think. "Wait a minute," she broke free to beg. "Maybe you weren't warning me about safe sex last weekend, but—"

A wicked grin crossed Jonathan's lips, erasing all sign of his earlier fatigue. "Don't worry. I'll protect you. I put more than lunch in the basket." He waited, not knowing if she would be pleased or dismayed by the direction he had hoped the picnic would take. He saw the question in her eyes, and whispered against her lips. "No. I didn't really expect this to happen, but I sure hoped it might."

Leigh could not fault him for that, and wrapped him in her arms. She did not want to ever let him go, and soon his deep kisses made her hungry for more than a fervent embrace. She heard a siren's faint wail in the distance and sat up slightly. She raked her hair out of her eyes, and looked around. "Are we really alone here?" she asked.

"A few birds might be watching," he conceded. "Shall I tell them to look the other way?"

"I don't care about birds," Leigh assured him, and she rose to begin a slow, wildly provocative striptease. After she peeled off her shorts and T-shirt, she tossed them over a low branch of the pepper tree. Then looking Jonathan right in the eye, she unhooked her white lace bra. She was petite, but her proportions were as perfect as any model's. Her legs were long and shapely, her hips gently rounded, her waist narrow, and her breasts delicious swells. Now clad only in whisper-light white bikini panties, she stepped back to flip her bra over a branch, and then rested her hands on her hips.

"Well?" she asked. "You could at least take off your shoes."

Fascinated by her charming indifference to her own near nudity, Jonathan had forgotten he was still dressed, and quickly yanked off his shoes without bothering with the ties. He rolled his socks into tight balls, and stuffed them into his shoes before he stood to face her. He slipped his hands under the elastic waistband of his shorts, but Leigh came forward to stop him.

"I'll do that," she offered in an enticing whisper. "Turn around." When he did, she pressed her breasts into his back, and rested her cheek against his shoulder blade. She then slid her hands down his flat belly, and into the front of his shorts to grasp his cock. She knew exactly what he would like, but after a few hard strokes, stopped to peel off his shorts. She then waited to see what he would do.

Jonathan had been with several women, but he had never had one come up behind him to simulate the way he pleasured himself, and that Leigh could do it so expertly was a delightful surprise. He turned to face her, wishing he had an equally imaginative way to get her out of her panties. "Come here," he ordered in a husky sigh.

Leigh didn't just step close, she raised his jutting cock, brushed the smooth tip across his belly, and thrust her pelvis against him. With a slow turn, Jonathan drew her down into the grass, and now positive nothing he could do would shock her, he pulled off her panties with a single, easy caress. He suckled at her breasts, teasing the pale pink nipples with his teeth and tongue while he slid his hand between her legs. She was already wet, and he put a finger to his lips to taste her.

Salty sweet, the flavorful drops were as delicious as her kiss and he worked his way down her lithe body, creating an adoring trail with his lips and tongue until he found the source of her essence. He felt the sun on his shoulders, but her inner heat was far hotter. He nibbled and lapped, and allowed her to guide him with the pressure of her fingers in his hair. He stroked the bud at the peak of her cleft, and then pulled back to let the glorious sensation subside before he gave her another exotic kiss.

Pacing his teasing attentions to her breathing, he waited until a small cry caught in her throat. Then pausing only long enough to protect her as he had promised, he shifted his position and entered her with a driving thrust. She arched up against him, and the final tremors of her climax pulled him deep. She was petite, but certainly not fragile, and he held none of his strength in reserve.

He knew how to slow his tempo each time his body began to crave release, and delayed his inevitable surrender until caught in Leigh's second orgasm and overwhelmed with desire. He kissed her long and hard, and then cradled in her arms, nuzzled her throat, and relaxed completely. He could not remember the last time he had felt so blissfully at peace, but did not want to crush her and raised up to move aside.

"Stay with me," Leigh urged.

"I'm not too heavy?"

"No. We fit together perfectly." She coaxed his head back down on her shoulder, and ruffled his hair. She assumed he must be thrilled to find her so uninhibited, but she could not take all the credit and felt she owed him an explanation.

"As you said, there are advantages to being married to a professor," she whispered, "but my husband was an actor, and while he never worked in porn films, we used to rehearse our own. We never filmed ourselves though, so you needn't worry that you'll ever see me on some late night cable show."

Jonathan raised up slowly. "I suppose this was an effort to expand his range?"

"Of course, but with an historian, I imagine re-enactments of some of history's most passionate couples might be far more appropriate."

Charmed by the idea, Jonathan responded with a lingering kiss, and then kissed her eyelids, and earlobes. "I think we've already begun with Adam and Eve, and thank you. It was paradise. I'd forgotten what it means to be truly alive."

Leigh framed his face in her hands. His smile was as warm as the day they had met, and she didn't want anything to jeopardize the happiness they had created here together. "We've had to be much too serious, haven't we? Circumstances haven't changed, but I hope that we have."

Jonathan rested his forehead against hers. "I don't even want to think about Mirasol, but I've a meeting scheduled this afternoon at my house and I have to get back." He kissed her again, and then moved aside.

Leigh watched him out of the corner of her eye as they got dressed. She would rather have lain in his arms until nightfall, but she wouldn't complain, nor offer more affection to make him late. She still wished she could really talk with him about why she had had to leave her husband, and about Mirasol as well, but there was no time today. He had brought avocados, tomatoes, and sprouts, and made their sandwiches fresh rather than offer one he had made at home that would surely have gotten soggy.

It had been making *love,* Leigh reflected with a satisfied smile, and while Jonathan talked about the prep school rather than what lay ahead for them as they ate, she did not feel slighted. It was much too soon to talk of where that day might lead them, but as she helped him fold up the blanket, tears filled her eyes. She turned away to hide them, but he quickly guessed why.

"Hey. Don't cry." Jonathan hugged Leigh as they started back to their cars. "We're intelligent people. We'll find a way to get along. At least I hope we will, but that doesn't mean I won't be at the council meeting tomorrow night to object to everything that's said."

"No. I expect that."

Jonathan stowed the blanket and basket in his van, and walked Leigh to her car. "Maybe we'll have to reserve Sundays for each other, and just shut out everything else."

Leigh could see how in some respects his suggestion was a very good one, but as far as she was concerned, one day a week with him wasn't going to be nearly enough. She was certain she was right about Mirasol's future, but it might take several years after the redevelopment was complete before he would be proven wrong. By that time, of course, she would be gone.

She raised her hand to caress his cheek. "I'll see you tomorrow night then."

Jonathan pressed a kiss into her palm, then waited until she had gotten into her car and shut her door. She watched him jog back to his van, but had no reason to follow him now. She pulled around the van and headed back into town. This had easily been the most remarkable morning of her life, but she still felt as though she and Jonathan had an awfully long way to go. She did not want to jinx whatever they might share, but she could not help thinking they had merely postponed their problems rather than taken any real steps toward solving them.

The highway straightened out as she entered Mirasol, but she found the road up ahead blocked by fire engines. She remembered hearing sirens, but in the heat of passion had been too distracted to care where the emergency vehicles were bound.

There was a crowd milling around in the street, and she had to park well back of the fire trucks, but as she left her car, she began to run. Cinders floated on the smoke-filled air, burning her lungs, but she knew she ought to be able to see the second story of Jonathan's house and it just wasn't there. She tore down the street and forced her way through the crowd. Firemen were still pouring water into the smoking ruins, but Jonathan's wonderful Victorian house had already burned to the ground.

Twelve

Leigh knew how much Jonathan's house had meant to him. That it had provided not only his residence, but his livelihood, made the fire even more tragic. She turned to look back down Mirasol Avenue and saw him running toward her. His anguish was etched so deeply on his features she knew nothing she could say would matter in the slightest. His whole world was gone, and sharing his pain, tears poured down her face. She reached out for him, but he brushed right past her in his haste to find the fire chief.

Leigh followed, carefully stepping over the fire hoses snaking across the sidewalk. The fire engines were the new pale chartreuse color. Diligently washed and polished, their chrome reflected the bright sunlight, but the beautiful machines were parked in front of charred ruins.

Leigh was at Jonathan's elbow a few seconds after he had reached the fire chief. She looked around for Ron Tate, thinking he would surely be at the front of the crowd, but the handyman was nowhere in sight. The motors were running on the fire engines, making it difficult to hear the chief, but Leigh leaned close so as not to miss a word.

"Looks like a gas leak, Mr. Reid. The explosion rocked all of Mirasol. You must have heard it."

Jonathan shook his head in disbelief. He had heard it all right, but Leigh had distracted him so thoroughly he had not cared what the noise was. "I was out of town," was all he would say. He followed the arc of the spray from the nearest fireman's hose, and fought the wave of revulsion that swept through him. "There was no leak," he swore.

"Houses don't just explode," the chief argued.

Jonathan was equally assertive. "I remodeled that house myself. It was rewired, and the gas lines were new. If there was a leak, then someone caused it." The motive was sickeningly clear, and while he did not want to accept the possibility that anyone he knew could have wished to hurt him so badly, he could come to no other conclusion. It made him as sick as losing the house did. That he felt like a complete fool compounded his distress.

When Jonathan turned toward Leigh, his mouth twisted into a hostile sneer. "How could you have been a part of this?" he asked, his words charged with loathing.

Frightened, Leigh took a step backward, and bumped into Eli, who caught her and gave her shoulders a comforting squeeze. "No," she gasped. "You can't possibly believe that I had anything to do with the fire."

Jonathan did not want to believe it either, but her job had drawn her too close to Eli to believe she could be innocent of the charge when his old rival surely wasn't. He wanted to rip off Eli's head and drop kick it clear down the block, but as he lunged toward him, the fire chief blocked his way. Dressed to fight the fire in a heavy yellow slicker, black hat, thick gloves, and rubber boots, the chief formed as formidable a defense for Eli as a samurai warrior, and Jonathan could only shout his rage.

"Hell, yes I think you're involved. Were you really that terrified of me, Eli, that you'd torch my house?"

"That's absurd!" Eli countered,

Jonathan scoffed at Eli's denial, then spit out his accusations in a bitter stream. "I know you wouldn't stoop to starting the fire yourself, but you sure as hell paid to have it done. You had me completely fooled, Leigh. I wasn't certain you'd accept my invitation, but you would have done anything to keep me out of town this morning, wouldn't you? Well, you earned whatever

Eli's paying you, and be sure to ask for a bonus for handling your assignment with such erotic abandon."

Leigh was quick to defend herself. "Jonathan, you're not making any sense. You came looking for me!"

"Yeah, I did, and you were right where you knew I'd find you. Jesus. Your husband wasn't the only actor in your family. You gave an academy award winning performance this morning, but you can dry those phony tears. If you wanted to stop my opposition to the redevelopment plan, you two should have blown up my house with me in it."

"We don't have to listen to this," Eli responded, and he draped his arm around Leigh's shoulders to pull her away. "Your anger is understandable, but you're no threat to me, and even if you were, I'd not have burned down your house."

"Jonathan, please!" Leigh cried, but after scorching her with a final searing glance, he turned his back on her. She looked up at Eli. "How can he even imagine that we did this?"

Eli wouldn't defend Jonathan by blaming it on hysteria, or grief, and just shrugged. "Come on. I'll drive you home and then come back later for my car."

Leigh didn't want to leave while Jonathan was spouting such furious nonsense, but when Denise ran up to him, he slipped his arm around her waist to pull her close. Leigh had believed she was the one he would turn to for comfort, but he had shoved her aside with a blistering disgust that left her feeling thoroughly defeated. She finally noticed how closely the crowd had pressed around them, and from the angry looks directed her way, it was plain a good many people believed Jonathan's accusations. She let Eli lead her away, handed him her car keys, and sobbed all the way back to her duplex.

Eli parked Leigh's Camaro in the garage, walked her to the backdoor, and followed her inside. "We need to talk, but you'll have to take a shower first. Jonathan's scent is smeared all over you, and it's making me sick."

Leigh could scarcely deny that she and Jonathan had been intimate when he had shouted about it at the top of his lungs.

It had felt so right, and she would have treasured the memory, but now he had crammed her into another ghastly mold without any consideration for how poorly she fit the role of conspirator. No amount of personal pain would excuse what he had done to her. The tragic fire had turned him into someone she did not even know, nor even want to. "I can't talk about anything now."

Eli was used to getting his way and insisted upon it now. He took her arm and marched her into the bathroom. "Yes, you can. Now clean up. I'll make us some coffee."

He slammed the door on his way out, but Leigh slumped down on the side of the bathtub rather than obey him. Jonathan's awful accusations kept ringing in her ears, but they were far easier to shut out than the memory of how quickly he had pulled Denise into his arms. She had believed the love that flavored his kisses was sincere, but if he could turn on her so viciously, and go back to Denise within hours of their becoming lovers, then she had not really known him at all.

He had misjudged her completely, but she felt equally betrayed. Sick to her stomach, she remained on the edge of the cold porcelain tub until she realized what Eli had said was true. She did smell like Jonathan. An hour ago she had not minded at all, but now it was an all too potent reminder of how foolish she had been to trust him. She stood, peeled off her clothes, and turned on the shower.

By the time Leigh walked out into the living room, Eli was on his second cup of coffee. She was wrapped in a paisley robe, barefoot, with her hair towel-dried and slicked back from her face. She looked so thoroughly miserable that he almost felt sorry for her. He was seated at one end of the sofa, and she curled up at the other.

"Do you want some coffee ?" he asked.

Leigh shook her head. "I'd just throw up."

"Good. Maybe it would help you remember what an appalling mistake you made today, so you'd not repeat it."

Leigh had taken some aspirin, but they hadn't begun to work, and her head was splitting. "Please, Eli. You're wasting your breath. I couldn't possibly feel any worse than I already do."

"Neither could I. I didn't like it one bit when you claimed becoming involved with me would create too many problems while you were working on the redevelopment project. I understood why you'd want to play it safe when you were so new to the job, but I'll be damned if I can figure out why you'd go right out and start sleeping with the man who's organizing the opposition. If you've got some logical explanation for what has to be the very worst of choices, I'd sure like to hear it."

Leigh snuggled down into her terry-lined robe. She couldn't describe what had happened between Jonathan and her as love at first sight, but it had been awfully close. "I don't have any excuse," she finally replied. "We were simply drawn to each other, and hoped to keep the redevelopment issue separate from our private lives. I know it must sound naive, or stupid."

"More like lunacy." Eli leaned forward to set his coffee cup on the table. "Jonathan was yelling so loud, half the town heard him compliment you on distracting him so creatively. There isn't anyone in Mirasol who's short on imagination, so by tomorrow night's council meeting, everyone's sure to hear you've been sleeping with the enemy. Jonathan should be in rare form tomorrow night. I hate to suggest this, but you might want to resign rather than try and continue to work for the city."

"Why? I've done nothing wrong," Leigh insisted, "other than follow my heart. I didn't compromise the redevelopment project in any way, nor would I ever do anything to undermine the city's plans. Besides, if I quit, Jonathan and his allies would assume I was admitting my guilt. Because he accused you of masterminding the fire, my resignation would also look very bad for you."

"I can take care of myself. It's you I'm worried about."

Tears welled up in Leigh's eyes. "Thank you. I told Jonathan I was afraid everything would go wrong, but I never dreamed it could be this horrendous. Do you suppose he has insurance?"

"Yes, I'm sure he does, but I don't give a damn about him.

I warned you he had the temperament of a pit bull, and you certainly saw his rabid side today. I don't want to see you hurt like this again. Are you smart enough to stay away from him now?"

Leigh sighed sadly. "I won't have to. He's not going to come anywhere near me ever again."

"You didn't answer my question."

"I never heard my parents argue," she replied, "and my husband and I didn't fight either. No one has ever attacked me the way Jonathan did. That he would do it out in the street in front of so many witnesses just made it all the more destructive. That he could regard what we shared as some evil seduction breaks my heart, and if he did it once, he'll just blame me for some other ridiculous crime later, won't he?"

"Yes. That's usually the pattern and verbal abuse is as harmful as physical violence. Denise doesn't have any better control of her anger than Jonathan, so the two of them will probably tear each other to pieces before too much longer."

That was no consolation at all, but when Eli smiled at her, Leigh reached out to take his hand. "I don't want to resign. Do you really think I should?"

Eli hesitated, but his response was firm. "No. If Jonathan wants to scream outrageous lies in the middle of the street, he just makes himself look ridiculous. If he does it again though, I'll sue him for slander." He wanted to stay with Leigh, but comfort wasn't all he longed to offer, and he knew she wasn't up to accepting anything more. The thought of making love to her so soon after Jonathan was a real turn off as well. He gave her hand a squeeze, then released it and stood.

"If you have any trouble at all today, with Jonathan or anyone else, I want you to call my private number. Do you still have it?"

"Yes. I do. Thanks, Eli."

"Why don't you take a nap? Things will look better when you wake up."

Leigh didn't see how, but just nodded and let him go. She

tried to imagine how she would have felt if she had arrived home to find the duplex had burned down. While there was little comparison between her modest apartment and Jonathan's Victorian, she knew she would not even have suspected, let alone accused him of having anything to do with the fire. His opposition to the redevelopment plan was frustrating, but not such a dire threat that anyone would have set fire to his house just to drive him out of town.

She knew instinctively that he wouldn't leave. The carriage house which served as a garage was set far enough back from the main house that it hadn't burned, so perhaps he would live there temporarily. Whatever he did, she would see him tomorrow night, and the prospect filled her with dread. She was completely innocent of his ludicrous charges, and not in the least bit ashamed to have slept with him, either. It had definitely been a conflict of interest, but not a criminal diversion to keep him out of town.

The council meeting was sure to have a trial-like atmosphere, however, and she would have to stride right in as though she had nothing to fear. Jonathan had been wrong about her acting abilities where he was concerned, but she was going to have to give the performance of her life tomorrow night. Wearily, she rose from the sofa and went into her bedroom, where her pillow was soon soaked with tears.

Jonathan had gone home with Denise rather than wait until the fire department had extinguished the last smoldering ember. She lived in a sprawling ranch style house south of town. It was furnished in the same smooth neutral colors as her shop, but that day he would not have found anything soothing. He sat down in a pale beige easy chair, and put his feet up on the ottoman.

Denise handed him a shot of Scotch, then refilled it when he swallowed it in a single gulp. She sat on the ottoman, and curled her hand around his feet. "Your house was a landmark in Mirasol," she recalled fondly. "Will your insurance allow you to rebuild?"

Jonathan finished his second drink, and leaned over to place his empty glass on the white rug before he replied. "I'm thinking of having it declared a monument. Then maybe Lloyd Channing can rebuild it along with the rest of the town."

Denise's dark eyes widened. "Would you really consider such a thing?"

"No, Denise. I wouldn't." Not surprised she hadn't gotten his bitter joke, Jonathan leaned back and closed his eyes. "Besides, I don't believe it's even possible to have a structure that's no longer standing designated as a historic site. The insurance will cover most of the work, but it will take a long time to rebuild a house with so much elaborate detail. My God," he sighed. "I never thought Eli would sink this low."

Denise had been standing close enough to hear his whole tirade against her ex-husband and Leigh, and didn't want to hear him repeat it. "It might be a good idea to wait for the results of the arson investigation before you blame him again in public. He has the money to slap you with an expensive lawsuit, and because the two of you have never gotten along, it's likely he'll sue."

"Fuck Eli. The bastard did it. You know he did."

"You really don't think it could have been an accident?"

"No way. The house was better than new." Jonathan was beginning to feel the effects of the Scotch, and welcomed the nubbing warmth. "I don't even have a change of clothes," he murmured to himself.

"Let's go into Santa Barbara in the morning and get you a whole new wardrobe." Denise took a breath, and lowered her voice to its most seductive level. "I want you to stay here with me, Jonathan. I have plenty of room, and I'll make you feel more than welcome."

"Yeah. I just bet you would." Jonathan had slept with Denise upon occasion, but it had never been the magical union he had found with Leigh. He was so disgusted with himself for falling

for her he couldn't stand it, but he did not want to compound
that error by moving in with Denise. She was a rare beauty, but
no longer nearly as exciting as he had found her in his teens.
She was a friend nothing more.

He opened his eyes, but his expression wasn't encouraging.
"Are you talking about living together?"

Denise licked her lips nervously, but her confidence didn't
waver. "Why not? We enjoy each other, and while I would much
rather that you had suggested it, I think it will work out real
well."

Jonathan was not even remotedly interested. "I've just lost
my house, Denise, not my mind."

Stung by that bitter taunt, Denise rephrased her suggestion.
"Please don't misunderstand me. I'm not asking for a commitment at such a difficult time. I'm merely offering to share my
home as any good friend would during a dire emergency. If
later we decide to stay together, fine. If not, there will be no
hard feelings."

But Jonathan already had too many hard feelings. Superim-
posed on the memory of water and smoke, he kept seeing
Leigh's shocked expression when he had accused her of deliberately keeping him out of town. He was positive she had to
have been in on the fire. A lot of people knew he liked to run
on the beach, but the arsonist couldn't have risked his coming
home early and discovering the device that caused the blaze,
and perhaps being trapped by it. So Leigh had been stationed
on the shore to keep him occupied.

She had carried out her mission with remarkable precision,
but he had not even suspected she could be so cruel as to prey
upon his emotions as she had. Wasn't losing his house punish-
ment enough? Why had she had to break his heart? Denise
began stroking his leg with her long fake nails, and he sat up
to avoid her touch.

"Thanks for the drinks, but I've got to be on my way."

Denise uncoiled from the ottoman in a graceful stretch. "But
where will you go?" she asked anxiously.

"I keep a sleeping bag in my van, so I'll survive the night."

Denise wrapped her arm around his as he started for the door. "Jonathan, perhaps you're in shock, because you're simply not thinking clearly. Why would you want to spend the night in a lumpy old sleeping bag, when you could stay here with me in comfort? I'll make you a delicious dinner, too."

Jonathan scraped her hands off his arm. "I've already thanked you for your kindness, Denise, but the answer is no. I'd like to be by myself tonight."

Denise kept still until they reached her front door and then she slipped in front of him. "I heard what you said to Leigh Bowman. Are you leaving because of her?"

Jonathan eased her aside and turned the doorknob to pull the door ajar. "You might say that. Look, Denise. We agreed a long time ago that neither of us owes the other any explanations. I obviously made a very bad mistake in trusting Leigh, and I'd like to be alone with it."

Denise was certain he would have stayed with her had Leigh Bowman not interferred. She didn't understand how Jonathan could have become infatuated with Leigh. Her pride aching, she dug her nails into her palms as she walked him out to his van. She would scream and throw things after he had gone, but for now, she appeared serenely unperturbed by his rebuff.

"I know how things stand between us, and I'm not complaining. I like leading an unfettered life too, but if you get sick of camping out, my door will always be open."

"Thanks." Jonathan quickly climbed into his van, and left without really having anywhere to go. He wondered why he hadn't seen Ron Tate at the fire, and supposed he must have been calling on a lady friend and missed the whole commotion. "Well, he'll sure have a hell of a shock when he comes by in the morning," Jonathan murmured to himself, and unable to stay there himself, he drove back out to the prep school.

He still had half a thermos of tea and some protein bars he kept handy for long trips, but he doubted he would ever get over feeling unclean. That Leigh thought nothing of using her

gorgeous body in a plot to ruin him made his skin crawl. He
turned on a sprinkler, shucked off his clothes, and scrubbed
himself thoroughly, but it didn't help. He had simply lost too
much in one day to regain any sense of composure and he ached
from the inside out.

On Monday, Leigh wore a simple black suit to match her
mood. Opal Lingard barely glanced up as she told her good
morning, and Leigh wondered if the whole town had turned
against her. If so, she would have no choice but to resign, but
unless she was absolutely forced to leave, she intended to stay
and do a magnificent job. She watered her philodendron, and
was reviewing the notes she had made on Friday, when Frank
Pierce came to the door.

"The fire chief just called. He says they've found a body at
Jonathan's. Looks like it's Ron Tate."

"Oh, my God," Leigh moaned. She rested her face in her
hands for a long moment and then looked up. "Did he have
family here?"

"No, but he sure had a lot of friends." Frank came on into
the office and sat down opposite Leigh. "I didn't know if you'd
have the courage to come in this morning, and I'm glad to see
that you did. Most people dismiss what Jonathan said about you
and Eli as sheer nonsense and blame it on the stress of the fire.
I know if I came home and found my house burned to the
ground, I'd be quick to look for something to blame, but I hope
I'd not take out my anger on innocent people the way he did."

Leigh was enormously relieved. "Thank you. I hope the rest
of Mirasol will be as understanding."

Frank pursed his lips thoughtfully. "There are a lot of merchants who are barely making it now, and the redevelopment
offers us a real chance to do well for a change. Frankly, if the
fire does turn out to be arson, there could be plenty of suspects,
but Eli won't be among them. He doesn't need Mirasol like the

rest of us here do. Jonathan was stirring up trouble; maybe he got more than he bargained for."

"The chief seemed certain yesterday that a gas leak caused the fire. Has he found evidence of arson?"

"Not yet, but he's making a careful search. Apparently Ron liked to nap on Jonathan's side porch. They found him as they started combing the rubble. Looks like the poor bastard never knew what hit him. One minute he was taking a peaceful snooze, and the next, he was at the pearly gates. That's a good way to go though. He didn't suffer."

Leigh had shed so many tears over Jonathan, that while her throat tightened, her eyes remained clear. "I liked Ron. He really made me feel welcome here. I hope there will be a memorial service of some kind. I'd like to attend, but not if there's any risk of Jonathan calling me a murderess."

"He wouldn't dare." Frank pushed himself to his feet. "I'm sorry to have brought such sad news. I'll let you get back to your work."

Certain she wouldn't be able to concentrate now, Leigh shrugged. After Frank left, she considered calling Eli, but he had ready access to information in Mirasol and she bet the fire chief had called him before he had called the mayor. "God, what an awful mess." Shaken, she went down to the water fountain and took a drink, then felt compelled to walk up to Jonathan's. She would take care to stand well back, but still wanted to go.

"I'm going into town for a while, Opal," she called out, and the receptionist waved.

As Leigh left city hall she walked slowly, but her chest ached as though she had run for miles. The pain was an all too familiar reminder of the despair she had come to Mirasol to escape. She crossed the street to approach Jonathan's from the library side, and found Bonnie and several others gathered at the patio gate to observe the scene of the fire. Firemen were surveying the damage, but Leigh doubted they would find much evidence of wrongdoing. Even the ornate chimney had been blown apart, and bricks were littered over the yard Ron Tate had tended so beautifully.

"Did you hear about Ron?" Bonnie asked. When Leigh nodded, the distraught librarian dabbed her eyes with a tissue, and sniffed loudly. "He was such a nice man. He always returned his books on time, and he used to bring me beautiful roses for the little vase on my desk."

Bonnie had been one of the few people Leigh hadn't seen at the fire scene, but she knew by now someone would have repeated every despicable syllable of Jonathan's tirade for her. She smiled at the others standing nearby. Some nodded, but a few turned away and whispered asides.

"I didn't have anything to do with the fire," Leigh assured Bonnie.

Bonnie looked horrified and drew Leigh away from the others. "I didn't think you did!" She peeked over her shoulder, then certain she wouldn't be overheard, she whispered. "Is it true that you've been seeing Jonathan though?"

"Is this just between you and me, or for public consumption at the Beauty Spot?"

Taken aback, Bonnie blotted her eyes another time, and took care not to ruin her mascara. "I know how to keep a secret," she stressed pointedly.

"Yes. I know you do. Frankly, I don't know how to describe what's happened between Jonathan and me. We liked each other, but the timing and circumstances were all wrong." Leigh glanced across the street and saw Jonathan coming around the side of the house or what was left of it. He hailed one of the firemen, and the two stood together talking. Yellow police ribbon had been strung all the way around the structure, but they were inside the barrier.

Leigh felt very much on the outside. Jonathan was wearing a gray sweatshirt streaked with soot and Levi's. It hurt very badly to look at him, and coupled with the sorrow of Ron's death, she did not know how she would survive the day, let alone last until the town was rebuilt. She waited, knowing Jonathan would turn toward her soon, and sick with the knowledge of how badly he would react.

She could wait for a furious glance, or for a bitter curse to pierce the air that still smelled of smoke, or she could seize the initiative. Too numb to decide if she were being very brave, or merely foolish, she bid Bonnie good-bye and crossed the street. She didn't duck under the yellow ribbon, but she walked right up to Jonathan and the fireman, and waited for them to sense her presence. Just as she had known he would, Jonathan was the first to turn toward her.

She did not wait for disgust to replace the surprise in his expression, and offered her sympathy quickly. "I'm so sorry about your friend's death. Ron was my friend too, and I'll miss him." She walked away then, holding her head high. She had not wasted her breath protesting her innocence. Either Jonathan believed in her, or he didn't, and because he had made his sentiments abundantly clear yesterday, she wouldn't engage him in a second senseless debate in the street.

She held her breath, half expecting him to hurl a brick at her head, but all that came her way was the force of his silent rage, and it hit her just as hard.

Thirteen

The fireman's lazy wolf whistle yanked Jonathan back to the present with a jealous snap. He was in his mid-twenties, and his blue eyes were aglow with a lustful sheen. Jonathan hadn't gotten much sleep, and he hadn't bothered with breakfast either. Other than the sandwich he had eaten yesterday with Leigh, he hadn't had a decent meal in nearly a week. He should have felt too light-headed and weak to take on a fireman more than ten years his junior, but he was eager to give it a try.

Jonathan knew he ought to have reached out, grabbed Leigh by the throat, lifted her clear off her dainty little feet, and squeezed the truth out of her, but he had been so astounded by how boldly she had approached him he had just stared at her. But not the way the fireman was staring at her. That he could still be jealous after the diabolical way Leigh had betrayed him defied logic, but he recognized the suffocating hurt for what it was, and couldn't simply swallow it.

"That adorable little brunette was a party to arson," he stressed darkly. "Wouldn't that be too much for a fireman to forgive?"

The fireman adjusted his hat, and laughed. "Not in her case. I know what you think, Mr. Reid, but we've never had any arson in Mirasol, unless you count the time Dan Kunkel built the fire out beside his hen house to keep the chickens warm on a cold night, set fire to the coop, and roasted his whole flock."

When Jonathan wasn't at all amused by the fireman's tale and just glared at him, the fireman raised his gloved hands. "All right, I agree that's a stretch and it was closer to stupidity than arson, but the point is, arson just doesn't happen here."

"This time it did," Jonathan insisted. He turned back toward what was left of his house. The second story had caved in on the first. The old wood had burned like the dry tinder it was, leaving a thick bed of ashes to sift through for the clues he was certain were there. If the fire department couldn't find the proof, then surely his insurance company could. If their experts also failed, then he would hire a private arson investigator, but damn it, this *had* to have been arson. The proof had to be there.

"It was a real pretty house," the fireman remarked in a conciliatory tone. "Are you going to rebuild it?"

"I sure am, and with a sprinkler system this time."

"It's a shame you didn't put one in earlier."

"Isn't it, though?" he ground out.

Jonathan would have to submit an inventory of everything that had been lost to his insurance carrier, but he did not feel up to beginning one yet. First thing that morning, he had bought Levi's and a few shirts, but he had been there when Ron's body was found. He was still reeling from that additional shock. When Leigh spoke to him, she appeared sincerely bereaved, but it had to have been a pose.

Feeling sick, he walked around to the back where he had parked his van, and crawled in. He had several padded blankets he used to wrap the antiques he often carried, and they made a better bed than his sleeping bag. Exhausted, he finally gave in to sleep, but it was only because he wanted to be at his best that night. He hoped evidence would be discovered by then so that he could confront Eli. Unfortunately, arsonist was much too tame a term for Leigh.

The council meeting opened with a moment of silence in tribute to the many ways Ron Tate had touched the lives of those in Mirasol. Leigh was grateful for an excuse to close her eyes rather than look at Jonathan and Denise in the front row.

Denise was shedding such copious tears that Leigh assumed she and Ron must have been extremely close. She wondered if he had brought her roses as he had Bonnie, but couldn't really picture him striding across the white carpet in her ultra chic shop in his work boots.

Denise was dressed in a denim sheath with a fringed yoke and tan boots. Leigh didn't recall ever seeing her in anything with Western styling before that night. She didn't carry such casual clothes in Silken Shadows, but Leigh supposed she might have been too depressed over Ron's death to dress with her usual sophisticated elegance. She looked splendid as always, but more subdued than haughty, which Leigh considered a definite improvement.

As for Jonathan, he was wearing a blue chambray shirt, and Levi's, but she didn't need to glance his way to feel his presence. It was as pervasive a force as the warmth in the auditorium, and grated on her already badly ravaged nerves. He was sure to occupy the same seat at every meeting, so she had no hope future Mondays would be any more serene. She chided herself for not thinking of Ron as the others were, but truly, she had remembered him fondly all day. Had he not lost his life in the fire, she knew he would have stood up for her. Sadly, he was gone.

Frank Pierce rapped his gavel lightly, then announced Ron's memorial service would be held Wednesday at the Methodist church. He then began the formal council meeting. "We had planned to show a video tonight that highlights three of the resorts built by Channing Enterprises, but it no longer seems appropriate with yesterday's fire on everyone's mind. Now I'm praying it wasn't arson as Jonathan supposes, but in hopes of putting an end to any nasty rumors that might have been circulating, I've asked Chief Perez to give us a preliminary report of his findings. Chief Perez."

The fire chief was wearing his navy blue uniform that night, and a deep frown that did not lift as he stood and came to the front of the room. He carried a small notebook, and quickly flipped to that day's investigation. There had seldom been a residential fire in Mirasol. Occasionally they had to put out a fire in a clothes dryer, or a grease fire in a kitchen, but to have a house burn to the ground was a rarity.

"We had an unusual situation here in that Mr. Reid stored paint thinner, varnish, and other flammable materials on his back porch. Once the gas leak ignited, those materials fed the resulting blaze. Thus far, we've found no evidence of arson from any incendiary device, but we'll continue our investigation until we're completely satisfied the fire didn't have a suspicious origin."

The chief scanned the crowd, and just as he had expected, Jonathan Reid raised his hand. "Yes, Mr. Reid?"

"I appreciate the department's fine work yesterday, Chief, and your thoroughness today." That was true, but Jonathan was bitterly disappointed that no evidence of foul play had yet been found. "I have just one question. Ron Tate died in the fire. When evidence of arson is found, will a murder investigation follow?"

The crowd leaned forward in a graceful wave, and the chief assured Jonathan it would become the police department's first priority. He knew Eli had something to say, and hoped he didn't have to prevent another fight while he was dressed in his good uniform. "Mr. Keene has an announcement, so I'd like to call on him."

Eli left his seat at the back of the auditorium, and regarded Leigh with an encouraging smile as he came forward. He took care to stand at the opposite end of the council table, however, to keep people's minds on what he was saying rather than remind them of Jonathan's charges. He had seldom been more serious, and looked it.

"In the unlikely event the fire does turn out to be the result of arson, I don't want anyone to believe that I support what could only be described as an act of urban terrorism. I've welcomed Jonathan's opposition to the redevelopment plan because he's forced us to sharpen our focus. If someone actually did set the fire to silence him, then they're guilty of the most heinous of crimes. The minute Chief Perez finds evidence of arson, I'm posting a reward of $10,000 for information leading to the arrest and conviction of those responsible."

Frank had to use his gavel to restore order as a surge of startled gasps and muffled comments disrupted the meeting. Eli thanked him for restoring order, and then continued. "Should anyone have any information that will help in the investigation, please give Chief Perez or the police a call. I've been assured all tips will be held in the strictest confidence, and investigated promptly."

When Eli finally sent Jonathan a questioning glance, he had nothing to say. Without proof, he would not make another accusation, but he couldn't bring himself to thank Eli for his generous gesture, either. Ten thousand dollars was pocket change to Eli, and in this case, undoubtedly a flagrant attempt to deflect suspicion from himself. Jonathan was tempted to rise and ask Eli where he had been Sunday morning, but he already knew Eli was far too clever to have been anywhere near the fire until his house was past saving.

He reached over and patted Denise's hand. She had taken Ron's death much harder than he had expected but he wouldn't urge her to hush. He was beyond tears himself, but he didn't begrudge Denise hers.

Leigh noted that tender exchange and had to fight back her own tears. Jonathan was either the most deeply confused man she had ever met, or one who cared so little about women's emotions that he could move from her to Denise without needing a second's delay to adjust his own feelings. She had seen him do it yesterday, but it still hurt to watch him display such solicitous concern for Denise again today. She took a deep breath, and hoped the council meeting would soon adjourn.

The president of the garden club was recognized next, and because Ron had had such an extraordinary talent with flowers, she suggested a memorial rose garden be planted in Keene Park. Leigh thought it a lovely idea, and was surprised when there were objections that it would set a precedent which might soon result in the park being portioned out in neat little floral plots with bronze plaques and leave no room for picnics and play.

Out of respect for Ron's memory, Rhonda Boyle had worn black that night, but her pantsuit was liberally adorned with gold braid. Her voice was low and hoarse but carried well. "I do not believe my ears," she exclaimed. "There's ample room in Keene Park for a hundred or more memorial rose gardens and it's unlikely Mirasol will produce three people a century who deserve them. Ron Tate most certainly did!"

She sat down to thunderous applause, and the memorial rose garden project was approved. The question then became one of what type of roses to plant, and after a lengthy discussion of whether red or yellow were most appropriate, the yellow were selected. Carl Brown then wanted to know if the city were paying for the memorial, or the garden club and another round of discussion began.

To Leigh, the evening had taken on a decidedly surreal quality. She tried to follow the discussion as it skipped around the auditorium, but all too often Jonathan and Denise were in the way. She looked down at her hands and just listened, but finally she could take no more petty arguments and raised her hand.

"Because Ron is so fondly remembered, I move that a memorial fund be established, and anyone who wishes to contribute may do so." She knew there was sure to be a question as to who would manage the fund, and turned to Bruce Sitz. "Would you be willing to be the treasurer, Mr. Sitz?"

Always pleased to be entrusted with money, the CPA readily agreed. The matter was put to a vote, and passed with no objections. By then it was nearly nine o'clock, and after promising to show the videotape the next week, Frank Pierce adjourned the meeting.

As the council members moved away from the table, Zoe Kunkel came over to Leigh. "Thank you for settling the memorial issue so sensibly. I'm embarrassed by how long some people can talk about nothing. I swear all they want is attention.

"Ron loved animals, so he came into my shop often. The last time he was in, he suggested I cross pit bulls with poodles, call them pitipoos, and sell them to people who wanted fierce watch dogs that wouldn't scare their neighbors."

Leigh considered the idea and smiled with Zoe. "I suppose a pitipoo would look sort of like a woolly lamb with sharp teeth, wouldn't it?"

"Sure would. Damnedest idea I ever heard, but I think Ron was just teasing me. I'm surely going to miss him, and I'll give Bruce a check tonight to start the fund. You take care now, honey." Zoe gave Leigh a hug before moving away.

Leigh sat down again and wrote out her own check. When she looked up, Eli was waiting for her. She passed the check down to Bruce, then stood to face Eli. "Considering what might have happened tonight, it didn't go too badly," she whispered softly.

"Not at all," Eli agreed. "How did your day go?"

"I didn't get a single hate call here at city hall, and turned off my answering machine so I wouldn't get any at home. It still hurts to be unjustly accused and have no way to prove Jonathan wrong."

"Chief Perez won't find any evidence of arson."

"I certainly hope not, but I'm sure there are people who will suspect a conspiracy even if none existed."

Eli looked around to make certain Jonathan was gone, then took Leigh's arm. "Your real worry is what Jonathan will think, isn't it? Don't worry. He prefers facts to wild theories and when he can't support his accusations, he'll be forced to retract them. Let's go over to the Marmalade and have a piece of pie. I want plenty of people to see us out looking confident of our innocence."

Leigh didn't really want any pie, but understood Eli's reasoning and met him at the cafe. It was decorated in a charming French Provincial style with an assortment of bright prints, and crowded after the council meeting, but they were quickly shown to a booth. Leigh felt uncomfortable with what was essentially a performance but Eli put her at ease when he began to talk about the hotel.

He handed her a manila folder. "Lloyd faxed me these designs today from his head office in San Francisco. Tell me what you think of them, and remember he'd like to use the same architectural style downtown for a unified theme."

Before she could look, a reed-thin waitress arrived to take their orders. The girl blew a stray curl out of her eyes, smiled broadly at Eli, and ignored Leigh completely. The same thing had happened frequently when Leigh had been out with her husband, but Doug had always insisted that she place her order first so she would not be forgotten. To his credit, Eli did also.

"Try the apple pie à la mode," he suggested. "They have a very light, thin crust, and just enough cinnamon in the apple filling."

Leigh would only have had tea, but Eli had made the pie sound so good she ordered it as well. She then opened the folder, and found a series of computer generated sketches. While there was some variation between them, they all featured essentially the same eight-story complex Jack Slate had shown them the night they had met at Eli's home.

"I like the waterfall at the entrance of this one," she said, "but none of the buildings sketched really seem suited to the valley. I'd rather see something low and sprawling, like what they did in Santa Fe, rather than a structure of eight stories."

Eli reached across the table to take her hand. "We agree, then. The only problem with the Santa Fe style is that it's too closely identified with Santa Fe. I want something more uniquely California. As for the waterfall, that one reminds me of Hawaii, and the valley just isn't tropical."

Leigh withdrew her hand from his and picked up that sketch so he would not think she was merely avoiding his touch, which she was. "You're right. I don't really like this that much, either. It's just the best of the lot. What are you going to do?" Their waitress returned with the pie, and when Eli took a bite before replying, she sampled hers, too. "Oh, this is good."

"Yes, isn't it? You have a lovely smile. After yesterday, I wasn't certain I'd see it again."

Leigh really didn't feel a bit better than yesterday. In fact, knowing Ron had been killed had deepened her melancholy. "Do I strike you as too shallow to remain depressed for long?"

"No, not at all—just the opposite in fact. I think you've been unhappy for too long. You've just absorbed the pain and put on a brave act."

Leigh sat back and wondered why Eli understood her so well, while Jonathan couldn't get past appearances. "You're a treasure, Eli. I'm surprised you haven't remarried."

"A wife like Denise will leave a man averse to commitment for a good long time. She wants a cut of the hotel, by the way, and I think that she sincerely believes she deserves it."

"What do you think?"

"I told her to go to hell, or words to that effect. Were you impressed by her tears tonight? It was all an act. I doubt that she'd spoken to Ron Tate more than once or twice. She isn't the type to make friends with gardeners—even good-natured ones."

Leigh did not have to ask who Denise had been trying to impress, she knew: Jonathan Reid. From the gentle sympathy she had seen him extend, the ploy had been effective. "How long have you two been divorced?"

"Five glorious years." Eli winked at her and took another bite of pie. "I wish that I'd divorced her earlier. I made the mistake of hoping that she'd mellow with age, and that we'd eventually have a happy marriage. Worst mistake of my life. Jonathan is welcome to her."

Leigh couldn't comment on that opinion and ate her pie in silence. It was so good she took tiny bites to make it last. Fortunately, an intriguing question quickly came to her. "If you had a wedding ring, what did you do with it?"

"I flushed it down the toilet." Eli noted Leigh's startled expression, and shrugged. "Well, I just wanted to be rid of the damn thing. Was that the wrong answer?"

"No. There isn't any right answer. It's just something I've wondered about." She didn't feel up to discussing her own dilemma, however, and promptly changed the subject. "I'm glad you offered the reward, even if there's no possibility anyone will ever collect it."

"I had little choice," Eli responded. "But I'll tell you something you mustn't repeat. I'm not a bit sorry Jonathan's house burned down. He's never missed an opportunity to cause me grief, and I'm glad to see he's finally had to deal with some. What goes around comes around, after all."

Appalled by the glint of triumph in Eli's eyes, Leigh had to take a sip of tea before she could swallow. She knew she hadn't had anything to do with the fire, but what if Jonathan's suspicions were correct, and Eli had hired someone to set it? It was almost too ghastly a possibility to accept. *Almost.* He definitely had the resources to do it, and an old rivalry coupled with a new conflict over the redevelopment plan to provide a motive.

He wouldn't have intended for Ron Tate to be killed, but the handyman was dead nonetheless. That she could be calmly eating a delicious piece of pie with a man guilty of arson and manslaughter—if not murder—was unnerving, but unlike Jonathan, she was far too concerned with making false accusations to give voice to unsubstantiated fears. Unable to take another bite, she pushed her plate away.

"It's been a long and difficult day, but before I go, please tell me what you plan to tell Lloyd Channing."

"I think I'll invite him to come back here alone, take him out to the valley, and make him sit there until he sees what we do. Then he can go back to San Francisco and tell Jack Slate we'd prefer the cement teepees they used to build for motels in the fifties to any of the designs he's come up with thus far. I'll make some sketches of my own if I have too, but I'm not plunking an eight-story hotel down in the valley, and that's all there is to it.

"Oh, one other thing," he added. "I told Miguel Fuentes that if he had any complaints about the hotel he was to bring them to me, and if he had complaints about Bonnie, he was to take them up with her, but that he wasn't to bother you ever again. I didn't offer him the job of maintaining the resort grounds, but hinted that I'd like to if he could reconcile his objections to the project. Essentially, I'm asking him to put aside his principles for a chance at a brighter future. Maybe that's underhanded, or just plain bribery, but I expect it to work."

Leigh didn't know how such a tempting offer could be accurately described either, but clearly Eli was pleased. It was a matter of principle, of course, and she was terribly afraid he might have set his aside as he expected Miguel to, and caused the fire at Jonathan's house. A shiver coursed down her spine, and she felt more lost than when she had arrived in Mirasol. Jonathan hadn't trusted her, and he had warned her not to trust Eli. The only person she could really trust was herself.

Miguel wound his fingers in Bonnie's hair, and nibbled her ear. "You know you don't want me to leave, *querida.*"

He had her pinned against the front door so she could not have opened it and demanded he go, but she was adamant all the same. "Yes, I do. You know I don't want you coming here."

"The council meeting will last for hours," he argued. "No one will see me."

"I can see you!"

Miguel silenced her protest with a deep kiss, and followed it with another, and another until Bonnie was too drunk with desire to murmur more than a faint protest as he led her back to her bedroom. He didn't need to turn on the light to undress her, and quickly stripped her nude. He pushed her down on the side of the bed, and unbuttoned his Levi's.

She knew what he wanted, and nearly swallowed his cock in her eagerness to please him. He stroked her cheeks gently to slow her down, and pulled back. He made her lean toward him, and then only allowed her to lick him with the tip of her tongue. She cupped his balls with one hand, and encircled his waist with the other. She made little slurping noises, as though he tasted better than candy.

Miguel combed his fingers through her curls. "Now tell me you don't want me here," he asked but he slid his cock back into her mouth before she could answer. "I can't hear you," he said, and thrust along her tongue. Her mouth was hot, and the rhythmic suction she created was so good he couldn't delay his climax nearly as long as he had intended. He pushed her down on the bed, stretched out over her, shoved her legs apart with his knee, and thrust deep as the bliss washed through him.

He savored it only a few seconds, and then quickly withdrew. He moved off the bed, tucked in his shirt, and buttoned up his pants. He leaned down to kiss Bonnie while she still tasted faintly of him, then reached for the light switch so there would be no mistaking his expression.

"Unless you finally admit that we're a couple, and welcome me here, we're through. I'm tired of being treated like a shameful secret when I'm proud to love you."

Until that night, Bonnie had never felt in the least bit embarrassed by anything she did with Miguel, but now she was acutely aware of her nudity. She was too thin to have much in the way of breasts, and as Miguel's dark glance traveled over her, her nakedness made her feel ugly and awkward. She would have grabbed up her clothes, but Miguel had tossed them clear into the corner. Obviously he had planned to humiliate her, and he had succeeded. She pulled the bedspread around her and started to cry.

"You know why I can't be seen with you," she sobbed. "A librarian has to be respectable and one look at you and everyone will know we're lovers."

"That's bullshit and you know it. It's not your job that keeps us apart, but mine. You're ashamed of me."

He turned away, and despite her embarrassment, Bonnie went after him trailing the fringed spread. "Miguel, please. Don't leave like this."

He paused in the hallway. "Do you want me to stay the night?

My truck's parked right out front where everyone will see it. Do you want me enough to finally admit that you love me?"

She ached with wanting him, but rather than a handsome young man, what Bonnie saw was her mother's shocked disappointment. It coiled around her stomach, and filled her throat with the bitter taste of bile. She had been carefully tutored to choose a man with money. Then, when he eventually abandoned her, she would still have enough left to prevent her from ever being poor. What would she have when Miguel left except a badly broken heart?

"We could drive to Nevada and be married tonight, *querida*. It's what I want. Will you ever agree?"

Sick with humiliation and fear, Bonnie collapsed against the wall, then turned her face away and wept with low, racking sobs. Her mother had worked so hard to make her daughter's life better than her own, but Bonnie couldn't remember any of the advantages now. She felt hopelessly torn, and needed comfort rather than angry ultimatums.

Miguel was more disgusted with himself than her. "Tell me this, then. Why did I put up with such a skinny, frightened girl for so long? What I need is a real woman, not someone who doesn't even understand what love is."

Miguel tore out the front door, and ran down the walk. He started his truck, and hoping to bring everyone who was not at the council meeting to their windows, gunned the engine. Then he left Bonnie for what he promised himself would be the last time.

Leigh had just begun to turn the corner on her way home when Miguel veered wide rather than slow down as he made the turn from the opposite direction and they came within inches of colliding. Although Miguel sped by her in a frantic blur, his tires squealing for traction, she recognized him and enough of the white lettering on the silver Chevy truck's door to see it belonged to the Elijah Keene Ranch. Badly shaken, she continued on down Aliso Street, and pulled into her driveway, but it took her several minutes to find the strength to get out of her car.

Eli may have thought he had influenced Miguel with veiled references to a better job, but it was clear to Leigh that he had not defused the young man's furious anger. Miguel had terrified her just now, and while she felt far from capable at the moment, she was certain Bonnie must feel worse. "Stay out of it," she told herself, but as she unlocked her backdoor, she feared she might very well have created this latest problem between Miguel and Bonnie, and that meant she couldn't just walk away.

Fourteen

Leigh stayed at her place only long enough to take a quick sip of water, and then went on to Bonnie's. There was no response when she rang the bell, so she knocked forcefully. Unlatched, the door swung open. Leigh didn't want to enter uninvited, but she could hear Bonnie sobbing pathetically from where she stood out on the porch.

"Bonnie?" she called. When her friend's cries increased in volume, Leigh decided her presence had been duly noted, and let herself in.

Bonnie was still slumped in the hallway, swathed in her bedspread. Leigh took one look at her, and feared the situation was desperate. She knelt down beside her, and rubbed her hand over Bonnie's shaking shoulders. "I think I'd better call the police."

Shocked out of her sorrow, Bonnie quickly wiped her eyes on the spread, leaving long black streaks of mascara on the pale pink chenille. "Whatever for?" she asked between loud sniffles.

"Miguel nearly ran me off the road just now, and look what an awful state he left you in. Don't tell me you had a simple lover's quarrel, because you'd not be collapsed on the floor if that's all that happened here."

Bonnie relaxed against the wall, but her expression was still full of misery. "Despite how I look, this isn't a matter for the police," she insisted. "Miguel left me, Leigh. He saw through my excuses, and he walked out." Her lower lip trembled, and tears again spilled over her lashes. "I always knew that he would. I just didn't want it to be this soon."

Leigh sat down opposite Bonnie. The hallway was lit by an overhead bulb in a crystal globe and bright enough for an extended conversation, which she was certain this would surely be. She hadn't expected Jonathan to leave her after they had shared only a single passionate interlude, well, perhaps two, but he had all the same. "There are times when I'm certain love is worth the emotional pain," she confided, "and other times, like tonight, when I'm afraid pain is all there is."

Bonnie wrapped her arms around her legs. "I was never ashamed of Miguel. Never. I can't bear to have him think that." She rested her cheek on her knees. "That's how it looked, though."

"It doesn't matter how things look," Leigh stressed. "It's how they really are that matters. Or at least that's the way it ought to be."

"I should have gone to the council meeting. Then I wouldn't have been home when Miguel came by. He knew I didn't want him coming here, so the instant I opened the door I knew we were in for trouble and he sure gave it to me."

"He didn't hurt you, though?"

"No. But he didn't take the time to please me, either, and he's never done that before." He had ruffled her curls with a tender caress as she had pleased him though, his love sweetening his touch, and she was heartbroken that he had not been able to overlook her reticence to declare her love for him.

"Well, then, if you hadn't been home tonight, he would probably have come by tomorrow or the next day. Miguel doesn't appear to have much patience."

Bonnie was afraid Leigh had seen only the worst side of Miguel, the side he had shown her that night in what had clearly been a well-planned performance. "No. He has a great deal. It's taken more than a year for me to exhaust it. Was my mother there tonight?"

Leigh took a moment to visualize the crowd. She skipped over Denise and Jonathan and scanned the first couple of rows before she found Beverly's wild heap of blond hair. "Yes. She was there."

Bonnie sighed dejectedly. "I guess now I'll have to tell her I've broken up with the realtor from Santa Barbara."

Leigh was amazed by how unerringly Bonnie made the wrong choices. "Are you just going to let Miguel go?"

"What else can I do? He wanted us to elope tonight but had me too rattled to even consider it. Everything's such a mess, Leigh. I know what I'm supposed to want, what it's smart to want, but that's not the way I feel."

Leigh found it easy to counsel Bonnie now. "Forget what your mother, or anyone else, might think of the suitability of a ranch hand as a husband for a woman with a college degree. Follow your heart. No matter what happens, you'll never regret taking a chance on love, but you will always be sorry if you don't."

She pushed herself to her feet, and reached down to catch Bonnie's hands. "Come on, I'll run you a bath, and pour in plenty of Sensual Harmony oil. I won't promise things will look better tomorrow, but maybe it will make you feel a little bit better tonight."

Bonnie didn't argue, but soaking in the fragrant oil only made her miss the joy she and Miguel had shared all the more. Leigh had a cup of soothing herbal tea waiting for her when she got out of the bathtub, and she drank it before going to bed, but her friend's thoughtful gestures weren't nearly enough to make up for the anguish of losing Miguel.

Denise had been so distraught that evening that Jonathan had reluctantly gone back to her place after the council meeting. He had stuck with coffee, but she had sipped cognac which had only made her all the more weepy. Thoroughly depressed himself, for the better part of two hours he had barely listened to her rambling conversation but caught enough to recognize she was simply grappling with her own mortality.

It was a common occurrence after the sudden death of a close friend or relative, but he had come to grips with the specter of death in the course of his history studies and Ron's tragic loss was affecting him differently. Even with Denise snuggled against him on the sofa, his thoughts were full of Leigh. She had looked pale and fragile rather than confident that evening.

Perhaps Ron's death had left her heavily burdened by guilt. That would account for her subdued mood even if she wasn't ashamed of what she had done to him. She had only glanced his way a time or two, and then had quickly looked down at her hands. Like Lady MacBeth, he imagined. He hoped Leigh came to an equally bad end.

He didn't blame her for avoiding him. He blamed himself for being so needy he had fallen for her in the first place. Maybe if he hadn't been filled with romantic illusions Ron would still be alive. Then again, maybe he would be dead along with him. That was such a ghastly thought, he straightened up slightly, and Denise finally interrupted her tearful monolog to look up at him.

"Stay with me tonight," she begged in a hoarse whisper. "I don't want to be alone after all that's happened. If you're right about Eli being behind the fire, then he might come after me next."

Jonathan was used to her wiles, and wasn't swayed by her plea. "I doubt he'd set another fire. In such a small town, it would be too great a coincidence."

Denise had applied waterproof mascara that evening, and while her face was slightly flushed, her make-up hadn't run. She dabbed lightly at the corners of her eyes with a tissue, and then regarded Jonathan with a wounded gaze. "Coincidence or not, I'd be just as dead."

Jonathan responded with a deep chuckle. "And you want me to risk perishing with you?"

Clearly he was highly amused by the possibility, but Denise surely wasn't. Haunted by the fire and it's deadly consequences, she scolded him. "Don't tease me. You've lost your beautiful home, and Ron Tate is dead. This is no time for humor."

Jonathan felt not the slightest bit of shame. He looked into Denise's tear-brightened eyes, and replied with the same hint of sarcasm as his last comment, "I've begun to think all of life is a very bad joke, Denise, and the only thing that keeps me sane is a sense of humor.

"I started clearing out the second floor of the carriage house this afternoon. I've been using it for storage, so it's rather crowded at present, but it will make a fine temporary apartment. It's been used for one in the past and has a small bathroom. That in the space of a week I've gone from a Victorian mansion to living over a garage is disappointing, but it's a heck of a lot better than what happened to Ron."

Denise had laced her fingers in his and was gripping his hand tightly, but confident she would survive the night without him, Jonathan broke free of her possessive grasp and stood. "I've got to be going. Try and pull yourself together. I'll see you at the memorial service on Wednesday."

Infuriated by his callous disregard for her grief, Denise came close to shrieking a colorful curse to damn him for walking out on her. She drew in a shuddering breath instead, and tried to appear merely disappointed rather than enraged. "Yes. I'll be there," she assured him.

She remained at her open doorway until the taillights on Jonathan's van disappeared in the distance. Then she closed and locked her door and went into the kitchen where she poured herself another cognac. She took a sip, and then unleashing the terrible temper she had used so often on Eli, she hurled the snifter against the wall. As the delicate glass shattered, the expensive brandy splattered across the white enamel, but Denise was too angry to care about the sticky mess and let it trickle on down to the floor and went to bed.

Jonathan parked in front of the carriage house, and then remained seated in the van. He knew he had been rude, and had nearly bolted out of Denise's house. In the future, he would sidestep her invitations and not go back. He felt uneasy around her now. He had been flattered by her interest when he had first returned to Mirasol, but gradually he had simply gotten bored with her.

The initial spark of chemistry between a man and woman was supposed to grow, and deepen into something far more meaningful, but it hadn't with Denise.

That it had with Leigh had become a constant torment. As he left his van, part of him wished he had kept right on driving to spare himself another look at the ruins of his home. Another part knew he would have to stay and fight for justice. He was angry enough to fight forever, but the prospect of sending Leigh to prison just didn't seem like much of a reward.

Leigh felt that she owed the city of Mirasol a full day's work, but Tuesday morning she did little more than sit at her desk and stare out the window. At lunch time, she took the carton of yogurt she had brought with her out to the demonstration garden behind city hall and sat alone on a bench to eat. It was a peaceful spot to enjoy a warm, lazy moment, but the garden's tranquility failed to lift her mood.

She had come to Mirasol with such high hopes, but had quickly become even more emotionally battered than when she had arrived. Whether or not there was an arsonist loose, the redevelopment project would survive. She wasn't certain she would. Her previous jobs had been such straightforward assignments and she had expected the same here, but her resolve was crumbling faster than the buildings downtown.

Perhaps she wasn't suited for this line of work after all. There were always opponents to any new city plan, and animosity frequently ran high until the benefits of redevelopment became clear. She had never been as personally involved as she was here, though, and it was a costly mistake she would not repeat.

She rose wearily, and tossed her yogurt carton and plastic spoon into the trash bin. She still had time left on her lunch hour, and on a sudden whim walked into town and went into Fins, Feathers, and Fur to visit the potbellied piglet, but there was a cage of guinea pigs where his plastic wading pool had been. She looked around for Zoe.

"Did you sell the piglet?" Leigh asked the shop's owner.

Zoe smiled sheepishly. "No. I decided he was too cute to sell, named him Sweetpea, and took him home. I'll reconsider though, if you want to buy him."

Leigh still couldn't visualize herself as the proud owner of a piglet. "No, thank you. I just came by to tell him hello, and you too, of course."

A perceptive woman, Zoe thought it likely Leigh had come seeking something more. "Feeling kind of down, are you? I know just the thing. I have the cutest little calico kitten you ever saw. She'd make the perfect pet for you, and I do mean *purr*-fect."

Leigh knew she would have absolutely no resistance to cute little furry creatures that day, and began to back away. "My life is already too complicated, Zoe, but thank you anyway. Goodbye."

Zoe followed, and caught Leigh as she reached the door and walked out to the sidewalk with her. "Jonathan came in a little while ago looking for the piglet, too. He seemed kinda lost, same as you."

Surprised by Zoe's insightful description of her mood, Leigh didn't know what to say, and pretended a rapt interest in the two poodle puppies in the window. Ginger colored, and full of rambunctious energy, they were chasing each other around and around in the shredded newspaper. "After the fire, that's not surprising, is it?" she asked.

"No, I suppose not, but I'll never understand why he blames you."

"Thank you, Zoe." Leigh hurried away, and just as she had on the way into town, she cut through the library patio rather than use the sidewalk opposite Jonathan's corner. She was sincerely sorry to learn he wasn't doing well, but because he had

Denise to keep him company, she knew he couldn't possibly feel as lonely as she.

The Methodist church was already crowded by the time Leigh arrived for Ron Tate's memorial service on Wednesday morning. She had walked over with Frank Pierce, but his wife had saved him a seat up front, and she preferred to sit in the rear. When Lester Cornell moved over to make room for her in the last pew, she sat down beside the janitor. They had exchanged only a few words at city hall, but she appreciated his welcoming smile.

Lester leaned close to whisper. "Ron wasn't much of a churchgoer. If he had been, he'd have been here Sunday morning instead of napping on Jonathan's porch, and there would be no need for a funeral."

Leigh nodded her agreement, and wondered how many of those present were thinking the same thing. Eli had not known Ron well, and had told her he did not plan to attend the service. He had advised her to be absent as well. She understood why being there might make her a target for abuse, but she had liked Ron too much to stay away out of fear. The memorial began with a hymn she had learned as a child. She shared a hymnal with Lester, but sang softly while his steady tenor carried well.

When everyone had resumed their seats, the minister described Ron as a man dedicated to service to others. He had been a veteran, and had led a varied life before coming to Mirasol in his forties. A caring friend, he was praised by George Culbert for bringing constant humor to the older men who crowded Mama Bee's counter every day for lunch. They jokingly referred to themselves as death row, but none had expected Ron to be the first to die.

"He was a damn good friend," George said, unmindful of the sacred setting. Looking very uncomfortable in the suit and tie he seldom wore, as he left the lectern, his eyes filled with the tears he could no longer hide. Rhonda Boyle, wearing a beaded black sheath more suitable for a cocktail party than for such a solemn occasion, came forward teetering on spiked heels. She praised Ron for maintaining the gardens of several of Mirasol's elderly residents without charging them a penny to keep their property looking nice.

"He was a true Christian," she declared emphatically.

A soloist from the church choir sang a poignant hymn in a lilting soprano and then Jonathan left his place down in front. As he moved toward the lectern, Leigh glanced over her shoulder to gauge the distance to the exit. She had been to several funerals where friends had shared their memories of the deceased the way George and Rhonda had today, but the possibility Jonathan might want to lace his comments with another arson charge had not occurred to her until that very moment, and she could not imagine a worse scene.

Lester leaned close. "Stay," he urged. A stocky man, who had come wearing his khaki work clothes, he looked ready to hang on to Leigh if she didn't obey.

Leigh sat back in her seat, but she hoped Jonathan had not noted her presence, and would not mention her name or Eli's. When he began the story of how Ron had come to work for him when he had first bought a home in great need of repair, she held her breath until it became clear he intended to praise his late friend for his talent with a hammer as well as a hoe, and pruning sheers. He spoke with the resonant assurance which had made him a popular professor and confided several amusing anecdotes that illustrated Ron's abundant humor and warmth.

Leigh had never been able to sit through a funeral without being overcome with tears, but by the time Jonathan brought his moving eulogy to a close by suggesting they should all remember Ron in the fragrance of a beautiful rose, and the kindness of a friend's smile, there were only a few in the crowded church who weren't weeping openly. They stood to sing, "Amazing Grace," as best they could in voices choked with emotion, and then Leigh hurried away before the others began to file out of the church.

Jonathan's words had touched Leigh deeply, but on such a sad day it was difficult to dwell on sweet memories as he had advised. She did so want to remember the few good times she had had with Jonathan rather than how quickly he had turned against her, but it was much too soon to possess the necessary perspective. She had seen Pam Akers at the church, and wondered if she shouldn't join the Fitness Center. Exercise was good for cutting stress, and she certainly needed something to help her cope.

Most of the shops in town had closed for the memorial service, and there were few people about as she walked back to city hall. It was a beautiful sunlit day, but having lost a chance for love, and burying a friend, she saw little to appreciate. When she reached the library, she stopped in to see Bonnie.

"How was the funeral?" Bonnie asked, and then quickly rephrased her question. "I know it must have been sad, but was it well-attended?"

Leigh provided a few details, and then lowered her voice. "I wanted to see how you're doing."

Bonnie shrugged. "We've not had many people come by this morning, so I've been able to catch up on things, but that's not what you meant, is it?"

Leigh shook her head. Bonnie then admitted to feeling desperately sad, but seemed resigned to it. Leigh wanted to help, but realized how ridiculous it would be to repeat her suggestion that Bonnie fight for Miguel, when she had been too demoralized by Jonathan's anger to fight her own battles. "Would you please show me where the relationship books are? I remember recommending them, but I'd like to read a few myself."

"Sure. They're right over here." Bonnie came out from behind the counter, and led Leigh over to the appropriate aisle. "I'm going to take your advice, and read them all." She plucked the first one from the shelf and perused the table of contents. "This sounds rather dry, but maybe I'll find a few good tips in it. Let me know if you can't find what you need." She tucked the book she had selected under her arm, and went back to her post.

Because relationship books frequently made the bestseller lists, Leigh recognized several titles, but she wasn't looking for advice on how to flirt, or how to analyze men's conversation as though it were a foreign language. She wanted something more scholarly than entertaining. She needed a book on how to survive absolute disasters and finally found one with a section on coping with loss that sounded helpful. She carried it up to the desk and checked it out on her new card.

"Have you heard from Miguel?" Leigh then whispered.

"No, but I didn't expect to. Some things just aren't meant to be, and he's one of them."

Leigh readily understood that sentiment, but still thought it a shame Bonnie didn't trust her feelings more. She picked up her book. "Let me know what you think of the book you chose. If it's any good, I'll read it, too."

"Sure. I'll do that. With no one else around, I might as well start on it now."

Leigh left the librarian scanning the introduction, and went on back to work. She slipped the book she had selected into the bottom drawer of her desk with her purse, and now focusing solely on Mirasol, got busy. The city had a fascinating history, but its current brochure detailed it in such an unimaginative way she wanted to update it and reprint it with the tourist family on the front cover.

She was busy revising her second draft when Eli came by that afternoon. "Lloyd Channing's coming back tomorrow," he announced as he dropped into the chair opposite Leigh's. "I think he's beginning to worry that I've gotten cold feet and may back out of the resort deal."

Leigh had come to Mirasol because its challenging redevelopment plan would include a spectacular resort. Rather than remind Eli of that fact, and how badly his comment had scared her, she searched his expression for the truth. "It's a big step, Eli. It would be natural to have some doubts."

Eli leaned over to feel the leaves on the philodendron he had given her. "This needs water. I'll get it some before I leave." He sat back and forced a smile. "Of course, I have doubts. Who wouldn't? But I've thought about doing this for years, and I know it's the right thing for Mirasol. It's just that I hadn't expected the architecture to present a problem. I thought we'd just build a resort. I didn't stop to visualize the place in detail, and that was obviously a mistake."

Be careful of Eli, Jonathan had told her, and Leigh rubbed her temple to dispel the warning. Eli was handsomely groomed and dressed as always, but as she looked at him, it suddenly occurred to her that while he supervised the running of the Keene Ranch well, this might be the first important project he had ever set out to do on his own.

"Every project begins with the initial concept, in this case a resort with ample recreational facilities, and then moves into the planning phase when the details are hammered out. That problems appear at this stage is only natural," she explained. "The main reason I'm here is to handle the city's problems, and because the resort is tied to the redevelopment, I expect to be involved with solving yours as well. Let's take this one step at a time."

Eli broke into a wide grin. "I love women who know how to take charge."

Leigh leaned back in her chair. If there was anything she absolutely couldn't abide, it was men who didn't take her seriously, and Eli obviously didn't. When she spoke, there was no mistaking her mood.

"The resort, Eli. Let's focus our attentions on the resort."

Feeling properly chastised, he attempted to appear contrite. "I'm sorry. Go on."

Eli was having such great difficulty looking serious, that Leigh was tempted to pick up her ruler and whack him one. "You're a very charming man," she complimented, "but I want you to save it for Lloyd Channing rather than waste it now on me."

Eli responded with a sly grin. "It's not wasted if you've noticed."

Leigh feared Eli was beyond redeeming, and continued as though she had his full attention. "You don't want a skyscraper in the valley, but Lloyd will argue eight stories is scarcely in that category. You'll concede the point, but remind him you have plenty of land, so there's no need to build anything over, what will you accept, four stories?"

Eli winced. "I'd have to drive into Santa Barbara and look at one of their old hotels to judge."

Leigh rose from her chair. "Let's go then."

"Now?"

"As I see it, with Channing coming in tomorrow, we don't have much time to make field trips. I'll drive this time, if you like."

Eli came out of his chair with a reluctant stretch. "I'll drive, but if we're going to Santa Barbara, we might as well stay, and discuss tomorrow's meeting over dinner."

Leigh knew exactly how he would behave at dinner, but trusted herself not to be impressed. "Sounds good to me." She bent down to get her purse, but she left the book she had intended to read that night in the drawer. She already knew how to cope with loss by diving into work, and regarded Eli's misgivings as an opportunity to do just that.

Fifteen

After Leigh dropped off her Camaro at home, Eli chose route 33 taking them past the prep school rather than the picturesque back road to Santa Barbara that they had taken on their first trip together. Leigh wondered if he had done it deliberately to remind her of her ill-fated tryst with Jonathan, then remembered he had no idea where it had taken place. Still, it was difficult to appear nonchalant as the faded sign came into view.

"We've not discussed the prep school," she remarked as casually as she could. "Have you considered reopening it?"

Eli frowned slightly. "If there's sufficient interest I suppose I would, but I've no plans for it now. In some respects it's like the Inn. It's part of Mirasol's history, but it's not a key element in the redevelopment."

"What's going to happen to the Inn?"

"Nothing for the time being. It should probably be torn down, but I'm too attached to the place to let go until I absolutely have to. That's one of my problems," he admitted with a rueful smile. "I hang on with a gila monster's tenacity when I should just say, 'The hell with it!', and let go.'"

"Yes. I know exactly what you mean." Leigh eased down in her seat, and the buttery smooth leather cradled her weary body in lush comfort. "It's also far too easy to just let things drift, even when they're headed in the wrong direction."

Leigh was studying the passing scenery, so Eli didn't have a clear view of her expression, but the wistfulness of her remark touched him. There was an issue between them that he had let slide, hoping there was no need to press it, but now he feared he had been wrong. "Leigh?"

"Hmm?"

"I didn't have anything to do with the fire."

There was no mistaking his seriousness now, and Leigh was grateful for it. "I'd hoped that you hadn't."

"But you weren't sure?" Eli was badly disappointed by that and winced. "I can't seem to get anywhere with you."

When he glanced toward her, Leigh thought, as she so often did, that when he dropped the superficial charm, he was infinitely more appealing. "I like it when you don't make any effort to be charming. I think you have a serious side few people in Mirasol ever see, but quite frankly, I prefer it."

Eli opened his mouth to argue that other women didn't complain about his approach, but fortunately he realized none of them had mattered nearly as much as Leigh and caught himself before he sounded as though he was bragging about his conquests. There had been a lot of women, but they had been so eager to sleep with him that all he had had to do was show up at their front door to be invited into their beds. He didn't pursue the ones who weren't easy, or at least he hadn't until now. It appalled him to think maybe he didn't even know how.

"I hope you won't mind if I laugh when it's appropriate," he offered.

"No, not at all." Leigh sighed softly, and closed her eyes. When Eli touched her shoulder to wake her, she was embarrassed to have fallen asleep. She sat up, and discovered she had slept all the way to Santa Barbara. "I'm sorry. I haven't gotten much sleep the last few nights, and—"

Eli leaned over and brushed her lips with a light kiss. "Don't apologize. I'm just glad I didn't agree to let you drive."

He tried to contain the width of his grin, but gave up when Leigh laughed along with him. "Come on. We weren't looking at hotels the last time we were here, but there are a couple just off State Street with several stories. They're far from new, but if we're just considering height, they'll do as examples."

Leigh was glad Eli knew Santa Barbara so well, and had brought her clipboard to keep notes and make sketches. "Maybe we ought to find a travel agent and pick up brochures for every resort this side of the Rockies," she suggested as they walked along State Street. "We're familiar with most architectural styles, and Channing Enterprises certainly has innovative designs, but maybe there's something more we're overlooking."

"I liked your suggestion of natural stone."

"That was just the first thing that occurred to me after driving through the valley."

"Sometimes the first ideas are the best. Straight from the heart, you know?" Eli took Leigh's arm when they came to the corner, then slid his hand down to hers as they continued on down the street. They paused in front of the Schooner Inn, but neither wanted to borrow any ideas from the stately old hotel, and hurried on. By sunset, they had wandered through the town, found some pleasing elements as well as a few awful ones, but were still excited as they sat down for dinner on the patio of a Mexican cafe. It featured an outdoor barbecue which scented the air with the smokey aroma of mesquite, and the Margaritas were strong.

Leigh licked her lips to catch the last bit of salt from the rim of her glass. "I can't remember the last time I had a Margarita, and they're always good." She noticed a couple of young women at an adjacent table eyeing Eli, and knew they must envy her. That she had been dumped by the man she really cared for, and was simply discussing business, wouldn't occur to the pair, but it didn't escape Leigh for an instant.

"The red marble fortress might be perfect for a stark desert setting, but the valley needs something far less dramatic." She took another sip of her drink. "Something bronze and gold, with sandstone, or lots of oak and thick bougainvillaea."

His mood mellow, Eli leaned back in his chair, and stretched out his legs. "What do you suppose it would cost to borrow heavily from Greene and Greene's craftsman style?"

"A fortune."

Eli tried not to look smug. "Fortuately, I have one." He finally noticed the attractive pair at the nearby table, but neither young woman interested him half as much as Leigh, and he gave no sign that he had seen them. "My grandfather didn't just own land in Mirasol, he also had some acreage in Los Angeles. Wilshire Boulevard runs through part of it."

He was describing some of the world's most expensive real estate and Leigh was appropriatedly impressed. "My God."

"Exactly. I wish I still owned it, but when my father parted with it in the fifties, he struck a very good deal, and invested the money wisely. I told you I wanted to rebuild Mirasol, open a resort, and get out, but I do have other options."

The waitress came for their orders, but neither had opened a menu. "I'm hungrier than I thought," Leigh admitted as she quickly scanned the list of steaks and chose one. When the waitress left their table, Leigh leaned forward slightly. "What do you mean, exactly?"

Eli knew he was being devious, but damn it, Leigh was a city planner, and if that were the only way to excite her, then he would damn well use it. "I've become more interested in the resort project than I'd expected. I might consider building it on my own if I can't find a quality developer like Lloyd Channing who'll build what we want."

"We?"

"Sure. You're the expert on planning. I'd probably have to begin with a small facility and expand, assuming of course that the resort is successful."

"How could it be otherwise?"

Eli raised his Margarita and touched her glass. "To success."

Leigh echoed his toast, but she recognized the gleam in his eyes for the challenge it was, and knew for the moment at least that winning her heart was his true goal. Perhaps it was the warmth of the evening, or the delicious kick to the Margaritas, but as she looked at Eli, her smile was the prettiest it had ever been. It was very nice to be wanted, and the objections she had given him when they first met now seemed foolish in the extreme. Eli wouldn't interfere with her work. Just the contrary, he was her most enthusiastic ally.

She thought he would be a tender lover, and she had never needed affection more. She reached for his hand, and gave him an encouraging squeeze. It was a small step, but enough to fill his gaze with the joy that was absent from her own. "I'm scared to death, Eli."

Eli leaned close to whisper. "That's okay, baby. So am I."

Leigh felt better though, and while she didn't invite Eli in when he took her home, she did kiss him good night as though she meant it, and she did.

On her lunch hour Thursday, Leigh went to the Beauty Spot. She had called to make an appointment, and prayed she wasn't about to make a horrible mistake by trusting Beverly MacNair to do her hair. "I'm having dinner with Lloyd Channing tonight at Eli's, and my hair's so long it keeps falling into my eyes. I'm afraid I'll mistake the centerpiece for the salad if you don't trim it for me. Not too much, though."

Beverly ran her fingers through Leigh's boyish cut, and fluffed it out. "Yes, this is a mite long for the way you've been wearing it. You have such pretty hair. Have you thought about letting it grow?"

"No. I like it short."

Beverly met Leigh's eyes in the mirror, and shrugged, but it was clear she thought it too short already. "Let's start with a shampoo." She took Leigh over to the sink, and once she was comfortably seated, lathered her hair.

Leigh heard the door open, but tilted back in her chair, couldn't see who had entered the shop. The manicurist and other beautician were at lunch so the three of them were alone. Beverly interrupted her gentle scalp massage to offer a greeting.

"I'll be with you in a second," she called out. "Lloyd Channing will be the guest of honor at Eli's tonight. I'd sure like to meet a man with his money. Have you met him?"

"No. Eli doesn't include me on his guest list any longer. I just came in for another bottle of Sensual Harmony. I'll leave the money here by your register."

Leigh recognized Denise's smooth alto, and didn't relax until she heard the door close behind her. She thought Lloyd would probably like Denise's type, but certainly wouldn't call Eli to suggest that he invite her to join them. She was afraid the evening's conversation was going to be combative at best, and thought the fewer people present the better.

"I ought to wrangle an introduction to Lloyd Channing myself," Beverly mused aloud. "Lord knows I could sure use a rich man."

"Money is nice, but wealth isn't nearly as important as character," Leigh responded. "In fact, wealth is probably the least important attribute a man could have."

Beverly gave Leigh's hair a final rinse, wrapped her head in a towel, and eased her up into a sitting position. "That may be easy for you to say, Ms. Bowman, but for me, a man would have to be Max Beadle's twin for money not to be enough."

Leigh readily grasped Beverly's use of the portly slob who owned the pool hall as an example, but she could not agree. "It looks as though you do well here, and because you can take care of yourself, you ought to be able to follow your heart rather than choose a man simply for security."

Beverly laughed as she walked Leigh back to her station. "I've followed my heart too often, or I'd not still be here in Mirasol cutting hair. No thanks. Give me a man who can provide a few luxuries, and I'll set my sights on him. Say, maybe you could help me meet Lloyd Channing. I cut men's hair, too. Tell him he's in desperate need of a trim and ought not to leave town without one, will you?"

"Wouldn't that be a little too obvious?"

"Who cares? It just might work."

Leigh gave up the effort to influence Beverly, and sat back in her chair. Despite her apprehensions, the beautician gave her a superb cut, and she went back to city hall knowing she looked her best. She didn't see anyone working at Jonathan's and hoped the fire department had completed their investigation. She believed the fire was no more than a tragic accident, but even if Jonathan finally accepted that, it would be far too late for them.

Miguel took a sip of his beer, and leaned back against the bar. Two of his friends were shooting pool, and he was waiting to play the winner. To get ready for the evening crowd, Max Beadle was working his way around the room emptying the ashtrays into a dented galvanized pail.

Miguel had spent countless afternoons there, but this was the first time he had really looked at the dingy bar and he didn't like what he saw. It had been several years since Max had had the place painted, and a greasy line encircled the room halfway up the wall where men leaned back and their dirty hair rubbed against it. The tobacco-colored carpet had wrinkles big enough to trip a sober man. Many a drunk had gone sprawling and been left to lie where he had fallen. Dried puddles of drool marked those places with dark stains.

Country Western music blared on the jukebox, and Miguel had never liked the nasal wailing. He had simply tolerated it, just as he tolerated everything else in his life. Almost everything, he corrected absently. Bonnie had been the single exception. She had bubbled with an intoxicating exuberance, and lit the times they spent together with a pure joy he feared he would never find again.

Mirasol was full of pretty girls, but Bonnie was the only one he had wanted to marry. With her he would have had a chance for something better than the life his father and mother had known. Without her, he couldn't foresee anything good happening to him.

Near tears, he gulped down the last of his beer, and then went over to the rack holding the pool cues. He grabbed one, and drawing a bead on the jukebox, walked over, and drove the end of the cue right through the glass. When that didn't stop the dreadful noise, he hit it again, and a third time. Glass showered around him, and with a wrenching screech, Tanya Tucker was silenced in mid-note.

Miguel's friends rushed toward him, while the few others wasting away the afternoon just tipped back their chairs, and laughed. Max Beadle wasn't amused, however, and made a dash for the bar where he kept a loaded forty-five handy. As a warning, he put his first shot through a ceiling already peppered with holes, then propped his chubby arms on the bar, and aimed for Miguel.

"You're not leaving without paying for damages!" he yelled.

Miguel turned, gripped the pool cue like a javelin, and hurled it toward the barkeep. Max ducked, and the cue shattered the mirror behind the bar. Miguel and his friends ran out the door before Max fought himself out of the falling glass. By the time he reached the door, Miguel's silver truck was tearing around the corner, and his friends were nowhere in sight.

"Son of a bitch!" Max screamed, and bounded back inside the pool hall to call the police.

"Focus," Leigh repeated softly before applying a sunny coral lipstick. She was convinced the secret to success was remaining focused on the task at hand, and that evening, she intended to help Eli convince Lloyd Channing an eight-story complex would be totally out of place in the valley. It was purely an aesthetic decision in her mind, and she did not care what the financial considerations might be and neither did Eli.

She dressed in a slate gray suit that conveyed her commitment to business in no uncertain terms, added gold button earrings, and after a final glance in the mirror, was ready to go. She concentrated on the evening traffic as she turned the corner at Signal Street onto Mirasol Avenue, but it was difficult not to glance toward what was left of Jonathan's house as she drove by. He had made his choice. Now she was forced to make hers. She gripped the steering wheel in a confident grasp and checked her watch. It was already a quarter to seven, and wanting to be on time, she speeded up as she left town and turned onto highway 150. The sun glared in her eyes, and she lowered the visor. Most of the residents whose houses were scattered along the road had already returned home and the traffic was light. Once she left the residential section behind and reached the avocado groves, she was alone on the highway until a silver Chevy truck pulled out of a side road and began to follow her closely.

The sun's reflection off the truck's windshield prevented her from seeing the driver, but when he came within inches of her back bumper, Leigh had a very good idea who he was. She increased her speed, and tried to recall how much farther it was to the entrance of the Keene Ranch. The Chevy stayed right on her tail.

"Damn it, Miguel. I've no time for your games," she cursed under her breath. She pressed down on the accelerator and her Camaro surged forward, but again the Chevy truck kept pace. She pulled over to the edge of her lane, lowered her window, and waved for him to go around. He didn't respond immediately, but after she had waved him on another time, he finally pulled out into the roadway.

The height of the cab prevented her from seeing his expression as he came alongside her, but she was certain he had to be snarling furiously. She just wanted him gone, but in the next instant, he made a sharp turn to the right and swung the side of the truck into her car, nearly slamming her right off the road into the avocado trees. Had Leigh not been so alert, she would have crashed into the grove, but she caught the wheel and hung on. She tried to increase her speed in another attempt to escape him, but he bumped her again.

"Miguel!" she screamed, but he couldn't hear her over their engines' roar. She didn't even consider stopping for fear he would stop with her and yank her right out of her car. She slowed down, but he slowed with her, and when she tried to trick him by flooring it to lurch ahead, the Chevy truck went flying on right beside her. They were nearing Eli's, but Leigh knew she couldn't make the turn through the arched entrance at the speed she was traveling.

The trees were a blur on her right, but she remembered the thickness of their trunks and didn't want to risk wrapping her car around one. She had been too tolerant with Miguel, she fumed, and look what it had gotten her. "I'll have you arrested for this, you bastard," she yelled. All she had to do was hold on until she reached Eli's, and then she would be calling the shots.

She thought the ranch was just up ahead, and the Chevy slowed, allowing her to pull away slightly. Then just as the road made a gentle curve, the massive truck came at her again, jolting into the side of the Camaro with the greatest force yet. Knocked sideways by the impact, Leigh lost control of the wheel, and as she skidded off the road, the tires caught on the edge of the asphalt and the sleek car flipped into the air.

Leigh screamed as the car left the road. She was wearing her seat belt, and it yanked her back into place as the car rolled in the air and came down on the roof. It scraped a shower of sparks as it slid along the edge of the highway, then with a wrenching dive, it nosed off the road and careened into the ditch.

Her window had been down, and the car filled with flying dirt as it tunneled several yards along the ditch before finally coming to rest. Dangling upside down, and choking on dust, Leigh hung onto the steering wheel. She had cut her forehead and she could feel blood running into her hair. Dizzy and nauseated, her first thought was that she couldn't meet with Lloyd Channing looking such a mess. Too badly shaken to release her seat belt, she looked out toward the road, hoping for help, but all she saw was the Chevy truck's tires.

"Oh God," she whispered. Her Camaro had stalled, but the truck's motor was idling with a deep rumble. Miguel hadn't gotten out, and Leigh didn't know which would be worst: to be abandoned for some passing motorist to find, or to have Miguel crawl into the wreckage of her once beautiful car. Both choices struck her as bad until she realized Miguel had clearly intended to harm her, and that he might very well wish to finish the job if he found her alive.

Her seat belt was cutting into her collarbone, and she was so sick to her stomach she feared she would vomit, but she closed her eyes, went limp, and hoped that she looked dead. She hadn't heard Miguel leave the truck, but thinking she might have been unconscious a minute or two, she didn't dare open her eyes. She waited, praying he would leave, but the faint odor of gasoline pierced her thoughts like a scream.

If her car caught fire, she'd die as quickly as Ron Tate in a horrible blast as the gas tank exploded. She lost all sense of composure then, and began to scream for Miguel. He had to get her out, he just had to, but as she shrieked his name a second time, he gunned the truck's motor, made a wide U-turn, and sped away.

Eli slopped the Bourbon over the side of the glass onto the table. "What was that?"

"What was what?" Lloyd asked. He was sorting the sketches he had brought, and continued arranging them on the coffee table.

"It sounded like metal scraping the road." The awful sound echoed in his mind, sending an anxious chill rolling through him. "I don't like this. Excuse me."

"An accident?" Lloyd called after him, but he wasn't sufficiently concerned to follow.

It was almost seven, and Eli prayed he would find Leigh climbing the steps, but Lloyd's Jaguar was the only car parked in the circular drive and there was no sign of her. It was more than a hundred yards out to the highway, but he sprinted the whole way. He saw the Camaro, or what was left of it, as soon as he burst through the stone arch.

Several of his men were already at the crash scene, and from the frantic way they were throwing dirt on the car, he feared the danger of fire was intense. He reached the accident scene just as they pulled Leigh through the open window. That her hair was matted with blood terrified him, but he reached out to take her in his arms. She looked up at him, her glance confused, then her eyelids fluttered, and she slid into unconsciousness.

"José, run to the house and call for an ambulance," Eli ordered. "Everyone else, get away from the car." He backed away, hoping the threat of fire was over, but not wanting to take the risk that it wasn't. A driver passing by stopped to help, and then another, but he was afraid he might already have exacerbated Leigh's injuries by carrying her in his arms and waited for the ambulance to come rather than risk transporting her in a car.

He sat down at the side of the road with Leigh drapped across his lap, and held his handkerchief to her forehead to stem the flow of blood, but the gash was long and deep. He kept his fingertips pressed against the pulse in her throat and counted the slow steady beats to keep himself from becoming hysterical. He could hear the sirens on the emergency vehicles from a long way off, but he was frantic with worry by the time the paramedics arrived in the ambulance. A fire truck and police car followed. The firemen would rinse away the gasoline spill, but Eli had forgotten the risk of fire.

As the paramedics left the ambulance, he called to them. "She was conscious when we pulled her from the wreck. Is that a good sign?"

The paramedics nodded, then eased Leigh onto a stretcher before taking her vital signs. Eli stood out of their way, and tried to make some sense of the grim scene. "Did any of you see anything?" he called to his men, but like him, they had heard only the sound of the crash, and come running. The twilight was growing dim, and Eli would not leave Leigh to search the road for clues, but he could not believe that she had simply run off the highway on her own.

She had fallen asleep while he was driving yesterday it was true, but he knew she was eager to meet with Lloyd Channing again and doubted she would have dozed off today. "This doesn't make any sense," he told the police officers. "Cars don't just fly off the road."

"Maybe she swerved to miss a rabbit or squirrel," one of the policemen replied. "Women do that all the time."

Eli followed as the paramedics lifted Leigh into the back of the ambulance. "I'm coming with you," he announced and he climbed right in. As they started into town, the siren again blaring, he finally remembered Lloyd Channing, and hoped he enjoyed the excellent dinner his cook had prepared. He felt sick to his stomach, and clasped his hands tightly so the paramedic tending Leigh wouldn't notice how badly he was shaking.

Eli didn't know Leigh well, but he could not even imagine her being so startled by the sudden appearance of a squirrel that she would lose control of her car. "Perhaps there was another car involved in the accident," he blurted out. "One that refused to stop."

"The Camaro will be towed into town and checked," the paramedic assured him. "If there's paint from another vehicle on it, it can be identified. Are you all right, Mr. Keene?"

Eli shook his head. "Just take care of Leigh. I'll be fine." But the closer they got to the hospital the worse he felt. He could think of only one person who would want to harm Leigh, and that was Jonathan Reid. If the crazy bastard still blamed him and Leigh for burning down his house, then he should have come after him rather than running Leigh off the road.

"Oh God," he moaned. When they reached the hospital, he waited until Leigh had been taken into the emergency room, and then he called the police to make certain they roped off the crash site. He requested a thorough search of the accident scene at first light, and that their forensic experts examine Leigh's Camaro for evidence of attempted murder. For the moment, it was all he could do, but if Jonathan had tried to kill Leigh, he wasn't going to wait for the legal system to exact justice. He intended to take it into his own hands and make it swift and lethal.

Sixteen

Jonathan burst through the emergency room doors of Mirasol's Community Hospital and rushed up to the desk. "The police told me Leigh Bowman is here. May I see her?"

The clerk had perfected a regretful look, used it to full advantage, and then suggested that Jonathan wait in the adjacent visitors' lounge. "Dr. Nelson will give you a full report on her condition just as soon as she can," she promised.

As Jonathan turned away from the desk, he saw Eli seated nearby but it wasn't until he was within a few feet of him that he realized the dark stains on his light blue shirt were Leigh's blood. It looked like a great deal of blood too, and he dove for a chair seconds before his legs gave out under him. "I was out jogging and saw the tow truck pull into George Culbert's with Leigh's Camaro. Can you tell me what happened?"

For a long moment, Eli simply regarded Jonathan with a blank stare, then he straightened up in his seat. If Jonathan had run Leigh off the road, then she would surely say so when she came to, so he kept his suspicions to himself for the time being. He couldn't resist needling Jonathan, though. He leaned forward slightly.

"I beg your pardon, were you talking to me? From what I recall of our last conversation, I didn't think we were still on speaking terms."

"We aren't," Jonathan assured him, "but I'm making an exception in Leigh's case. Now either you tell me what you know, or I'll beat it out of you right here where you'll have ready access to medical treatment when I'm finished."

Eli laughed easily at that surly threat, and sat back in his chair. "If you saw Leigh's car, you already know about as much as I do. She was coming to my place, but somehow landed upside down in a ditch."

Not nearly satisfied with that terse account, Jonathan pressed him for more. *"How* did she end up in the ditch?"

Eli's glance turned cold. "Suppose you tell me."

"I wasn't there!" Jonathan exclaimed, and the clerk at the desk put her finger to her lips to warn him to be quiet. "Damn it," he whispered. "Cut the cryptic innuendos and just tell me how you got covered in Leigh's blood."

Eli looked down, appeared to be shocked by the sorry state of his clothes, and then shrugged. "She cut her head."

"Does she need blood?"

Eli looked away. "This is the same woman you accused of burning down your house, Jonathan. Now you want to donate blood?"

Giving up on Eli, Jonathan stood and went back to the clerk. His legs still felt weak and he had to lean against the desk to remain upright. "Is Ms. Bowman going to need a transfusion?" he asked.

"That I wouldn't know, sir. Why don't you just wait in the lounge, and the doctor will speak with you when she can."

The lounge held only a dozen chairs, and that Eli occupied one of them made the whole area unappealing, but Jonathan couldn't leave. He was forced to return to his seat. Mirasol had only a small hospital where local physicians delivered babies, and treated heart attack victims. He had no idea whether or not the emergency room staff was any good.

"Is this the best place for Leigh to be?" he asked Eli.

"Probably not, but it was the closest. They'll transfer her if there's a need."

"Besides cutting her head, did she have any broken bones or internal injuries?"

Eli gave another lackadaisical shrug. "I'm not licensed to practice medicine. Why are you asking me?"

"Christ!" Jonathan slumped back in the plastic chair. The fire department still hadn't turned up a single clue that pointed to arson, but he wasn't about to retract his accusations. He crossed his arms over his chest, dug his fingers into his armpits, and stared at the floor until a policeman entered carrying a black handbag and pair of pumps he recognized as Leigh's. Rather than taking them to the desk, the officer carried them over to Eli, who placed them on the chair beside his.

"We didn't find any skid marks, Mr. Keene, but we'll be able to see more in the morning. Maybe by then Ms. Bowman will be able to tell us what happened herself."

"I hope so. Thanks." As the policeman left, Eli picked up one of Leigh's shoes. It was a size five, and looked no bigger than a child's to him. He caressed the soft black leather, and then set it aside. Had Jonathan not been observing him, he would have opened Leigh's purse, and sorted through the contents just to feel close to her. Wearing her blood didn't provide any comfort, but he didn't want to go home and change. He would have to call someone to come get him, he realized, and they could just as easily bring him a clean shirt, but he just sat there, too frightened for Leigh to make the call.

Eli's emotions were so easy to read, Jonathan could no longer ignore them. "You really care about Leigh, don't you?"

Eli nodded. "Far too much to sleep with her and then call her vile names in front of half the town."

"I didn't call her any vile names," Jonathan argued, but he knew Eli was right. He had shouted rude insults, which was just the same. He had seen the betrayal so clearly on Sunday, but now, well, now he just knew Leigh had been hurt and he was sick with worry. He kept thinking about Princess Grace. He thought she had died as a result of a stroke rather than from the auto accident she had been in, but she was dead all the same.

He got up and began to pace. He was still shaky, but kept moving until an attractive young woman who didn't look old enough to have graduated from medical school finally appeared. She had thick auburn hair knotted atop her head, bright brown eyes, and a reassuring smile. She sent him an inquiring glance, and he followed her into the lounge and sat down to listen to her report. She wore a name tag which read, Marsha Nelson, M.D.

"Ms. Bowman needed more than twenty stitches to close the gash in her scalp," the physician explained softly, "but her hair will hide the scar so she'll have no permanent reminder of the accident. X-rays don't show any injuries other than a concussion, but she has some bad bruises, and we'll keep her here a couple of days just to make certain she's all right. There's no reason for either of you to stay here any longer. Come back tomorrow afternoon during visiting hours."

"I want to see her tonight," Jonathan insisted.

"She's asleep," Dr. Nelson replied.

"I don't care. I just want to see her."

"So do I," Eli added. "If she's asleep, there can't be any harm in us just looking in on her." He rose intending to follow the physician.

Marsha Nelson stood as Jonathan came up out of his chair. Tall and slim, she wasn't intimidated by his size. "We respect our patient's privacy here. Would either of you gentlemen want her looking in on you if you'd been in an accident?"

"Yes!" the two men responded in unison.

"I'd be flattered rather than offended," Eli explained. "If I collapse from an anxiety attack out here, then you'll have two patients rather than one. Please let me see her."

Because Eli was so well known in Mirasol, the physician thought she could trust him. "I suppose you're also a close personal friend of Ms. Bowman's?" she asked Jonathan.

"I sure am."

Somewhat amused by the men's devotion to Leigh, Marsha allowed them to follow her into the treatment area, but she remained with them. They had no other emergency patients that night, and with Leigh sound asleep, she could not see any real harm in it. Even in the disheveled state she had met Leigh, she could readily understand why her patient was so popular.

Jonathan had not expected Leigh to look as though she had been beaten, but she had a black eye, and a long bruise crossed her neck and collarbone where the seat belt had caught hold of her. She was discreetly covered by a blanket, but still looked all too vulnerable. Her playful striptease under the pepper tree was still vivid in his memory, and he didn't want this sad image to replace it. He took her hand, and squeezed her fingers lightly.

Eli studied Jonathan rather than gazing at Leigh. For a man who quite possibly had wanted her dead, Jonathan was surprisingly concerned with her welfare. Leigh was sleeping peacefully, and reassured, Eli turned away, but after thanking Dr. Nelson for her kindness, he waited for Jonathan by the desk.

"Not that you'll take my word for it, but Leigh didn't have anything to do with the fire at your place—and neither did I," Eli told him. "I can understand why you'd accuse me of arson, but not her. She didn't deserve that any more than she deserved today's accident. If you're half the man some of the people in this town believe you to be, you'll do everything you can to make it up to her."

"You're right," Jonathan replied crossly. "I won't take your word for anything."

Giving up in disgust, Eli crossed to the lounge, picked up Leigh's shoes and purse, and then went to the pay telephone to call home. He had completely forgotten about Lloyd Channing, and was surprised to find the developer was still there. He couldn't bring himself to reschedule their meeting until he knew for certain that Leigh could join them, but he did extend his apologies for leaving him so abruptly that night. When he got off the phone, Jonathan called to him from the lounge.

"I'm not leaving," Jonathan told him. "Leigh might not wake until morning, but I want to be here when she does."

Eli briefly considered asking the police to post a guard by Leigh's room, but quickly decided to keep an eye on Jonathan himself. "Then I'm staying too," he announced, and he returned to his seat where this time he kept Leigh's purse cradled in his lap.

When Leigh awakened in a private room, she ached all over, and her head felt as though it had been split in two. White miniblinds at the window filtered the morning sun, and threw narrow bands of light across her bed. She didn't recognize her surroundings, but hoped she hadn't lost more than a single night.

She turned her head slowly in time with the throbbing pain, and found both Jonathan and Eli slumped in chairs along the wall. It didn't surprise her that Eli was there, but Jonathan was certainly out of place. A wave of dizziness swept through her, and she had to close her eyes quickly. The next time she opened them, Jonathan was standing beside her bed. She felt the warmth of his hand on hers, and was thoroughly confused.

"Good morning," he whispered, trying not to wake Eli. "How do you feel?"

"Half dead," Leigh answered truthfully. "Is that what it takes for you to care?"

Jonathan was encouraged that she felt well enough to insult him, but it was also a disappointment. He squeezed her hand slightly but her fingers remained limp. "No," he assured her. Her eyes were glazed with pain, and he pressed the call button to summon the nurse. When the woman arrived, she woke Eli, and tried to hustle them both out of the room.

"Just a minute," Eli said, and he went to Leigh's bedside. "I won't ask how you feel because I know it can't be good. Can you remember what happened?"

Leigh pulled her hand from Jonathan's to take Eli's but even as sore as she was, she noticed a profound difference. Jonathan's touch held a familiar strength, while Eli's grasp was tentative and cool. She knew it was unfair to compare the two men, but it had come as second nature.

"It was Miguel Fuentes," she responded in an anguished whisper. "He forced me off the road. He came back, but just watched. I could smell the gasoline seeping out all around me, and called to him, but he drove away."

Huge tears welled up in Leigh's eyes, and Eli leaned down to kiss her. "God help me," he exclaimed as he straightened up. "You told me Miguel had been obnoxious, but I never dreamed he could be brutal."

"That's enough, Mr. Keene," the nurse cautioned. "Can't you see that you're upsetting her?"

The solidly built woman outweighed Eli by a good thirty pounds, and he backed away from the bed rather than wrestle with her. "I'll send the police after Miguel," he promised Leigh. "I'm just sorry I didn't do it sooner."

As Eli strode out the door, Jonathan followed right on his heels. "I didn't catch all of that, but if Miguel had been bothering Leigh, why hadn't you fired him?"

Eli had no intention of justifying his actions to Jonathan, and didn't dignify his question with a response. He had had one of his men drop off clean clothes and his Porsche, but the hospital was in the same block as the police station and there was no need to drive. When Jonathan came up beside him, he simply ignored him and increased his pace. He reached the front door of the police station first, but Jonathan was only a step behind.

Eli hurriedly explained to the officer at the desk that Leigh Bowman had identified Miguel Fuentes as the cause of her accident. "He has to know he can't get away with it, but I don't want him taken at gunpoint. I'll talk him into giving himself up, but I'd like to have a patrol car follow me out to the ranch with a couple of your best men to bring him in."

Sergeant Randall had curly red hair and a thick red mustache that looked as though they had come from a child's kit of disguises, but he went about his duties with a deadly serious demeanor. "There's no need of that, Mr. Keene. Fuentes is already in custody for vandalizing the pool hall yesterday. He's expect-

ing you to come and bail him out. It looks as though he's going
to be sadly disappointed."

"When did you arrest him?"

"Must have been about seven this morning. We should have
had him yesterday, but he gave us the slip. We'll send a detective
right over to the hospital to take Ms. Bowman's statement. Do
you want to see Fuentes?"

Eli was so angry he could scarcely contain himself. He
glanced toward Jonathan, and saw the same fierce determination
etched on his features that he knew must mark his own. "Yeah.
I'd like to see him alone for about ten minutes. Can you arrange
it?"

The sergeant readily understood Eli's intention, and shook
his head. "No, sir. The chief doesn't allow any kind of private
interrogations."

"Then I don't want to see him," Eli swore. "I've carried his
whole family for years, and that he would repay me like this is
unconscionable. I thought I knew him, but not after this. Send
that detective over quick, will you? I don't want anyone else
bailing Miguel out before a charge of attempted murder can be
filed."

"Don't worry, Mr. Keene. Fuentes isn't going anywhere."

As they left the police station, Jonathan opened the heavy
plate glass door for Eli. "Leigh mentioned Miguel once. I got
the impression that she liked him."

"Well, he sure as hell didn't like her, did he?" Eli grumbled
darkly.

"Apparently not, but running her off the road is a bit extreme."

Eli came to an abrupt halt. "So was burning down your
house, but that hasn't occurred to you yet, has it?"

Jonathan had a slight advantage over Eli in height, and used
it as he swept him with a menacing glare. "I wouldn't put anything past you." He spun on his heel before Eli could reply and
beat him back to the hospital. It was plain Leigh wasn't thrilled
to have him there, but it was where he needed to be. Awful

things tended to occur in threes, and he was afraid all he could do was sit and wait for the victim of the next catastrophe to be carried in on a stretcher.

Joe Wheeler had been a detective for six years, but still didn't own a suit that fit his lanky frame. His bony wrists dangled below his sleeves like knotted rope, while the cuffs of his baggy pants pooled out over his shoes. With slicked back hair, a sharp, jutting nose, and small, close-set eyes, he resembled a hatchet in profile, but despite his comically severe appearance, he had received numerous commendations for the excellence of his work.

Standing beside Leigh's bed, pencil and notebook in hand, he tilted his head, and listened attentively to her account of the accident. As he asked questions, his voice had a gravely catch to it, but his manner was relaxed until he had heard Leigh's description several times. His attitude shifted then, and he honed in on a detail that perplexed him.

"You're positive the truck belonged to the Keene Ranch?" he asked.

Leigh knew she had said so quite emphatically but attempted to keep her impatience out of her response. "Yes. I recognized the truck when Miguel first began to follow me. Then when he pulled alongside, I could read the name of the ranch clearly."

"Clearly," the detective repeated as he wrote himself an additional note. "I know this is difficult for you, Ms. Bowman, but try and tell me when you first caught sight of Miguel Fuentes."

Leigh licked her lips and took a deep breath to stave off her rising panic. Eli had told her Miguel had already been arrested so she knew he could not hurt her again, but that he had done so once still terrified her. Forcing herself to recall the attack, she tried to answer Detective Wheeler's question accurately.

The sun's glare on the truck's windshield had hidden Miguel's face when he had driven up behind her so it hadn't been then. Nor had it been when he had come up beside her, she realized.

"We were driving toward the setting sun," she explained, "and the height of the Chevy's cab made it impossible for me to see inside, but it was Miguel. He nearly ran into me Monday night. I saw him clearly then, so I recognized the truck, and how erratically he drives."

"But you didn't actually see his face?"

The pain and fright of the crash was far sharper than Leigh's memory for detail, and she finally had to concede the point. "No, but he'd threatened me, and no one else from the Keene Ranch had any reason to harm me."

"So it had to be Miguel Fuentes?" Wheeler stressed.

"I have absolutely no doubt of it," Leigh replied. "He wanted me dead."

Joe closed his notebook, and straightened his tie. "I may need to ask a few more questions later. I know keeping the details of the accident fresh in your mind will be painful, but try and go over the sequence as often as you can so you'll be able to respond correctly at the trial."

"I won't forget," Leigh promised.

When the detective left Leigh's room, he went down to the lounge to find Eli. "I have a question or two if you don't mind, Mr. Keene."

Eli was on his feet in an instant, while Jonathan remained seated and simply regarded the rawboned detective with a curious gaze. "Several of my men reached the accident scene before I did," he began.

"Yes. I have all that," Wheeler said. "I need to know how many of those silver Chevy trucks you own."

"I've got four of them."

"Who drives them?"

"I do sometimes. Miguel uses one fairly often for errands. In fact, he treats it as though it were his. The other two get constant use by the other men. The ranch is large, and we need transportation to get around it easily. Some years I've had as many as six trucks, but right now I'm down to four."

"Where are they parked when they're not in use?"

"They're out by the barn. We do our own maintenance on the trucks and tractors, just the way the Army runs a motor pool, and the barn doubles as our garage."

"And the keys?"

"They're left in the ignition, or placed on the rack just inside the barn door."

The detective surveyed his notes, and seemed satisfied. "I'll need you to call out to the ranch and tell your men not to drive any of the trucks until we've had a chance to go over them thoroughly. We'll get it done today so it won't be a hardship for you."

"I appreciate that, but isn't Miguel's truck the only one you need to see?"

Joe Wheeler had noted just how closely Jonathan Reid was following their conversation, and did not care to reveal anything more in front of him. "Step over here, will you, Mr. Keene?" The detective moved ahead of Eli, and then turned his back toward the lounge.

"We may have a problem," he confided in a hushed whisper.

"What sort of a problem?" Eli drew himself up to his full height. "I don't want this case to be thrown out of court on some trivial technicality. If you need to impound the blasted truck, go ahead. I'd rather get along without it than risk your blowing the case."

Joe pursed his lips thoughtfully. "It's not the truck that worries me, Mr. Keene. It's the driver. She didn't see him."

Eli shot Jonathan a quick glance. "What do you mean she didn't see him?"

"Just what I said," the detective repeated. "She got a real good look at the truck, and swears it came from the Keene Ranch, but she can't identify the driver. Besides Miguel Fuentes, does Ms. Bowman have any other enemies that you know of?"

"Yeah. Jonathan Reid, and he's sitting right behind you in the lounge."

Wheeler glanced over his shoulder. The whole town knew

what Jonathan Reid thought of Eli and Leigh. "Does he still believe you and Ms. Bowman burned down his house?"

Eli responded with a derisive snort. "So he claims."

"Then he had a motive." Wheeler smiled to himself, thanked Eli for his cooperation, and turned to approach Jonathan. "I wonder if you can give me a bit of help, Mr. Reid."

Jonathan stood to face him. "Sure. What do you need?"

"Ms. Bowman's accident occurred about five to seven last night. Where were you then?"

Astonished by what the detective's question implied, Jonathan stepped back slightly. "You've got to be kidding. I didn't have anything to do with Leigh's accident."

"I'm glad to hear it. Now, where were you at 6:55?"

Jonathan jammed his hands into his hip pockets. "I was at home, or what's left of it, getting ready to go for a run."

"But you weren't actually out running where someone might have seen you going by?"

At best Jonathan had a tenuous hold on his temper, and even that faint restraint began to slip away. "No. I was probably tying my shoelaces about then, and that doesn't usually draw much of a crowd."

Joe Wheeler closed his notebook with a careless flip of his wrist. "Right. I understand. Thank you. I'll talk to you again if need be."

Jonathan waited until the detective had pushed through the hospital doors, and then confronted Eli. "That was low even for you," he challenged.

"What are you raving about now?"

"I'm not the one doing the raving," Jonathan shot right back at him. It had been years since one of their arguments had come to blows, but he sure wanted to punch Eli in the face now and smear his too perfect features all the way around to the back of his head. "Why did the detective need to know where I was at the time of the accident?"

Eli debated a long moment, and then told him Leigh hadn't actually seen Miguel Fuentes. When Jonathan merely appeared confused rather than alarmed, he elaborated. "He asked about enemies, and I thought you qualified. It had to have been Miguel, though. The truck belonged to the ranch, and none of my other men would have gone after Leigh."

"Yeah? Where were you when she landed in the ditch?"

"I was with Lloyd Channing. Do you want a notarized statement from him?"

"Gentlemen, please," Dr. Nelson urged as she joined them. The previous evening she had been clad in the shapeless green shirt and pants the hospital provided, but today she was wearing a dress in a delicious orange sherbet shade topped by a lab coat. With her glossy auburn hair caught at her nape with an orange bow, she looked stunning. "If you can't keep your voices down, I'll have to ask you to leave."

Jonathan and Eli regarded each other with sullen stares. "I'm going home to clean up," Jonathan finally announced. "I'll be back when visiting hours begin."

"Take your time. I doubt that Leigh will miss you if you don't make it back," Eli replied. For an instant, he hoped Jonathan would swing at him, because he sure as hell wanted an excuse to hit him back, but Jonathan just sneered, and turned away.

Intrigued by the men's hostility, Marsha Nelson smiled knowingly when Eli glanced toward her. "I'm sure Ms. Bowman must be deeply flattered to have two such attractive men fighting over her, but please don't disrupt the hospital routine with your arguments, or I'll have to ban you both."

Dr. Nelson was a beauty, which made following her orders only marginally less difficult for Eli. Her perfume was light and subtle, but horribly distracting. "I'm sorry if we were too loud," he apologized, but he gave no promise to behave in the future. "I'd appreciate it if you and the nurses would keep a close eye on Leigh while she's here. I have to go home for a while, but perhaps I'll see you again later."

"Yes. It's possible." Marsha watched him walk out before she turned away, but as long as Eli Keene was prepared to fight

Jonathan Reid over Leigh Bowman, she was definitely going to stay out of his way.

Adelita Fuentes was waiting for Eli when he got home. A petite woman who wore her long, dark hair in a single plait, she grabbed hold of his arm as soon as he left his car. "Mr. Keene, please. You know my Miguel is a good boy. He would never harm anyone. I know he made some trouble at the pool hall, but that's a small thing. He would never cause an accident. Please help me get him out of jail."

Eli pushed away from her grasp. "Adelita, please. If there's no evidence to link Miguel to the accident, the police will quickly release him. If there is, then I'm warning you now that I won't play any part in his defense."

Adelita's dark eyes widened in horror. "How can you believe him guilty? You have known him his whole life."

That was what really rankled Eli. He had trusted Miguel, and that mistake had nearly cost Leigh her life. "Maybe none of us really knew him," Eli replied. He left Adelita on the porch and went on inside. As he entered his room, the bed was tempting, but he did want to observe whatever procedures the police used for examining his trucks and walked right to the bathroom. He did not feel any better after a shower and shave, but trusted his appearance was much improved.

By the time he reached the barn, the police had arrived. He walked up to Detective Wheeler, who was quizzing José Blanco, the mechanic who kept all the Keene vehicles running well. José gestured toward the line of trucks.

"You see, one, two, three, four. They are numbered, and always parked in the same spaces."

"Miguel Fuentes usually drives number one?" Wheeler asked.

"Yes, sir. That is Miguel's. He washes it every week and treats it like his own."

Eli walked around to look at the passenger side of the first

Chevy expecting to find evidence of a collision, but there wasn't a single dent or scrape of white paint anywhere on number one. "Are you sure Miguel was driving this truck yesterday?" he called to José.

José gestured helplessly. "All the trucks were out yesterday. It's possible he took another, but I doubt it."

Detective Wheeler frowned pensively as he approached Eli. "I took a good look at the truck, too. It's clean. It's number three that draws my attention. Check that one out."

Eli moved down the line and sure enough, the telltale streaks of white paint that he had expected to find on number one began at the fender, and extended clear across the passenger door. He reached out, but not wanting to risk destroying the evidence, jerked back his hand. "Son of a bitch," he cursed. "Miguel obviously cared more about his damn truck than Leigh, and used this one to run her off the road."

"It's possible," Wheeler agreed, "but your mechanic says he thinks number one was the only one out when he quit at 5:30."

"So what? Miguel must have come home after that. Swapped trucks, and gone after Leigh."

The detective looked over at a shiny new tractor nearby. "You take real good care of your equipment here, don't you, Mr. Keene?"

"Of course. It would wear out much too quickly otherwise."

Joe Wheeler nodded. "That it would. I try and do my work with the same care. We're taking fingerprints from inside your Chevy number three, and a sample of the white paint from the scrapes to make certain it matches Ms. Bowman's Camaro, but for now, we've got nothing to place Miguel Fuentes in it."

First, Leigh had been unable to positively identify Miguel, and now there was a question about the truck. Eli feared what he had considered an airtight case was springing more leaks than the conscientious detective could plug. His stomach tightened painfully and he realized he had not eaten in a long while.

"Look, yesterday Miguel went on a rampage at the pool hall, which is a pretty clear indication of a foul mood. Then he went after Leigh. It would be just like him to switch trucks, too. Maybe he was trying to throw the blame onto someone else rather than merely protecting his truck from damage, but he's your man, detective. He has to be."

"Granted, we've got a dead jukebox, a young woman in the hospital, and a truck with some suspicious scrapes, but the only eye witnesses were at the pool hall, Mr. Keene. We can charge Miguel for the ruckus at Max Beadle's, but that's it. I'd be happy to arrest your Chevy number three, but no judge is going to believe it caused Ms. Bowman's accident by itself."

Incensed by that ridiculous taunt, Eli poked the detective in the chest. "Interrogate everyone on the place. Find a witness, but don't you dare release Miguel just because he's a hell of a lot smarter than you are and switched trucks!" Eli walked off cursing the justice system for protecting criminals rather than victims, but if he had to pull every string he held in Mirasol, he wasn't going to allow Miguel Fuentes back on the streets.

Seventeen

Bonnie tiptoed into Leigh's room carrying a bouquet of delicate multicolored sweet peas. She set the vase down on the bedside table, and then stepped back when Leigh opened her eyes. "I didn't mean to wake you."

Leigh smiled wanly and sat up. Her head still ached, but she was getting used to it. "I was just resting. Thank you for the flowers. They're lovely. Can you stay a minute?"

Grateful for the invitation, Bonnie pulled up a chair. "I was afraid you wouldn't want to see me. Is it true that you're blaming Miguel for your accident?"

Leigh had expected that question, but didn't feel well enough to debate the issue. "Yes. I know you don't want to believe it, but it's true."

"It just can't be," Bonnie argued convincingly.

Leigh's mouth was dry, and she took a sip of water before replying. "Look at me. It happened."

Squirming in her chair, Bonnie sent a trembling hand through her tangled curls, then adjusted her hoop earrings. "I wasn't home last night to notice that you didn't get in. When did the accident happen?"

Leigh feared Bonnie would repeat everything she said to Miguel, who would quickly weave the information into a tight alibi, and refuse to supply any details. "I don't think we ought to discuss this, Bonnie. The police are still investigating, and I don't want to confuse things in any way."

Bonnie scooted to the edge of her chair, then smoothed her

flowing skirt over her knees. Her nails were polished in an iridescent fuchsia that clashed with the pale earth tones of her floral skirt and sweater. "Are you worried that I'll tip Miguel?"

Projecting her usual naïvete, Bonnie appeared sincerely pained by that possibility, but Leigh remained cautious. "Perhaps not intentionally, but it could happen. That wouldn't be fair to either of us, or to Miguel, either."

Bonnie's shoulders sagged dejectedly. "You don't trust me."

Leigh brought her hand to her temple in an attempt to massage away the pain but it continued to throb in a relentless cadence. "Let's not make trust an issue," she begged.

The librarian fought back tears. "Trust *is* the issue. Otherwise you won't know whom to believe, but whether you trust me or not, what I'm about to tell you is true. Miguel was with me last night," she confided in a breathless rush. "He called me about 5:00, but he was so excited he didn't make much sense. At first I thought he'd hit Max Beadle with a pool cue, but he swore he hadn't hurt anyone. Neither of us had had a moment's peace since that awful fight Monday night, and I was so happy that he had called me, I asked him to meet me at our favorite motel in Santa Barbara.

"When I closed the library at 6:00, I met him there. I wanted to talk, but we didn't get anything settled." Embarrassed that they hadn't, Bonnie pulled her lower lip through her teeth, then realized Leigh already understood why. "We made love all night, and came back to Mirasol in time to go to work this morning. Miguel intended to call Max and arrange to pay for the jukebox he broke.

"I heard about your accident soon after I opened the library. Then Max Beadle came in and bragged about how he'd had Miguel arrested. I was horrified, but thought Eli would surely put up his bail before noon. Then my mother called to tell me Miguel had run you off the road. She thought I'd want to know because we're neighbors. She still doesn't have any idea that I know Miguel."

Dizzy and weak, Leigh followed Bonnie's halting narrative

with growing alarm. Mirasol was only thirty miles from Santa Barbara, and if Bonnie's version of yesterday's events was accurate, then something was desperately wrong. "Wait a minute" she said. "Was Miguel already at the motel when you arrived?"

Bonnie grasped the sides of her chair and leaned forward slightly. "Yes. He'd parked around in back like he always does, but he met me out in front."

Of course, Leigh thought. They had always been discreet, and Miguel wouldn't have wanted anyone to see a truck from the Keene Ranch and place him there with Bonnie. She reached out to touch one of the fragile blossoms Bonnie had brought and tried not to panic. "What time was it?"

"It must have been 6:45, maybe a few minutes earlier. I was so worried about Miguel that I'd driven faster than I should have. He's always been so calm and steady, but he'd just lost it at Max's, and I knew it was all my fault. I'm the one who ought to pay for the jukebox he smashed, and I will. How much do you suppose they cost?"

"I've no idea." Leigh glanced up, saw Jonathan waiting at the door, and wondered how long he had been standing there. She vaguely recalled speaking with him earlier in the day, and knew she couldn't have been cordial. "You need to go over to the police station and ask for Detective Wheeler, Bonnie. Tell him exactly what you've just told me."

"Then the whole town will know we're lovers," Bonnie exclaimed, her eyes wide with dread.

Leigh brushed her complaint aside. "So what? The police will surely ask Miguel to account for his whereabouts yesterday. Then they'll check his story. Will the motel clerk remember what time you two checked in?"

Bonnie shook her head. "We take turns renting a room, and yesterday I went into the office alone. He didn't see Miguel."

"Then you're the only alibi Miguel has, Bonnie. Do you expect him to keep your affair a secret if it means he'll be charged with attempted murder?"

The color drained from Bonnie's face as she finally realized how serious the charges against Miguel truly were. "Don't the police need proof that he tried to harm you to hold him?"

"Someone driving one of Eli's trucks ran me off the road. I thought it was Miguel, but if he was with you, then it can't have been him. Perhaps Miguel will keep quiet to protect you, but you mustn't let him do it, Bonnie. Even if he means nothing to you, do it for yourself. Tell the truth, and stand up for him. Wouldn't you expect him to do the same for you?"

"There has to be another way," Bonnie argued in an anguished whisper. "Couldn't I just make an anonymous call?"

Leigh's body ached from head to toe, and even knowing she lacked the necessary stamina to break through Bonnie's stubborn resistance to do what was right, she kept trying. "What would you say, that Miguel was with you last night, but that you won't give your name? I doubt that you'd be believed."

Bonnie rose and as she moved her chair back toward the wall she noticed Jonathan standing by the door. She sent Leigh an anxious glance and then spoke to him. "How much did you hear?"

"Enough to know you need to speak with Detective Wheeler right away," Jonathan replied. "I'll go with you now if you like."

"No. This isn't a good time. I have to get back to the library." Bonnie darted past Jonathan, and hurried away.

"You shouldn't have been eavesdropping," Leigh scolded.

Jonathan entered the room, and not wanting to give someone else an opportunity to overhear their conversation, he took the precaution of closing the door. He noticed the sweet peas, and felt guilty he had come empty-handed. "I wanted to bring you some flowers too, but they reminded me so much of Ron that I couldn't buy any."

Leigh had found Bonnie's visit upsetting, but just looking at Jonathan caused a profound sense of loss. She didn't want to cry, but the threat of tears stung her eyes. "Because you miss him, or because you still believe that I caused his death?"

With her head swathed in gauze, and her right eye ringed with deep purple, Leigh looked every bit as forlorn as Jonathan felt. He moved closer to the bed, and took her hand. "I've really made a mess of things, haven't I?"

Leigh wondered if that were his idea of an apology. She didn't want him to get down on his knees and beg for forgiveness, but she would have preferred a more straightforward admission that he had misjudged her. Lacking the strength to demand it, she simply agreed. "Yes. That pretty well sums it up."

Leigh laced her fingers in Jonathan's, creating a fond clasp. "Things were perfect for us for a few hours on Sunday, but now I just feel hollow, as though my insides have been eaten away, while my head's ready to burst with painful thoughts. I can tell just by looking at you, that you don't feel any better."

Moved by her description of his mood, Jonathan leaned down to kiss her cheek, and then barely touching her fair skin, he slid his lips to the corner of her mouth. When she turned her head to meet him, he had to grab for the metal headboard to keep his balance. He kissed her with a sweet tenderness, and then drew away before the need for more overwhelmed him.

"I should have had more faith in you," he whispered.

Leigh raised her free hand to caress his cheek. Jonathan had made a truly horrendous mistake, and she did not want to compound their problems by making one of her own. "Love can't exist without trust," she replied, "and clearly you have none in me. That breaks my heart. Perhaps I expected too much too soon, but you must have expected nothing."

Jonathan pressed a kiss in her palm. "No. I expected everything to go wrong, just the way you did. My house meant the world to me, and when I saw it was gone, I thought I'd lost everything that mattered and struck out at you. It was a wonderful house and I'd filled it with beautiful things, but all I really miss is you."

Before Leigh could respond, Eli came bursting through the door, saw he was interrupting what appeared to be a tender scene, and cleared his throat loudly. "Your concussion must have been more serious than Dr. Nelson believes, or you'd not be holding hands with a man who regarded you with open contempt until you landed in the hospital." He nudged Jonathan out of his way, and placed a spectacular arrangement of red roses beside the little vase of sweet peas.

"Are you feeling better?" he asked.

"No," Leigh replied regretfully. She admired the roses and thanked him, but wished they had come from Jonathan. She described Bonnie's visit, and wasn't surprised when Eli responded angrily.

"She's lying," Eli swore. "She and Miguel might have spent the night together, but he couldn't possibly have been in Santa Barbara by 6:45."

Leigh waited for one of the men to take Bonnie's alibi a step further. Eli was adamant about Miguel's guilt, but Jonathan didn't condemn the young man. "What did the police find out at your place?" he asked.

Eli shrugged slightly. "Just what they'd expected. One of my trucks was involved."

When he didn't meet her gaze, Leigh became suspicious. "There's something you're not telling us."

Eli took Leigh's hand, and gave her fingers a reassuring squeeze. "Well, I suppose there is. It isn't the truck Miguel usually drives, but that doesn't mean he wasn't driving it yesterday."

Jonathan saw the doubt in Leigh's eyes, and voiced it. "What if Miguel was in Santa Barbara with Bonnie, Eli? Then who was driving that truck?"

Eli's expression filled with loathing and Leigh knew he was going to accuse Jonathan. "Don't say it," she begged. "It wasn't Jonathan."

"How do you know?" Eli countered. "You admit you didn't see the driver."

Leigh had noted the sorrow etched on Jonathan's features when he had first entered her room. Regret rather than guilt colored his every gesture, and she had no doubts about his motives. "I just know is all," she assured him. "I trust him."

"Well, he sure as hell doesn't trust you," Eli reminded her.

Dr. Nelson pushed the door open a crack. "Gentlemen, please. I can hear you way down the hall and you can't possibly be aiding Ms. Bowman's recovery. I'm going to have to ask you to leave."

"Do you want us to go?" Eli asked.

Jonathan was regarding her with a look of awkstruck wonder. Clearly he had not expected the vote of confidence she had just given him, but she had been sincere. "I'm awfully tired," Leigh answered. "Thank you again for the roses."

Eli would have kissed her good-bye, but with the physician and Jonathan observing so closely he was reluctant to display his affection. "Can I bring you anything? Dinner from the Marmalade, or something to read?"

"I don't feel well enough to eat or read, but thank you," she said.

Jonathan waited until Eli had stepped out into the hall, then leaned down to kiss Leigh. He wanted to thank her for believing in him, but didn't know how when he had been so quick to turn on her. "I'll talk with Bonnie," he promised instead, wanting to be useful.

Leigh reached out to catch his hand. "Wait. Give her time to go to the police on her own first."

"And if she doesn't?"

"Then I'll tell Detective Wheeler what she told me, so that he can check Miguel's alibi, but I want to give Bonnie the opportunity to do the right thing for a change."

"That's what really matters to you, isn't it?"

He seemed surprised, but Leigh could have made no other choice. "Of course. If Miguel didn't do this to me, then I don't want him sitting in jail just because he's the most likely suspect. I'd also like for Bonnie to finally find the courage to follow her heart."

Because Jonathan knew just how much courage that required, he promised Leigh that he would hold off speaking with Bonnie, but he did not intend to wait long. If the person who had caused her accident were still at large, then there could be no further delays in tracking him. As he left Leigh's room, Eli was speaking with Dr. Nelson, but Jonathan had heard all that he needed to from Leigh, and left quietly on his own.

Bonnie had gone to see Leigh on her lunch break, but she couldn't eat when she left her and went straight back to the library. Needing time to think, she sat down at her desk. There was some paperwork she had left unfinished that morning, but all she did now was shuffle the forms. She had known from her first date with Miguel just how much trouble an affair with him could cause her, but she had continued to see him anyway. It hadn't been simply for the incredibly good sex, either. It had been for the way he made her feel when they were together.

She had had plenty of boyfriends before him, but the others had all disappointed her in some important way. Most had not called again after she had slept with them a time or two. The few who had wanted more had not been her favorites, and she had soon grown bored and broken up with them. There were times she feared she expected too much from men, and others when she knew she hadn't asked nearly enough.

She had come a long way following her mother's advice, but she certainly couldn't go to her now. The library had gotten busy yesterday, and she hadn't had a chance to read more than a few pages of the relationship book she had chosen with Leigh. Now there wasn't time to study it for answers. She was on her own, and it was a very uncomfortable feeling.

Leigh had asked what Miguel would do, and Bonnie knew he would have gone straight to the police station had she been arrested, but she had waited for Eli to bail him out. After she had heard he had been implicated in Leigh's accident, she had convinced herself the police would soon discover they had the wrong man and again stayed away. She agonized over what Miguel must think of her. She knew the police wouldn't mistreat him, but being in jail couldn't possibly be a pleasant experience, especially for an innocent man.

Miguel had given her so much love, and she had treated him very badly in return. She knew what she would have to do, and near tears, asked the clerk to cover for her for the remainder of the afternoon and to lock up. She nearly ran down to the police station, but she was shaking so hard by the time she arrived, she feared they would think her hysterical.

"I need to see Detective Wheeler," she announced to the red-haired officer at the desk, and in a moment she was shown into one of the small rooms used for interviewing suspects or witnesses. The walls were painted a pale green, and the metal furniture was gray. There were no pictures on the walls, or magazines to look at while she waited, and the stale air smelled faintly of disinfectant. She soon wished she had accepted Jonathan Reid's offer and come with him so she would not feel so horribly alone.

"Ms. MacNair?" Joe Wheeler called out as he entered.

Bonnie leapt from her chair. "I'm going to pay for the jukebox Miguel broke," she assured him immediately, "so you needn't hold him for that, and he was with me yesterday, so you can't charge him with running Leigh off the road."

Startled by the pretty young woman's outburst, the detective gestured toward the chair she had just left. "Sit down, Ms. MacNair, and let's go over things one at a time."

Bonnie was far too nervous to display the requisite calm of a good witness, and after she had repeated her story three times, Joe Wheeler still couldn't decide if she was a very poor liar, or simply telling the truth poorly. "How did you pay for the motel room, Ms. MacNair?"

"I usually paid in cash, but yesterday we hadn't made plans to meet early enough for me to stop by the bank so I used my credit card." She fumbled through the clutter in her purse, dropped a lipstick and pack of gum she bent down to retrieve, then extracted a wrinkled receipt from the motel, and thrust it into his hands.

The detective smoothed it out, and read the date. "Thank

you. It's a good thing you saved this, but maybe you just wanted to have it handy when Miguel needed an alibi."

Bonnie missed his meaning completely. "I always save my receipts, because otherwise it's too easy to forget how much I've charged, and I don't like to be surprised when the bill arrives. The interest on the account is ruinous, so I pay off the balance every month."

"That's very wise," Wheeler agreed, nodding at the totally irrelevant information. "How often have you and Mr. Fuentes met at this particular motel?"

"Oh, my goodness," Bonnie exclaimed. "I'd have to check my diary to make certain, but we've been there at least once a week for more than a year."

"Perhaps sixty times?" the detective asked incredulously.

"Yes, I know it's expensive. We used to split the cost, and then decided to just take turns."

"How modern. You're not married, are you, Ms. MacNair?"

He was being so stern, Bonnie feared she had already outraged his sense of morality. "No. Of course not. Miguel and I just enjoyed getting away from Mirasol. There's nothing wrong in that." The detective had such cold little eyes, he made her feel even more uncomfortable than she already was. She fiddled with an earring then dropped her hands into her lap.

"Will you release Miguel now?" she asked.

Joe Wheeler had seldom met such a nervous young woman, and he equated her restlessness with guilt. "Ms. MacNair, perjury is a serious crime. Now I can understand why you'd want to provide your boyfriend with an alibi, but are you prepared to go into court and swear that he was with you in Santa Barbara at 6:45 last night? Think about it a minute before you answer. If there's a possibility you could be mistaken about the time, I'll make no record of this conversation. You can just walk out, but I hope you'll be more careful in the future about the company you keep."

Bonnie had had more than a year to consider what people would think of her should they learn she was seeing Miguel.

That Detective Wheeler believed she could just walk away when Miguel needed her made her ashamed she had ever insisted upon keeping their affair a secret. It had never been merely an affair either, she realized now.

She leaned forward slightly and spoke with stunning sincerity. "Not only am I prepared to repeat my story in court, I'll be proud to do it. It will make you look like a fool though, won't it? After all, if you've interviewed a witness who can place Miguel Fuentes in Santa Barbara at the time of the accident, then why was he ever charged with the crime?"

Because Joe Wheeler had had serious misgivings from the instant he learned Leigh Bowman could not place Miguel at the accident scene, he chose not to argue. Bonnie MacNair might be a class A flake, but she had definitely made her point. He pushed himself out of his chair, and gestured toward the door.

"I'll call Max Beadle and see if he'll drop the charges against Miguel in exchange for your promise to pay for the damages he caused. If Max agrees, then we'll release Miguel."

Bonnie couldn't leave and just hope the detective would keep his word. "I'll wait for him," she said, but she went outside where there was fresh air to breathe, sat down on the bench, and tried to think of a way to tell her mother that despite all her warnings, she had fallen in love with a man who owned nothing but the good name it had taken her far too long to come forward and save.

Leaving nothing to chance, before Joe Wheeler spoke with Max Beadle, he called the motel in Santa Barbara to make certain Bonnie MacNair and Miguel Fuentes were indeed frequent visitors. Because the pair had never resorted to using assumed names, that was readily done. Max Beadle had been astonished to learn Bonnie wished to pay for the damages to his jukebox, but trusted her to keep her word. His last call was to Eli Keene, but the rancher was out, and he had to leave him a message.

As Wheeler walked Miguel to the door, he offered two conditions. "You're not to leave town without checking with me, and you're not to set foot in the pool hall until Max has a new jukebox and long mirror. Is that clear?"

"Yes, sir," Miguel responded, without a shade of respect. "Am I still a suspect in Ms. Bowman's accident?"

"Possibly," Wheeler advised.

Disgusted anyone had ever considered him capable of hurting the young woman, Miguel pulled on his denim jacket, and pushed out the door. When he found Bonnie waiting for him, he halted in mid-stride. "You shouldn't have had to come down here," he said.

Bonnie rushed into his arms and gave him an exuberant hug. Then she couldn't let him go. No other man had ever felt so right in her arms, and she clung to him until he gave her a gentle push and stepped back.

"Hey," he cautioned. "Someone's sure to drive by and see us out here."

"It's about time, don't you think?" She laughed at his surprised gasp, and took his hand as they started up Ventura Street toward the library. "I meant for us to talk last night," she insisted. "There's so much I've never told you about the way I was raised, and it kept us from ever becoming close."

Miguel swept his thick, black hair out of his eyes with his free hand. "Bonnie, we're as close as two people can get."

"No, not really," she insisted shyly, "not when I wouldn't admit to myself, or to you, how much I love you."

Amazed to have finally wrung that confession from her, Miguel pulled her around to face him. There was a gentle sweetness to her expression that was new, but he couldn't help but wonder why she had chosen that particular day to reveal her true feelings. "If I'd known I had to get thrown in jail for you to realize that you love me, I'd have busted up Max's place months ago."

Bonnie knew that was how it must look, and felt ashamed. She looked away for a moment, but now that she had finally spoken the truth aloud, she recognized her mother's admonitions for the pathetic fears they were. They no longer held any power to sway her emotions. "When my father left my mother, she blamed herself for ever loving him and leaving herself open to pain. I don't think she ever let herself love any of the other men she met; then she blamed them when they drifted away. Her mistake wasn't following her heart, but being afraid to. Until I met you, I didn't expect a man to stay with me, either."

Bonnie's newfound insight made her desperately afraid, and her eyes filled with tears. "How can you possibly love me, Miguel?"

Miguel pulled her back into his arms and hugged her tight. "You are so easy to love, *querida*. So easy."

Bonnie rested her head on his shoulder. He was young and strong, and she always felt safe in his arms. "Well, easy is certainly true."

Miguel laughed, released her, then took her hand. "That wasn't what I meant. Shouldn't you be at the library?"

They were almost there, but Bonnie didn't feel like going back to work. "I took the afternoon off."

"I wonder if I still have a job. I've stood up to Eli so often that he may have decided he doesn't want me around any more. I wouldn't blame him, either."

"If he fires you, you'll find other work. We'll get along."

"We?"

Bonnie glanced up at him. "You proposed to me on Monday. Have you forgotten?"

Miguel winced. "I remember too much about last Monday. I shouldn't have treated you like that, Bonnie. I keep remembering how hurt you looked when I turned on the light. That was such a stupid thing to do, and I haven't slept well since."

A seductive smile curled across Bonnie's lips. "You did all right last night."

"I don't remember either of us getting much sleep." They had reached the library parking lot, and Miguel walked Bonnie to her car. "Will you give me a ride to the ranch?"

It pained Bonnie that he had to ask, but after she had been

impossible to pin down for so long, she could not blame him. "If you like, but I'd rather take you home. You can call your mother from there and let her know you're free. Then I'll call my mother and ask her to help me plan the wedding."

"You want to take me home," Miguel repeated numbly.

"Would you rather live out at the Keene Ranch? Assuming you still work for Eli, of course, but I doubt that he'd give you two houses, and I don't want to share your mother's. I'm sure she's a lovely person, and that your brothers and sisters are adorable, but we'll have to pay for the jukebox and mirror before we go away on a honeymoon, and—"

Miguel stilled her worries with a lengthy kiss. "I don't want anyone crowding us either," he said. He pressed her against the side of her car. It was a beige Honda with more than 100,000 miles on it, but at least she would not be making so many trips to Santa Barbara before he could buy her a new one. He rubbed his hips across hers.

"Let's go home," he breathed against her throat.

Breathless, Bonnie reached into her purse, felt around for her car keys, and then handed them to Miguel. "I think you better drive." She circled the car to get in on the passenger side.

Miguel had to force himself not to exceed the speed limit on the way to her duplex, but then throwing away all restraint, he raced her across the porch, and through the front door. The important telephone calls they had intended to make were forgotten, and in their excitement to be together again they peeled off each other's clothes on the way to the bedroom. Bonnie grabbed for the bedspread to roll it back, but Miguel yanked it out of her hands, and draped it around her like a royal robe.

Bonnie slid her fingers through Miguel's hair as she leaned forward to kiss him, then pulled him down with her onto the bed. "You are so very handsome," she whispered.

"I am not nearly handsome enough for you."

Bonnie giggled as his hands began to wander beneath the spread. "I have pretty eyes, but I'm much too thin."

"*No, querida.* You are delicate, like a fawn," Miguel argued.

Bonnie savored that graceful image as his caress strayed up her inner thigh. "What if I have ten babies in as many years and look more like a hippo than a deer?"

Miguel leaned back slightly. He could not even imagine Bonnie getting fat, but he definitely liked the idea of having babies. "Do you really want to make babies with me?" he asked, suddenly fearful that she might not.

A shadow of doubt crossed his gaze, and Bonnie knew her former reluctance to accept his love was to blame for his uncertainty. "I think we'll make very beautiful babies, Miguel."

Miguel studied the gentle curve of her lips. She looked different somehow. Her smile was softer, as he had noted earlier, but there was something else as well. Then he realized that while he had often spoken of love, it wasn't until today that she had dared to let her love for him show. It lit her whole face with a joy he hoped would never fade.

He kissed her lightly at first, and then more deeply as his fingertips dipped into her slippery wetness. While the police had released him, he knew he might still be in serious trouble. He might be out of work when he had more dependents than any twenty-six year old ought to have, but he could not wait to take on another.

Bonnie's breathing quickened, and he varied the pressure of his strokes until he felt her muscles begin to contract around his fingers. The bedspread was in his way then, and they both fought the tangled chenille until with a fierce cry of exhilaration Miguel finally tore it away. Later he would make love to Bonnie slowly with his lips and tongue, but now, he entered her with a savage thrust that carried him deep. She wrapped her legs over his thighs to hold him, but his searing kiss carried a heartfelt promise that he would never leave.

Eighteen

By the end of visiting hours, Frank Pierce and all the members of the city council had come by to see Leigh. The men had merely looked in on her, offered their sincere regrets for her accident, and embarrassed by their inability to do more, had quickly excused themselves. Only Zoe Kunkel had stayed for a lengthy chat.

Leigh appreciated Zoe's efforts to amuse her with stories centered around her pet shop's multitude of exotic pets, but she couldn't seem to follow along closely enough to smile at the appropriate times. When she could no longer hide her fatigue and yawned openly, Zoe had finally brought her visit to a close. Hoping for a nap, Leigh was still attempting to find a comfortable pose when Dr. Nelson entered and asked how she was feeling.

"I'm not any better than I was when I awoke this morning," Leigh responded truthfully. "I feel as though I've been run over by a steamroller, then scraped off the road."

"Ouch." Marsha's frown was sincerely sympathetic. "Give it another day. You're sure to feel better tomorrow."

The physician's confident prediction failed to lift Leigh's spirits. There wasn't an inch of her body that didn't hurt, and despite the medication she had been given, her headache had barely begun to fade. "I just want to rest."

"Would you rather not have visitors this evening?" Marsha read Leigh's dilemma in her averted glance. "Perhaps there's one visitor you'd like to see, but not others?"

Leigh would have liked to have seen Jonathan again, but couldn't bar Eli when he was so deeply concerned about her. "That wouldn't be fair," she said, "and it would only make things worse than they already are."

"I'll tell the clerk at the desk that you're not accepting visitors then, but I wonder if you'd satisfy my curiosity. I know from personal experience just how difficult it is for a successful woman to capture a man's interest, but you have two men fighting for the chance to impress you. It makes me very envious. Do you have a favorite?"

More amused by that question than Zoe's stories, Leigh produced a faint smile. "Why, Dr. Nelson, I'm shocked that you'd ask."

"Was it terribly unprofessional of me?"

"No, merely human." Had Leigh not been in an accident, she might have accepted more of Eli's tender affection last night, and after seeing Jonathan again, she knew it would have been a horrible mistake. Jonathan touched her in ways Eli never would, but she was fond of him, too. "I'm sorry. Could we discuss men another time? I just don't feel up to it today."

"Sure. Another time, then. I'll stop the visitors." Marsha closed Leigh's door behind her, but remained where she stood when she saw Eli coming her way. "The afternoon visiting hours are over," she reminded him softly.

"I don't care. The police have released the man we all believed to be responsible for Leigh's accident. I don't think she's safe here."

Marsha took Eli's arm, and drew him away from Leigh's door. "I'll alert security," she whispered, "but I don't want Ms. Bowman informed. The accident left her badly battered, and she doesn't need the addition of mental anguish as well."

Alarmed, Eli stepped back slightly and broke the contact between them. "She is going to be all right though, isn't she?"

"Yes, of course she is. I fully expect her to be able to return to work next week. Now what about you? You can't have gotten much sleep last night, and you've been in and out of here all day. You'll not do Ms. Bowman any good if you become ill yourself."

Eli wondered if the attractive redhead was always so attentive to her patients' visitors. Because he was used to getting plenty of attention of his own, he doubted it. "Do I look that bad? Perhaps I ought to come by your office for a physical."

Marsha had to cover her mouth to muffle her laugh, and then apologized. "I'm sorry, but men frequently ask me to examine them, and that's really not the way I want to build my practice."

Marsha was a charming woman with gorgeous hair and sparkling eyes, and had it not been for Leigh, Eli would have suggested they continue their conversation about health care over dinner. "I understand. If the hospital doesn't have sufficient security staff to station a man outside Leigh's door, then I'm going to call the police and request an officer."

Marsha hoped she and Leigh would become good friends, and Eli's concern with danger scared her. "Do you really believe she's in danger?"

"I hope not, but I don't want to take any chances."

Marsha scanned the long hallway. Leigh's room was near the nurses' station, and keeping her under close observation would not be a problem. "I'll have a security guard monitor this corridor. I've been looking forward to the redevelopment myself, and I can't believe anyone would resort to murder as a protest."

"Maybe the creep just wanted to frighten Leigh, and things got out of hand." Eli walked with Marsha to the end of the hall, and then wished that he hadn't when he saw Denise standing at the desk. She had brought an orchid with a single white bloom, and was arguing for permission to deliver it to Leigh's room herself. Flustered, the clerk gestured toward Dr. Nelson.

"Are you Ms. Bowman's physician?" Denise asked. "I know I'm a few minutes late, but I've a boutique to run and can't always meet other people's schedules. I promise not to stay more than a few minutes, but I do so want Leigh to have this beautiful plant."

Marsha quickly took it from her. "Ms. Bowman is asleep, but I'll see this is sent to her room when she wakes."

Peeved, Denise sighed unhappily. "Well, I suppose it would be an imposition to wake her, but I did want her to know I was concerned about her."

"She'll be deeply touched," Eli promised. He had been ready to leave, but not wanting to escort Denise to the parking lot, he propped his elbow on the desk, and got comfortable. Denise looked splendid as always in a beige sheath sparked with jet buttons, but he had already seen enough of her to last him a lifetime. When she turned away with her usual graceful sway, he caught Marsha's eye and shuddered

"You should probably check my blood pressure," he suggested. "My ex-wife has never been good for my health."

"Really? I must say I admire her taste in clothes," Marsha hesitated, and Eli's quizzical glance prompted a more revealing confession. "And in men," she added.

Eli laughed. "Thank you." Hoping he had given Denise enough of a head start, he headed for the door, but when he reached it, he turned back and waved. While he couldn't be certain, he thought Marsha was blushing, and that tickled him all the more. Then he saw Denise waiting beside his Porsche, and his smile disappeared beneath a dark frown.

"I didn't want to quiz Leigh's physician," Denise told Eli when he reached her, "but were her injuries severe?"

Surprised by her interest, Eli did his best to curb his constant sense of irritation where she was concerned. "No, thank God, but she's badly bruised and sore. I swear I don't know what Mirasol is coming to when a woman isn't safe on the roads."

"I heard the police arrested one of your men."

"Yeah, they did, but they bought his alibi and let him go."

Denise released a dramatic sigh. "What kind of a heartless brute could have done such an evil thing, Eli?"

Eli jangled his keys and she moved away from his car door. "Beats me, but the police will get him. Now you'll have to excuse me. I need to get home." He got in and started the engine before she could steer their conversation in another direction, which he was certain she was about to do. He really did need to get home and decide what he was going to do about Miguel Fuentes. He had always liked Miguel, but lately he had sure been more trouble than he was worth.

That evening, Bonnie called her mother to make certain she would be at home. Wanting to deliver her news in person, she and Miguel drove over to her place. Beverly lived in the little stucco house where Bonnie had grown up. The yellow paint was faded to a pale cream, and the flowerbeds overgrown, but Bonnie still regarded the modest house as home. The porch light was on, and as they walked up to the door, Bonnie caught her mother peeking out at them through the organdy curtains at the living room window.

She tried to smile bravely, and clutched Miguel's hand as they waited for Beverly to open the door. "Hi, Mama," Bonnie greeted her.

Rather than invite them in, Beverly pulled the door open only a crack, and peered out. She recognized Miguel Fuentes, but couldn't imagine what he was doing with Bonnie. She knew one thing for certain, however: she didn't want his kind in her house.

"I thought he was in jail."

"How do you do, Mrs. MacNair?" Miguel responded politely. Bonnie had warned him things might not go well here initially, but she had high hopes that eventually her mother would warm to him. Now that he was stuck out on the porch, he wondered if Bonnie hadn't been overly optimistic.

Bonnie had expected her mother to at least say hello to Miguel, even if she weren't cordial, but Beverly was being positively rude and staring at him coldly. "Aren't you going to invite us to come in, Mama?" she asked.

"Not until you tell me why he isn't locked up."

"He's not just a 'he,' Mama. His name's Miguel, and we've

been going out for a long time." Bonnie saw a confused hurt fill her mother's gaze, and guilt stabbed her with the sharpness of a thousand pins. Miguel slipped his arm around her waist to give her an encouraging hug, but it wasn't nearly enough to counter her mother's scorn.

"You have got to be kidding," Beverly exclaimed. "What if that nice realtor from Santa Barbara finds out that you date ranch hands?"

Bonnie licked her lips. That afternoon she had finally done what was right, and no matter how badly it hurt now, she wouldn't allow her mother to twist it into something ugly. "There isn't any realtor. I just made him up to keep you happy while I was seeing Miguel."

Beverly opened the door a little wider, but it wasn't to welcome them in. "Because you knew damn well I wouldn't be happy about him! Tell him to get lost, and then get in here. You and I are going to have a long talk."

Bonnie was ashamed that Beverly was so lacking in manners. "I can't do that. We're going to be married, and we'd like you to help us plan the wedding."

Beverly stepped through the doorway, and for an instant Bonnie thought she was going to embrace her, but instead Beverly drew back her hand and slapped her so hard her head snapped back at a painful angle. She would have fallen off the porch had Miguel not been alert and tightened his hold on her. Badly hurt, and horribly embarrassed, Bonnie shrank away from her mother.

Miguel moved between them. "No one, and I mean no one, is going to abuse Bonnie." He had had no idea Bonnie had lied to her mother about him, but he could see why she had done it. "Bonnie's of age, and we don't need your permission to marry. Now we came here to do things right, but neither of us is coming back until you accept the fact your daughter's a grown woman, and can treat her with respect."

"I'll treat Bonnie any way I please," Beverly replied, and with a snotty strut, she went back inside and slammed the door.

Miguel wheeled Bonnie around, helped her down the porch steps, and guided her back to her car. He helped her in, and then got in on the driver's side. "I'm not asking you to choose between your mother and me," he stressed, "but you don't have to take that kind of abuse from anyone, least of all your mother. Why didn't you tell me about her?"

Miguel's eyes were blazing with a fierce light, and rather than give an all too obvious answer, Bonnie turned away. Her mother had turned off the porch light, and that final insult broke her heart. "By the time I was two, she had my whole life plotted out for me. A lot of her ideas were good. She insisted that I do well in school and go away to college, but it was never to fulfill my potential. It was always to get the most I could from every man I met. She doesn't even remember what love is."

Miguel leaned forward to turn the key in the ignition, then decided they weren't ready to leave and sat back. "If you're sorry you said yes, say so now, and we'll forget all about the wedding, but please don't wait until you're Mrs. Miguel Fuentes to decide I'm not good enough for you."

Bonnie put her hand on the door handle. "I'm the one who's not good enough, Miguel. Only me." Certain of it, she opened her door.

Miguel reached across her to pull the door shut. "This is your car, Bonnie. If anyone's getting out, it has to be me."

Bonnie didn't know whether to laugh or cry. She could see her whole life laid out in a colorful comic strip, but there wasn't a trace of humor in her mother's endless manipulations. She had fought her all year by seeing Miguel, and finally her independence was real. "I know my mama's wrong," she sobbed, "but she's all I have."

Miguel pulled Bonnie into his arms. "No, *querida*. Now you have me, and I come with a whole family who'll be proud to love you."

Bonnie snuggled against Miguel's shoulder. "What if they're not, Miguel? What if they're as awful to us as my mama?"

Miguel eased her out of his arms, and gave her a quick kiss. "They won't be, but let's go and see."

Bonnie wiped away her tears with her fingertips, and fastened her seat belt. She wanted to believe Miguel, but her doubts were too strong. "Tell me about your brothers and sisters again. I know I'll never get them straight, but I do want to try."

"My family isn't *that* large," Miguel protested. "Aurora is sixteen, and Linda's fourteen. They're both students at Mirasol High. Felipe's ten, and Daniel's seven. They're good boys. Daniel can't remember our father, so he's probably the most attached to me, but that's normal."

"Aurora, Linda, Felipe, Daniel," Bonnie chanted the names in an effort to remember them. Then fearing she would sound ridiculous to Miguel, she repeated them silently to herself. "What about your mother? Does she date at all?"

"Not really, but José Blanco, he's the ranch mechanic, spends a lot of time with her. Maybe when I move out, he'll find the courage to propose."

"What was her name, Estelle?"

"Adelita."

"Oh, no. I'm never going to get the names right."

"Do you get this frantic running the library?" Miguel thought Bonnie's worries absurd. She was the woman he wanted for his wife, and his mother would never be rude to her. As for his brothers and sisters, they were always teasing him about girls, but none of them knew he had been dating Bonnie for as long as he had.

"That's just keeping track of books," Bonnie replied. "It's not the same at all."

In no mood to argue, Miguel flipped on the radio, and let the strains of Guns and Roses' "Patience," fill the silence as he drove home. He had called his mother from Bonnie's house to provide the tardy news of his release, but he hadn't given her any hint that he wouldn't be coming home alone. Now he wondered if he shouldn't have at least warned her.

As they left the Honda parked beside his house, Miguel

thought he was probably more nervous than Bonnie, but he flashed a wide grin so she wouldn't guess the truth. As they climbed the steps, his family spilled out on the porch. The kids were all staring at him wide-eyed, and he didn't know if it were because he had been arrested or because he had never brought a woman home before.

"I know you," Daniel announced excitedly. "You work at the library."

Bonnie prayed the little guy was Daniel rather than Felipe, and answered him with the confidence she showed at work. "That's right, Daniel. I do. Weren't you there on a field trip just before school was out?"

Daniel beamed with pride. "You remember me?"

"Of course. You're as handsome as your big brother, and you are too, Felipe."

Turning bashful, Felipe nearly twisted himself into a knot trying not to look proud, but truly both he and Daniel resembled Miguel closely. Aurora and Linda favored their mother, and rather shy, hung back behind her. Adelita, however, smiled warmly as Miguel introduced Bonnie.

"We have had such an awful day, but now that Miguel is home, you must help us celebrate," Adelita said.

Miguel waited until they were all inside the living room to say more. The furniture was worn, and the floor cluttered with the boys' collection of plastic dinosaurs, but he saw only the familiar warmth of home. "There's something else to celebrate," he told his family. "I've asked Bonnie to marry me, and she said yes."

"Does that mean we'll get free books?" Daniel asked.

Everyone laughed, and then came up to give Bonnie a welcoming hug and kiss. For a moment, she was simply dazed, but then her smile grew as wide as Miguel's. "Thank you for being happy for us. I'm afraid I can't get any books free, Daniel, but maybe you and Felipe can come into the library on Saturday, and check out some of the new ones."

Adelita reached up to whisper in her son's ear. "It is about time, *mijo*. She is lovely."

"Yes. Isn't she?" Miguel caught Bonnie's eye, and thought as he had so often, that he was a very lucky man. He knew it took a while to plan weddings, and that everyone would have to have new clothes, but he didn't want to wait a minute longer than they absolutely had to to make Bonnie his wife.

Bonnie sat down on the floor so Daniel could show her his dinosaurs, and she was impressed that he knew all their names. She had never expected to feel so at home there, but it was easy to relax when surrounded by smiles and happy laughter. She suddenly realized this was what a family was supposed to be, and she gave Daniel a fond squeeze.

"I have some wonderful dinosaur books at the library," she confided. "I'll set them aside for you." Daniel gave her cheek another shy kiss, and her mother's stinging insults were forgotten. It may have taken her too long, but she had made the right choice, and had no regrets. The girls ought to be visiting the library too, she decided, but she would make certain they thought the idea had come from them.

Miguel sat down to join them on the floor. "Was I right?"

Bonnie's blissful smile assured that he was. She felt safe, and the sparkle in her eye promised she would thank him in her own way later tonight, and for a great many nights to come.

Jonathan arrived at the hospital carrying a box of Godiva chocolates. When he was told Leigh wasn't accepting vistors that evening, he immediately assumed the worst. "She was fine this morning. What's gone wrong?" he asked anxiously.

"She's tired is all," the clerk replied. "You'll be able to see her tomorrow. You can leave the box of candy here if you like, and I'll see she gets it first thing in the morning."

Because he had planned to hand it to her himself, Jonathan hadn't brought a card. "I need to write her a note first. Do you have any paper?"

The clerk tore a sheet from a tablet, and Jonathan carried it over to the waiting room. He sat down, intending to use the bottom of the box as a desk, but he couldn't think of anything to say that wouldn't sound ridiculous. There was so much he wanted to tell Leigh, but the words just wouldn't come in a logical sequence and he gave up the effort. He wrote a brief message to let her know he had come by, signed his name, and stood.

As he started back toward the desk, several people came in, blocking the clerk's view, and on a sudden impulse, he ducked down the hall and went to Leigh's room. The lights were turned down low, and she was curled up on her side sound asleep. Her brow was furrowed slightly, and he feared she was in pain.

He longed to reach out and touch her, but had to settle for leaving the gold box of candy on the table beside Eli's roses. He turned to tiptoe out, but just as he opened the door, a burly security guard made a grab for him. The guard shoved him back into Leigh's room, and turned on the lights.

Had the men's scuffle not awakened Leigh, the lights surely would have, and she propped herself up on her elbow. "It's all right," she assured the guard. "He's a friend."

"I don't care if he's your identical twin, Ms. Bowman. He shouldn't have been in your room when you asked not to be disturbed."

Leigh covered a wide yawn. "Identical twins are always the same sex," she informed the guard, "otherwise, they're not identical."

Confused, the man considered her comment, and then nodded. "Okay, so it was a poor comparison, but the fact is, no visitors means no visitors. He'll have to go."

"I'm sorry," Jonathan interjected. "I knew better."

Jonathan was attempting to look suitably contrite to impress the guard, but the corner of his mouth twitched slightly, and Leigh could see it was an effort. "Now that I'm awake, let him stay. The least he can do is sit with me awhile until I get back to sleep. Otherwise, I might lie here wide awake for hours."

"Ten minutes," the guard offered. "Then I'm coming back to escort you out."

"Thank you." Jonathan waited until the man had left, then grabbed a chair, set it close to the bed, and dropped into it. "I brought you some candy. Do you feel well enough to eat a piece?"

Leigh settled back down into her pillows. "No. Why don't you have one, though?"

Jonathan had never felt less like eating candy. "I'll wait until you can join me. Bonnie went to the police on her own just as you'd hoped, and they released Miguel."

"That's good. Have they arrested anyone else?"

"Not yet, which has me worried. Mirasol used to be such a sleepy little place, and now in less than a week, I've lost my house, Ron's dead, and you were nearly killed."

Leigh didn't want to dwell on those tragedies. She was happy Jonathan had gotten past the guard, but his charming smile filled her with guilt rather than gratitude. "There's something I should have told you on Sunday. I was afraid to even approach the subject, which was cowardly of me."

She saw Jonathan's posture stiffen. Eli's responses were subtle: a gently arched brow, or slight smile, while Jonathan's reactions were so broad they were impossible to mistake. She scolded herself silently for again comparing the pair, when it was a disservice to them both.

"I'd like for you to just listen," she explained. "You needn't say anything before you go, and if you don't come back I'll not think any less of you." Leigh paused a moment to gather her thoughts, and her courage. "My husband and I were college sweethearts. We married at twenty-one, and expected to be together forever. Sadly, it didn't turn out that way."

Not wanting to miss a single word, Jonathan leaned forward slightly as Leigh's voice softened with the anguish of her memories. She had already told him Doug was an actor, but now described her ex-husband as a man of great charm, but little substance. She didn't use those precise words, but as she related

Doug's penchant for play over work, Jonathan readily understood. Part of him wanted to stop her hushed confession as unnecessary, but an even greater part needed to hear it all.

Leigh hurried to sum up before the guard returned. "I wanted a family, but I couldn't get Doug's attention long enough to discuss having children. He was too much of a child himself, you see, to be a good father. I couldn't pretend the happiness I didn't feel, but he didn't even notice how silent I'd become. When I began to fear I'd take my frustrations out on Doug, when he simply couldn't change, I left him."

Leigh could barely hold back her tears. "I asked you not to force me into your wife's mold, but I'm afraid I might be more like her than I care to admit. Like Cheryl, I put my needs first, but I knew I couldn't make our marrige work all alone. Maybe it was selfish of me, but I could have made no other choice and survived as the type of person I want to be."

Jonathan knew that even if he couldn't manage anything profound, he ought to say something at least meaningful, but the painful knot in his throat choked back the words. Like Leigh, he saw the parallels between Cheryl's choices and hers, but he didn't want to comment before he had thought them through. He got up, turned off the light so Leigh could sleep, and then after giving her a hasty kiss, left the room.

Feeling abandoned when she had needed him most, Leigh gave into her tears, and her head began to pound with a fresh burst of pain. She had expected some response from Jonathan, if only a terse good-bye, but that he had kissed her before walking out left her thoroughly confused. He wouldn't be back. She was positive of that, but shouted insults would have been easier to bear than a silent rejection.

She doubted she would sleep at all that night, but closed her eyes. Almost immediately she felt the same terror she had experienced just prior to her crash. The scene was so vivid in her mind, but as it replayed, she could find no way to make it end differently. The Chevy truck had simply been too heavy and powerful to battle and the avocado groves too dense to offer refuge.

She fought to force her memory past the lettering on the truck's door, but her field of vision had extended no higher. She had not seen the driver, but if it hadn't been Miguel, were there others like him who worked for Eli and also regarded the resort hotel as a threat to the ranch they loved? Maybe every last one of his workers hated her enough to want her dead. It was a chilling thought.

She believed Eli must surely know his men's views, but they could not have gone after him without jeopardizing their livelihood to an even greater extent than the hotel would have. Knowing what Eli thought of Denise, he would not have left the ranch to her in his will, but she wondered who would inherit it. Perhaps he had a great many relatives he had not mentioned.

Leigh shifted her position, striving to find one that didn't aggravate her aches and pains, but remained no more comfortable than she was with her tortured thoughts. If the fire at Jonathan's had been set, then it must have been by someone who feared he might actually stop the redevelopment plan. Whoever had come after her, however, must have wanted to stop the project. She wondered if the culprits were friends like Ron Tate and George Culbert had been, who argued constantly, but never changed each other's views.

She remembered the map she had made with the discreet plus and minus signs, but didn't want to recall the names of those opposed to the redevelopment and regard them as suspects in her accident. She hoped it had been someone she had never met whose violent tastes ran counter to the town's. How could coming to Mirasol have brought such tragic results? she agonized.

When at last she did fall asleep, her dreams were filled with images of twisted wreckage and the pungent scent of gasoline. She awoke long before dawn sick with fear and a numbing sense of loss. She had left Doug to begin a new life, but this wasn't the life she had envisioned, and perhaps it had all been a terrible mistake. Maybe every choice she made was wrong, and she would have been better off had she died in the accident.

Jonathan also found it difficult to sleep. He lay stretched across the ornately carved bed he had planned to refinish until it became the only bed he owned. He would still refinish it, but the need scarcely seemed urgent. Memories of how small Leigh had looked in the hospital bed tugged on his conscience and he couldn't help but fear his bitter accusations of arson were partly responsible for putting her there.

He sifted through the names of the others who were as opposed to the redevelopment as he, but it was difficult to regard friends as suspects in the crime. He had known there were plenty of people who considered rebuilding the town ill-advised if not downright disastrous, and had taken pride in being their spokes-man. Now he was merely ashamed to think his stubborn oppo-sition to the project had inspired such a hateful burst of violence.

It was far easier to think of the accident than examine his own life, however, and he postponed thoughts of Cheryl until the sun had turned the sky a vibrant gold. Drawn in the starkest comparison, his ex-wife and Leigh were exactly alike. Each had longed for something her husband had been unable to provide, and so each had ended her marriage.

He hated viewing it that way though, and spread it out more clearly in his mind. Cheryl had wanted a career in politics, and an eccentric husband had stood in her way. Leigh had wanted her marriage to include children, and Doug had not even lis-tened, let alone understood her need. She had provided only a brief sketch of their marriage, but it was clear Doug had been dependent on her, making her more of a mother than a wife. Knowing she must have felt desperately lonely, his heart ached for her.

"And just what do you have to offer her, Mr. Reid?" he asked himself. He sat up, glanced around the crowded apartment that was now his home and doubted love would be enough.

Nineteen

When Jonathan arrived for visiting hours Saturday morning, Eli was already in Leigh's room and arguing with Dr. Nelson, while Detective Wheeler looked on. Leigh was sitting up in bed, and following the disagreement with the scanning motion of a spectator at a tennis match. The detective acknowledged his arrival with a curt nod, then locked his hands behind his back and rocked back on his heels.

"What's going on?" Jonathan asked. When Leigh's eyes widened, he didn't understand why she appeared to be surprised to see him. She still looked frail, and her black eye had taken on a hint of green in the purple, making her look all the more pathetic, but he was pleased that she felt well enough to sit up. He winked at her, then thinking he had every right to be there, he sent the physician an expectant look to prompt a reply.

It was Eli who answered. "The good doctor says Leigh's well enough to go home, but I think she needs someone to look after her, and Dr. Nelson doesn't. Wheeler here doesn't particularly care where Leigh is as long as he's informed, so I want Leigh to come home with me where my staff can look after her."

Jonathan moved over to the bed. "I don't think you should be home alone either, but I don't want you to go with Eli. Come home with me."

"Get off it, Jonathan," Eli cried. "You don't even have a home. All you've got is an old carriage house."

Jonathan continued to gaze into Leigh's eyes. "That's true, and it's crammed with old furniture in varying states of disrepair, but I hope you won't mind." He took her hand, rubbed his thumb over her palm, and whispered enticingly, "Come home with me."

Leigh closed her fingers over his. She could lie in bed elsewhere just as comfortably as she could there at the hospital and was eager to go. Accepting Eli's hospitality would send the wrong signal, but taking Jonathan up on his offer might prove equally unwise. Jonathan's relaxed smile made it plain she had misjudged his reaction last night, and she regretted it badly. Feeling torn, she really didn't know which would be best, to go home alone, or to go with Jonathan when they continually misunderstood each other.

Out of the corner of her eye, Leigh saw Marsha Nelson observing Eli with a fond glance, while Eli was facing the bed, waiting for her answer. A startling question popped into her mind, but it presented the perfect means to help her make the right decision. "Will you tell me something please, Jonathan? If you had a wedding ring, what did you do with it after your divorce?"

"Oh, Christ," Eli moaned. "It is a test after all."

"No, it isn't," Leigh insisted. "I'm just curious."

Dismayed, Jonathan searched Leigh's dear bruised face for clues to her real question, but he found only keen interest rather than any sinister intent. He looked away for a moment, then chose his words with care and hoped his explanation wouldn't sound utterly ridiculous. "I had a ring, and kept it to remind me of a time when I was deeply in love, so I'd not lose the hope that I'd fall in love again. It was lost in the fire, but it had served its purpose. I don't need it anymore."

Eli swore under his breath, and Marsha released a poignant sigh. Touched by Jonathan's endearing comment, Detective Wheeler cleared his throat, then whipped out his notepad and scrawled a hasty note in an attempt to hide the tears in his eyes.

Leigh felt like crying, too.

"That's a beautiful thought. Thank you. If I'd not be in your way, I'd like to go home with you."

Eli's disgust became firmly etched on his aristocratic features, and after giving the doctor a curt nod, he walked out. Joe Wheeler spoke on his way to the door. "You'll be close to the station and I'll have our patrol car keep an eye on the place, Ms. Bowman. Let me know should you remember anything more about the accident."

"Yes, thank you. I will."

Unable to suppress her smile, Marsha resembled the cat who had swallowed the canary. "I guess I have the answer to my question too," she said.

"What question was that?" Jonathan asked.

"It was just between us," Leigh assured him.

Marsha gestured toward the purse and shoes Eli had laid at the foot of the bed. "You can't leave in the clothes you were wearing when you arrived, and you'll surely need more than this. Would you like to send Mr. Reid to your home to pack a few things?"

"Will you do that for me if I make a list?" Leigh asked.

"Sure. I'll be happy to." Jonathan pulled his note off the box of candy he had brought so she could write on the back, and handed her a pen.

"I'll see to the paperwork for your release," Marsha called as she slipped out the door. She doubted she could overtake Eli before he reached his car, but he was waiting for her just outside Leigh's room. Delighted, she tried not to let her happiness show when she feared Leigh's choice had hurt him badly.

Eli gave her a sad smile. "I saw that one coming," he revealed, "so I don't feel too bad now, but I'm afraid I might take a sudden turn for the worse later. Do you make house calls, Dr. Nelson?"

Few men had the confidence to date a female physician, but Marsha had seen enough of Elijah Keene III to know her profession would never be a problem with him. "Upon occasion," she admitted. "If there's a dire need."

Eli handed her his card. "You can't miss the gate to the ranch.

If you come by about seven, I'll take you on up to Santa Barbara for dinner."

"That sounds fun, but it might be dangerous for you to overdo."

"As long as I have a physician with your considerable talents along with me, I'm sure to survive." Eli started to walk away, and then came back. He was completely serious as he spoke. "Leigh and I are just good friends. It was never anything more."

Before he turned away again, Marsha responded with a knowing smile that invited a great deal more than friendship. Pleased, Eli discounted the fact he was on the rebound, and vowed to make the most of it. "See you tonight then."

"Tonight," Marsha echoed, and she couldn't wait for the day to end.

Jonathan drove up to Leigh's duplex, and having nothing to hide from the neighbors, let himself in the front door. He glanced around the living room, and was surprised that while the furnishings were handsome, they clearly belonged to the apartment, giving the room the stark feel of a motel. Leigh had only been in Mirasol a short while, but he had expected to find ample evidence of her personality in her home.

He stepped into the kitchen to get a drink of water, and again was impressed by the lack of clutter. There were no dirty dishes in the sink, nor clean ones stacked on the counter. Thursday's newspaper was folded neatly on the table. Thinking he better not leave anything out of place, he washed the glass he used and returned it to the cupboard.

On impulse, he opened the refrigerator and was relieved to find it stocked with wholesome food. "Well, at least she eats," he murmured.

The bottle of Sensual Harmony oil caught his eye in the bathroom. It wasn't on Leigh's list, but he grabbed it before gathering up her cosmetics. He paused to admire the framed print of Monet's *Nymphéas,* a luminous depiction of sky, clouds, vines, and waterlies on a pond. The towels repeated Monet's deep blues and had been folded and hung with care.

Leigh's home reflected the same neat perfection with which she dressed but it wasn't until Jonathan entered her bedroom and saw the spectacular star splashed quilt that he felt he had learned something new about her. It was wildly romantic, and although a trifle modern for his tastes, he liked it. After he had carried the clothes she had requested out to his van, he came back and folded up the quilt and pillows to take as well.

He chuckled to himself as he drove to the hospital but Leigh's gasp of amazement when she climbed into the van and saw the quilt in the back convinced him he had done the right thing. "I wanted you to feel at home with me," he explained. "You were complimentary the one time you were in my house, but now that I've seen your place, I'll bet mine looked awfully crowded to you."

Leigh had to concentrate on fastening her seat belt, and was grateful they wouldn't have more than a couple of blocks to drive. She didn't want to insult Jonathan now after being so careful the day he had just recalled, but feeling far from well, it was difficult to find sufficient tact. "That was the Victorian style, wasn't it?" she replied.

"Yes, but you didn't really like it, did you?"

Leigh struggled to find an innocuous reply. "Let's just say it wouldn't be my first choice."

"Be honest, Leigh. You hated it."

"Jonathan, please. The house is gone, so what does it matter?"

While not entirely satisfied with that noncommittal response, Jonathan did see her point, and reluctantly agreed. "You're right." He pulled into his driveway, and parked close to the carriage house stairs. "I've worked all week to arrange the furniture I had stored upstairs here so that I'd have a path to walk through. I'll clean some more stuff out just as soon as I get you settled. I don't want you to feel claustrophobic."

Leigh touched his arm as he turned to open his door. "It's

only for a couple of days," she stressed. "There's no need to rearrange things."

Jonathan's glance darkened. He wanted to hold her forever, but he could sense she was on the verge of flight and did not want to risk frightening her away. "Hey," he reassured her softly. "We're not moving in together or anything like that. You're just staying with me until you feel better."

Leigh was relieved he understood, but angry with herself for not making the terms of her visit clear before they had left the hospital together. "Thank you." She waited while he walked around the van to open her door, but the instant she released her seat belt, he scooped her up into his arms.

"Jonathan! Put me down. I can walk up the stairs."

"What if you get dizzy and slip? I can't risk having you fall and getting a second concussion."

"Yes. I see what you mean. Perhaps we should be cautious." Leigh looped her arms around his neck, but as he started up the stairs, she feared she was going to prove too heavy for him. She held her breath, afraid they might both go bumping down the stairs like Winnie-the-Pooh, but he made it to the top without even having to draw a deep breath.

Jonathan set Leigh down on her feet while he unlocked the door. "The previous owner of this property was a dear little old woman who had a man who looked after the gardens and served as her chauffeur. This was his apartment. He used to eat his meals in the kitchen, so there's no stove, but I bought a microwave and little refrigerator last week so we'll get by."

Leigh had thought Jonathan must surely be exaggerating when he had described clearing a path, but the single large room above the garage truly did resemble a furniture warehouse. A narrow aisle ran from the front door to the bathroom at the opposite end, but as she walked down it, she discovered he had cleared sufficient space to arrange a massive bed, dresser and chairs beneath the dormer windows. It was precisely the bed she had visualized him sharing with Denise. The sheets were a plain cream-colored cotton rather than edged with lace, and she prayed Denise had not actually slept on them.

She sat down on the side of the bed while Jonathan went back to his van to bring her things. He then needed two more trips to fetch all the flowers she had received. After he had placed the bouquets on the dresser, she stood to help him spread out her quilt.

"Did you just happen to have this marvelous bed, or had you used it before the fire?"

Jonathan smoothed out the beautiful quilt, and added the pillows. "I had a bed in the house. Why would I have been using this one out here?"

"I don't know," Leigh hedged, ashamed to describe her lurid daydream. "It's very pretty."

"Yes, it is, but it needs to be refinished. The mattress is brand new though, so you should be comfortable." He patted the bed. "Come on, into bed. I promised Dr. Nelson that I'd see you got plenty of rest."

Leigh kicked off her tennis shoes, and climbed up on the bed. She had asked him to bring a comfortable pair of Levi's, and knit top, so she was ready to nap in her clothes and curled up obediently. Having her own quilt was rather nice, and she traced the outline of a star with her fingertips. "Dr. Nelson seems like a nice person, doesn't she?"

"Yes. I'm afraid Eli and I gave her a hard time the night you were hurt, but neither of us could go off and leave you."

Leigh waited until Jonathan had pulled up an ornate platform rocker and sat down. She hoped Marsha wouldn't object to her confiding in him, and did so. "I think she's rather taken with Eli."

"Good, that will keep him out of our hair." Elated by that thought, Jonathan rocked back too far and had to catch himself before he went over backwards. Certain that clumsy show couldn't have impressed Leigh, he was silent until he grew too uncomfortable with his thoughts. "I know you can't feel up to discussing anything heavy, but I want you to know after the terrible week we've had our running argument over the rede-velopment project seems trivial in the extreme."

"That's certainly true. Eli's leaning toward Greene and Greene architecture for the resort. It would require lots of Craftsman style furniture, Stickley, mission style, whatever. Do you know where to find it, or have replicas made?"

"They're called reproductions." Thinking Leigh had certainly hit the ground running, Jonathan's temper flared, but cooled just as quickly. "What are you trying to do, use my interest in period furniture to tempt me into working on the resort?"

He appeared to be amused rather than outraged, although Leigh was positive she had caught a glimpse of something darker before he had spoken. "Blatant manipulation, isn't it?"

Jonathan glanced out the window at the cloudless sky. "It sure is." He thought about it though. "Lloyd Channing can't have suggested California bungalows. Whose idea was it?"

"Eli's. He's more sensitive to preserving the beauty of the valley than you might have realized."

Jonathan had great difficulty even imagining Eli possessing any good qualities, but he had shown himself to be devoted to Leigh since her accident. Perhaps the guy wasn't entirely worth-less after all. He wasn't about to admit that aloud, however. "Now I'm beginning to suspect that you might have come here just to lobby for Eli's side."

Leigh snuggled into a deeper curl. "No."

She closed her eyes rather than say more, and Jonathan didn't press her. He just waited for her to elaborate on her own, but after a few minutes he realized that she had fallen asleep. Mov-ing out more furniture now would surely disturb her, so he stayed put. It would take months to rebuild his home, so for the time being, he would have to do business out of the carriage house. That was certainly going to be a challenge, but the pros-pect of supplying the furniture for an entire resort excited the hell out of him.

If only it hadn't been Eli's hotel.

* * *

Leigh rested all day, and by evening felt well enough to join Jonathan in the supper he picked up at the Marmalade Cafe. He pulled out a gateleg table from his collection, set it up by the bed, and found himself a rosewood chair to sit opposite her. She couldn't decide if it were an extremely romantic setting, or like eating on a stage set for a play.

The honey barbecued chicken was so good, she ate a wing with her fingers. "I can't even remember the last time I ate a full meal. It must have been Wednesday night." With Eli in Santa Barbara she dared not add. "Jonathan?"

"Hmm?" He took a sip of wine to wash down a mouthful of chicken.

"Eli and I are just friends. It was never what it is, or was, with you." Embarrassed that she had had to explain, Leigh stared at her plate, and scooped up a bite of coleslaw.

"Is," Jonathan stressed. "What it *is* with us." When she nodded, he felt confident enough to continue. "I thought about what you told me about your husband, and there's no comparison between you and Cheryl. You wanted more from Doug, and she didn't want anything from me. People change over time, but I'd like to believe they grow wiser, and more concerned about others rather than simply becoming so self-centered no one else's feelings matter. I'll promise you right now that I won't disappoint you the way Doug did."

Expecting him to demand a similar assurance from her, Leigh held her breath, but Jonathan resumed eating as though they had merely been exchanging polite dinner conversation rather than making plans for the rest of their lives. She had heard the only people who insisted they were trustworthy, weren't, and so hesitated to invite his trust. "You have such beautiful hair," she said instead. "The silver highlights are so handsome with your brown eyes."

Startled by her compliment, Jonathan sat back in his chair. "You don't think the gray makes me look too old?"

"Too old for what?" Leigh asked in a throaty whisper.

Jonathan responded with a rich, rolling laugh. It had easily been one of the worst weeks of his life. He had lost his best friend, his beautiful home, and nearly lost the spirited young woman he adored. "Thank you. When my hair first started turning gray, Cheryl asked me to dye it. I told her I'd rather shave my head, which really set her off."

"You don't mean it."

"Oh, but I do. That's when I began to suspect she merely regarded me as window dressing. I thought if you loved someone, it didn't matter what color their hair was. Cheryl obviously disagreed. I don't miss her one bit, but you still miss Doug, don't you?"

Leigh hadn't expected that question, and it really hit her hard. Her eyes filled with tears, and she had to blot them away with her napkin. "We grew up together," she explained softly. "I'll always miss him. I'm sorry. It must be the accident. I'm not usually so emotional."

"You needn't apologize. If you're finished eating, I'll run the bath for you."

Her appetite gone, Leigh slid off the bed. "Thank you, but I can manage on my own." The big old bathtub had clawed feet, and when Leigh sank down into the hot water she had scented with Sensual Harmony oil, she nearly disappeared below the rim. It was relaxing though, and she added hot water several times to keep the water warm enough to sooth away her lingering stiffness and pain. It wasn't until she got out that she realized she had neglected to bring her nightgown with her. She wrapped herself in a towel, and left the bathroom to get it.

Jonathan had cleared away the remains of their meal, and turned down the bed. He no longer owned a television set, but had a couple of books, and he thought he might read one aloud until Leigh fell asleep. When she appeared in one of the new cream-colored towels he had purchased that week, the deep bruise at her collarbone made him wince.

"I forgot my nightgown."

Jonathan remembered searching through her dresser to find one. She owned half a dozen, and he had chosen one which was more ecru lace than satin. The night was warm, and she probably wouldn't need it. Not wanting her to need it, he walked toward her.

Jonathan raised his hand and ran his fingertips along Leigh's jaw. "I'm getting used to your black eye, but I'll be glad when it fades and we won't have a constant reminder of the accident." He bent to kiss her cheek. "I want to stay with you, but if you don't feel up to it, I have a sleeping bag in my van."

Leigh laid her hand on his shoulder to encourage a more devoted kiss, and he brushed her lips lightly with his. Sleepy and warm, she tightened her hold on him and this time he kissed her deeply. He was the one making her dizzy now, not the concussion. She felt safe and loved. "Stay with me," she murmured when he broke away.

"I'm afraid I'll hurt you." He kissed her bruised collarbone, but didn't want to unwrap her towel for fear her slender body would bear far more gruesome reminders of her near fatal ordeal.

Leigh slid her arms around his waist, and laid her head on his shoulder. "Then just sleep with me," she suggested.

"I couldn't just sleep."

Leigh wondered why he was being so difficult. "I thought you didn't want me to be alone."

They were standing so close, Jonathan knew Leigh could feel how rapidly he was losing this argument. "I suppose I could call the paramedics, and put them on alert. Then if you need them—"

"I won't," Leigh insisted as she began to unbutton his shirt. She did not really feel well enough to make love, but she needed to be with him too badly to care. "Someone may have tried to kill me, but I'm not ready to die."

That softly voiced vow put an end to Jonathan's resistance. He gave a hushed cry, then gathered Leigh up in his arms and laid her across his bed. She flung away the damp towel, and he

was greatly relieved to find the ugly bruise on her collarbone
the only damage she had suffered. Still, he could not look at
her without remembering how terrified he had been when he
had seen her car being towed down the street. He was ready to
kill the son of a bitch who had hurt her, but hid his anger as
he yanked his shirt out of his pants.

What she needed from him that night was exquisite tenderness, not rage, and he took a deep breath to steady himself
before he peeled off his clothes and joined Leigh on the starry
quilt. He drew her into his arms, and began to make love to her
with all the devotion that filled his heart. His knowing touch
was petal soft, and his kisses sweet until the enthusiasm of her
response assured him he need not treat her as an invalid. Still,
he fought to temper his passion with tenderness until she moved
astride him and he no longer had to fear he might crush her
with his weight.

Leigh wasn't strong enough to tease him with enticing gestures as she would have liked, but she was skilled enough to
coax the last pleasure-blurred thrill from Jonathan's lean body
before she stretched out over him to enjoy her own. She loved
everything about the man: the taste of his kiss, the warmth of
his touch, the way their bodies melted together into one with a
heat that seared her soul. She didn't mean to fall asleep still
sprawled across him, but she was so relaxed in his embrace,
she forgot to move.

Not wanting to disturb her rest, Jonathan lay perfectly still,
his body awash in contentment, while his restless mind replayed
every conversation he had heard that week. Someone had to
have said something suspicious, or made a careless error that
he and the police had failed to catch. Mirasol was too small a
town for people to cause the havoc he and Leigh had suffered
without leaving clues which would lead to their arrest.

Why couldn't he find them? He and Leigh hadn't been tar-
geted by spirits, but by beings whose flesh and blood was as
dense and warm as their own. He had to find them before they
struck again, and succeeded in killing him or Leigh. He could

not bear the agony of that possibility, but at the same time he could sense they were being stalked and it took him a long while to fall asleep in a room filled with the antiques which would make a spectacular funeral pyre.

Leigh did not awaken until mid-morning Sunday. Warm and content, she remained languidly curled around her pillow until she began to wonder where Jonathan had gone. She raised up slowly, guarding against the headache she felt was sure to come, but it was faint now, rather than blinding. Her towel was draped over the arm of the rocking chair, and once wrapped in its folds, she glanced out the window.

The blackened ruins of the house filled her with sorrow, but in the next instant she saw Jonathan picking his way through the wreckage. He was dressed in his jogging shorts and T-shirt, but she doubted he had left her to drive out to the coast and run. Eager to see him, she made up the bed, got dressed in the clothes she had worn yesterday, and went outside.

She called to Jonathan as she ducked under the yellow police ribbon. "Is it safe for you to be in there?"

Jonathan's ready grin lit his whole face with the happiness she had brought him. "Probably not, but when the fire department couldn't find proof of arson, my insurance company saw no reason to investigate. There are private experts in arson, but I've not found one who's available. That means I'm on my own."

Leigh climbed over a charred rafter. "I'll help you."

Jonathan's clothes were streaked with the soot that clung to his arms and legs, but he was more worried about her moving back home than getting dirty. "You probably ought to stay in bed another day or two," he suggested. "I've had about enough for today, so I'll come in and clean up and get us some breakfast."

"No, let's wait. It's nice being outside and I don't want to go back in yet. The fire chief blamed a gas leak for the fire. Did he ever pinpoint a source?"

Jonathan was standing in what was left of his dining room, and gestured toward the kitchen. "The fire started in the kitchen, so it had to have been the stove, but all that's left of it is a mangled heap of iron."

Leigh picked her way over the debris to reach him. "I don't know anything about arson. How do people usually start fires?"

Her question was asked with such charming innocence, Jonathan hated himself anew for ever blaming her. "The fire department searched for an incendiary device. Some sort of a time bomb, I suppose. When they didn't find one, they discounted the arson theory."

"Wouldn't it have taken a professional to build such a device?" Leigh saw a china cup that was blackened, but unbroken. She picked it up and set it atop the rubble to be collected later. The remainder of the set had been destroyed when the china cabinet had burned around it. She had to step with care as she headed into the sorry mess where his once pretty kitchen had been.

Jonathan followed her. "Yes, and a professional would have charged a bundle. Who, besides Eli, would have had the money to hire one?"

"Jonathan, please. Eli didn't do this, and where would he have found an arsonist anyway? *Soldier of Fortune* magazine?"

"I don't know." Jonathan gave the blackened sink a desultory kick.

Leigh glanced toward where the side porch had been. She had gone out that way the day Jonathan had invited her to have brunch. It had been an inviting spot, but also the place Ron Tate had died. That he had not suffered was scant consolation.

"Now I know you weren't responsible," she began, "so please don't mistake my intentions, but what if you had wanted to burn down the house to collect the insurance? How would you have done it?"

Jonathan put his hands on his hips, and regarded her with a confused glance. "How would an amateur start the fire, is that what you mean?"

"Exactly. The fire chief mentioned paint thinner and solvents."

"Right. There were plenty of them here, but I was careful. I didn't leave heaps of oily rags lying around to spontaneously combust."

Leigh pushed him further. "Did you lock your doors when you went to run?"

"The front door was always locked, but not usually the back. I used to consider Mirasol a safe place to live."

Leigh bent down to pick up a plate, thinking it was still usable, but it had a chunk knocked off the rim and she laid it back down in the ashes. "How many people know you like to jog on the beach every morning?"

"Damn near everyone who knows me."

Leigh made her way over to the stove. The explosion had twisted its shape, and the oven door was hanging askew. The knobs for the burners were angled this way and that, but they all appeared to be turned on. "Jonathan," Leigh mused aloud. "Let's say someone waited for you to leave, then came in the backdoor, passed through your work area, and helped themselves to some paint thinner. They could have come in here, slopped it around, blown out the pilot light on the stove, and turned on the gas. Could they have left a candle burning? Would that have ignited the gas?"

"No. The gas would have consumed the oxygen, and snuffed the candle."

"Damn. That was a good theory."

Jonathan's rueful laugh made his opinion plain. "With that scenario, you'd need a Molotov cocktail."

Leigh looked around. "Then the person could have come in, splashed a trail of paint thinner back to the workroom, turned on the gas, gone outside to a safe distance, and lobbed in a Molotov cocktail."

"Well, I suppose it's possible," Jonathan agreed grudgingly. "I've just imagined something far more sinister."

"Isn't this idea sinister enough? The one time I was here, I was talking with you the whole time, but I think I remember the layout of your kitchen. There was a door into the hallway, and another to the porch you used as a workroom. There were windows above the sink which looked out on the side porch where Ron was asleep, but no one would have come onto the porch and tossed a flaming cocktail over him. Were there windows on the other side of the room?"

Jonathan was beginning to feel sick. "Just one." He pointed. "It would have been right over there."

Leigh turned in that direction, and stepped on what she thought was another piece of broken crockery, but as she moved her foot, she caught a glimpse of bright blue among the ashes. Intrigued, she bent down and picked it up. It was only the circular bottom of a bottle, but she recognized it as coming from Tŷ Nant, the spring water Denise served.

"What did you find?" Jonathan asked.

Not wanting to dwell on the time Denise and he were together, Leigh was about to toss it aside. "Nothing really, just part of a Tŷ Nant bottle."

"Are you sure?" Jonathan took it from her and ran his fingers around the raised lines that ringed the bottom. "My God," he moaned.

"What's wrong? Isn't that from Tŷ Nant?"

Jonathan looked up at her, his dark eyes filled with pain. "You know who drinks it?"

"Denise served me some once."

"Yes. She buys it by the case, but I don't drink Tŷ Nant, and she never brought any here." He turned to look over his shoulder where the window had been, and shuddered. He could have hired a dozen experts, but in the ruins of a kitchen strewn with broken dishes and glass, would any of them have known the significance of a single shard of brilliant blue glass?

"I think I'm going to be sick." Leigh grabbed for Jonathan, and he caught her as she fainted into a dream of dancing flames.

Twenty

Miguel Fuentes' eyes were the shade of bittersweet chocolate, but Leigh didn't recognize him until after he had replaced the cold washcloth on her forehead and stepped back from the bed. Bonnie was standing beside him, fidgeting nervously. Leigh was back in the cluttered carriage house, on the massive bed, but she didn't know how she had gotten there.

"Where's Jonathan?" she asked.

Bonnie's silver bracelets created a musical tingle as she flung her arm in a wild gesture. "He went downstairs to use the phone in his van. How do you feel? Are you all right? We went to the hospital to visit you, and were told we'd find you here. Jonathan said you'd just passed out and asked us to stay with you while he called your doctor."

Leigh licked her lips. It was plain Jonathan had not confided what had prompted her to faint. She felt numb with the terror of their discovery, but would not reveal the cause either. "Would one of you please stop him? I'm sure there's no reason to bother Dr. Nelson."

Miguel turned away from the bed, but Jonathan was already making his way toward them. The strain showed in his expression, but when he saw Leigh had revived, he relaxed visibly. "Marsha Nelson isn't on duty today, but I asked her service to page her. She should give me a call right away. I'll have to get back to the van to wait for it, but I needed to check on you."

I needed to check on you. Leigh liked the way that sounded. "I guess I should have stayed in bed after all," she replied, "but

I'm fine now, and there's no reason to disturb Marsha on her day off. When she calls please tell her it was a false alarm."

Jonathan nodded to acknowledge her request, but didn't agree. He read the warning in her veiled glance, but wasn't even tempted to share their suspicions with Bonnie and Miguel. "Miguel asked for a chance to speak with you. I hope you don't mind."

Leigh smiled as she glanced toward the young man, and Jonathan left to await Dr. Nelson's call. "Why would I mind?" she asked. "Unless, of course, you plan to yell at me the way you usually do, Miguel. I'm just not up to a confrontation today."

Miguel shot Bonnie a hasty glance, and she nodded to encourage him. Still, he appeared to be horribly embarrassed. "I had no right to say what I did to you, and I want you to know how sorry I am. Bonnie told me how much you've helped her, and I'm real glad you came to Mirasol. I just want you to know that no matter how many arguments we might have had, I'd never have tried to run you off the road. Neither would anyone else at the ranch. That was the work of a coward, and to drive off and leave you when there could have been a fire—well, none of us knows a man that low."

"They'll catch him soon," Bonnie said. "He's probably some nut everyone will describe as being so nice, and quiet. It's always that kind who does such awful things. He probably even returns his library books on time."

Leigh now had an inkling of who it might have been, but she wanted to discuss it with Jonathan before she revealed a name. "Let's talk about something more pleasant. It's good to see the two of you looking so happy together."

Bonnie slipped her arm through Miguel's and blushed with pride. "We're going to get married real soon. My mother's not speaking to me, but you know something? I really don't care. You were right. I was listening to her bad advice instead of following my heart, and that's why I was so unhappy."

"Shakespeare said it best: 'To thine own self be true.' It isn't always easy, but it's very wise."

Miguel broke into a wide grin. "That's a line from Hamlet. We saw the movie with Mel Gibson. I don't read as much as I should, but I'm not stupid, and I don't plan to be a ranch hand much longer. I had a long talk with Eli yesterday, and he told me he's scaling back his plans for the resort so it won't take so much good land. He wants me to help with the grounds, and I told him I would if he'd pay me enough so I could buy some land. I want my own ranch, Ms. Bowman. I was born right here in the valley, and I want to be able to call a few acres my own."

Bonnie was looking up at Miguel with such an adoring gaze, it was readily apparent she had revised her opinion on the value of remaining in Mirasol. Leigh was grateful to have had a part in helping her find the courage to follow her heart before it was too late. "Thank you so much for coming to see me. I better try and rest a while now."

Bonnie pulled Miguel away from the bed. "We'll see you again soon. I want you to be part of our wedding. The ceremony will have to be small, but it can still be elegant, don't you think?"

"Definitely. I'll look forward to it." Leigh closed her eyes, and waited until she had heard the door close after them to sit up. She set the washcloth on the windowsill, then crossed her legs, propped her elbows on her knees, and held her head. She still felt badly shaken by their discovery, but with that single ominous clue, everything fell into place. She looked up as Jonathan joined her.

"Marsha's with Eli at the Inn," he explained as he sat down on the foot of the bed. "I told her you'd had a damn good reason to faint and she was relieved to hear how quickly you'd revived. She said to stay in bed, and that she'll stop by this afternoon to check on you."

"I wish you'd talked her out of it. I don't want to ruin her day off."

"Maybe she'd just like a break from Eli, but her schedule

isn't our problem. I've thought all week that someone who stood a real chance to gain from the redevelopment set the fire, and that foes must have gone after you to retaliate. But if Denise set the fire, my whole theory was wrong."

"She was married to Eli," Leigh reminded him. "I'll bet any amount you name that she knows how to drive his trucks."

Jonathan had already considered that fact and come up with the very same answer. "The fire and your accident had nothing to do with the redevelopment then. It was just about Denise and me. I was never interested in anything serious, but she'd begun pressuring me for a commitment long before you arrived in town. It was subtle at first, merely a hint of us becoming a couple, but gradually she had grown more demanding.

"I'm ashamed to admit I didn't take her seriously. After the fire, she offered me the use of her home, with her included, of course, but I refused to consider it. I was rude, in fact. I couldn't understand why she was so broken up over Ron's death."

"Eli told me it was simply an act."

"I doubt it. She must have thought that if I lost my house I'd turn to her for comfort, and perhaps even become dependent on her. Not only did that ploy fail, but she'd killed a man. Her tears were definitely real, but as usual, they were for herself, not Ron." Jonathan shook his head sadly. "God. I don't know what I ever saw in that woman."

"Neither does Eli, but she's very beautiful, and sometimes it takes a while to realize there's nothing behind it."

"You saw right through her though, didn't you?"

Leigh recalled the first time she had walked into Silken Shadows and a chill shot down her spine. The white orchid on the dresser suddenly took on a whole new significance, and Leigh knew it had never been meant to wish her well. "She had an icy calm that was unsettling, but I never dreamed she was capable of arson, or what she did to me—if she did it."

"What do you mean, 'if'?"

"I don't believe the police will accept our conclusions without proof, no matter how logical they might be. Just because

Denise drank Tŷ Nant, doesn't mean she hurled one of the bottles through your window to start the fire. Nor does the fact she might know how to drive a truck make her the one who came after me."

Jonathan had no such doubts, and rested his hand on Leigh's knee. "Take a nap. I'm going to clean up, and then walk over to the boutique. It's open Sunday afternoons, and I'll have a friendly chat with Denise. Maybe she'll let something slip with me that she'd hide from the police."

"If she's responsible for both crimes, that could be dangerous. I think you ought to call Detective Wheeler right this minute."

Jonathan got to his feet. "Unlike you and Eli, Denise and I were more than friends once, and while this may sound ridiculous, I really think she'd be more willing to confide in me than the police. Maybe I owe her that chance."

Like hell, Leigh thought, but she bit her tongue, and tossed him the damp washcloth. "I know you won't do anything stupid, but be careful."

Jonathan leaned down to kiss her. "I'll be the soul of tact."

Leigh watched him walk toward the bathroom, his stride long and sure, but she had absolutely no intention of allowing him to confront Denise alone. The woman was a viper, and ought to be caught with a forked stick. She curled up on the bed, and closed her eyes, but only pretended to be asleep. When Jonathan left, she waited a few minutes to make certain he would have crossed the street and rounded the corner, then got up to follow.

Totally focused on the conversation he wished to have with Denise, Jonathan didn't once glance over his shoulder to notice he was being tailed. When he reached Silken Shadows, he drank in the perfume-laced air. The delicate harmonies of a string quartet were playing softly on the stereo system, but he now knew Denise's elegant tastes hid the soul of a murderess. A customer he didn't recognize had just made a purchase, and he waited until she had left to approach Denise.

"Why, Jonathan, what a delicious surprise. I hope you've come to see me rather than to select a gift."

She was dressed in a simple ivory top and slim skirt that enhanced her dark hair and eyes, but as she came out from behind the counter, Jonathan had to force himself not to back away. "You'd better lock the door."

Denise responded with a seductive smile. "I didn't think you'd missed me that much."

"I haven't missed you at all," Jonathan countered, "but I've found proof you set the fire at my house, and I don't think you want anyone coming in while we're discussing it."

Denise's expression betrayed none of her dismay, but she reached out to grab hold of the counter. "What have you found?"

That she hadn't even bothered to deny the deed galled Jonathan, but he strove to keep his temper in check. "Damning evidence, Denise, and because Ron Tate was killed in the blaze, you'll be charged with his murder."

Denise moved back behind the jewelry-filled counter. "First you blamed Eli, and now me? Really, Jonathan. Don't be absurd. I know you miss your house, but continuing to make wild accusations when the fire department can find no evidence of arson only makes you appear delusional."

Her voice was always sultry, but it had taken on a husky edge Jonathan ascribed to panic. He threw in a bluff in hopes of pushing her into making an incriminating slip, if not an outright confession. "Your fingerprints are on what's left of the Tŷ Nant bottle. The police will be here in a few minutes, but I asked them to let me talk to you first. Things are sure to go easier for you if you admit what you did to me and Leigh."

"Leigh?" Denise gasped. "I barely know the woman. Why would I wish her any harm?"

"People do crazy things in the name of love, and you saw

her as a rival. You were right, by the way. I intend to marry her."

Denise reached for the handgun she kept on the shelf beneath the cash register and with a graceful ease, leveled it at him. "I think not."

Jonathan had not even dreamed she might own a gun, but remained in control, and gave her a calmly voiced order. "Put the gun away, Denise. Shooting me will only compound your problems. A clever lawyer will have the murder charges reduced to manslaughter, and Leigh wasn't badly hurt in the accident you caused, so that could be classified as an assault. I doubt you'll spend more than five years in prison, and—"

He saw her finger tightening on the trigger and lunged across the counter to catch her arm and ruin her aim, but Denise fought him so hard he went rolling right on over the counter and plunged down with her into the narrow aisle behind. Without releasing the weapon, she tried to rake his face with her nails and his elbow scraped the wall as he blocked the attempt. Over their labored breathing the mellow tones of a cello merged with the higher notes of a violin and then a shot reverberated with a deafening intensity.

For one dreadful second, the smell of warm blood filled Jonathan's nostrils and he didn't know which of them had been hit. He waited for a jolt of pain, but it didn't come. He raised up slightly, and saw Denise's beautiful face had been completely blown away. Her body was still twitching slightly, but it was only the shuddering reflex of death. He scrambled off her and got to his feet just as Leigh and Eli came through the door. He saw the horror in her eyes, and looked down, but the blood splattered across his shirt wasn't his.

"I'm okay, but stay where you are," he begged, and he leaned on the counter to catch his breath.

Eli brushed past Leigh and rushed to Jonathan. "Marsha and I were on the way to your place and heard a shot." He glanced past Jonathan and saw what was left of his ex-wife. "Oh, dear God," he moaned.

Marsha had been right behind Eli, and hugged Leigh to move her out of the way. "Sit down before you faint again," she ordered, and Leigh made an obliging slump to the floor. Marsha hurried around behind the counter, but with a large portion of her brain ripped away, Denise was past saving. Marsha reached for the telephone, then dropped it when she heard the sirens coming their way.

"Tragedies come in threes," Jonathan breathed out in an anguished sigh. This is finally the end of it, thank God."

Even after the police arrived, Leigh remained seated just inside the doorway. When Detective Wheeler questioned Jonathan, she listened attentively as he described how quickly his conversation with Denise had turned violent, but she had little to add when it came her turn to speak. Eli, however, denounced Denise as a selfish bitch who resorted to temper tantrums whenever she didn't get her way. He assured the detective she was fully capable of arson and stealing one of his trucks would have been no challenge for her.

Leigh suddenly remembered something, and rose unsteadily to her feet. "The day of the accident, I was in the Beauty Spot. Denise came in, and Beverly told her Eli was having a dinner party for Lloyd Channing. I'd forgotten all about it, but that's how she knew when I'd be on the highway. She was waiting for me too, and drove out of a side road to follow me."

Satisfied he finally had all the answers, the detective gave them permission to go, but a crowd had formed outside on the sidewalk, and Eli reached out to stop Jonathan before he and Leigh opened the door. "Let's let this be the end of it. I've always admired you, and regretted the fact Denise got in the way of our being friends. I think we could work together, and turn Mirasol into a town where we'd both be proud to live. What do you say?"

Jonathan gave Leigh's hand a fond squeeze. "Are you really going with Greene and Greene for the resort?"

Eli smiled at Leigh. "Yes, and I've even got Lloyd Channing interested in doing it as more of a retreat than a convention complex. It's in his best interests to do an occasional project the environmentalists will love, but regardless of his motivation, his firm will build it the way we want it built. The town project is still on, and with your academic credentials, I think we can make a go of the prep school."

Jonathan didn't dare look at Leigh now. "Well, I suppose I could live in the headmaster's house, and oversee the organization of it, but that wouldn't mean I'd want to stay on after we got it running again."

When Jonathan had said, "we," Eli knew he had him. He offered his hand and Jonathan took it. "Let's duck out the back door so we don't have to answer any questions. After this horror, I'm not going to feel up to working for several days, and I don't want to pressure Leigh either, but whenever you feel up to it, Jonathan, we'll get to work."

"Wednesday," Jonathan promised, and he and Leigh followed Eli and Marsha out the backdoor.

"I don't think I've ever seen a more beautiful sunset." Leigh leaned back against Jonathan, and for a long while they watched in silence as the sun turned a flaming orange and slowly disappeared into the sea. It was as perfect a moment as the first time they had made love. That had been a glorious taste of paradise, and she intended to fill all their days with the same delicious sense of wonder. She turned to look up at him.

"I came to Mirasol expecting to work on a project that really excited me. I'd no idea just how exciting life was going to be here," she confided.

Jonathan wrapped his arms around her more tightly. He felt certain Leigh had heard him tell Detective Wheeler that Denise had drawn her gun when he had said he intended to marry her. She hadn't asked him to repeat the statement, but he didn't want it to be the only proposal she heard.

"Leigh?"

"Hmm?"

"Do you know why I asked Eli for the headmaster's house?"

Leigh looped her hands over his. "Is that a trick question? I thought it was just because you'd rather not live in the carriage house while you rebuild your own house."

"No." Jonathan wished it weren't too dark to explore the tide pools, and then decided he had already made the most extraordinary find of his life there. "I love you dearly, and I'd like you to marry me, and that house would make a fine place for us to start out. I'm afraid if I kept you in the carriage house, you might get so upset with the clutter that you'd leap out the window after a day or two."

"It's a real possibility," Leigh admitted. She had a bandage on her head, and a black eye, but she had never felt more comfortable in his arms. "I love you, too," she murmured softly. "It's going to take a long time to rebuild Mirasol, open a resort, and reopen a school. Our work may not be finished for years and years."

"Did you just agree to marry me?"

"Yes, I did. I didn't expect to live in Mirasol more than a few years, but now I doubt there will ever be a reason to leave."

Jonathan pulled her down into the sand, and then remembering her bruises, held her in a tender embrace. "I can sell antiques anywhere, Leigh, so if ever you want to leave, I'll go with you." He saw the glimmer of tears in her eyes, and kissed them away. "What's wrong?"

Leigh raised her hand to caress the soft silver hair at his temple. "Absolutely nothing," she assured him. The sea breeze scented the air with the fragrance of dreams, but he had already made hers come true.

Note to Readers

The town of Mirasol, and all its quirky residents, exist only between the pages of this book, but it was inspired by Ojai, California, a charming artists' colony located in the verdant valley I described. Should you ever have the opportunity to visit Ojai and explore, as I did while writing *PARADISE,* you're sure to find the townspeople friendly and the arts and crafts exceptionally fine.

While writing this book, I became intrigued by the question Leigh asks about wedding rings. If you are divorced, and found a unique way to either dispose of your wedding ring, or create something new from it, will you please write and share your story? I'll print some of the more unusual responses in my newsletter. I would also appreciate hearing any other comments you might have on *PARADISE*. Please write to me, c/o Zebra Books, 850 Third Avenue, New York, NY 10022. Please include a legal size SASE to receive a newsletter and an autographed bookmark.